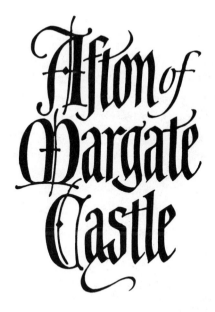

Afton of Margate Castle

Angela Hunt

Tyndale House Publishers, Inc.
Wheaton, Illinois

For Gary

Library of Congress Cataloging-in-Publication Data

Hunt, Angela Elwell,   date

  Afton of Margate Castle / Angela Hunt.

     p.   cm. — (The Theyn chronicles)

  ISBN 0-8423-1222-6

  I. Title.   II. Series: Hunt, Angela Elwell, date   Theyn
chronicles.

PS3558.U46747A69   1993   93-7201

813'.54—dc 20

Printed in the United States of America

99 98 97 96 95
10 9   8   7   6   5   4   3

The heart of the human problem
is the problem of the human heart.
—Anonymous

Name	Meaning	Pronunciation
Afton	"one from Afton"	'Af-tun
Agnelet	"little lamb"	Ag-nuh-'lay
Ambrose	"immortal"	'Am-broze
Arnoul	"strong as an eagle"	Ar-'nool
Calhoun	"warrior"	Cal-'hoon
Charles	"manly, strong"	Charles
Clarissant	"blonde beauty"	Clare-iss-'ahnt
Corba	"maiden"	'Core-buh
Endeline	"woodlark"	'En-duh-line
Fulk	"from the field"	Fulk
Gislebert	"shield bearer"	Zheel-'bear
Hildegard	"woman of strength"	'Hill-deh-guard
Hubert	"bright mind"	Hyoo-'bear
Jarvis	"keen with a spear"	'Jar-vis
Josson	"God helps"	Joe-'sahn
Kahlil	"good friend"	Kaa-'lil
Lienor	"light"	Lee-'nor
Perceval	"pierce the valley"	'Pur-seh-vuhl
Raimondin	"wise protector"	Ray-'moan-din
Reynard	"mighty fox"	Ray-'nar
Wido	"from the village"	'Wee-doh
Zengi	"fierce warrior"	'Zen-gee

GLOSSARY

bailey—the outer wall or any of several walls surrounding the castle

barbican—tower or gate

boon work—work done at the request or demand of a feudal lord

burnous—a hooded cloak made of one piece of cloth, worn by Arabs

castle keep—the strongest and securest part of the castle

destrier—war-horse used especially in tournaments

enciente—a wall surrounding the castle; served as a defensive barrier

fief—an estate controlled by a feudal lord or king

guimpe—a veil-like covering draped over the head and shoulders and around the neck and chin

machicolation—an opening in a castle wall, through which projectiles could be launched upon attacking forces

motte—a hilltop site for a medieval castle

pottage—a thick vegetable or vegetable and meat soup

quintain—used in training young knights; consisted of a post with a rotating crossbar that had a target on one end and a sandbag on the other

scapular—a cloth covering worn over the shoulders and falling over both the front and back; part of the monastic habit

scutage—a tax on those tenants of a knight's estate that did not offer him military service.

verjuice—the juice of crab apples or of unripe fruit, usually sour

villein—a common villager; bonded to the lord

FEASTS

Feast of St. Agnes—January 21

Feast of Hocktide—the Monday and Tuesday following the
   second Sunday after Easter

Feast of St. John the Baptist—June 24

Feast of Mary Magdalene—July 22

Feast of St. Michael (or Michelmas)—September 29

TABLE OF CONTENTS

WIDO
A.D. 1119

"Two things I ask of you, O Lord;
do not refuse me before I die:
Keep falsehood and lies far from me;
give me neither poverty nor riches,
but give me only my daily bread.
Otherwise, I may have too much and disown
you and say, 'Who is the Lord?'
Or I may become poor and steal,
and so dishonor the name of my God."

PROVERBS 30:7-9, NIV

ONE

Wido grunted with satisfaction as he settled into his bed next to his wife, Corba. It had been a full day, but a good one—filled with hard work in his own furrows—and he laced his fingers together across his broad chest and breathed deeply. Across the room, he could hear the regular breathing of his six children, five strong boys and the girl, Afton. Next to him lay Corba, his wife, the full lines of her pregnant body silhouetted in the shadows. Wido lifted a hand to rest it lightly on her hip, though he was careful not to wake her. It felt good to lie alone in the dark and think.

Not that Wido never had time alone. As a ploughman he was often alone in his narrow field or in the fields of Lord Perceval. Still, his thoughts when behind the plow were centered on the incessant cycle of plowing, sowing, and harvesting: which fields should be planted with drink grains, which with bread grains, and which should lie fallow? Of course, in Lord Perceval's fields Wido did as he was told, but in his own meager strip he was careful not to offend the laws of God and nature. One miscalculation, one failed crop, and his livestock or his family might not make it through the winter.

Today his thoughts had been of the upcoming festival of Hocktide, when he and Corba would have to present a full basket of eggs to Lord Perceval's steward. Sixteen eggs they would have to bring—two for each person who lived in their small hut. Sixteen eggs! Wido crossed himself and hoped that Corba had said the proper incantations and prayers to keep the hens laying. If they were even one egg short, Wido would have to load timber for the castle or spend an extra day in Lord Perceval's fields while his own chores waited.

As if she knew his thoughts, one of Wido's hens stuck her head out from under his bed and squawked. Wido smiled. "Yes, little friend, ye have work to do," he whispered, his gruff voice breaking the stillness of the night. "We cannot be even one egg short."

Corba stirred, the hay in their mattress creaking softly. "Is all well?" she whispered, raising her head from her pillow. Her beautiful wide-set eyes were drowsy. "Are the children all right?"

"All is well," Wido assured her, turning on his side to look at his bride. Dim moonlight streamed through the open window, and Wido was struck again by his wife's beauty. He loved her. Indeed, he loved her more now than he had on the day they were wed in front of the church—a fact that amazed him. "I was reminding the hen of our need for sixteen eggs," he said with a smile.

"Ah." Corba nodded and her head dropped back on the rough wool of her pillow. "Lord Perceval must be satisfied. What do ye think his steward will do if we only bring fifteen?"

"Old Hector will want to extract an arm or a leg," Wido answered, his voice light. He nuzzled his wife's shoulder. "Or perhaps Lady Endeline will covet instead your golden hair. But I will not let ye pay the price. My life would be forfeit instead."

"Ye talk like a fool," Corba answered, smiling drowsily.

"Ye would not have married a fool," Wido answered, caressing her pregnant belly with his rough hand. The child within her womb was awake, too, and Wido felt a decisive kick against his palm. "Did ye feel that? Our child agrees that his father is a wise man."

"A wise ploughman," Corba answered, her blue eyes closing. "What is the use of such a man? Does the ground

4

care who plows it? Does the ox know who drives it? Does the seed notice who throws it?"

"No," Wido agreed. "But the wife knows what her husband is, and the children follow in the footsteps of their father. Wisdom has its place, even among unfree ploughmen."

"Does it?" Corba asked softly. She turned toward her husband and gently kissed the tip of his nose. "Will wisdom make your eggs sweeter than those of your friend Bodo?"

Wido held her hand and squeezed it. "No. But I have chosen a wife even more beautiful than Lord Perceval's."

Corba smiled and a dimple appeared in her cheek. "Alas, Wido, I was wrong. Ye are wise beyond measure."

The day dawned bright with rare sunshine. Wido and Corba hustled their children out of their hut and joined the other villagers on the road to Margate Castle. The air was filled with cries of merriment, and Wido noticed that even the dour Father Odoric seemed jovial. "Who knows but that even Father Odoric will dance today," Wido whispered to Corba as they followed the crowd.

"That's not likely," Corba answered, breathing heavily. She was carrying their basket of eggs on her right arm and balancing their youngest child on her left hip. Wido stopped and lifted the baby into his arms.

Corba was right, of course. The church took a dim view of dancing and merriment, especially on religious holidays. Wido often wondered how God could create such wonderful things as animals and sunsets and babies and women and yet make work so hard and church so somber. Wido made a mental note to ask the priest for an answer.

The castle road led the stream of villagers out of the village and through the forest, where they gathered greenery and wild blossoms. The procession then wended its way to Margate Castle, home of Perceval, earl of Margate, and his wife, Lady Endeline. Wido's village was one of many manors overseen by Perceval and his steward, Hector, but it was the only one directly affiliated with Margate Castle.

Wido had had occasion to talk with ploughmen from other manors and knew that his lot was often better than theirs. Lord Thomas of Warwick, a knight who had received his estate from Perceval's father after the first mighty expedition of God to the Holy Land, charged his tenants three eggs per person at Hocktide. Wido understood the discrepancy. Those who held land owed tribute and service to their lords, and the tribute was ultimately paid by the villeins, the feudal slaves on the estate. The villeins of the estate who belonged to Thomas of Warwick paid service and tribute to Thomas, who gave tribute to Perceval, who gave tribute to King Henry. "The more lords a man 'as," another ploughman once confided to Wido, "the less a man eats."

Wido and his family ate—usually—depending upon the land's bounty. Wido wasn't sure whether he held land or the land held him. As a villein on Margate land he and the land could be bought, sold, or traded at Perceval's pleasure. But within the Margate acres he had his own furrows to plow, a garden to plant, and a hut in which to shelter his wife and children. He had a bed, a sheep, a cow, four chickens, two pigs, four bowls, and two complete sets of clothing, gifts from Lord Perceval at Christmastide.

Wido's time was more or less his own. True, he did owe three days of work each week to Perceval's fields, and the call for boon work came frequently during the harvest. These days of work on demand were usually rewarded, though, and the villeins had pet names for them: *hungerbidreap*, when the villeins were given nothing; *waterbidreap*, when they were given water at the end of the day; and the *alebidreap*, when each villein was allowed a long drink of the lord's ale.

Corba was not exempt from Perceval's service. Three days a week she left Afton in charge of the little boys and went up to the women's quarters behind the tall walls of the castle. In a private hedged area, the villein women and the female servants of the castle wove linen or wool. Sometimes they were dispatched to the sheep pens for shearing.

Wido had the distinct impression that Corba enjoyed these days with the other women. She always came home with a secret gleam in her eye, and she would never tell him what it was women talked about. Wido finally stopped asking. Other men assured him that women were tools of the devil, and the less a man had to do with them the better off he'd be. Wido could believe nothing bad about Corba, but still—better to be ignorant and happy than wise and sorrowful.

The deforested pasture surrounding Margate Castle gleamed in the sunlight, and the castle's imposing stone walls were gilded in a covering of early morning dew. Flags with Perceval's family crest fluttered in the slight breeze from the imposing twin towers, and Wido idly wondered how a place built for battle could look so inviting. The gates were open and the drawbridge down, with the men, women, and children of Perceval's manor, free and unfree, streaming into the castle for their annual reward.

The outer courtyard had been filled with tables, and soon the castle servants would serve the Easter feast. But first there was necessary business. Under a canopy near the gate, Hector the steward had set up his accounting table and was making notes in his ledger book. Hector was ruthless in his devotion toward Lord Perceval. Wido crossed himself and thanked God that the hens had come through. Not only were there sixteen eggs, but Corba, his wise wife, had set two extra eggs aside for their unborn child.

"If he asks eighteen, ye will be prepared," Corba had told Wido as she placed the basket in his hand. "And if he asks sixteen, the two extra will bring ye favor in his sight. That favor may do us good in months to come."

In her twenty years as a villein, Corba had learned the advantages of bribing the lord's steward. Wido had to consciously smooth his face when he thought of her, so great was his urge to beam with pride. His friends would have thought him addled if they knew how much he adored his wife; their admiration was reserved for oxen, fields, and sheep. A young and fertile wife was something to be desired, but to adore a wife was mere foolishness.

Wido adored Corba more fervently than he adored the Blessed Virgin. His young wife had suckled six healthy children, who all survived infancy—an unheard-of accomplishment—and she remained strong enough to carry yet a seventh. Best of all, five times she had borne sons stamped in the image of dark-haired, wiry Wido himself. Lord Perceval himself would not have as many fine sons, probably not even King Henry.

And there was the girl, the firstborn. Wido had been bewildered at her birth. *What is this squalling, red-skinned creature?* he had wondered when the midwife showed the child to him. *Surely it is not bone of my bones!* Time had not lessened his confusion. Eight years had passed and the girl had grown tall, blonde, and fair like her mother. Once as Afton trudged alongside the ox with the goad, Wido had studied her profile and thought that not one bit of him was reflected in the child, save perhaps his temper.

She was not a brawler, as Wido had occasion to be when he was under the influence of ale, but he had seen her eyes flash fire and steely determination when she was angry. Wido first saw her anger when, as a babe, she came naked out of the baptismal font, wet and shivering. She had glared at the priest before bursting into furious wailing. Since then Wido had been careful to keep those cool gray eyes from turning too often in his direction, but common sense told him his behavior wasn't natural. A man should not be afraid of any woman, especially his own daughter.

"Wido." Hector looked up appraisingly, seeming to weigh even the flesh on the ploughman's bones. "Six children, one wife, and yourself—that will be sixteen eggs."

"If it please ye," Wido said, proffering Corba's basket, "my wife sends eighteen eggs for ye and Lord Perceval."

Hector nodded and dipped his quill pen into the ink-filled cow's horn attached to the table. His left hand took two eggs out of Wido's basket and disappeared under the table. "Wido's tribute is paid," he said as he set the basket aside. "You may sit at the upper tables."

Breathing a sigh of relief, Wido moved away. Behind him, Bodo, another ploughman, was explaining why he was five eggs short. It would not go well with him, for Hector did not appreciate shortages.

Wido led his family to a long table, where they sat and waited for the food to arrive. In front of each of them was a trencher—a large, stale piece of bread that served as a plate— and each place had its own knife and fork. Wido was pleased. The upper tables were furnished with utensils, but the tables farthest away were bare. Poor Bodo would certainly be sitting at a lower table.

A flush of excitement lit Corba's face, her cheeks glowing like roses. Afton squirmed next to Corba, the baby on her lap. Next to Afton, Wido's other sons lined the table like a neat row of growing corn.

The flourish of a trumpet silenced the restless peasants, and a barred wooden shutter on the second floor of the castle keep—the strongest and securest part of the castle—was thrown open. A handsome man in a white-and-purple tunic approached the window and held up his hand.

The crowd stilled as if God himself had signaled them. At twenty-eight, Perceval, the earl of Margate, was a commanding presence. He stood taller than most men, his height accentuated by his straight carriage and regal bearing. His shoulders were broad, and his body tapered neatly down to a trim waist, where his polished sword hung ever ready. Like his father before him, Perceval tolerated no ambition but his own.

"My people." Perceval's voice carried easily over the crowd. It was a voice accustomed to giving orders. "As a father welcomes his children for dinner, so welcome I you." He smiled down on his tenants. "It has been well said that May is the joy month. After dinner, select for yourselves a lord and lady of the May to preside over your games and dances. Perhaps we can even get Lady Endeline to crown your lady of the May."

The crowd cheered, and Wido saw Endeline obediently draw near to the window as her husband gestured to her. Younger than her husband, she was tall, thin, and regal, but there was no trace of a smile upon her face.

Perceval clasped the hand of his lady and outstretched his free arm to the crowd. "Eat, drink, and enjoy the hospitality of Margate Castle," he said. "And long live England's King Henry!"

"Long live King Henry!" the people responded, Wido joining in with the others.

Perceval withdrew, the barred window was again shut, and Wido and his family set about enjoying the food set before them. The people did not need Perceval's instructions, for this was their holiday, long established in tradition and mutual agreement. They worked for the lord all the year long, and in return, he gave them a feast at Easter and Christmas. They gave him three days a week; Perceval gave them a week's holiday at Easter and a two-week vacation from Christmas Eve to Epiphany. The villagers brought firewood for the castle, and Perceval allowed them to cut wood for their own fires from his forests. Each man knew his place in the scheme of things.

Wido caught Bodo's eye at a table on the far side of the courtyard. "Bodo!" Wido called, waving a loaf of brown bread to catch his friend's eye. "How did it go with ye?"

Bodo grinned, his black teeth showing plainly. He walked over and folded his scarecrow frame to kneel in the dust behind Wido. "I'll be cleaning the stables for a month now," he said, putting a hand on Wido's shoulder. "Would a friend like ye be willing to join me?"

Wido took a bite of bread and answered while he chewed: "And who's to finish planting my ridge and furrow?" He swallowed. "Corba wants oats, peas, beans, and barley this year."

"That's what it will take with another mouth to feed," Corba answered quietly, chewing a piece of the rough bread. She took a chewed bit out of her mouth and gave it to her youngest child. "Ye should have had a talk with your hen, Bodo."

Bodo raised an eyebrow. "'Twouldn't do any good. But that reminds me, Wido, I have need to talk to ye."

"Talk." Wido took a drumstick off a platter that was being passed.

"My son is ten, ye know, and I want ye to remember I've come to ye first."

"About what?" Wido turned a bewildered gaze upon his friend.

A corner of Bodo's mouth slowly curled in a half-smile. "Marriage. Your daughter and my son. We could arrange it now and let them marry when ye are ready."

Wido was stunned for a moment, then erupted in a hearty laugh. "Are we putting on airs now, Bodo? Since when do we arrange marriages like the master? It is not our choice, anyway. Lord Perceval must agree to any marriage in the village."

"Ye know full well the lord does not care what we villeins do. Did he object to your marriage? To mine? I do not think he will object to this, either."

Wido shook his head. "I don't understand your hurry. They are yet children."

"Yours is a special child, Wido. Have ye looked at your daughter?"

Bodo's eyes had left Wido's face and were turned toward Afton and her brothers. Wido turned to look over the head of his wife at his daughter, while Bodo spoke. "Straight nose, gray eyes, little red mouth, high forehead, pink skin—ye have a beauty in your house, Wido. Men will pay dearly to have such a wife."

Something in Bodo's words and tone made Wido's skin crawl. His hand grabbed Bodo's tunic roughly and held the scrawny ploughman in a fierce grasp. "I'll not talk of this," Wido snarled, the words hissing between his teeth. "Ye'll not look at my daughter in that way. Now leave."

Wido's powerful hand thrust Bodo away, and the

11

hapless ploughman fell back into the dust. "'Tis a pity ye were not born a knight," Bodo said, raising an eyebrow. He stood and wiped the dust from his rough tunic. "Such a sense of honor! But, my friend, if ye don't give her to wife, someone will take her, and then where will ye be?"

Wido snarled and made a move to stand, but Bodo threw his hands up in defense and backed away, smiling. "Peace be unto ye, brother," he said, chuckling as if at a bad joke. "It will be as God wills it."

TWO

Afton was bored with the feast. The food was a treat because figs, dates, raisins, oranges, and pomegranates never found their way to Wido's house, and for a while it was interesting to watch Lord Perceval and Lady Endeline as they ate on their raised table at the entrance to the huge stone castle. But they ate little and talked even less, and after a while, Afton tired of looking at them.

When the tables were cleared and the games begun, Afton found that the holiday had become sheer torture. Corba expected her to keep watch over her five younger brothers, and Jacopo, Marco, Matthew, Kier, and Gerald had more room to run and more avenues for mischief in the castle courtyard than at home.

She was too young to be a candidate for lady of the May and too busy watching her brothers to join the May dancers. After two hours of chasing the energetic boys, Afton noticed Wido leading Corba toward a quiet bench in the shade of a tall hedge around the women's quarters. Afton herded her brothers toward their mother and stood silently at her side.

She and her mother had always understood one another. As the boys swarmed over Corba's lap, Corba saw the question in Afton's eyes and nodded. "Yes, daughter," she said, sighing. "You may go play."

Afton turned and scampered away.

There was much to see within the castle walls. Outside

the kitchen buildings, two sheep and a calf were penned, awaiting slaughter for the lord's dinner. A group of richly dressed nobles lounged on benches outside the mews, where the lord's hunting hawks roosted, and Afton slipped quietly by them, not wanting to attract attention. She paused outside the stables—horses were so beautiful, so majestic! Just like the rich people who owned them.

After circling for the space of half an hour, Afton decided there was no safe place to play inside the castle walls. She knew she ought not to visit the horses, for they were the lord's. Besides, she was frightened to death of the knights who lounged outside the huge stone tower that served as a garrison. The castle itself was off-limits, of course, for the lord and lady actually lived inside; Afton feared she would be clamped into prison if even her shadow fell upon one of those august persons.

She tiptoed quietly through the rowdy crowd of merrymakers until she spied an open field of green grass through the imposing barbican that opened the castle to the world outside. In a flash she was through the castle gate, bolting for the meadow. Its openness was delightful, not at all stuffy like the castle courtyard. She skipped through tall grasses that had not yet been devoured by hungry sheep and cattle and collected an armful of flowers: bluebells, buttercups, daisies, dog roses, and red poppies.

Breathing deeply, she buried her face in the blossoms, lost in pleasure. "What are you doing there?" An unfamiliar voice startled her and she nearly dropped her load of flowers. Looking about, she wondered if it was against the law to pick the lord's wildflowers. For a moment she was frightened beyond reason, but then she saw who had spoken. It was a boy who looked a little older than she, and who obviously had been overwhelmed by the feast too. Why else would he be out here in the meadow?

"I'm gathering flowers," she said simply, stooping to pick another bunch of daisies. "I'm going to make a garland for the queen of Sheba."

"I've never heard of her," the boy answered, coming closer.

Afton cocked her head and studied the boy. He was not from her village, but the castle was filled with people from many of Perceval's estates. The boy was finely dressed, though, without even one hole in his tunic or surcoat. His eyes were the color of the creek water when it ran clear, with the same sparkle. His hair reminded her of the golden flax of wheat, and his smile was open and frankly curious. He allowed her to look him over without interrupting, then he repeated himself: "I've never heard of the queen of Sheba."

"She lives in the village," Afton replied, tossing her head. "In my house."

"Really?" His tone was curious, not challenging. "Can you show me?"

Afton considered a moment, then nodded. "If ye help. I've got to get a few more flowers so I can weave a crown. The queen loves flowers, and I like to make her a crown as often as I can."

"Will these do?" The boy tugged at an unfamiliar plant, breaking off a twig loaded with small white flowers and shiny black berries.

"Bee-utiful." Afton tucked the berries into her bouquet and they continued through the meadow, running from flower to flower until their arms were full. Then they sat breathless in the grass and Afton showed the boy how to weave the flowers and twigs into a wreath.

"That's a very large wreath," the boy said when they were done. He frowned. "How big is the queen's head?"

Afton's laughter echoed through the stillness of the meadow. "It doesn't go on her head, silly, it goes around her neck. Come, and I'll show ye."

"All right, but tell me your name." The boy's eyes shone with friendly interest.

"Afton. What's yours?"

"Calhoun."

"All right, Calhoun, let's go." Together they held their wreath and walked down the road toward the village.

A stand of oak trees lay between the pasture outside Margate Castle and the village, lonely sentries for the army of oaks that dwelt deeper in the depths of King Henry's forest. "I know this spot," Afton said, skipping ahead of her companion. "Would ye like me to show ye a magic place?"

"There are no magic places in the forest," Calhoun answered, lifting his chin. "My father and I hunt in these woods, and he would have told me if such a thing existed."

"He can't know everything, though, can he?" Afton asked. It seemed to rattle the boy that there was laughter in her voice. "Can *anyone* but God know everything?"

After considering her words, he nodded. "All right, show me this place." He threw the floral wreath over his shoulder. "Lead on, girl, and I will follow."

Afton laughed and scampered into the trees. The ground at the edge of the forest had been recently flattened by the footsteps of eager villagers searching for greenery, but Afton moved quickly into the deep woods, where the brush grew thicker and footing was more uncertain. Calhoun looked up uneasily as the trees thickened and daylight disappeared from around them.

He struggled to keep up. The wreath was awkward and scraped against his side. He would have thrown it off, but he was anxious to present it to the mysterious queen of Sheba. He also found it difficult to keep his footing in the leaves that carpeted the forest floor—his previous journeys into the forest had been on horseback; never had he actually walked through it.

He was tired and a bit cross when he finally caught up to the girl, who stood before a pair of massive oak trees. "I call them the twin trees," she said, her eyes shining as she gazed upward. "See how the trunks have wound around each other? Why did they do that, do ye know?"

Calhoun made an effort to close his mouth and quiet his breathless panting. "I suppose they grew together," he answered, his voice sharp. "Does it really matter?"

Afton shook her head. "No. But up there, where both trunks bend together, they point to my secret place."

Calhoun's eyes followed her hand. Perhaps twenty feet from the ground, both trunks jutted sharply westward, then seemed to recover and reach again for the warmth of sun and sky. He looked from the tree to the west—what place could this simple girl have found?

He was about to ask when she suddenly smiled and whirled away from him. She ran about twenty paces to the crest of a hill, then jumped down and out of sight.

Calhoun followed, then gasped at his delightful discovery. Beyond and below the hill lay a perfectly round pool, shimmering like an emerald in a dark and lush earthen setting. No human footsteps had crushed the dainty vegetation surrounding this pool. Indeed, the boy wondered if anyone but this blonde sprite had ever visited the place.

Afton sat on a rock at the edge of the pool, her long legs gently skimming the surface of the water. "It's nicer than ye might think," she told him in a conspirator's whisper. "Ye can swim here and no one will bother ye. I call it the Pool of the Twin Trees."

"How did you find it?" Calhoun asked, his voice sounding strangely loud in the stillness. "Does your tutor let you enter the King's forest—"

"My what?" She crinkled her nose and grinned, and he noticed for the first time that she was missing two front teeth. "I come here when my mama says I am free to play. I learned to swim here, too. Watch."

Without warning, she kicked off the simple slippers she wore, shimmied out of her outer tunic, and dove smoothly into the water. He was amazed that the water was transparent; its emerald quality came from moss growing on the bottom. He could see every movement the girl made, and soon her head and shoulders appeared at the far end of the pool, her soaked chemise clinging to her skin. "Come in," she called, her teeth chattering. "It's cold, but ye'll get used to it."

17

Calhoun pondered his situation. He had learned to wrestle and fight, to throw horseshoes and handle a horse. But never had he learned to swim. Yet, the girl made it look easy, as simple as jumping in and sailing underwater to the far side of the pool. But what if it were not easy? What if he floundered and sank? Drowning would be better than asking for help, but neither choice was attractive.

"I want to go see this so-called queen of yours," he called, his chin jutting from his youthful jaw. "My patience grows thin."

Afton dove and again became a rippling watery angel, then reentered the world of light and air when she climbed out onto the bank. She threw her tunic over her head and stepped into her slippers. "We can go now," she said, passing Calhoun without a backward glance. "But I could teach ye to swim."

After passing the hedge that sheltered the village, Afton walked resolutely to her house. "I'm sure no queen lives here," the boy said, tilting his head and peering at the rustic cottage. "My father says only villeins and a few free men live in the village."

"Your father didn't know about the Pool of the Twin Trees, and he doesn't know about the queen of Sheba, either," Afton replied, grabbing the boy's hand. "Come on in, and I'll show ye."

The boy allowed himself to be led inside. Afton waited for his eyes to adjust to the darkness, and she wondered why he looked so curiously at the furnishings: a table, a bed, several straw mattresses on the floor, chickens, and a huge presence over in the corner of the room.

"Is that—"

"The queen of Sheba, our sheep," Afton answered, taking the wreath from his hand. She placed the wreath gently over the ewe's head and watched while Sheba began to nibble contentedly on the flowers. "See? I told ye she loves flowers."

The boy sat uneasily on a small wooden stool and looked around. "You live here?"

"Yes."

"You left the feast to come here? Why?"

"Because I was tired of taking care of my brothers." She tilted her head and gazed at him. "Why did ye leave?"

Calhoun shrugged. "I wanted to find some excitement. Maybe a fight. I'm a good fighter."

"I'm not going to fight ye." Afton walked over and stroked the soft nubby wool of the newly shorn sheep. "Don't ye think Sheba is wonderful? I love her. My father loves her. She's going to have a lamb, ye see, and that's good for us, my father says."

"I want to find a real queen and pledge myself as a knight. I want to fight battles, maybe even in Jerusalem, and kill the infidels."

Afton turned blank gray eyes on the boy. "What's an infidel?"

"You don't know? Why, they are heathens who are not Christian," Calhoun said, pounding his palm with his fist. "The enemies of the church! My uncle the abbot tells me about them all the time."

"Oh." Afton grew quiet and sat on a bench. "I don't want to kill anybody. I want to stay here with Sheba and the chickens."

"That's because you're not a man," Calhoun said, standing up. He stretched to make himself as tall as he could, and Afton was impressed, even if the boy could not swim.

"We ought to return to the castle," Calhoun announced.

"Yes," Afton agreed. They left the house, where Sheba munched contentedly on her wreath of poppies, berries, and daisies.

The next morning when he opened his eyes, Wido knew something was wrong. Flies that usually attached themselves to the shredded ferns Corba hung in the corners of the room were swarming in the darkness. There was a strange odor in the room, too, something more than chickens and sheep and eight people.

He rolled off his hay mattress and slipped on his tunic. Over in the corner, not far from where his children lay sleeping, Sheba lay on the dirt floor. With one touch Wido knew she was dead.

Wido dragged the carcass out of the house without waking Corba. Around the ewe's neck were the remains of one of Afton's floral wreaths. Wido fingered the usual flowers, then pricked his finger on an unfamiliar leaf with a sharp tooth. There were berries on the branch, and Wido knew instantly what had happened. "Baneberry," he muttered under his breath, silently cursing the field where it had grown. The berries, highly poisonous, had killed not only the family's ewe, but the lamb that was owed to Perceval at Michaelmas, only four months away.

THREE

Wido stood before Hector's desk and shuffled his feet uneasily. "What is it?" Hector snapped, looking up from his ledger books. "I've a full day planned, ploughman, so state why you've come."

"It's about the lamb for my tribute," Wido said, clearing his throat. "My ewe has died. I wondered if ye would give permission to make a substitution at Michaelmas. My wife would gladly weave the lord a tunic or surcoat, or perhaps his lady would like a linen cloak? My wife does fine weaving."

"So does every other woman in the village," Hector replied, scratching in his ledger with his quill. "I'll think on it, ploughman, and we'll arrange for a substitution."

"I could capture a wild hog from the forest," Wido offered.

"The hogs in the forest already belong to Lord Perceval," Hector sneered, glaring up at Wido. "And hunting is prohibited there by the king's order."

Wido looked at the ground in embarrassment, and Hector paused to dip his quill in the cow's horn of ink. "I'll make mention of your dead sheep in the ledger," he said, "and I will decide later what you shall give at Michaelmas."

Lady Endeline gave a curt nod to her maids. "You may leave my chamber," she said, her tone sharp. "Lord Perceval is on his way."

When the maids had curtsied and left, Endeline slipped

21

off her heavy fur surcoat, loosened her hair, and reclined regally on their bed. Her silk tunic clung to her slim body; perhaps Perceval could be distracted this afternoon. She had already bade Hector send two cows to the church, and the priest had promised to pray for her. As an afterthought she had quietly commanded one of the village women to buy a fertility charm from a carnival witch. The charm now dangled between her breasts, and Endeline smothered a smile. *My brother the abbot would threaten me with hellfire if he knew I had resorted to witchcraft,* Endeline thought. *But whether through the powers of heaven or hell, I want another child. Three are not enough.*

She heard the sound of Perceval's boots on the stone floor and absently pulled all but one curtain down around her bed. When Perceval came in and saw her thus . . .

But Perceval was not alone. Behind him was Hector, and neither man even glanced at the bed when they entered the room. "I want a careful accounting," Perceval said, tossing a ledger book on the table. "King Henry may visit in September and the stores must be replenished before then. Have all the manors sent in their due?"

"Aye," Hector nodded. "And more is due at Michaelmas."

"Perceval," Lady Endeline interrupted.

"Michaelmas is not until the end of September!" Perceval fretted, pulling energetically on his beard. "Could we demand an earlier accounting? If we required the annual payment in August, would our store be sufficient to do the king honor?"

Hector scratched his bald head thoughtfully. "August is harvest month, my lord. The villeins will be hard pressed to harvest their crops as well as yours."

"Perceval." Lady Endeline's patience was growing short. What if the witch's charm would not last for more than the day?

"Why don't we take the annual tribute in July? We could call for the rents on the day of St. Mary Magdalene."

22

"Hay month, my lord? The villeins will be so busy—"

"All right, then, June."

"A plow month?"

Perceval lost his patience. "How long does it take for a villein to bring his required rent? The annual tribute is well known and planned, so what difference will it make if we call for the rents early?"

Hector bowed his head in the face of Perceval's anger. "None, my lord, but in the unusual cases. For instance, Wido, a ploughman in the village, must pay tribute of one lamb. But his ewe has died, and he will need time to come up with a suitable substitute."

"And what is a suitable substitute?"

"I do not know, my lord. Perhaps you can tell me."

"What does the man have to offer?"

Hector shrugged. "Chickens. A small garden plot. His wife, who weaves." He smiled. "His wife's best talent is producing children. A healthy baby every year, to serve you, my lord."

Endeline's temper flared. "Perceval!"

Perceval turned toward his wife, then stared in bewilderment. "What are you doing, woman?"

Hector bowed and left the room. Endeline rolled onto her stomach and kicked her bare legs playfully. "I want another baby, my lord," she whispered, her voice husky. "Give me another child."

Perceval shook his head. "For this you interrupt a meeting with my steward? I have given you three children, and I am not to be blamed for your barren womb."

Perceval turned to leave, but Endeline ran to him, her bare feet skimming the floor. She went to her knees before him, flinging her arms around his waist. "I gave two cows to the priest. I sent for charms from the witch at the carnival. I've done all I can, Perceval. But you must give me a child!"

Perceval scowled in impatience, but she would not let him go. For seven years she had longed for another child, and lately the feverish longing would not be denied. She clung steadfastly to his belt, perspiration dripping from her forehead, her hands trembling. She desperately hoped her body would convince her husband; her words had evidently failed.

Perceval laid his hand on her head. "Come, my dear," he said, helping her to her feet. He walked her to the bed, and her eyes were alight with hope. But Perceval shook his head. "No, Endeline, I cannot stay with you now. But you should not carry on this way. If God wills another child, it will be. Didn't your brother assure you of this?"

"I am barren because the first animal I saw after Lienor's birth was a mule," Endeline moaned softly. "A sterile mule. My handmaid said it was so, and I believe her."

"You must not believe her." Perceval sat on the bed and draped his arm around her thin shoulders. "You have three worthy children, lady, what others could you want?"

Endeline shook her head. "Would you be happy with only three horses? Only three fields? Only three manors?"

"That's a different matter."

"No, it is not." She raised her head and looked him in the eye. "I am married to a great man. I should raise great and noble children, as many as I can bear in a lifetime."

"Then raise noble children."

"How?" Her voice was flat.

Perceval stood and smoothed his surcoat. "Wido the ploughman has a wife who has a baby every year. He also owes me tribute. Go to him with my blessing and take what you desire."

Endeline wasn't sure what she would find at Wido's house. The mud cottage with its freshly thatched roof looked neat enough for the house of a lowly villein, but out of it emanated odors and sounds she couldn't identify.

She nervously jiggled the reins in her hand and nodded to Sir Jarvis, the burly knight who had accompanied her to the village. He dismounted from his horse and called into the dusty courtyard of Wido's house: "Lady Endeline is at your door, villein! She asks to see Wido the ploughman or Corba, his wife."

A woman's dust-streaked face appeared at the window, then she hesitantly stepped through the doorway. "I am Corba," she said, wiping her hands on her apron.

Endeline's gaze froze on the woman's belly, where the rough tunic stretched tautly over the round shape of her unborn child. "My husband, Lord Perceval, tells me that your sheep has died," Endeline said icily, forcing herself to look into the woman's faded blue eyes. Her horse stamped a hoof impatiently, and Endeline shifted in the saddle. "I have come to choose a substitution for your annual tribute."

"Aye," Corba answered, bowing her head respectfully. "What do ye have in mind, my lady? I weave very well and I could make ye a nice cloak."

"I would like to see your children."

Corba blinked rapidly, but stepped back into the cottage. Endeline studied the sky, where a squawking flock of crows flew overhead. *Troublesome birds,* she thought. *I ought to have Jarvis kill them all.* Presently a boy stepped out of the house, then another, until five dark-haired children stood blinking in the sunshine. Endeline gazed at them hungrily.

The youngest boy was but a baby, a chubby bundle of delight. The next was dark-skinned. Two were of the same size and manner, both shyly studying the trappings of her horse. The tallest boy stood defiantly, a challenge in his eyes.

Endeline bit her lower lip. Perceval would choose the tallest boy, no doubt, but she knew the choice was not so simple. The child who would live with her noble children must possess a brave heart, adaptability, and charm. Most of all, he should reflect well upon the earl and his lady.

Jarvis interrupted her thoughts. "Are these all the children?" he called to Corba. "I heard there were six."

"There . . . is a girl," Corba replied, her voice uneven.

Endeline frowned. The woman's frantic handwringing was distracting. With a disdainful lift of an eyebrow, Endeline turned her head away and looked toward the horizon.

25

Corba cleared her throat and spoke with an effort: "My daughter is with her father in the fields of the lord."

Endeline glanced at the woman dispassionately, then lifted her horse's reins. "I must see the girl, too," she said, relieved that her decision could be postponed.

"I will lead you there," Jarvis offered, and Endeline pulled her horse's head to follow Jarvis to the fields, ignoring the sputtering woman, who apparently did not realize the honor Endeline was about to bestow upon her and her peasant family.

When they arrived, Lady Endeline saw that several villeins were plowing in the wide wheat field, but only one ploughman was accompanied by a young girl. Endeline watched the pair from the edge of the field, carefully noting the child's slender form, her height, and her agility. "She moves well," she said, watching Afton leap from ridge to furrow as she goaded the ox. "She could be a beautiful dancer."

"She would do well with you as her teacher," Jarvis answered, displaying the tact that had earned him the distinction of being Perceval's most trusted knight. "But no child of a ploughman will dance as well as a nobleman's daughter."

"How old would you say she is?" Endeline mused. "She's about Lienor's age, is she not? And the blonde hair will be more seemly in my household," she added, thinking of the row of black-haired boys at Corba's house. "She would almost be able to pass for Perceval's child."

"No child of a ploughman—" began Jarvis, but Endeline silenced him with a stern look.

"Go tell the ploughman I've chosen his daughter," Endeline said, turning her horse's head toward the castle road. "The girl should be brought when the rents are collected next month."

Wido's steps were heavy as he led the ox home. Afton scampered ahead of him, happily splashing her slim legs and tunic in the rutted road's muddy puddles. How could such a child find a home in Lord Perceval's castle? Why had Endeline not chosen one of his sons? He had five sons, fine sons, but only one daughter!

Wido was not a man of learning or sophistication, but he had the good sense to prize the few rare treasures life had sent his way. Corba was one treasure, more beautiful and gentle than the rough village girls he had known as a young man. He had been honored and humbled when she consented to become his wife. Afton was like her mother, all golden hair and sensitive spirit.

The ox snorted behind him, anxious to be back in the community pen, and Wido thought of what his neighbors would say. "Ye are fortunate to lose her," the men would agree, "for what is a girl child but an obligation to pay a dowry?" Sons were strong and valuable, and Wido was particularly blessed with sons.

But there was something about this sprite who had been born to him first. Endeline had recognized it; even Bodo, wretch that he was, had desired it. Wido could not define the quality that made Afton unique, he only knew she had always unsettled him. Perhaps it was God's will that the girl leave. He had never felt she truly belonged to him . . . a fact that somehow saddened him.

Afton sprinted toward the cottage, and the ox quickened its pace now that its pen was in sight. Wido dreaded breaking the news to Corba. He led the ox into the pen, fastened the gate, and stooped to affectionately rub the tousled heads of Matthew and Kier, who were spinning their wooden tops on the impacted earth. Was it only a few days ago that he had felt like a king of the earth with a beautiful wife, five sons, a daughter, and a sheep?

Now he knew full well that he was not a king.

Corba was waiting in the doorway. "Lady Endeline was here," she said stiffly, a broom in her hand. "We are to lose one of our children in place of the sheep that died."

"I know," Wido answered, patting her shoulder as he passed. He settled onto a stool near the table. "The annual rents are to be paid next month instead of at Michaelmas."

"So soon?" Corba's hands flexed instinctively over her unborn child. "The babe will not yet be born."

"It's not the babe she wants," Wido said, trying to keep his voice calm. He reached for the round loaf of brown rye bread on the rough table and broke off a generous hunk. "She wants the girl."

Corba abruptly drew in her breath and sat down. In the corner of the room a chicken clucked, a sure sign their best laying hen had laid yet another egg.

"Nothing else will do?" Corba asked, her voice strangled.

"Nothing else," Wido answered, chewing his bread though it seemed tasteless in his mouth. He swallowed it with great effort. "It would not be wise to argue, in any case."

Corba straightened her shoulders. "Then there will be one less mouth to feed and a dowry we may not have to pay, if all goes well," she said, her eyes dark and wide. "If the girl minds her manners, she may stay as a handmaid for many years. It will be good for us."

"Aye." Wido agreed. He muttered the words Corba wanted to hear even though he did not believe them: "This is a good thing."

The family ate supper together as they always did, the children scrambling for bread and scooping thick pottage from their wooden bowls. Wido found his eyes irresistibly drawn to Afton. She ate with her usual concentration, but once she looked up and frowned. "Mama," she asked, one eyebrow raised delicately, "can't we get some pomegranates for supper? They were delicious."

Wido shook his head. By all the saints, perhaps it was a good thing she was leaving.

As the sun set, Corba bedded the children on their mattresses while Wido stirred the coals on the hearth in the center of the house. A fire was hardly necessary since the weather was so warm, but the glowing red embers comforted him.

Wido watched the coals until he heard the regular breathing of sleeping children, then he joined Corba in their bed. Her back was to him, and when he touched her, he felt her body convulse in soundless sobbing. He held her until she lay exhausted from crying.

The moon was shining through their open window when she spoke. "I never thought of us as poor," she said, her voice remarkably clear. "We have each other, we have a home, we have children."

"We are not poor," Wido said. "Even when my crops have failed, the lord's generosity has sustained us."

"I have never counted that as charity," Corba said, wiping her face with the light woolen blanket that covered them and rolling to look at him. "We give Perceval his due as lord, and he gives us our due as his villeins. It is a partnership."

"Aye," Wido answered.

"But today has taught me what poverty is. It is not that we lack clothing or furs, for we have what we need and no more."

Wido lightened his voice. "Ye have to agree, dear wife, that we could find use for a cow."

"No." Corba's voice was emphatic and she gazed steadily into her husband's eyes. "We are poor because we have no power. We have no voice. If we had twenty cows, we would still own nothing. All that we call ours is the property of Lord Perceval. We do not even own the children we and God have created."

Wido was silent, thinking. "The voice of God is our voice," he said, finally. "And he has sent us another child to replace the one we will lose to Perceval. God is our judge, as he is Perceval's. Father Odoric tells me so, and I do not believe a priest can lie."

"Aye, but will God comfort Afton when she is flogged for making a mistake in the castle? Will he teach her when she grows wise to the ways of women? Will he defend her chastity when a knight desires to have her?"

Wido felt a slow burn begin in his stomach. "I will make it so," he said slowly. "Ree is our best laying hen. If we give her to the priest—"

"We will starve," Corba interrupted. "Surely there is another way."

"No," Wido shook his head stubbornly. "I will give God our best, and he will see the strength of my heart and watch over our daughter in the castle—for he knows her villein father cannot hope to protect her there."

The village churned with activity the day before the feast of St. Mary Magdalene. Work in the fields was suspended while the villagers prepared their rents. Each farming family had to pay one sheep, one woven tunic, and ten smooth planks of oak. For the past month Corba had been weaving continuously, and Wido had spent his evenings polishing oak planks. Afton watched the bustle with little concern and enjoyed the extra commotion in the cottage. If she was good, perhaps her father would even let her journey to the castle with him tomorrow.

"Afton, come here." Afton came in from the courtyard and stood in front of her mother. Corba placed her hand beneath Afton's chin and inspected for dirt, a critical examination usually reserved for church days. Afton saw herself reflected in her mother's worried eyes, and smiled at the two tiny girls with straight noses, wide eyes, and smudges of dirt on their cheeks.

Corba dipped a cloth in her water bowl and swiped Afton's cheeks. "You're fine," she pronounced, stepping back. "Tomorrow ye will go with your father to the castle. And ye will wear this."

Corba pulled a tunic from her workbasket, a blue tunic finer than anything Afton had ever possessed. It was lightweight, woven from cotton instead of the usual rough wool, and a blue silk ribbon had been woven into the neckline. "It's beautiful," Afton murmured as Corba laid it across her arms. "It is really mine?"

"It is really yours," Corba answered. "Now put it away so that it doesn't get dirty before tomorrow."

The next morning Afton felt a gentle hand on her shoulder. "Time to dress, daughter," Wido told her. "We are going to the church."

To church? Without the family? Afton swung her legs off her mattress and yawned. The boys were still sleeping, and it was not yet fully light outside. Why were they rising so early? Then she remembered her new gown and eagerly slipped it on. She whirled gently, the full skirt circling around her legs like a whirling top. She giggled.

From her bed across the room, Corba called. "Let me brush your hair." Afton danced over to her mother and allowed herself to be pulled down onto the bed. Her mother brushed Afton's golden hair vigorously, then locked her daughter in a hug so fierce Afton could barely breathe.

"You'll crush me like a blueberry," Afton complained.

Corba sniffled. "Lady Endeline has taken a special fancy to ye," she said quickly. "Ye are to live in the castle beginning today." Her words streamed like a raging river. "I will see ye when I go there to work, of course, and ye'll see your father, too. But ye will not be returning here to sleep in this house."

"No?" Afton pulled away, eyes wide. Surely there was some mistake.

Corba shook her head somberly. "No. Go now with your father to the church. Say your prayers and be a good girl. Always remember that ye are the daughter of Corba and Wido."

Afton looked curiously at her mother and took her father's hand. Wido was carrying Ree, the noisy hen that laid the most eggs, in his left hand. "Why are we taking Ree to church?" she asked as they left the house.

"You'll see soon enough, child," Wido answered. The villagers were beginning to stir, and several villeins were already out in their courtyards, checking their stores to make sure all was in order for Perceval's steward. Wido waved to Bodo, who was inspecting his lamb to make sure it had no deformity. Only the best could be given to the lord.

The village church stood at the northernmost point of

the village. It was a sturdy structure with a large oak door and two windows, and Afton had often thought the church looked like a face, with a stubborn nose and two gleaming eyes to watch over the small village houses. Wido once told her that God lived there, and it was comforting to think of him watching over her, even if the face of the church did not have a mouth. *If it did have a mouth,* Afton wondered, *would it smile or frown?*

Wido knocked on the church door. It would be hours before the church opened for Mass, but Wido knew Father Odoric rose early for prayers.

The good priest opened the door slowly. "I've come for a blessing for the child, Father," Wido said. "I've brought my best laying hen as an offering."

The priest nodded and held his right hand above Afton's head. He murmured lyrical words Afton did not understand, made the sign of the cross above her head, then his smooth thumb firmly traced the sign of the cross on her forehead. "May God go with you," he said, holding his hands out for the chicken.

Wido handed the hen to the priest, then took Afton's hand again. "Thank ye, Father," he said, stepping away from the church. He did not speak as they began walking on the castle road, but Afton looked up once and caught her father wiping something from his eye.

The Latin phrases of Mass still echoed in Hector's head as he left the castle chapel and hurried toward his own house. The villeins would begin to arrive soon, and Perceval was most anxious that the day's bounty be well counted. It was not a day for mistakes.

A hulking man with a child stood outside the door already, and Hector quickened his pace. Was he so slow? Or was the man early? Hector glanced at the villein and squinted, trying to place the man's face. "Wido, isn't it?" he asked, going past the man to his door. "Allow me a moment. You're early."

"I am bringing the tribute Lady Endeline requested," Wido said, his voice and manner solemn. "I could not do this in front of the eyes of others. I will return later with the planks and the garment."

Hector's eyes widened and he turned from the door. Oh, yes, this was the man who was to give his daughter! So he was going to do it—surrender the girl without a fuss. Of course, it wasn't a question of *if* he would bring his daughter, but *how*. Any dispute or reluctance at all would have resulted in a much higher fine, most of which would have ended up in Hector's pocket.

"This is the child my lady specified?" Hector said, peering at Afton. "She is healthy? Without defects?" He reached for the edge of her tunic to inspect her more closely.

Wido growled. "She is perfect. Take your hand off her."

Hector backed away and waved his hands in the air. "Fine. I will leave you to answer if a problem arises." He went back to his door, his keys jingling with importance. "I'll mark your entry in the book, Wido, when all is paid in full." Hector gestured impatiently to Afton. "Follow me, child."

Wido did not let go of her hand. "You're not going to leave her here all day?"

Hector pushed his door open and frowned at Wido. "What else am I supposed to do? I haven't the time to take her into the castle just now."

Wido stepped forward and flexed his mighty arms. "Do it," he said, glaring into Hector's eyes. "Afton is to be taken to Lady Endeline. I will not have her kept waiting here like an animal."

Hector would have liked nothing better than to remind the man of his lowly status, but he had neither the time nor the force, for the knights who were to stand guard at his desk were not yet at their posts. His eyes gleamed in derision. "I will take her up myself," he said slowly, as if the idea were repugnant to him. "But only for the sake of Lady Endeline. And I expect you to return here with not only the planks and garment, but a chicken as well, for the consideration I have shown you."

Wido scowled, but he backed away and released his daughter's hand.

Afton clung to the hand of the elderly man who hurried her across the dusty castle courtyard. They did not stop at the kitchen buildings or at the animal pens, but walked straight through the rugged doors of the stone castle itself and up a staircase to the second floor. Afton tried to look around her, but the man rushed her up the stairs so briskly that she had no time to see anything but stone walls, wooden floors, and a timbered ceiling.

The staircase opened into a large hallway, and through an arch she saw a group of people gathered. Men in armor sat around tables, ladies in beautifully colored dresses sat conversing with them, and one lady in particular caught Afton's eye. She broke away from the others as soon as she saw Hector, and her narrow face lit up in a smile as she came to greet them.

"Finally," she said, her eyebrows arching across the white of her forehead like the wings of startled birds. "I thought this day would never come." She opened her arms and looked down at Afton. "Hello, dear. I hope you understand that from this day forward you will live with us."

Afton did not answer, but involuntarily clenched the hand of the old man who had brought her to this place. The man shook his hand free. "Her name is Afton," he said, folding his own hands and bowing respectfully to the lady. "Though, of course, you may change it to anything that pleases you."

"Afton pleases me very well," the lady replied, still looking at the little girl. "Very well indeed." She knelt on the floor and looked directly into Afton's eyes. "I am Endeline, dearest. Won't you come to me? We will have a wonderful time together."

Afton found her voice. "I want my mother," she said clearly.

"Of course, dear." Endeline's face did not change its expression, but she regally stood and nodded at Hector. "Keep the child with you now and go at once for the child's mother. Bring them both back here."

Hector bobbed his head nervously. "But my lady, the rents are due today and the villeins are even now lining up at my house—"

"Do as I say!" Endeline snapped, glaring at the older man. "And be quick about it!"

Afton's hand was snatched again, and Hector hustled her down the stairs and out of the castle as if the hounds of hell were after him.

"Is there a problem, my lady?" Perceval left the group of knights he had been entertaining and stood at Endeline's side. "Don't tell me the child of your dreams wants nothing to do with you."

"It is only natural for a child so young to be diffident with strangers," Endeline answered, forcing a smile upon her face. "How do you think your children would fare if they were taken to another man's house?"

Perceval's eyes darted to the small side room where his three children were playing. Charles and Calhoun were deeply involved in a game of chess; their sister, Lienor, was watching in fascination. "I think my children could live anywhere," Perceval drawled. "For they know what they are."

"Charles knows he is your firstborn and heir," Endeline replied, her dark eyes sweeping over her children. "But does he know he must marry soon? His interests lie more in the fields."

Perceval shrugged. "He will discover women in time."

"Calhoun knows he is the noble son of Perceval," Endeline spoke again. "But does he know what he must endure to become a great knight?"

"He will learn," Perceval answered, irritation edging his voice.

"And Lienor, our daughter," Endeline said, more softly. "She must marry well, and her only possible choice is a son

35

of the king. It is for her sake, dear husband, that I welcome the villein's child." Endeline took her husband's hand as he led her to their seats at the raised table. "She is too much with the boys, and too unlike a lady. She is eight years old and should begin to know a woman's place."

"You think a villein can teach her how to behave like a lady?" Mischief danced in Perceval's eyes.

"I will teach her," Endeline answered, smoothly adjusting her gown. "The village girl is to be her companion—and her competition."

Perceval's eyebrow shot up. "Explain yourself."

"Certainly." She nodded gently toward their daughter. "You may not have noticed, my husband, but Lienor is not beautiful as men count beauty. Her hair is too rough, her features too irregular. The ploughman's child, on the other hand, has smooth skin and hair like the rays of the sun. When Lienor looks at this girl day after day, she will pay heed to the lessons I will teach her. She will yet be fit to marry the son of the king."

Perceval sighed and stood up. "I still think you would do better to keep this child in a servant's place," he said, patting his golden belt contentedly. "What will happen when she grows up a lady? What will you do with her then?"

"I will do whatever needs to be done," Endeline whispered, but Perceval was no longer listening. He gestured to his knights and led them out of the room.

Afton's legs felt as though they would fall off from running behind the old man, but he had taken her home! Hector stood outside her cottage and called for Corba, who came out immediately, her eyes puffy and red. When she saw Afton there, she wiped her face on her apron and smiled tremulously. "Did the girl not suit Lady Endeline?" Corba asked, her eyes shining with hope. "Would Lady Endeline like a woven tunic instead?"

Wido appeared in the doorway, his eyes widening with joy at the sight before him. "Hector, my deepest gratitude," he said sincerely. "I must do something for you to deserve this unmerited favor."

"It's nothing to do with you," Hector snapped. He looked at Corba. "Lady Endeline would like you to return to the castle with me. We must go at once."

Corba dashed into the house and came out a moment later with a shawl tossed over her disheveled hair. "May the saints be praised," she whispered to Afton as Hector set a furious pace back to the castle. "Your father said God would keep his eye on ye."

The hall was ominously quiet when Hector returned with Corba and the breathless little girl. Only Endeline was in the room, her face lined with impatience. She scowled at the sight of Hector, but her face brightened when Corba and the child followed him into the room.

"Hector, keep the child outside until I call you," Endeline said, nodding graciously. "I wish to speak to this woman alone."

Hector pulled Afton's hand again and led her outside the hall. He was beginning to feel sorry for the girl. She'd been dragged up and down the castle road three times, and the simple blue tunic she wore was streaked with grime and dust. He forced himself to look away. No matter. She was Lady Endeline's worry.

But a barb of curiosity pierced his thoughts. What sort of servant would this girl be? Endeline had never taken this amount of trouble with a servant girl before.

"Corba." Endeline spoke her name gently, and the woman seemed to blush. She was pretty, for a villein, and very large with child. Endeline ignored the dart of jealousy that penetrated her heart. "I understand you could not pay the tribute this year."

Corba bowed her head in respect. "'Tis true. Our sheep died. Wido says it ate baneberry."

Endeline smiled in pity and walked over to where Corba stood. "And now you give me this girl. I promise you that she will be cared for. I don't intend for her to be a mere serving girl, you see. I wish her to be a companion for my own daughter, Lienor."

Corba's face fell. *She thought I had changed my mind,* Endeline realized. *The poor fool.* She spread her hands out in a gesture of generosity. "Of course, just as Perceval is a father to all who live on his lands, I will be a mother to your child, too."

"Thank you, my lady." Corba's voice was flat.

"But a child can have but one mother."

Corba's face was uncomprehending. Endeline pressed on and gently placed her arm around Corba's shoulders. "You must turn the child against you."

Corba smiled in surprise. "I cannot. 'Twould be unnatural."

"Not really," Endeline purred. "You must simply do as I tell you, then all will be well. Do as I say and promise never again to speak to the girl should you see her at the castle."

Corba chewed her knuckle in fear. *What a peasant,* Endeline thought. She put her hand on Corba's pale cheek and turned the woman's face toward hers. "If you want all to go well with your family from this day forth, you must do what I tell you. . . ."

"Hector!" The old man heard his mistress' voice, and he looked at Afton. She stood up and willingly placed her hand in his. Perhaps now she could go home.

Endeline and Corba stood together in the hall, a study in opposites. Endeline was a tower of power, and Corba was a stumpy tree, bulging with hopelessness. Endeline smiled at Afton when Hector brought her into the room, but Corba would not meet her eyes.

"Afton, darling, this woman has something to say to you," Endeline said, leaving Corba's side. "Hector, you are free to go attend to the rents."

Hector slipped out of the room in relief, and Afton ran to her mother, pillowing her head in the coarse wool of her mother's skirt. Corba was silent until Endeline sat on a bench against the far wall.

"Get away from me, ye hateful child," Corba said suddenly, her voice trembling. With both arms Corba pushed Afton away, holding her at arms' length. Her face was contorted in fury. "We don't want ye with us, you're to stay away," she screamed, her voice cracking.

"But Mama—" Afton's own voice broke in confusion and pain and tears began to stream down her face. Never had her mother spoken to her in such a tone.

Corba released her iron grip on Afton's shoulders and Afton once again rushed toward the security of her skirt, but Corba's hand swung back and slapped Afton's face with a resounding crack. The shock of it left Afton speechless.

Corba covered her face with both hands and turned away, sobbing wordlessly. "Mama?" Afton sobbed, reaching again for her mother.

"Stay away!" Corba shrieked and her arms and fists flew in Afton's direction. Afton ran instinctively for protection to the only other person in the room, the calm lady who held out her arms. Once Afton's sobbing head was buried against Endeline's neck, she nodded at Corba, who flew out of the room and down the wide stairs.

ENDELINE
1119-1123

Like arrows in the hands of a warrior
are sons born in one's youth. . . .
They will not be put to shame
when they contend
with their enemies in the gate.

PSALM 127:4-5, NIV

FOUR

In Endeline's arms Afton found comfort. "There, my pretty one," Endeline whispered in the child's ear. "You are safe with Lady Endeline. No one will harm you here at Margate Castle. You are under the beneficent protection of Lord Perceval himself."

Afton wasn't sure what "beneficent" meant, but she had often heard her parents speak of Lord Perceval in the same hushed voice they used to speak of God. In fact, Afton's family prayed for favor from Perceval as often as they prayed for it from God. Indeed, Perceval had a much more direct role in their lives. If Perceval willed it, they had firewood. If Perceval granted his favor, Wido was allowed to hunt in the forest. If Perceval called, Wido and Corba were commanded to obey. God, who lived in his little church with Father Odoric, only asked for goodness and that the villagers adore the Virgin, whose statue lived in the church with him.

Afton felt overwhelmed with confusion. Why was she to remain where Perceval and his lady lived? She did not feel especially good or holy. And why were the revered hands of Lady Endeline actually stroking her hair? She lifted her tear-stained face and cautiously pulled away from the woman who held her, half-expecting to find herself at the feet of a maid or surrogate mistress, not the divine lady herself.

But this woman was neither servant nor statue. Endeline's eyebrows arched as she smiled, and her breath was sweet as she spoke: "You are a lovely child, Afton, and we

43

will enjoy having you with us. Things will be quite different for you here at the castle, and I want you to forget all about the things you knew before. Here you will find happiness, playmates, and protection. As long as you remain here, no one will ever strike you again."

Afton's hand went involuntarily to her cheek, which still stung. More painful than the blow, however, was the memory of Corba's face contorted in anguish and her harsh words of rejection. Afton choked back a sob, and the blessed lady pulled her into softly scented robes, cushioning Afton's head against the delicate skin of her breast. "My brave, brave girl," she whispered. "I know you will bring us honor. And you will have pretty dresses, and lessons, and—"

"Pomegranates?" Afton whispered, pulling away. She looked wistfully at the gracious woman at whose feet she knelt. She had often asked for things at the feet of the Virgin, but the Virgin had never smiled as generously as this woman. "If I am very good, can I have pomegranates?"

Endeline's laughter rang through the hall. "As many as you like, dear heart."

Afton buried her face in the woman's neck, overcome with gratitude. She could find no reasons for this exceptional honor, just as there were no natural explanations for the angelic visitors who often visited the saints. She only knew that God sometimes chose simple folk to spread his message. In the same manner, for some unearthly reason, Lady Endeline had chosen her.

Afton could have worshiped at Endeline's feet for the rest of the day, but the purified atmosphere dissipated when two boys burst into the hall. Both boys were carrying bows and quivers of arrows, and the shock Afton felt at seeing weapons in what she felt was a holy place was quickly surpassed by incredulity when the older boy actually complained to the revered lady: "Mother, Jarvis is supposed to meet us in the courtyard but we can't find him."

"Hush," Endeline answered. She slipped her slender

arm loosely around Afton's shoulders. "I would like both of you to meet Afton. She will live here at the castle as a companion for Lienor."

The boys came closer, reluctantly, and the older boy barely glanced at Afton before looking away. "This is Charles, my eldest son," Endeline said, pointing to the taller boy. Afton noticed that he resembled his mother, sharing the same dark eyes and slim build.

"And this is Calhoun, my second-born." Afton's eyes locked with the second boy's and she recognized her companion of weeks earlier. His eyes were as merry now as they had been on that sun-drenched day when he had helped her make the wreath for Sheba. In fact, his eyes were twinkling with their secret, and he removed his cap and bowed gallantly from the waist. "I am pleased to meet you, my lady," he said.

"There's no need for that, Calhoun," Endeline reproved him. "Afton is only a child. But you and your brother will do your best to make her feel welcome, will you not?"

Charles mumbled something in reply, and Calhoun smiled broadly. "But of course, Mother," he said, holding his cap over his heart. "It is my sacred duty as a knight and a nobleman to protect women and children."

"Be off with your foolishness," Endeline answered, shooing her sons from the hall. "If Jarvis said he would meet you in the courtyard, you will find him there, not here."

The boys scurried out of the room, and Endeline stood from her chair in one fluid motion. Her hand sought Afton's and held it tightly. "You will now meet Lienor, Afton. You will be her playmate and companion. I think you will get along well together."

A girl's playmate! Afton felt another indescribable rush of gratitude to the tall woman at her side. In her fondest dreams, Afton had never dared to hope that she would be able to play while at the castle—and with a girl!

Afton followed Endeline out of the spacious hall and ascended another staircase, this one of wood and very steep.

To the right of the staircase landing lay a spacious chamber, whose chief furnishing was an enormous curtained bed. Afton was led through this chamber to a smaller room.

Here a girl sat at a heavy table with a solid-looking woman, whose plump face was framed by a coarse cotton wimple. Afton glanced at the woman, then gazed hungrily at the girl. The girl returned Afton's scrutiny with a scowl.

"This will be your chamber," Endeline said gently. She pointed to a stack of stuffed mattresses against the wall. "You will sleep in here with Lienor and my maids. Lienor, dear, greet your new companion."

The girl frowned and her brows rushed together. "Hello."

"And this is Gwendolyn, who is giving Lienor a lesson in Latin. Do you read, Afton?"

Afton shook her head, and Endeline nodded curtly. "Then you shall be taught. You will learn to read, write, and speak Latin and French. You and Lienor will be unsurpassed in your ability to sing and tell charming stories." She patted Afton's shoulders and laughed softly. "You two girls will be the most accomplished young women in King Henry's kingdom."

"Lienor has written you a poem, Lady Endeline," Gwendolyn spoke up, pointing to a scrap of parchment on the table.

"I will hear it later," Endeline said, dismissing Gwendolyn with a gesture. "Now I would like you to fetch Morgan and Lunette. We're going to give this child a bath and get her into decent clothes."

Afton's world expanded with each passing moment. Morgan and Lunette, Endeline's two young maids, made no secret of their curiosity and zest for their lady's latest endeavor. They bustled Afton to another small room off the bedchamber. Glancing around, Afton saw nothing in the room but a wooden tub lined with thick cloth. She stood and hugged herself, not knowing what to do. Lunette put her hands on her hips. "Don't just stand there, miss, strip off zat tunic," she ordered in a heavy French accent. "You're in need of a good scrubbing, zat's for sure. When ees the last time you had a bath?"

Afton's eyes widened. *Strip? A bath? A scrubbing?* What were they planning to do to her?

Morgan sighed. "Excuse me, miss, but Lunette thinks everybody in the manor knows what a bathtub is. I know better and I know you likely 'aven't seen one, but Lord Perceval fairly loves the thing. He even takes it with 'im when 'e travels."

"So strip!" Lunette ordered, moving toward Afton. "Get ready to take ze bath, or I'll 'af to take your clothes off myself."

Afton unloosed the ribbons that held up her tunic and let it fall to the floor. Morgan jiggled a spigot and water began to flow into the tub. Afton couldn't believe her eyes. "Where does the water come from?" she asked, her voice a mere squeak under the sound of running water. Did Lord Perceval have the power to make the walls give water?

"The water comes from the roof," Morgan explained, raising her solid arm and pointing upward. "A cistern up there collects rainwater, and it comes down through the pipes when we need it."

"Ze rain even flushes ze lavatory," Lunette added. She crinkled her nose and pointed to a niche in the stone wall. "So we pray for rain." She nodded toward the filled tub. "Step on ze stool and hop in, little lamb."

"What does the rain flush?" Afton asked, stepping into the tub. She shivered. The water was cold.

Morgan's head jerked toward the opening in the wall again as she began to scrub Afton's skin. "The lavatory. Where you will relieve yourself. A long pipe against the outside of the castle wall carries everything down into the moat. The lord's very proud of his lavatory, 'e is, and I hear 'e's planning to build them all along the outer wall for the knights, too."

47

"It's just like him to keep up with everything," Lunette added, pouring something cold and oily into Afton's hair. "If King Henry's castle adds a thing, Lord Perceval doesn't blink an eye before he's adding it, too."

Afton glanced over at the famous lavatory. It was a dark recess, a wooden shelf with a single hole, and a pile of hay lay off to the side. "For what does Lord Perceval use the hay?" she asked shyly.

Lunette covered her mouth and giggled. "Honestly," she squeaked when she had caught her breath, "Where did ze mistress find you? Out in ze fields?"

Morgan silenced the younger maid with a stern look, and Afton shivered while the two of them continued to scrub her hair and skin. Yes, she had come from the fields, and what of it? She had come from a small mud hut with sunbleached grass on the roof and chickens underfoot. But in that rough home had been babies, and laughter, and the earthy smells of hardworking people and nurturing animals.

Afton clenched her chattering teeth and shut her eyes tightly to block out the most recent and vivid memory of home: Corba in a rage. Surely her mother could not have done those things! But the sound of the slap, the sting of her flesh, and the flurry of arms and legs that literally kicked her away were still in the forefront of her memory.

In contrast, the Lady Endeline was tall and darkly beautiful and smelled faintly of roses and summertime. Her arms had been extended; her words, honey-sweet. Her realm held soft mattresses to sleep on, lessons to learn, and a girl playmate. And a boy with smiling eyes.

Lunette stopped rubbing the coarse cloth across Afton's neck, and Afton opened her eyes. "You really should bless ze star you were born under, you know," Lunette said. "Eet's not every girl who gets ze chance to live with the lord's family. Me, I have been 'ere two years, and a more noble family is not to be found."

Lunette gave Afton's hair a final rinse, and Afton told herself Lunette was right.

After the bath Morgan dressed Afton in a simple white cotton tunic. From her bed, Endeline nodded approval and snapped her fingers at her daughter. "Lienor, dear, show Afton around the castle," Endeline commanded. "We want to make her feel at home."

Lienor grumbled as she rose from her study table, but she grabbed Afton's hand and reluctantly led Afton out of Endeline's chamber. Her reluctance vanished, however, as soon as they were down the wooden staircase and out of Endeline's sight. Suddenly she seemed more relaxed and pleasant.

"There is a room for my brothers up above my mother's chamber," she explained, pointing overhead. "And a room for my father's chaplain. The chapel is up there, too, of course. But the hall is on this floor."

Afton wanted to explain that she had already visited the great hall, but Lienor pulled her through it and kept up a steady stream of chatter. "Those little rooms off to the side are for the pantler and cupbearer, but my brothers and I play in there during the day. The servants sleep in here at night." She nodded at the great hall around them. "Everything happens in here, or so it seems."

Afton nodded numbly, and Lienor pulled her out of the hall and down the great stone staircase to the first floor. "Here and below are the cellars," Lienor explained, skipping toward the huge arch that served as the entrance to Perceval's home. "You will not want to go down there. I have been down there only once and found it a dark and creepy place. Not even my brothers venture down to the cellars."

The girls passed through the archway and into a narrow hallway, beyond which Afton glimpsed the blue of open sky. She followed Lienor willingly into the gentle afternoon sunshine. They crossed the sturdy drawbridge that carried them over a lily-padded moat and went into the castle yard. As she trotted behind her new friend, Afton gathered her courage to make an observation. "I thought you did not want to come out. A moment ago, when your mother asked you to take me—"

"I hate doing what mother tells me to do," Lienor interrupted, whirling to face Afton. "She's always telling me what I have to do to be a lady. I actually like wandering around the castle, but I'm not permitted to go out alone, and the maids are always busy. But now that you're here, I hope I'll be able to do what I like."

Afton was shocked by the force behind Lienor's words. How could anyone hate the gracious Lady Endeline? But Lienor's eyes burned with the fire of righteous indignation, and Afton did not want to risk angering her chosen companion. She managed a weak smile. "What do you like to do?"

Lienor's eyes twinkled and she tilted her head. "Whatever my brothers do. Come on, I'll race you to the kitchens."

Lienor turned and sprinted away. Afton ran behind her for two steps before she slowed to a steady jog. It was probably not wise, on her first day in the castle, to outrun Perceval's fiery little daughter.

"Before William the Conqueror set sail for England in 1066, Margate was a crude castle," Gwendolyn said, rapping the table for emphasis. Afton struggled to pay attention, but her traitorous eyelids only grew heavier. She had not slept much the night before, and she was not accustomed to sitting still at a table for lessons.

Gwendolyn continued. "The people here were at the mercy of the Saxon master who ruled from the top of this hill. But the Conqueror from Normandy and the Battle of Hastings changed everything." Gwendolyn glanced at Lienor, who gazed out the window with a bored expression on her face. "What happened after the battle, Lienor?" her teacher asked.

Lienor didn't take her eyes from the window. "The Saxon ruler was killed," she responded, her voice flat. "His lands were confiscated, and all English lands were combined into fewer than two hundred estates."

"Aye," Gwendolyn nodded in satisfaction. "This estate

where you now sit, Afton, was awarded to Lionel, Lienor's grandfather. Today your lord Perceval rules these lands."

Afton nodded. That much she knew.

"Lionel civilized Margate Castle, enlarging the castle and building a larger wall around the castle estate. He was a strong ruler, and our lord Perceval has continued in his father's way. Margate is now one of the largest and finest castles in England."

Gwendolyn raised her head proudly, and Afton nodded slowly. There was no need to convince her of the castle's greatness, for it contained riches and luxury that eclipsed everything she had ever known.

Gwendolyn looked again at Lienor, and a frown crossed her face. "I suppose that is enough for today, girls," she said, crossing her arms. "Run along outside. I have other work to do."

Lienor smiled for the first time that morning and bolted for the door, pausing only for a moment to make certain that Afton followed. The girls flew down the stairs, out of the castle, and into the courtyard.

Outside the main castle keep and its shallow moat were other buildings that Afton had not yet fully explored: a two-story kitchen, the stables, a mews for housing Perceval's hunting falcons, a smithy, an orchard and garden, a women's work area, Hector's humble house, and a walled pool near the back of the castle wall.

"That's for the horses and the laundresses," Lienor said, jerking her chin toward the water. "Though sometimes my brothers like to splash around in there."

"Where does the water come from?" Afton asked, looking for magical spigots like those in the castle.

Lienor shrugged. "From outside. There's a stream outside the wall, and a pipe or something lets the water in. We can play there sometimes, but the maids will tell Mama if they see us."

Encompassing the castle courtyard and its outbuildings was a larger wall, the *enceinte*, which was twenty feet thick and eighty feet tall. Two imposing towers rose up from the wall to remind all who approached of the powerful man who resided in the castle and the powerful king the lord represented. An impressive barbican, or fortified gate, was built into the new wall around Margate Castle and reinforced with sliding iron gates and a drawbridge. The barbican offered the only way in or out of the castle.

For all intents and purposes, Margate Castle was impregnable.

Afton felt Lienor tug on her hand. "Come on," Lienor urged, "I want to go to the stables."

Afton trudged wearily behind Lienor as they wandered into the spacious stable, empty now since Perceval's knights had taken the horses on patrol throughout the surrounding manors. In the cold stone castle buildings, Afton felt alien, as though she were from a distant land of animals and earth. But here in the stables, surrounded by hay and the pungent smells of animals and manure, she felt at home. As Lienor scampered about on the hay bales, Afton snuggled into a fresh pile of hay, closed her eyes, and drifted to sleep.

Her new cotton tunic was damp with sweat, but the sweet-smelling hay was cool. Afton heard the gentle rustle of the hay as she turned in sleep, and for a moment she imagined that she was back on her own straw mattress. But when she opened her eyes she saw Charles playing in the loft above her. It was not a dream. She really was in the castle.

She stretched lazily and watched the swaying of a rope above her head. It was attached to a pulley in the roof and fell to the ground somewhere behind her, but Afton did not have time to reflect upon its purpose. Suddenly she saw a bale of hay fall from the loft, and before she could move, something cut into her ribs and hoisted her into the air. She screamed in alarm and fear, and below her dangling feet she could see Lienor laughing.

"Oh, that's a worthy trick!" Lienor called up to Charles, who peered over the edge of the loft. "It's the best idea you've had, Charles!"

Afton forced herself to be quiet. She saw what held her aloft; a rope had been tied around her waist while she slept and Charles had apparently slipped the other end around a bale of hay.

"Oh, Charles, it is too funny!" Lienor screamed, rolling in the hay beneath Afton. "We've strung her up! My little pet villein!"

"Let me down!" Afton shrieked, her fear crystallizing to anger. "Let me down right this minute or I'll—"

"What will you do?" Charles asked calmly. He clambered down out of the hay loft and stood below her, an inscrutable look on his face.

Afton thought of her most recent deliverer. "I'll tell Lady Endeline. She has promised that no one will hurt me."

"She is nothing to you, villein," Charles answered. He sat down in the hay and leaned against a post. His voice was oddly sharp as he added: "But she is *my* mother."

"Let me down right now," Afton said, glaring at Lienor, "or I won't go anywhere else with ye. I won't do anything with ye at all."

"If you don't, you'll be sent back to the village," Lienor said simply, sticking out her tongue. "And given a good whipping, too."

Afton grew silent. Was that true? She had heard her father speak of men who died under whippings administered by the lord's men. Perhaps it was better just to dangle in silence until their little game was done.

Lienor giggled a few minutes more, then grew disappointed when Afton did not respond. "You're not fun at all," she pouted. "Come on, tell me what you're going to do about this, villein." She walked directly under Afton's dangling feet. "Threaten me."

Afton folded her arms and remained silent.

"This is boring," Charles said, standing up. "I'm going to find Jarvis and play horseshoes."

Charles walked off and Lienor glanced anxiously at his

retreating form. "Let me down, please," Afton called, trying to sound pleasant. "I can play horseshoes, too."

Lienor turned and ran out of the barn after Charles. "I don't know how to let you down," she called over her shoulder.

With that, Afton was left alone in the barn, spinning like a rag doll above the stone floor of the stables.

Her anger dissolved into fear, and her fear arched into overwhelming loneliness. Afton bore her helplessness as long as she could, then let a loud sob escape her. Was she taken from her home only to be abused by those who were supposed to be her playmates? Why was Lady Endeline allowing this to happen?

The sound of approaching hoofbeats interrupted her tears, and Afton wiped her face with her sleeve. What if she was found by a knight? Would she be beaten? Left to starve? Turned out into the forest?

It wasn't a knight on the bulky horse trotting into the barn, it was Calhoun. He slowed his horse to a walk and bent over the beast's neck, gently stroking the lathered animal. Afton didn't know whether to call out or remain silent.

As she debated with herself, Calhoun walked the horse into a stall to dismount. He swung his leg over the horse's rump, glancing around as he did so. When he spotted Afton he paused, then came out of the stall for a better look.

"For a moment I thought my eyes had trespassed upon an angel," he said simply, looking up at her. The twinkle was gone from his eyes. "But you are not of the heavenly realm yet. If you were intending to hang yourself, you have placed the noose incorrectly."

"I didn't do this," Afton answered, unable to keep the anger out of her voice. "Lienor and Charles did it for sport."

Calhoun stood motionless, and Afton was afraid he would walk away, too. "Are ye going to let me starve up here?" she finally demanded.

"No," Calhoun answered, smiling up at her. "I was just

enjoying the sight. It is easy to see why my eyes mistook you for an angel. Hair of gold, eyes like morning fog—"

"Get me down!" Afton shrieked, covering her ears.

Calhoun maneuvered the weighted bale of hay to which the rope was tied so that it was directly under Afton. Then he pulled a dagger from his belt. "I'm going to cut the rope and you will fall," he said, looking up. "I will catch you."

"Is there no other way? I don't want to fall."

"I said I would catch you. Don't you trust me?"

Afton bit her lip. "No."

Calhoun shook his head. "A knight always keeps his word," he said solemnly. "I will catch you."

She nodded and held tight to the rope around her waist. Calhoun swung his dagger in a wide arc and as it bit through the rope, Afton squealed and dropped to the ground like an iron weight. She landed squarely on top of Calhoun, the impact knocking him off his feet. Both of them lay sprawled in the hay.

When she had caught her breath, Afton pushed herself up and away from her rescuer. "Ye didn't catch me," she said, her voice unsteady. "But thank ye for breaking my fall."

Calhoun spat hay out of his mouth and lifted his head. He grinned at her. "Next time, I will catch you."

She scrambled further away. "Ye will not have to rescue me again," she said, brushing the hay from her tunic.

In an instant he was beside her. "Nay, but that is a knight's duty." He ran his hands lightly over her shoulders and arms. "Are you certain you are all right? You are not hurt?"

"I am not hurt," she answered, studying his face. His touch surprised and affected her, for no man or boy had ever touched her with compassion. In his eyes she saw concern, friendliness, and care—the qualities she had always ascribed to God and the king alone.

I know this, she thought. *No son of the king's, or even the king himself, could be more beautiful than Calhoun.*

"Lienor and Charles will not play these tricks again," Calhoun told her, taking a step back. "You can be sure of it."

He returned his dagger to his belt and went to tend his horse, and Afton sat silently in the hay, watching him, a strange and unnerving emotion growing within her. In that moment, for the first time in her eight years, Afton knew what it was to value someone else's life above her own.

FIVE

Life soon fell into a comfortable routine. Every morning Afton awoke in the dormitory she shared with Lienor, Morgan, and Lunette. Under the maids' careful supervision, the girls washed their hands and faces in a basin, said hurried prayers, and dressed quickly and neatly. Afton found an endless delight in dressing. Her clothing was dyed in brilliant jewel colors, and it seemed that each day she was given a different long-sleeved tunic and sleeveless surcoat to pull on over her long linen chemise. In October, when the weather turned cool, she and Lienor were given graceful fur-lined mantles that fastened at the neck—hers by a simple gold chain, Lienor's by a golden brooch.

After the girls were dressed, the maids braided their hair. Lunette usually braided Lienor's into intricate designs, while the more down-to-earth Morgan braided Afton's. One morning Lienor rebelled against the daily ritual and pulled away from Lunette's nimble fingers. "I'll wear my hair down today," Lienor said, her back toward the wall. "I won't be all trussed up like a horse."

Lady Endeline stepped calmly into the small room. "Lienor, you will have your hair braided, and you will wear your cap, as a young lady should," she pronounced. "A lady's hair should always be beautifully braided. Wild hair, my daughter, is permissible only in mourning, and you are not in mourning"—she arched an eyebrow—"yet."

Lienor returned to the stool in front of Lunette, but the

sulky look did not leave her face. Endeline patted her daughter's shoulder gently and smiled coyly. "A beautiful braid will do much to attract attention even as you are walking away. Knights and lords have their swords, girls, but one of a woman's most effective weapons is her hair."

Lienor's scowl only deepened, but the lady's words fell on Afton's ears as true gospel. She sat motionless while Morgan finished braiding her hair and tied the close-fitting cap on her head. Soon she would be old enough to wear the tall veiled hats or beaded caps that Endeline favored, and Afton resolved to do nothing to weaken her lady's favor. Her world revolved around Endeline's instructions and gentle admonitions.

Lienor never failed to scowl when her mother imparted pearls of womanly wisdom, but Afton could never hear enough. She followed Endeline's example in word and deed, even wishing her own blonde hair were dark so she could undergo the bleaching treatments Endeline and Lienor endured once a week to give their dark hair a lighter color. "Why should you wish such a theeng?" Lunette once reprimanded her privately. "Even nature itself saves ze color gold for its best creatures—look at ze golden eagle! Your 'air, gold as nature intended it, is by far the more lovely."

Afton enjoyed the compliment, but she didn't believe Lunette. She wanted to be like Endeline in every way, and she was simply inferior. Why else was she left out of the most important weekly rituals?

Every Monday morning, after washing and bleaching their hair, the maids massaged Endeline's and Lienor's scalps with olive oil. Then Endeline endured the ritual every highborn woman favored—her scalp was partially shaved. Afton watched in horror the first time she saw Lunette shave Endeline's widow's peak and an inch of scalp to enlarge the lady's forehead, but Endeline merely smiled at Afton's frightened expression. Wide foreheads, Endeline assured Afton, were the fashion. After the lady was suitably bleached, oiled, and shaved, her remaining hair was combed, braided, and covered with a dainty cap.

With their daily grooming accomplished, the ladies met the rest of the family upstairs in the tiny chapel for Mass with Raimondin, Perceval's chaplain. After the Mass and prayers, Afton and Lienor went downstairs to their chamber for lessons with Gwendolyn while Charles and Calhoun stayed upstairs for lessons with Raimondin. While the children learned their lessons, Endeline went downstairs to discuss with Hector the details of the dinner and supper preparation.

Afton was always amazed at the grandness of the lord's dinner. The meal began promptly at ten o'clock in the morning, and the girls were excused from lessons just in time to rush to their places at the children's table in the great hall. They ate with Gwendolyn, Raimondin, Charles, and Calhoun. Their table was one of many, for three rows of tables filled the hall. At these tables were seated the other members of Perceval's household: the *mesnes,* or military personnel, such as knights, guards, squires, men-at-arms, and watchmen; and the domestic staff, such as clerks and high-ranking servants. Visiting vassals from other manors dined as well, and Afton saw new faces in the dinner crowd every morning. She often forgot that she was supposed to keep her eyes downcast while she ate. It was much more interesting to look around and take as much in as she could.

At the front of the spacious hall was a raised platform, upon which sat Perceval's table. From this vantage point, Perceval, Endeline, and Hector surveyed the members of their estate. Perceval often regaled his audience with tales of his bravery or his latest acquisition, while Endeline directed the servants with discreet nods and gestures.

Afton loved dinner. Not because of the adults around her—whom she ignored for the most part—but because of the laughing eyes that usually were less than two feet away from her. For there, across the rough table, sat Calhoun.

He talked constantly, keeping up a continual current of conversation under his father's orations from the dais. Afton loved hearing about the boy's exploits with the knights, or his horse, or the latest trick he had conspired with Charles to pull on Raimondin.

As for Charles, he said little, a fact that Afton found strange in an elder brother. Her brothers could not be kept quiet. When Charles did speak, it was to Lienor, and his eyes rarely lifted off his trencher. He ate dutifully and purposefully, never beginning one food until he had finished the first, and never, ever looking in Afton's direction. After a while, Afton was convinced that he hated her.

When dinner was done, Perceval led the men outdoors to hunt or go hawking. Charles and Calhoun usually amused themselves in the castle yard with archery or horseshoes, and Endeline kept Lienor and Afton by her side in the orchard as she conversed with her handmaids or visiting ladies. While the men participated in physical sports, the women took part in verbal exploits—telling stories, exchanging riddles, and playing gentle games.

Endeline's skill as a verbal gymnast fascinated Afton, and though she often did not understand what Endeline's coy words and upraised brow meant, her effect upon the other ladies was evident. Often they blushed, sulked, laughed, or went pale—but nothing upset Endeline. She was mistress of the castle and of the conversation, and no one dared contradict her.

When many outside visitors were present, Endeline's garden meetings often revolved around pure gossip. During these sessions, Lienor was expected to remain by her mother's side, but Afton was free to wander through the garden, weaving garlands of flowers or circlets of daisies. When the visiting ladies retired into the castle for a nap, Afton would take her floral offering and kneel to place it in Endeline's lap. Her efforts never failed to earn her a hug and a cry of "Oh, you darling girl!" Afton felt that no offering had ever been so well rewarded.

During the quiet afternoons when there were no guests, Endeline taught Afton and Lienor how to embroider. "You should create tapestries suitable for the finest castle or for a priest," she told them. "Leave the simple work for the villeins. Beautiful ladies should create beautiful things."

Lienor did not find needlework to her liking, and her finished works usually brought a frown to Endeline's delicate face. But Afton took to sewing naturally, for Corba had already taught her the basics, and the richly colored threads and fabrics available in the castle made embroidery a sheer joy. Best of all, Afton found that her skill in needlework surpassed Lienor's. Whenever Afton struggled to catch up to Lienor in her study of Latin and French, she took comfort that at least she could embroider beautifully.

At the end of the day, when Perceval and his knights came in from hunting or traveling, the ladies dropped whatever they were doing and ran to make the master comfortable. Endeline snapped her fingers and brought servants running with bowls to wash his hands and feet. Endeline herself brought comfortable slippers for him to wear while she hung on his words and admired his labors. It was Lienor's job to bring her father a pint of ale, and Afton's to bring a pillow for his head. She shrank from the job at first, hardly daring to approach the man whose name she had only heard breathed in dread or fear. But Perceval largely ignored her, and each day she found she accomplished her slight task more easily. Even so, she never lingered, never spoke, and never allowed her flesh to touch his head, shoulder, or hands.

After the lord had rested, a light supper was served in the hall, attended by only Perceval's immediate household. Even this group, however, was considerable, for it included the family, the steward, the knights, the chaplain, and the high-ranking servants. As a result, Afton learned to feel comfortable in the castle company. As each day passed and Perceval neither spoke to nor acknowledged her, she was sure that in the lord's eyes she remained a blessedly anonymous presence.

In truth, though, Perceval did not matter to the young girl. There were others who occupied her mind and heart:

Endeline taught her, Morgan and Lunette spoiled her shamelessly, Lienor tolerated her, Charles left her alone, and Calhoun often smiled at her.

And, as Endeline had predicted, Afton's memories of an earthen hut and five hungry brothers began to fade.

Two days before King Henry's scheduled arrival at Margate Castle, the household was a flurry of activity. Perceval lost his grand aloofness at meals and constantly called for Hector, Endeline, or Jarvis with real and imagined concerns. Endeline lost her mask of self-control and lashed out at the servants and her children. Afton slipped in and out of the castle, remaining in the shadows as much as possible.

Dozens of villeins from the village had been ordered to work at the castle, and Afton had never seen such sweeping and dusting. She peered through the crowd of women who worked in the kitchen, wanting to catch a glimpse of Corba, but relieved when Corba was not among them. Wido she had seen from a distance, carrying logs from the forest for the hearth fires. He looked as strong and dark as ever.

The annual rents of livestock, lumber, clothing, and other commodities that Hector had collected from the villeins were now put to use: sheep were slaughtered and salted for later use; oak planks were used to repair flooring in the castle; the woven garments were hung inside the wardrobe adjoining Perceval's chamber.

The children's lessons were interrupted when Hector led his new assistant through the lord's chamber. From the small dormitory where she sat, Afton saw the boy—a thin lad in his late teen years—burdened with a load of furs. "Lay them down carefully, Josson," Hector called, his reedy voice disturbing the quiet of the room. "Then go fetch the tapestries and candles that remain downstairs."

The boy put the furs next to Perceval's store of gold plates in the wardrobe, then turned to leave. As he passed the girls' dormitory, though, his eyes caught Afton's. He looked at her with frank curiosity, and she felt herself blushing.

"Afton!" Gwendolyn's sharp voice brought her back to her lessons. "You are not reading!"

Lienor closed her Psalter with a snap. "We can't read today, Gwendolyn," she said, peering out the arched doorway. "We want to watch Hector."

Gwendolyn sighed, but it was clear her curiosity had also been aroused by the procession of valuables from the outlying manors. "Let us watch, then," she conceded, moving closer to the doorway. "But mind you don't bother the gentlemen as they work."

Presently Josson returned with a crateload of candles and a tapestry rolled up under his arm, but Afton didn't care about the treasures in the wardrobe. She wondered instead about the boy. Where had Hector found him, and what would the future hold for him at Margate Castle? It was obvious that he was a servant, for Hector ordered him with impunity, but intelligence and honesty were written in his face. His hands, Afton noted, were not stained with earth, so this boy was no villein.

"Our lord is so rich," Gwendolyn whispered to Afton as they watched Josson bring a load of fabrics and a jeweled cask into Perceval's storeroom. "How could any one man use so much?"

"Aye, he will use all this and more," Lienor answered dryly. "I heard my father say that it must be displayed and given freely when King Henry visits."

"'Tis true," Gwendolyn said with a nod. "A lord is judged by his generosity, and he is only truly rich if he has many friends. The richest friend of all," she added, with a wry smile, "is, of course, the king."

As Lady Endeline approached the chamber, she saw that Hector and Josson were leaving. Good. Surely the girls had been distracted from their lessons, because today they needed to learn lessons of another sort.

Endeline swept through the chamber and into the girls' dormitory. "The king arrives in two days," she announced, though, of course, everyone in the castle was aware of the approaching visit. "It is time for you girls to have a lesson in manners. Come, put away your books. Gwendolyn, you are dismissed."

The girls stacked their books on the end of the table and followed Endeline into her spacious main chamber. Endeline sat on the edge of the bed and motioned for Afton and Lienor to be seated on a nearby bench. "Lienor," she began, folding her hands primly as she searched for the proper words, "you are nearly nine, the age of betrothal. As the daughter of an earl, we cannot marry you to anyone of lesser stature. There are, of course, a few families with sons whose rank equals yours, but why marry a partridge when you can marry an eagle?"

Endeline paused delicately, but it was clear from the girls' baffled expressions that they had no idea what she was talking about. She tried a more direct approach. "You are not too young, Lienor, to begin to think about your future husband." Her voice was sharper than she intended it to be, revealing her natural impatience with her boyish daughter. She paused, taking care to soften her voice. "King Henry has a son, you know. Prince William. Since you cannot marry beneath your station, you would do well to study the king's son. Find out what he likes, what pleases him."

"Do I have to?" Lienor's tone was almost a whine, and Endeline resisted the impulse to box her ears.

"Yes, you must. Look at Afton here. She acts more like a lady than you do."

Lienor scowled at Afton, and Endeline saw Afton blush. Why wasn't her own daughter as soft, pretty, and pliable? "Notice how Afton walks, straight and gentle, like a doe. A lady must not walk like a man, Lienor. You must not look like a man, or look *at* a young man as if you'd like to play with him. A lady should not glance at a man, for glances are messengers of love, and men are prompt to deceive themselves by them. From now on, the only man you should look at is Prince William."

Afton was listening carefully, Endeline noticed, but Lienor seemed more intent on studying the floor. Could it be possible that a fairy sprite had switched the two girls at birth? Endeline sighed and went on.

"A lady does not scold, swear, or eat or drink too much." Endeline stood up and paced in front of the girls. "If you are wearing a hood or a veil, you must remove it before King Henry, to show that you honor him. You must respond when the king salutes you."

Endeline paused for a moment and studied her daughter's scowling face. Perhaps it would be better if the king did not get too close a look at Lienor. "On the other hand, given your young age, perhaps it would be better to keep your face downcast, out of respect. And remind Lunette to bring you a glass of wine before dinner—it will bring out the red in your cheeks."

Neither girl gave any sort of response to Endeline's instructions, and she grew exasperated. Was she wasting her breath? Perhaps it would be better to keep Lienor out of sight until the king's visit had passed. If he got one look at her frowning face or her boyish hands—

Endeline snapped her fingers. "Put out your hands."

Both girls thrust their hands into the air in front of them, and Endeline inspected them closely. Afton's were perfect, her nails clean and cut close to the finger. Much to Endeline's displeasure, however, Lienor's hands were disgraceful. Her nails were long and ragged, and a definite crescent of dirt showed itself under each nail and in the creases of her palms.

Without a word, Endeline went out to the staircase. "Lunette!" she shrieked. "Come at once and cut this girl's nails to the quick! Scrub her, too, and make her presentable." The fine lady's tone of voice revealed her doubt that such an act would really be possible.

"Cut them to ze quick, my lady?" Lunette asked, coming breathlessly up the stairs and into the room.

"Cleanliness is better than beauty," Endeline answered,

sweeping regally past the maid. "I'll be back in a moment with the quicklime, so be sure those nails are done."

Afton scrambled to stay out of Lunette's way as she followed Endeline's orders. Before long, the lady returned, carrying a bowl in her hands. Afton felt genuinely sorry for Lienor when she saw how quicklime was used. The faint shadow of dark hair across Lienor's upper lip was swabbed generously with quicklime, then Endeline told Lunette and Morgan to hold Lienor down on the bed while the quicklime dried. When the mixture was dry, Endeline approached the bed with steely determination in her eyes. "Hold her tightly," she told the maids, reaching toward her daughter.

"No, mother! No!" Lienor screamed as Endeline scrubbed the dried quicklime from the delicate skin between Lienor's upper lip and nose. "Ouch! It stings!"

"One must suffer to be beautiful," Endeline replied, swatting Lienor's flailing legs. "Now be still!"

Afton turned her back and cringed each time Lienor howled. Was having Prince William as a husband really worth this much pain? The young girl shook her head, reminding herself that Lady Endeline had said it was necessary. In her heart, Afton knew she'd gladly undergo such a ritual if Endeline asked her to.

"Afton! Come away from the window."

She turned obediently back to Endeline, who was now standing with her back to her weeping daughter. Lienor sat drying on the bed, her upper lip raw and red. But there was no longer a shadow of dark hair.

"Make sure Lienor breakfasts on anise and fennel the morning the king arrives," Endeline told Afton as she wiped the dried quicklime from her fingers with a towel. "Her breath will then be sweet when she greets the king. Lunette, you will make her skin white with sheep fat." She frowned at Lienor's tan. "You will need to use a lot. She spends too much time outdoors with her brothers."

Lienor continued to weep silently, and Afton stared in amazement. Often she had seen Lienor in a fury, fighting and screaming. Many times she had wondered if the girl would destroy a room with her rages. But never, in the whole time Afton had been at the castle, had she seen Lienor weep like this—silently, painfully, as though something inside had broken.

"Quiet, Lienor." Endeline tossed the dirty cloth to Morgan. "I expect all of you to behave as well as you can. Perceval's honor must be upheld during the king's visit, for the future of our house depends on it. We will do our best to make King Henry comfortable and to please his son William. Is that understood?"

"Yes, my lady," Afton answered dutifully.

Still weeping, Lienor answered in a whisper: "Yes."

Endeline's eyes narrowed as she looked at her daughter. Then she turned to Afton and smiled. "Help me with my wildcat daughter, my dear, and perhaps we will present you to the king as well. Unless you are instructed in that regard, however, you will stay out of sight."

Afton nodded. She had not expected to meet the king. It was enough that she could help Endeline.

The next morning, a messenger carrying the banner of King Henry galloped through the gates of Margate Castle. His message to Perceval was simple: King Henry's ship had landed safely in England and the king was en route to Margate. Furthermore (the messenger added in an unofficial aside), His Majesty was in a jubilant mood. The war to reunite the Norman and English halves of the kingdom of William the Conqueror was nearly over, and Henry would doubtless be the victor.

Perceval breathed a sigh of relief. He knew full well that opening his home to the king was much like inviting a tiger into his private chamber. While the beast was truly powerful, beautiful, and awe-inspiring, it could eat a man alive. Still, honor demanded that he take the risk. He only hoped that honor would not cost him more than he could give.

Endeline roused Lienor before daylight the following morning, and Afton listened sympathetically to Lienor's quiet complaints as she was bathed vigorously and her hair washed in clove-scented water. Lunette braided Lienor's hair with fresh roses, and Morgan worked the same magic on Endeline. Afton was quietly granted permission to stay out of the way.

Gratefully, she dressed and scampered out of the chamber and down the staircase until she was in the castle courtyard. Life was busy here, too. The sun had barely begun to climb in the sky, but outside the kitchen the cooks were butchering lambs and calves for dinner. Afton felt queasy at the sight of so much blood, so she ran for the quiet of the orchard.

From the safety of an apple tree, Afton watched Perceval's garrison of knights mount up and ride out to meet the king's traveling party. As she watched the knights depart, the girl smiled. If the knights were gone, then the garrison tower would be empty—and the view spectacular. The towers were the only buildings that stood above the outer walls of the castle, and the only vantage point from which she would be able to see the king approaching.

Afton shinnied out of the apple tree and darted through the throng of servants in the busy courtyard. The tower's heavy wooden door intimidated her for a moment, but she yanked it open and scurried up the narrow, winding staircase until she reached the circular room at the lookout point.

Looking around, she spied an open space above an outcropping that jutted toward the castle road. She started toward the window, and jumped when someone moved in the shadows beside her.

It was Calhoun, and he seemed as embarrassed to be discovered in the tower as she was frightened. He turned his face from her. In a flash, she forgot her fears and leaned on the wall beside him. "What's wrong?" she asked, concerned. She could not imagine what could cause him embarrassment.

"Nothing you would understand," he answered, jerking his hand across his face and wiping his eyes. He closed his lips firmly together, looking out the window, but words seemed to rise unbidden from somewhere in his soul. "How am I supposed to be a knight if they won't let me do anything? I'm as brave as they are!"

"You are," Afton agreed. "Remember how brave you were when you freed me from the trap in the barn? I might have hung there for days and starved to death."

Calhoun smiled at her in spite of his misery. "That wasn't bravery. That was chivalry. Knights are *supposed* to help women and children."

"It was brave to let me fall right on top of you," Afton insisted, laughing, glad to see his smile. "I could have crushed you!"

"You're a slip of a girl. You couldn't crush anybody," Calhoun answered skeptically. Then his face clouded over again. "But today I asked Jarvis if I might ride out with the knights to meet the king. He . . . he told me to run along and stay out of the way." Calhoun's chin quivered and his face grew red. "To stay out of the way! He has never said that before."

"I'm sure he didn't mean to be cruel," Afton answered softly. She knew how much anything Jarvis said meant to Calhoun—and how much those words must have hurt. "It's just that everyone's upset about the king's visit. But Jarvis knows that you are brave and very able. Perhaps he has something better for you in mind, something you can do later."

"I shall be too busy staying out of the way," Calhoun answered, staring moodily out the window. Suddenly he stiffened and pointed down the road. "Here they come! The king's riders!"

Afton peered over the edge of the battlement. A row of splendid stallions, all decked in armor and wearing the king's red and purple, cantered abreast down the road. Behind them were chariots and other knights on horseback. Among these Afton recognized many of Perceval's men.

Then her eyes were drawn to one man. Wearing a simple

red robe and a purple mantle, he rode alone on a magnificent white stallion.

"That's the king," Calhoun whispered in awe. "King Henry Beauclerc."

Afton was fascinated. The riders were still a fair distance away, but behind the king she could see richly loaded wagons, which, along with the riders, formed a parade that seemed to stretch endlessly into the distance.

As the entourage drew closer, Afton was able to examine the king's company more closely. The wagons behind the king were loaded with cloth, bottles, and food. One wagon held a bathtub that was even bigger and more sumptuous than Perceval's! Another wagon carried three little girls who huddled together holding hands. Afton drew in her breath sharply when she noticed that the three girls were guarded by mounted knights who rode stiffly alongside them.

"Who are the girls?" she whispered to Calhoun, pointing. "Look, Calhoun, they're no older than we are. Who are they, and why do they look so sad?"

Calhoun looked, then shrugged. "Perhaps they are children King Henry has rescued. Orphans, maybe. Mayhap we will hear the story at dinner."

The first riders were at the castle gate now, and Calhoun turned and began leaping down the stairs, taking them two at a time. Before the circular path took him out of view, he paused and called up to Afton: "Aren't you coming?"

"Not to dinner," she answered, her eyes fastened to the wagon that held the three girls. "Lady Endeline asked me to eat with the servants today."

"All right, then, but I'd hasten out of the tower if I were you," Calhoun answered. "King Henry's knights are the fiercest in the world, and they'll be coming here presently." With that, he continued bounding down the stairs.

Afton waited only a moment before following him, pondering all that had happened already that day and wondering what more could possibly take place.

Six

Margate Castle could not hold all of King Henry's entourage. Tents sprouted like mushrooms in the field outside the castle walls to house the king's barber, a bloodletter, a doctor, a dentist, cooks, messengers, musicians, and a large part of the royal army. Henry's knights were garrisoned with Perceval's in the tower, and the royal counselors and the various nobles traveling with Henry were housed inside the castle's great hall. More than one hundred guests streamed through the gates of Margate Castle and, with Perceval's household in attendance as well, more than two hundred and fifty people sat down to dinner that day.

"It's a great feast," one of the young kitchen maids told Afton after returning from the great hall. "The lady has the best tapestries on display, and the king sits with Perceval and Endeline at the high table."

"Has the king met Lienor yet?" Afton asked, anxious about her friend.

"No, he only talks of the war for Normandy," the girl answered, filling a basket with fresh loaves of white bread.

"What of the three girls with him?" Afton asked. "Who are they and why do they travel with the king?"

"They sit and eat silently," another servant answered. "But I've heard it said they are the granddaughters of the king."

"Granddaughters of the king? But Prince William is not married."

The younger maid smirked. "Don't you listen to the gossip, girl? King Henry has other children, not legitimate, of course. These are the girls of his daughter Julienne. He has taken them from their home in Normandy."

Although Afton had no idea where Normandy was, the idea of having a royal grandfather was fascinating. She had never known her own grandfather, who had died at the old age of forty-five. How proud these girls must be of their grandfather the king! But why did they look so sad in the wagon? Were they frightened of the guards at their sides?

"The king must love them very much," Afton remarked to the servant, "if they are protected by a guard at all times."

"That kind of love I could do without," the kitchen maid replied. "Now out of my way, child. The king will be wanting fresh bread soon, and it'll have to be hot out of the oven."

After three days of the king's residence at Margate, Afton was convinced the old castle had disappeared and something new had taken its place. Nothing was the same. King Henry now slept in Perceval's chamber, and his counselors occupied the girls' dormitory. Perceval and Endeline slept in the boys' room above, and the boys were relegated to sleep downstairs in the great hall with the king's most esteemed traveling companions. Lienor, Afton, Lunette, and Morgan slept in the hayloft of the barn, with a knight assigned to guard them. The king's three granddaughters, strangely enough, slept in the highest part of the lookout tower, with a host of knights below them.

The pleasant pace of life that Afton had come to know was gone, and she worried that King Henry would never leave. Calhoun, on the other hand, seemed to thrive on the excitement. He acted as a page for the king, running to fill the royal goblet, to fetch His Majesty's counselors, or to order fresh bread from the kitchen.

At the end of the day, when the men had retired, Calhoun met Afton in the stable and reported everything. His eyes shining, he described the king's exploits in Normandy and the victorious battles in which Henry had fought. Often he stood up and embellished the tales by acting them out, frequently "dying" in the hay with great emotion and drama. Afton couldn't understand why Calhoun loved these tales of battle. She much preferred Endeline's gentle stories of King Arthur and fair Guinevere.

But Afton rarely saw Endeline these days except from a distance, for the lady of the castle was kept busy attending to her royal guest's needs. It wasn't until Henry announced that he would leave after dinner on the morrow that Endeline seemed to relax and exchanged her stiff smile for a more pleasant one. And that night Afton snuggled into her hay bed in delight, knowing that soon she'd be back in the castle next to her beloved benefactress. Life would resume and all would be peaceful once again.

Endeline actually stopped and patted Afton's cheek on the day of the king's departure. "Why don't you join us at dinner, Afton?" she asked, her voice gentle. "You've not had a good look at the king, have you?"

Afton shook her head. All her glimpses of the August Majesty had been from a distance. To her, Henry was merely a stick figure in red and purple.

"Put on your best tunic, then, and we'll find a place for you in the hall. You may sit with Morgan and Lunette. Calhoun will be serving the king, and Lienor will sit with me at the king's table."

Afton's jaw dropped when she entered the hall between Morgan and Lunette. Every table in the castle had been crowded into the great hall and put together end-to-end so that they stretched from the rear doorway right up to the dais where the king would sit. Bright tapestries hung from the walls, each one brilliantly decorated in the emblems of the royal crest and Perceval's family herald. Already the tables were crowded with Perceval's and King Henry's knights and nobles, and the colors of the two houses blended together in a rich mix of red, purple, and white.

Morgan and Lunette ushered Afton to a small table that was against the wall near the royal dais. Afton was delighted, for she could observe all that went on at the king's table and yet not be seen.

She glanced over the assembled company. The tables nearest the king's table were filled with richly dressed men in ermine-trimmed robes. The king's counselors, Afton assumed. She had heard Calhoun speak of them as "rich men who talk of war while knowing little of it." Behind the counselors were men with swarthy faces and simple red robes, the royal knights. Perceval's knights, in their white-and-purple tunics, were intermingled in their midst, and behind the knights were the various high-level servants and the men-at-arms who traveled with the king.

Afton was surprised to see the king's granddaughters sitting at a table directly across from her, on the far side of the room. They were silent, sitting in stillness, their eyes trained on the trenchers in front of them.

"Lunette," Afton whispered, tugging on the maid's sleeve. "See the granddaughters over there? Have you had occasion to talk to them this week?"

"Shh, not I," Lunette whispered, laying a finger over her lips. "Hush now, ze king approaches."

A trumpeter shrilly proclaimed the king's arrival, and the entire company stood and bowed as King Henry entered. Perceval, Endeline, and Lienor followed him and took their places at the raised table. When the king had been seated, the entire group sat and centered their attention on the grand meal set before them.

The dinner was impressive. Perceval had saved his best foods for the king's farewell dinner, hoping to impress his sovereign with Margate Castle's seemingly endless supply of palate-pleasing delights.

Afton sniffed the air in appreciation as the highly sea-soned foods were passed down the tables. Her mouth watering, she scanned the black puddings, sausages, venison and beef, eels and herrings, freshwater fish from the lake, and round and flat sea fish. The meats had been seasoned with sauces of vinegar, verjuice, and wine, and each gave off a most delicious aroma. One roast that passed by her was studded with cloves; steam and the scent of ginger rose from another tray of boiled snails. Almonds, a rare treat, were sprinkled over the foods in abundance.

Murmurs of appreciation rose from the men and women who indulged themselves at Perceval's table, but Afton was speechless. Compared to the common fare she had been eating with the servants, this food was an unimaginable excess of richness and variety.

At King Henry's right hand sat Perceval, and at his left sat Endeline, Lienor by her side. Afton glanced up at her playmate and smothered a smile. From the satisfied look in Lady Endeline's face, her plan was apparently proceeding well. After today Lienor's destiny would be set.

Endeline felt a vast feeling of relief settle over her, but she forced herself to remain vigilant. All was going well, but it was not yet time to celebrate. Perhaps, though, it *was* time to seal a royal marriage.

She smiled carefully at the king. "If it please Your Majesty, may we inquire about the health of your son, William? Our hearts were laden with sorrow when we heard he would not be joining you here with us."

"My son remained behind, but he does well," Henry answered, nodding. "He is a brave and valiant knight. He will do justice for England and Normandy when he wears the crown."

"He cannot do wrong, but with the proper wife he will do better still," Endeline said gently. "Has your royal son given thought to marriage?" She looked down and idly stirred the pottage in her bowl. "My daughter, Lienor, is of noble blood. Of course, I know I do not need to remind you, Sire, but her grandfather, Lionel, was a close ally of your father's."

"I heard my father speak of Lionel often," Henry said

with a nod. He glanced at Lienor, who sipped her pottage with her eyes obediently downcast. "And surely your daughter carries the same noble heart. There is a spirited look about her."

Endeline felt like kicking Lienor under the table. *What had the king seen?* Endeline had tried to keep Lienor's wild nature concealed, but obviously she had failed. "Aye, her grandfather's spirit flows in her, but a more womanly girl could not be found," Endeline answered, her cheeks reddening. "Do you not agree, My King? A free spirit can certainly be a virtue."

The king did not answer, but Perceval scowled in Endeline's direction. His look clearly said, *Quiet, woman! You will make matters worse.* Perceval cleared his throat. "We should like to host Prince William sometime," he said evenly. "Perhaps he can share his gracious company with us after his return from Normandy."

Henry nodded and patted his bulging stomach. He had eaten enough for three men. "It is a convenient place for resting from the sea journey," he said. "I will suggest it. And, of course, Perceval, earl of Margate, we thank you for your hospitality."

"It is no more than my duty demands," Perceval answered, bowing his head. "It is but right, my lord, that whenever you come, all doors should be thoroughly opened to you. Whatever you desire, you have but to ask."

"I have asked, and you have given," Henry said, quietly belching. Endeline blanched, but listened carefully to what followed: "And I will return the favor to you, noble Perceval," Henry continued. "You have but to ask, and your request shall be granted."

Endeline sighed in relief. There. The king had given his promise. All Perceval had to do was suggest an alliance between their two houses, and Lienor would be betrothed. Henry's visit had been a success.

Endeline sighed in relief and slipped her arm around Lienor's shoulder. *Her Royal Highness Queen Lienor,* she thought, a smile playing around the corners of her mouth. She knew Perceval would stall a moment, then he would tell the king his daughter needed a husband. William would be suggested; the two noble families would merge.

But before Perceval could speak, a clamor arose outside the hall. A messenger in the king's colors rushed up through the rows of tables and knelt before the royal table. "Your Majesty, I come from the port with news of Normandy," he exclaimed, breathless, holding up an envelope. "An urgent letter from Prince William!"

King Henry took the letter, broke the seal, and read it. Endeline drew in her breath—something had to be wrong, else the message would not have been so urgent. She only hoped that, whatever it was, it wouldn't spoil the king's positive impression of his visit to Margate.

King Henry put down the letter and closed his eyes. The audience of nearly three hundred waited in silence, many with spoons and tankards upraised in suspended animation, as the king of England sat in contemplation, a frown upon his face.

The king finally opened his eyes. "Bring me the daughters of Julienne," he whispered, his hoarse voice carrying to the farthest corner of the silent room. A guard left the king's side at once to escort the girls from their table. Henry rose to his feet, his eyes scanning those assembled in the room. "Hear me, all of you," he roared, his face reddening. "My own daughter in Normandy, Julienne, did she not give me her three daughters in trust and faith?"

"She did, my lord," one of the king's counselors spoke up from a nearby table. "To assure you of her love and familial devotion."

"Did I not give her to be the wife of Eustache de Breteuil, and did I not give them the chateau of Ivry?"

"You did, my lord," another counselor added. "A most generous gift."

"Why then," Henry shouted, shaking the letter in his hand, "does our rightful son William write and tell me that

Julienne, along with her traitorous husband, has stood at that selfsame chateau and fought against the armies of Henry of England?" Henry's voice rose to a shrieking crescendo. "Why has she put on armor and shaken her fist in the face of her father and king?"

Not a soul moved. Not a counselor dared to speak. Henry closed his eyes in resignation, and Endeline felt a trembling begin to rise from somewhere inside her chest. The king's wrath was boiling and it would be poured out on someone, somehow. *Please, God,* she prayed, *may heaven and the saints preserve us! Perceval and I have done nothing to deserve the king's anger.*

"Bring Julienne's children to me," Henry commanded. The guard sent to fetch Julienne's daughters stepped up to the king's table. The three girls, not one of them taller than Lienor, walked silently past the knight and stood in front of the king.

"Kneel before me," he commanded. The oldest girl, who must have been Lienor's age, knelt promptly at her grandfather's feet. The second girl hesitated a moment after looking up into the king's fierce face, and the youngest girl, a blonde cherub with baby-fine hair, looked to her older sister for instruction before teetering down to her knees and putting her hands together in the traditional position of prayer.

Endeline's teeth began to chatter, and she quickly clenched them together.

Henry unsheathed his sword and handed it to a nearby knight. "Put the point of my sword into the fire until it glows red," he said, all emotion erased from his face. "Then put out the eyes of these girls, for their mother does not recognize her father."

The knight took Henry's sword and walked over to the hearth. He set the point of the king's sword into the flames.

"And you, loyal friend—" Henry looked at Perceval— "as you love me, noble Perceval, obey my command now."

"As you wish, my lord," Perceval said, standing stiffly to his feet.

"Draw your sword and cut the noses from these three faces," Henry commanded, "so no man will bear their mutilation and take them to wife. The seed of my Judas Julienne must not be allowed to continue."

As Perceval withdrew his sword and held it above the face of the youngest girl, blackness rushed from the walls of the room and blocked the sight from Endeline's eyes. She fell forward into her empty bowl in a dead faint.

Henry was gone, but like fish fossils on high mountaintops that give evidence to powerful flood waters, traces of his brutality remained. Memories of the grisly scene in the great hall woke Afton from her sleep night after night, and Lienor did not fare much better. One night as both girls lay sleepless in the dark, Lienor confided to Afton that she would rather jump from the castle tower than marry the son of King Henry. "I'll take a vow of chastity," Lienor mumbled, "and give my life to God rather than to the son of such a man. Every night for a month now I have prayed for William's death. I pray that he will drown in the ocean and be eaten by sharks before he ever sets foot in England again."

"Lienor, you should not say such things!" Afton whispered, truly horrified. "That's treason! Calhoun says the punishment for treason is death, and—"

"I would gladly die rather than be married to the son of King Henry," Lienor whispered fiercely, her hushed words echoing in the stillness of their tiny chamber. "If God requires my life for my freedom, I will give it."

Since the king's visit, Afton, too, had been thinking heavy thoughts of God and man. Was it honorable for any man, king or not, to disfigure three children who had done no wrong? Endeline had taught her that the king was God's sovereign representative on earth; in fact, the touch of a royal hand had been known to heal the sick. Endeline had also taught Afton that God was good—but how good could the Almighty be if he allowed his holy representative on earth to commit such heinous deeds?

79

Afton closed her eyes and remembered how, in her child-hood, she had heard Wido and Corba pray often and loudly. Even so, her parents' prayers were more like incantations to the earth to bring forth food and rain; they bore little resem-blance to Endeline's eloquent prayers to a just and wise God. Though Father Odoric had taught Wido and Corba to end every incantation with "So be it, Lord!" they knew little about God except that his whims and ways controlled the weather and, consequently, their lives.

In Perceval's household, however, religion was dutifully practiced. Endeline's brother, Hugh, was the abbot of a nearby holy house that Lionel had established years before. The family still generously supported the Benedictine abbey where Abbot Hugh ran his monastery, and he counseled the family often in spiritual affairs. With such influences in the family, Afton knew Lienor's murderous and suicidal thoughts could not go unnoticed. For her friend's own sake, Afton felt Lienor should seek counsel.

That next morning, she begged Lienor to talk to Raimondin, the chaplain who led the family in daily pray-ers. When the family had departed from Mass, Afton led Lienor to confide in Raimondin. As a cure for her hatred and bitterness he prescribed silent prayer and meditation. "Women, being the weaker sex, are more prone to sin," he advised the girls. "So you must guard against improper thoughts that question the king's decisions. Because you have not husbands to watch over you, our Lord himself will do it if you raise your thoughts and voices in supplica-tion to him."

What Lienor did with the chaplain's advice Afton did not know, but she found a peculiar comfort in praying in the stillness of night. She did not yet know all the Latin prayers that Lienor and Endeline recited frequently throughout the day, so her prayers typically reflected both the elegance of Endeline and the brute strength of Wido: "Our Father, who art in heaven, blessed be the fruit of the earth. Blessed be Endeline and Lienor and Lunette and Morgan. Blessed be the fields and the knights and the villeins. And blessed be Calhoun. But may King Henry not be blessed. Amen."

After praying, Afton would roll over on her feather mattress and feel greatly comforted.

Abbot Hugh came for his annual visit in the late spring. Afton was relieved that this visit did not turn the household topsy-turvy as had King Henry's. Each family member stayed in his own room, the meals were no more plenteous or fragrant than usual, and Abbot Hugh arrived only with the company of one young monk, whom he called his "son." Afton instinctively liked the abbot, even if he did have a bald spot cut into the top of his head.

She was more than a little surprised when Abbot Hugh sought out her company one afternoon in the orchard. Endeline and Lienor retreated quietly, and the abbot looked Afton squarely in the eye. "I will be honest with you, child. I have been concerned about your presence here at the castle," he began, his clear voice resonating in the orchard. A small flock of birds flew out of the tree where they were nesting. "My sister Endeline tells me you have been here for almost a full year. You are a villein of lowly birth, but you are consorting with noble men and women. What say you about this arrangement?"

Afton was baffled. No one had ever asked her opinion. "I have nothing to say," she said, spreading her hands in the familiar gesture of speechlessness that Endeline often used. "I was brought here, taught to read and speak and behave as a gentlewoman, and I do what I am told."

"Do you never long for your parents?"

Afton cringed involuntarily. The frightful scene with Corba was still a painful memory, one she could not put behind her. "No, sir, I do not. I try not to think about the day of our parting."

"Do you pray, my child? Do you love God?"

"Oh, yes sir. Every morning and every night I pray. The chaplain here has taught me."

"And do you listen to the chaplain as you would listen to the voice of God?"

Afton thought a moment. She thought of the chaplain as a rather dour teacher, not a spokesman for God. She answered slowly: "I listen for the voice of God in the wind, in the fields, and in here." She touched the side of her head.

The abbot shook his head. "That is a dangerous heresy, my child. The voice of God is relayed to man through his ministers, his priests. Your heritage as a villein is showing, for with your talk of wind and fields you are reverting to a pagan practice."

He sat down on a garden bench and motioned for her to sit next to him. "How shall I explain it to you?" he said, gazing off into the distance. "In the beginning, my child, the entire world was much as this garden. The trees brought forth fruit bountifully, and roses bore no thorns. Adam and his wife, Eve, were equal, and they spoke with God."

He looked down at her to see if she was listening, and Afton squirmed uncomfortably.

"Then sin entered into the world," the abbot continued. "The perfection of earth was ruined, and sin stood between man and God. The trees gave fruit grudgingly, and to enjoy the flawless beauty of the rose, men had to bear the suffering of her thorns." He paused as a sparrow lit on a nearby apple tree. "Do you see what I am saying, child?"

Afton grimaced, then lifted her head with hope. "That I shouldn't pick roses?"

Abbot Hugh sighed and shook his head. "No, my child. I would have you know that sin and suffering has brought division into the world. A great gulf stands fixed between man and God, and between men and other men. A priest is nearer God than a nobleman, and a pious nobleman is nearer than a villein. You, child of the earth, should remember that you cannot be what you are not, and listen to the priests, who speak God's truth."

"Yes, sir."

The abbot stood up and shook out his dark robe. "Be a

good girl, and I will tell my sister no harm will come to any-one if you stay here. Obey your mistress and be a good com-panion for Lienor."

"I will, sir."

The abbot traced the sign of the cross on her forehead and left Afton alone in the orchard.

Endeline was nearly through the castle doorway when she heard her second son's impassioned cry. "Jarvis!" Calhoun called, racing across the courtyard from the doorway of the tower. "In the distance, a royal messenger approaches! He carries the king's banner!"

Endeline felt her knees weaken. There had been no news from the king in the many months since his visit, but, despite the ghastly scene at the final dinner, she still had high hopes that a match would be made between Lienor and Prince William. Was this the news the messenger brought?

She dropped the armful of roses she was carrying onto a bench and strode purposefully for the stable. "Get a fresh horse for the messenger," she snapped to a groom who lin-gered outside. "He will doubtless be in a hurry."

Perceval and Jarvis came out of the mews in the same moment the breathless royal messenger galloped into the courtyard. The man saluted Perceval. "Greetings in the name of the king. I am come with a woeful message for His Majesty, and I need a fresh mount to speed my journey to London."

"A horse is being made ready for you," Perceval said, taking the reins of the lathered horse. "What is this terrible news?"

"I have come from the seaport," the messenger said, sliding out of his saddle, his face contorted in anguish. "Prince William, fresh from victory in Normandy, has been lost at sea with all his companions and many other noble souls. The ship was split on a rock, and not a soul has come safe to land."

Endeline's hand flew to her throat. Could it be true? Was William truly gone?

Perceval was stunned. "We will pray for their souls," he managed to answer, "and for our king."

"Pray, too, for William's new bride, now left a widow," the messenger said, untying the banner with the king's herald from his saddle. "It is a mournful day for England, to be sure."

"His new bride?" Endeline asked, her voice choking on the words. Henry had allowed William to marry someone else?

"Aye," the messenger answered. He swung expertly into the saddle of the fresh horse Calhoun held for him. "A bride now with neither husband nor heir. The throne of England has no heir but Matilda, the king's legal daughter."

"Go in peace," Perceval replied automatically, and the messenger situated his banner in his stirrup, saluted Perceval, and spurred the horse.

Endeline marveled at the way the exchange of a few breaths could change the course of life so completely. She walked to Perceval's side and stood there numbly, like one who walks in sleep.

"Our plans have come to naught," she remarked as they watched the messenger gallop away.

"Perhaps greater glory lies ahead," Perceval answered, folding his arms. "Matilda is a woman and not a worthy heir. Soon England's throne will sit empty, and when it does, noble men from many families will rise to hold England and Normandy together. The next king must have noble qualities, and we have three excellent and suitable children, my lady. Charles will learn how to control and enlarge lands. Calhoun will study fighting and battle for glory. And Lienor . . . " Perceval shrugged. "If she does not marry a king, she can bring us to God."

SEVEN

In the two years after Prince William's death, the rhythm of life in the castle changed little. By the time she passed her eleventh birthday, Afton's education was nearly complete: she knew how to cultivate rosebushes, how to keep linens clean, how to dance and sing. She could play cards and handle a hawk with ease. She stumped visiting ladies with her clever riddles and arithmetic games, and she could recite the age-old formulas of women to provoke fertility in animals, prevent nightmares, and prompt the earth to productivity. She was, quite simply, a graceful, accomplished, and confident young lady in the bud of womanhood.

One afternoon Afton took her usual place by Lienor in the garden, where Endeline was entertaining several visiting ladies from other manors. "You must be quite proud of your daughters," one of the ladies remarked. "They are quite a study in opposites, one fair and dark, the other fair and light."

Endeline's smile was brief. "Yet they are not both my daughters, my lady, for one came from my womb and the other from my hand. Afton is Lienor's companion, brought from the fields of the villeins."

The ladies gasped in surprise, and Endeline tilted her head delicately. "Yet she brings honor to this house, does she not? She and Lienor have been most excellent pupils."

Afton recognized the unspoken command to prove Endeline's words. She gave the women a genteel smile and lowered her sewing. "I've heard it said," she began, "that to make a man prefer one son to another, he should be made to eat the tips of his dog's ears. If the child eats the other half of the tips, by the truth of the gospel, they will scarcely be able to bear being apart."

"Is that true?" a visiting lady asked, leaning toward Endeline. "I've noticed how Lord Perceval favors your eldest, Charles. Did you feed him the tips of his dog's ears?"

Endeline dropped her embroidery into her lap. "By the relics of St. John, I did not," she sniffed. "It was not necessary, for love of the land pulls Charles and Perceval together. Charles is destined to be Perceval's heir, and it is his right to take his father's place."

"And what of your handsome second son, Endeline?" The question was asked by an older woman, whose eyes gleamed brightly over the crescents of flesh that time had imposed upon her cheeks. "What purpose have you for that worthy boy?"

Endeline raised her chin proudly. "Calhoun knows it is his place to honor his father's valor in knighthood." She picked up her embroidery and stabbed the needle into the cloth with short, abrupt stitches. "He will be leaving soon to serve as a squire at Warwick Castle. Whether he serves in this household, the king's, or another, it is his choice."

Afton stopped sewing. Calhoun leaving? It was impossible! She would have known; he would have told her. Endeline must be mistaken, for Calhoun would never leave without discussing it with Afton. For three years he had shared his innermost secrets and dreams with her and her alone. He trusted her, he confided in her . . . and she was sure that he loved her! In fact, Calhoun and all of the emotions surrounding him made up the one constant thread of security in her years at the castle. He simply couldn't leave.

The answer was simple: Endeline was mistaken or deluded, there was no doubt about it. Or perhaps this was a subtle way for Endeline to prod Afton's heart, for the lady seemed to resent the friendship between the young girl and her affectionate son. In the past months Afton had realized how fickle Endeline's affections could be. Although Endeline had not done anything to separate Afton and Lienor, she seemed to grow increasingly less interested in the girls' instruction. Last year she had taken a baby boy from a villein, and now her passion was devoted to raising that chubby child.

Lienor had not seemed to notice that her mother no longer took an active interest in her upbringing. Since the news of Prince William's death, Lienor had become more and more introspective, giving up her boyish ways in exchange for a burning religious devotion born of gratitude to the Virgin. She played games only when begged, spoke only when directly addressed, and gradually exchanged roles with Afton: Afton became the leader, the bold and brash explorer; Lienor was content to be a mere shadow.

Afton gave no thought to her role in the castle, for like all children, she had a poor concept of time and consequences. Charles, now fifteen, was still as distant as Perceval, and neither of them acknowledged her presence. Morgan and Lunette regarded her as a bright little pet, the other servants deferred to her respectfully, and she often caught the knights peering at her with open curiosity. The only person who talked with her as a friend was Calhoun.

Afton stopped listening and pretended to concentrate on her stitching. As the women's conversation droned around her, she decided to ask Calhoun if this rumor was true. Her stomach tightened anxiously. What if it were? What would she do if Calhoun went away? Her heart froze, and her hand stopped pulling the needle in midair as she thought for the first time of the future. What would castle life be like without Calhoun?

Endeline stopped embroidering and stared at Afton. In the girl's three years at the castle she had grown from a very pretty child to an exceptionally beautiful young woman with delicate features, rosy cheeks, golden hair, and eyes that were forever open in curiosity. In the early years Endeline had secretly fretted because Lienor looked positively monkeylike next to Afton's inborn elegance, but now that she and Perceval had agreed that Lienor should take the veil, Lienor's physical shortcomings were not important. A nun had no need for beauty. And as long as Afton remained pleasant and docile, there was no harm in her staying as a maid and companion for Lienor.

But Endeline noted how a line had creased Afton's smooth forehead and intuited that something in the ladies' conversation had upset her. A prowling suspicion thrust its head into the light of Endeline's sophisticated understanding, and she decided to deal with Afton's misguided notions on the spot.

"I have an idea," Endeline said smoothly, putting aside her sewing. "Let us play 'The King Who Does Not Lie.'"

"How delightful!" the visitors bubbled, pulling their seats closer to Endeline.

"I shall play the king, and whatever I ask, you must give a truthful reply," Endeline said, nodding regally. "Lady Regan of York, we will start with you. Is it true that you languish of love for the handsome Matthew, son of Lord Gerald?"

The young Lady Regan giggled and hid her smile behind her palm. When she had composed herself, she spoke gravely. "Yes, my lady—excuse me, Sire, it is true. Can you speak to my father for me, O King?"

The other girls giggled in response, and Endeline raised a dark eyebrow. "We shall see. Now, Lady Udele of Berkhamsted, wife of Roger, I've heard it said that you entertain a young knight when your husband is away. Are these things true?"

Lady Udele was no giggling girl, but she was sophisticated enough to trust Endeline's discretion. She matched Endeline's gaze carefully. "Only a fool can misread the direction of the wind," she answered cryptically, and Endeline smiled in understanding. Lady Udele took a great risk with such an answer, for her husband could have her killed for infidelity.

"Afton, my dear." Endeline smiled pleasantly, keeping her voice light. "Of all the young men at Margate Castle, surely there is one special man who has caught your eye? Have you tasted yet of love?"

Endeline noticed that Afton's cheeks grew rosier. "I believe I have," she replied, keeping her eyes on her embroidery.

Endeline raised a finger and pretended to scold her young charge. "If you love, you know it. Do you love a valiant knight?"

Afton shook her head. "No."

"A groom, perhaps."

"No."

"Perhaps you love one of our frequent guests."

"No."

Endeline made an effort to keep smiling, but her voice sounded hard, even in her own ears. "Who is it you love, my dear?"

Afton raised her chin. "I love your noble Calhoun, my lady. I have loved him for years."

The old woman with the puffy eyes whispered loudly, "Who did she say? The handsome second son?"

Endeline kept her face smooth and under control, but her heart recoiled at Afton's answer. It was a horrible thing for the girl to say, like a rat declaring its love for an eagle. It was improper, indecent! Her son could no more love a girl like Afton than—

Well, her common sense reminded her, *with men being the way they are, he could love her if he wanted to.* Endeline's mind shrank from the memory of the time she caught Perceval kissing Lunette in the wardrobe. The passion of men was an unpredictable thing, and powerful men had no compunction about releasing it whenever they chose. But love was one thing, and marriage quite another. Calhoun could never marry the daughter of a villein, someone who once lived and slept with farm animals!

Endeline studied Afton, who continued sewing as if she

had done nothing more momentous than declaring the sky to be blue. *I have trained the girl myself,* Endeline realized, *and I do not think she would agree to any love outside lawful marriage.* Of course, it was impossible to know such a thing for certain, but Endeline trusted the standards of morality she had instilled in Afton. Still, it was a good thing Calhoun was going away.

Endeline stood to her feet and motioned for her maids. "Ladies, the men will return for supper soon," she announced. "I must go make preparation for things to come." She left the garden, Morgan and Lunette close behind her.

Afton slipped through the garden into the orchard. She had always been able to collect her thoughts amid the quiet of the apple and pear trees, but today was different. She had openly declared her love for Calhoun, and Endeline had not smiled in approval.

The stillness Afton sought was disturbed when a voice from the leafy branches above her called, "Look out down there!" Four apples fell out of the tree and landed on the soft ground by Afton's feet. She picked one up and wiped it on her sleeve, then bit into it. "Hey!" the voice yelled again. "That was mine!"

Calhoun lowered himself through the sprawling limbs of the tree and dropped to the ground. There was no anger in his eyes as he pocketed the other three apples and, when he bowed to Afton, she saw the teasing twinkle in his eyes. "If you're really that hungry, I'll fetch you a basketful of apples," he said.

Afton shook her head and chewed her apple slowly. At thirteen, Calhoun was still very much a boy, but his voice had deepened in months past and he seemed taller than he had been the week before. He was worthy of her love, she knew it—more worthy than any man in the castle or village—and she could not understand why Endeline did not approve. Surely she could not doubt that her son was good enough for Afton, and as for Afton, had she not been trained as well as Lienor, who was deemed fit for a prince? Afton made an effort to swallow.

"Are you really going away?" she blurted out. "Your mother told the ladies you were leaving soon."

Calhoun grinned. "Aye. This afternoon Jarvis said I might go on a cavalcade with the knights. We will be gone at least three days, perhaps a week."

He wasn't going to Warwick, he was going on a cavalcade. That was worse, and Afton couldn't stop a shudder. Stark fear laced her earliest memories of the knights' cavalcades. Once she had been with her father in his narrow field when a cavalcade of the lord's knights approached, dismounted, and brandished their swords. One burly knight cut her father's face with impunity and warned Wido that Perceval was lord and master. She had wet herself before the knights finally rode off, their war-horses trampling her father's meager field. Afton closed her eyes to block the memory of her father's blood-streaked face.

"Please, Calhoun, don't hurt anybody," she whispered, and Calhoun laughed.

"Why do you think we take this journey, girl? We go to find the enemies of the king's peace, those who would steal and break the king's laws or trespass in his lands. We go to ensure that all who live under Perceval's protection are living justly." He gestured broadly. "We would never hurt the innocent, Afton. A knight's duty is to—"

"Protect women and children," Afton finished for him. "I know. But envision each law-abiding villein you see as your friend, I beg you. Remember that I am the daughter of a villein."

"I cannot forget who and what you are," Calhoun answered. His expression changed subtly, and Afton thought she saw sadness and resignation in his eyes. Before she could speak, he turned and sprinted out of the orchard.

"I'd like you to oversee the women who work today in the women's quarters," Endeline told Afton after morning prayers. "The villeins are working on a special tapestry for the feast of St. John the Baptist. You have such a lovely touch with a needle, Afton. Will you make sure the work goes well?"

Afton was flattered and agreed easily. Endeline usually oversaw the villein women herself, and Afton took the request as a sign of Endeline's increasing confidence in her. She dressed quickly and went downstairs to the women's quarters, which were separated from the rest of the castle courtyard by a tall hedge.

The summer sunshine was warm, so she loosened her cap to catch the slight breeze and walked through the castle yard with an easy step. She had left Lienor praying in the chapel. That was all Lienor voluntarily did these days, and Afton thought Endeline seemed frankly relieved. It was better to have a daughter give her soul to God than walk mannishly and never be a proper gentlewoman. *It is quite surprising,* Afton thought as she waited for a group of knights on horseback to pass, *that Lienor grows more gentle every day that she prays. I wonder what it could be that is changing her?*

Afton hesitated outside the tall hedge that surrounded the women's enclosure. Morgan once told her that no man had ever entered the women's domain. Not that any man would want to. Even though Perceval felt quite at home in the girls' dormitory and the chamber he shared with his wife and her maids, he would never have lowered himself to walk into the women's enclosure where the villein and village women met to work. Such secrets as were told in there were not fit for men's ears.

Afton lifted the iron latch on the gate and stepped inside. Standing in the gateway, half-hidden by the thickness of the hedge, she could hear the women quite clearly and not be seen. She had never been to the women's enclosure alone. When she had visited with Endeline, she was aware of curious stares and veiled looks, but no one had ever spoken directly to her. She did not know how the villeins would react to her by herself.

A sudden gust of wind rattled the gate and startled Afton so that she stepped forward, in full view of the women. Though her eyes were cast down in their habitual discipline, she felt the pinpricks of probing eyes from every woman in the enclosure.

She glanced up. The worn eyes of the village women were judging her, from the quality of the fabric in her tunic to the tightness of her cap. *Oh no,* Afton realized, *her cap was too loose. Gentlewomen simply did not walk around with their caps undone, heat or no heat.* One woman shook her head disapprovingly, another bit her lip.

Sensing the censure in their faces, Afton raised her chin, determined to stare them down, one by one, individually. She was Endeline's emissary, sent on a justifiable errand. She was hot, so her cap was loose. Her eyes raked defiantly around the circle of women, causing them all to drop their appraising eyes, until she came to one tired and familiar face.

Corba.

Dear God! Afton thought, *My mother is an old woman already!* The face at which she stared was crinkled and leathered from the sun, and wisps of gray hair dangled rebelliously from the edges of her mother's cap. Corba's front tooth was black with disease, and jutted away from the others at an odd angle.

Despite the sun's heat, Afton felt a chill close around her heart, as if she had fallen through ice into the river. She jerked her head away from Corba's shy smile and forced her eyes to focus on the tapestry in the center of the group. "Lady Endeline sends me to look after the progress of the work," she said, her voice unnaturally loud. "I shall tell her all goes well. Will it be completed by the feast of St. John the Baptist?"

No one spoke for a moment, but then one stout woman nodded slowly. "Aye, the work will be done. You may tell her that Wilda gives ye this assurance."

"I will." Afton turned to leave even though she could feel Corba's faded blue eyes pulling her back. Something in

93

her wanted to run to her mother, to bury her head in her lap and cry away the pain of the years they had spent apart, but an iron discipline held her to her course. As a child she had been a carefree villein, but she was a child no longer. Engrained in her now was a new code of duty and obligation, a rigidly inflexible code of behavior.

She counted her steps to the gate. On the tenth step, she lifted the latch, swung the gate open, and left the women's enclosure. She did not look back.

The castle was alive with activity as always, but every room seemed empty without Calhoun's boisterous presence. He had been gone three days, and Afton went about her routine joylessly. *Endeline must have been joking when she said he would leave for Warwick Castle,* Afton thought. *Even she could not bear this lifeless castle if he were gone.*

The cry of the sentry warned of approaching riders, and Afton dropped her book and skipped down the steps from Endeline's chamber. Jarvis, Denton, and Calhoun were back, dismounting beside the stable. Afton lingered in the doorway, feasting on the sight of her friend. Life would be fun again.

At supper that evening Calhoun regaled the people of Margate Castle with stories of his cavalcade. He so graphically described the fierce bear they had seen in the woods that goose bumps rose on Afton's arms. He rose from the table and acted out Jarvis's defense against the pack of wolves that had followed them on the road, and he briefly described the man they had apprehended and charged with stealing chickens from a family in a nearby village. Denton, Calhoun reluctantly admitted, had chopped off the man's hands as punishment for his crime.

Afton cringed at each story, particularly the latter tale, amazed and a little horrified that Calhoun found excitement in such blood-chilling and blood-spilling adventures. But she excused his exuberance. Without his love of adventure, he'd be as plodding and shy as Charles, who exhibited neither enjoyment nor displeasure unless he was out in the fields.

The sun had begun to descend in the west when she found Calhoun alone in the stables. He was brushing his favorite horse, but he paused when he saw her step into the stall. "I'm glad you're back, Calhoun," she said simply. "The castle wasn't the same without you."

Calhoun didn't answer, but looked at her a moment, then dropped the brush onto the earthen floor and swung himself onto the horse's bare back. "Come on," he said, grasping Afton's hand firmly. "Ride with me."

Without a moment's hesitation Afton flung herself at the horse, throwing her leg up and over, not minding her skirts. She put her arms around Calhoun's waist, and he walked the horse quietly out of the stable and through the courtyard, then spurred the animal to canter out of the castle gate and down the road.

The ride was exhilarating. Afton and Lienor did not ride much, and when they did it was usually at a snail's pace. No wonder Calhoun loved his adventures! Under the sprinkling of stars and a blushing sky, Afton felt the warm wind caress her face and send her cap flying back off her head. As the horse gently cantered down the road, her braid loosened and wisps of hair fluttered around her neck.

She settled into the easy lope of the horse and rested her cheek against Calhoun's shoulder. They rode comfortably for several minutes, and Afton was disappointed when Calhoun pulled back on the reins and the horse slowed to a trot, then to a walk.

"Are we stopping?" Afton lifted her head. "Do we have to?"

Calhoun pointed to the sky. "It's growing dark. And there's a curfew. Only the enemies of peace go out after dark."

"We're not enemies of peace," Afton said, watching as Calhoun pulled the horse's head around and headed back up the road to the castle. "You're going to be a knight and I'm—well, I'm not an enemy of peace."

"Are you sure?" Calhoun asked. "I've had no peace, thinking of you."

She couldn't see his face, and his voice was flat, so she didn't know if he was teasing. "What do you mean?" she asked, wishing he would turn and look at her.

The horse trotted slowly up the road and Calhoun cleared his throat. "I'm going away soon," he answered, his voice growing deeper as the night grew darker. "I'm to serve as a squire at Warwick Castle. I'll be trained as a knight there."

"Why can't you be trained here at Margate?"

Calhoun shook his head. "A knight must not seek preferential treatment. Here I would always be Perceval's son. At Warwick I will be just another squire."

You'll always be more than that to me, she thought, and her arms tightened around him.

She thought he understood what she was feeling, because he patted the arms she had entwined around him. Then he made a clicking sound with his tongue and kicked the horse into a gallop.

The trees on the roadside flew by in a blur, and Afton blinked back tears as the wind stung her eyes. The castle would no longer hold happiness for her if Calhoun was gone. He was the only person who cared for her at all.

Suddenly, Calhoun gave the reins a sharp jerk and the horse reared, his front hooves pawing the air. Off-balance, Afton frantically grasped Calhoun, and he calmed the animal expertly. The horse stood still, twitching his ears as if wondering why they had stopped on a moonlit road. Calhoun turned on the horse's broad back.

"It was here in this field that I met you," he said, pointing to the broad field outside the castle walls. "We picked flowers for your sheep. You took me to your special swimming place in the forest. Do you remember?"

"I have not thought of that day in months," Afton answered, laughing softly. "But I remember you would not swim. And our sheep died. The very next day. . . ." A new thought struck her. "Maybe there was something poison in our wreath—"

"It doesn't matter," Calhoun broke in. Afton had never seen such seriousness in his eyes. "It is not our place to question God's providence. Whatever means he used, he brought you to me."

Afton couldn't answer. She could only think that if God had brought her to Margate Castle, it was highly unreasonable of him to take Calhoun away. But this thought—and all others—suddenly fled when Calhoun leaned toward her and placed his lips briefly on hers. The boyish kiss was both startling and welcome, and Afton wished it would never end.

But it did. Calhoun pulled his lips from hers, then turned without a word and kicked the horse once again. Before Afton had collected her thoughts, they were through the castle barbican.

"Who's there?" a guard called out. Afton heard the unmistakable clink of metal as a sword was drawn from its sheath.

"It is Calhoun," Calhoun answered, slowing the horse.

Jarvis showed himself in the torchlight. "By the sword of St. Denis, it is Perceval's second son," Jarvis said, sheathing his sword. He grinned at Calhoun and winked. "The boy who has grown to be a man."

Afton slipped off the horse and hurried toward the castle while Calhoun dismounted and walked with Jarvis into the stables. What they talked about, she didn't know. She only knew that the embers that had glowed in her heart at the mention of Calhoun's name had now burst into bright flames.

EIGHT

Once a month Perceval opened the castle doors to his vassals and dispensed justice to any and all who required intervention. On these occasions, the hall was cleared of tables, the best tapestries hung on the walls, and evidence of Perceval's wealth and power was conspicuously exhibited. It was a display designed to intimidate, and the villeins and lessor lords from the outlying manors seemed usually to creep into the hall, no matter how bravely they strutted when outside the castle.

Endeline considered it educational for the children, including Afton, to witness the proceedings in the great hall from a side room. Calhoun loved these trials and usually sat on the edge of his seat as he heard the cases that the petitioners brought before Perceval. Often he whispered to Afton what *his* verdict would be if he were presiding, and Afton found that she usually agreed with him. If they talked too loudly, either Endeline or Hector, who served as a scribe during the hearings, would glare at the two and remind them to be quiet.

On this day the first dispute was between two knights. One had insulted the other's honor, the second had promptly returned the insult. To settle the dispute and keep them from killing each other, Perceval sent each of them away: one to join with the Knights Templar, who protected pilgrims to the Holy Land, and the other to tour the outlying manors in a two-year cavalcade. "After two years you may return to Margate, and we will see what kind of love you hold toward each other," Perceval said, nodding to each of his knights. "In the meantime, you will do service to your lord and to the king."

The second case involved a forester and a villein caught trapping badgers in the king's forests. "You have stolen from the forests of King Henry," Perceval said, motioning for the aged Hector to write. "Therefore, your house and lands are confiscated in the name of the king. Your house will be razed and your animals will be forfeit to me. A decree regarding this judgment will be forwarded to His Majesty, the king."

"A good judgment," Calhoun whispered to Afton. "The king will be pleased."

"A boring case," Afton whispered back, concentrating on her embroidery. "Only a fool steals from the king's forest. Who are the next petitioners?"

"Two villeins from the village," Calhoun answered.

Afton did not even look up until she recognized the voice that reached her ears—Wido stood before Perceval. She lost custody of her eyes as she stared in fascination at the father she had not seen in over three years.

He was as she remembered him, broad and strong, but now there were streaks of gray in his dark hair. He stood tall and resolute before Perceval, his peasant's cap in his hand, and Afton felt an unfamiliar and unwelcome flush of pride in his appearance. Beside him was another peasant whose name she couldn't remember.

"I am Wido," he said.

"I know the name," Perceval answered dryly.

"My son Matthew was killed last week by this man's dog. My wife grieves deeply."

Afton counted on her fingers—Matthew had been five when she left home. He was eight, then, maybe nine . . . and he was dead? Killed by a dog? She gasped in horror.

"What's wrong?" Calhoun asked, turning to look at Afton. "It is not so horrible. It happens all the time in the village."

Afton blinked. Calhoun didn't even know this man was her father. Matthew was—had been—her *brother*.

Perceval stared at the nervous man next to Wido. "Your name?"

"Geoffrey."

"Geoffrey, is this man's report true?"

Geoffrey kept his eyes on the floor in front of him. "Aye, my lord. Sad, but true."

"What is it you wish me to do?" Perceval asked, turning back to Wido.

"He was but a child, but his life had value to us and to you, my lord," Wido responded. "We ask for recompense for his life."

"It is true that there will be one less villein to work in my fields," Perceval said. He gestured to Hector. "Make sure this Geoffrey pays two sheep for the life of the boy. One sheep to Wido, the father, and one to me." Perceval glanced up at Wido. "Is a sheep not a worthy price for the life of a villein's child?"

Afton saw a muscle shift in Wido's jaw, but her father did not answer. Perceval smiled. "Make it so," he told Hector. "Next."

Geoffrey and Wido bowed and left the hall. A tear fell on Afton's embroidery. Her father had not even glanced in her direction.

The next morning Afton heard the far-off blare of a trumpet, and she flew to the window of Endeline's chamber. Four knights on horseback approached on the road, and something was wrong—one of them was thrown over his saddle like a sack of potatoes. Afton's heart froze in fear. Had Calhoun gone out with the knights that morning?

She was about to run down the stairs, but a stern look from Lienor stopped her. "Stay here," Lienor said calmly, picking up a Psalter. "We will do no good when there is men's trouble afoot. It is better to stay here and pray."

"Pray?" Afton's voice squeaked. What good was praying

when it could be Calhoun out there on his horse, possibly wounded—or dying? He was too young, too untrained. He should never have been allowed to go out with the knights before his training was completed.

Afton paced in the chamber while Lienor chanted psalms in a voice like flowing rainwater. Soon Perceval burst into the chamber, Endeline and the knight Denton in his wake. "Tarry, my lord, tarry a day or two," Endeline was begging. "Surely this vassal Gerald knows what folly it is to displeasure you. This rebellion is only in his mind, he has not yet raised an army against you."

"I will not give him time to do that," Perceval snarled between his teeth as he sat on a bench and cast off his soft boots in favor of sturdier footwear. "It is enough that one of my own men has died from his wounds. Our honor, lady, is at stake. We ride today. Jarvis is in the village now, equipping the free men to fight."

"In the village?" Mortified that she had spoken, Afton covered her mouth with her hand. One did not speak to Perceval unless spoken to first.

But he seemed not to notice. "All free men who go with me today shall have a share in the honor," he said as Denton expertly pulled a suit of mail over Perceval's tunic. Perceval rubbed his hand over the smooth chain link of his suit and picked up his sword. A faint smile flickered across his handsome face. "Prepare a feast for our return, lady. Your lord will doubtless be the victor."

Endeline sank onto the bed, and Perceval sheathed his sword and grabbed a silver helmet out of the wardrobe. Afton was stunned at the sight of Perceval in armor. He was a fearsome sight, tall and gleaming in his anger, most certainly a man to be feared.

Ignoring Endeline's weeping, the lord and Denton stalked out of the room.

The battle ended as Perceval had predicted: the hapless Gerald, who had grown tired of paying allegiance to Perceval, raised his voice and his sword to Perceval's knights without preparing an army. Now he and his wife lay dead; his land, villeins, and servants seized by Jarvis. The few knights of Gerald's castle who had not fled in fear immediately swore their continuing allegiance to Perceval and followed him to Margate Castle.

Endeline instructed the servants to serve the feast she had ordered, and Afton followed behind her to help with the preparations. "We will have a tournament after supper," Perceval told his wife as Denton removed his armor. "It is not good to send knights into battle so briefly. The anger they roused in anticipation of a fight has not dissipated."

Afton noted with surprise that Perceval's observations were correct. The knights, fresh from their victory, were more interested in fighting than eating. The sumptuous food Endeline had prepared was passed over quickly, and the knights were quick to leave the great hall for the pasture outside the castle walls. Perceval did not even seem offended at his knights' lack of proper appetites. He merely shrugged and smiled at his wife. "There is a time for eating and a time for jousting," he said, rising from his place at the table. "The time for battle has come."

Like a boy plunging into deep water for the first time, Calhoun found the entire experience of that day both dangerous and exhilarating. Just yesterday life had been routinely predictable, but Gerald's fit of rebellion had brought new life into Perceval's settled knights. The men whose highest challenge had been browbeating villeins now blazed with the ardor of victorious warriors. They had won a quick, decisive battle for Perceval! And they would win a tournament for glory, honor, and the smile of fair Endeline!

Calhoun was offended when Denton flatly refused to allow him to ride in the tournament. He was needed on the sidelines, Denton said, to keep the spectators from venturing onto the bloody field of battle. And, after the first clash of mock battle, it would be Calhoun's job to ride out to the field and rescue wounded knights unable to continue in the tournament.

His horse shifted uneasily beneath him, and Calhoun made gentle clucking sounds. If only he were already a knight! He and Charles had been trained in jousting, horsemanship, and swordplay since they were small children, but Charles had never entered into the spirit of competition. Calhoun yearned to fight, to learn the secret of knighthood that went far beyond mere fighting techniques. There were mysteries Calhoun had yet to discover, and he was dying to know them.

A trumpeter blew a shrill blast, and the assembled crowd of spectators from the countryside and castle quieted themselves. Lord Perceval, Lady Endeline, and Hector stood in the walkway of the castle wall, high above the crowd. Calhoun thought he could see Lienor and Afton through a machicolation of the stone wall, but he wasn't sure. The opening was too far away and dark to see things clearly. If they were there, though, Calhoun imagined that Lienor was probably praying and Afton's gray eyes were wide with interest. He smiled to himself. She reminded him of a little mouse, usually quiet, but always about, watching everything. Of course, she was the most beautiful mouse he had ever seen. . . .

Perceval held up his hand, and the crowd was silenced. The late-afternoon sun gleamed off his golden hair and beard. "Before we begin the evening's tournament, I wish to reward a free man who has served his lord admirably in the day's battle," Perceval said, his voice echoing through the field. He beckoned to someone near him and a balding man in a common brown tunic stepped out into full view. "Hubert, free man of Margate village, because it was you who killed the rebel Gerald, I bestow upon you this day a fief of the mill in Margate village, to hold forever for you and your descendants."

Perceval then handed a straw to Hubert, who accepted it and fell to his knees. Perceval clasped Hubert's two hands in his own, like a father comforting a son, and kissed Hubert on both cheeks. The crowd roared its approval, and Hubert stood up and gave them a victorious salute.

"Now, knights of Margate Castle, do your best to declare our honor to the knights of Gerald whom we welcome in love and forgiveness." The air was still except for the impatient pawing of horses, and Calhoun drew in his breath. Perceval's face turned toward the east, where the line of knights from Gerald's castle waited with the sun in their eyes. "If there be any deceit in the hearts of Gerald's knights, may God seek it out and trample upon it today."

Perceval's knights were lined up on the west side of the castle gate, the knights from Gerald's castle facing them. Sunlight glinted off the knights' conical, open-faced helmets and shone steadily on their bright shirts of mail. A slight breeze blew the manes of the waiting horses, who snorted in their impatience.

Perceval gripped the standard that bore the emblem of his house, and the raucous sound of his father's voice startled Calhoun. "For the glory of Margate Castle and its fair Lady Endeline!" Perceval shouted, and he dipped the standard of his colors. From opposite sides of the open meadow, riders spurred their horses and charged each other.

Calhoun had to keep a firm rein on his own mount, so great was the mare's urge to run with the pounding hoofbeats of the knights' huge destriers. He bent and patted her neck as the pounding of hooves gave way to the clash of lance against mail and sword against shield. Several knights from Gerald's castle turned from the fight and fled through the forest, with Perceval's knights in pursuit. Others lay scattered in the field.

When the rush of knights had passed, Calhoun gave his mare a gentle kick and rode out to the open grass. The first knight he approached was merely stunned, blinking his eyes in the sunlight. The second knight, wearing Gerald's colors, was dead. Calhoun found two other dead knights from Gerald's house, one of whom was missing an arm. Calhoun slipped off his horse, roped the dead bodies under the arms, and tied the ends of the rope to his saddle. He mounted again and dragged the corpses through the castle gates. The servants would bury or burn the dead later. Though held for sport, the deadly consequences of the tournament varied little from those of warfare.

Any knight captured by an opposing knight would have to buy his freedom with money, horses, or armor. The victors would be pleased, for the life of a knight contained few luxuries. As the contest ended and the battle-scarred knights began to reenter the castle, Calhoun was relieved to see that only one knight from Gerald's castle had bested any of Perceval's men. This knight, a huge, surly-looking man with a livid cross-shaped scar upon his cheek, rode to the castle gate with two horses in tow, a sure sign that two of Perceval's proud knights had ransomed themselves immediately rather than be led into the castle as the man's captives.

"Who is that man there?" Calhoun asked a servant who had come with the contingent from Gerald's castle. "The man with the scar."

"He is called Fulk," the servant replied. "He was new to Gerald's house, recently come from the expedition of God to the Holy Land. Some say he branded himself with God's mark to show his devotion to our Lord."

Calhoun nodded. If the man was righteous, surely God had willed that he be spared.

Endeline found her eyes irresistibly drawn to the knight Fulk at dinner the next day. Even Perceval seemed to be fascinated with the man, hardly touching his meat, so intent was he upon staring at the alien knight.

Endeline wondered why this knight should be different from any other. True, he was massive—a head taller than most men—and his laughter rang loudly above the timid laughs of others. And he did bear that unusual scar upon his cheek, which made his already remarkable face less attractive, but much more arresting.

After studying him throughout dinner, Endeline decided that Fulk's uncommon quality was simple fearlessness. He bowed to Perceval upon entering the room, but his salute lacked the deference ordinarily bestowed upon a master—his obsequiousness was form, not function. Even more surprising was the fact that his brazen eyes and manner did not bring a stern rebuke from Perceval.

During the meal Perceval banged his spoon upon the table and the unruly knights quieted. "I wish the knight Fulk to approach me," he said, and Fulk rose from his table without hesitation.

Endeline felt herself grow uncomfortable as the man approached. She kept her eyes cast down at her soup. Hector fidgeted uncomfortably in his seat, and Endeline could feel his frightened squirrel eyes dart to her face in search of assurance. Knights were a rowdy, impetuous group, and Jarvis had always controlled those at the castle with a firm hand, leaving Hector free to manage the lord's estate. Endeline knew that with Jarvis away at Gerald's castle, Hector felt threatened, especially when approached by the fearless Fulk.

Fulk knelt in front of Perceval's table.

"My man-at-arms, Jarvis, is detained at Gerald's castle until I can find a trustworthy overseer," Perceval told Fulk. "Denton serves me in his place." He gestured toward the table where Calhoun and Charles sat with Raimondin, the chaplain. "But my son, Calhoun, is to be engaged as a squire at Warwick Castle and now finds himself without a mentor. Will you fill this role in my service?"

Fulk bowed his head. "I would be pleased to accompany your son. And I will teach him all he needs to know to serve my lord Perceval and the king."

"Precisely." Perceval's eyes narrowed, but he smiled. "I have a feeling you know more than the average knight," he said evenly. "And I entrust my son to you. If he loses his life on the battlefield, it will be as God wills and I will not hold you accountable. But if he loses his life in any other way, you will not escape my vengeance."

"I understand."

"You will leave tomorrow morning," Perceval said, standing up. Fulk bowed and stepped aside. Perceval smiled and extended his arms to his dinner guests. "Now, my people, the servants will clear the room and we shall have an afternoon of dancing."

There weren't many suitable women with whom the knights could dance, so Lienor, Afton, Morgan, Gwendolyn, and Lunette were sent upstairs with Endeline to dress for the occasion. Surges of conflicting emotion nearly overwhelmed Afton as she and Lienor went into their small chamber. The idea of a victory dance was exciting, but because it came on the day before Calhoun's departure, Afton did not think her feet would obey her heart. How could she dance when Calhoun would soon be leaving the castle? Another thought struck her—what if she were to dance with him? To stare into his eyes, to feel his hands on hers . . . might not a dance bring them together and reveal to him how much she loved him?

She reached eagerly for a deep blue tunic, but Endeline corrected her. "Wear the white one, my dear, it suits you better," she said warmly, placing her cool hands on Afton's shoulders. "And I do want you to look your best. You will have a wonderful time today."

Afton shivered in unexpected delight. Endeline had not spoken so warmly to her in weeks. Perhaps she had come to understand Afton's declared love for Calhoun! But still Perceval was sending Calhoun away in the morning.

Afton resolved to make it a day worth remembering. She slipped into the white tunic with its gauzy sleeves and selected a light blue surcoat to go over it. She buckled a slender gold belt tightly around it to show off her tiny waist. There! Certainly she looked as good as Lienor in her yellow gown, and nearly as regal as Endeline in her red silk gown with a squirrel collar.

Afton loosened her hair and picked up a circlet of roses she had brought in from the garden. Why not wear it? It was unconventional, but if Endeline didn't mind . . .

She place the circlet gently on her head, careful not to prick herself with the thorns, and turned questioningly to Endeline. A flicker of reproof passed across Endeline's face, but then she laughed. "Why not?" she said, waving her hand. "You look like a fairy sprite." She adjusted her gown and smiled at Afton. "You have found favor in the eyes of your lord, and it is time you were rewarded. Stay close tonight, for there will be news that concerns you."

Afton could scarcely breathe, so great was the hope rising in her heart. She glanced at Lienor for some hint of what was to come, but Lienor was taking pains to secure every single wisp of hair at the nape of her neck. Lienor apparently had no romantic illusions, nor did she seem interested in feminine speculation.

Afton sighed and waited for Morgan and Lunette. It would not be proper to go down alone with the great hall full of knights, but if she had less than one day left with Calhoun, she wanted to spend every available moment with him. After his training as a knight, he would come home, and they could be married. They would raise children in the castle, who would be brave and headstrong and—

"Afton, go down with me." Endeline's voice was edged with impatience, so Afton sprang to her feet and followed her mistress down the stairs.

The dance was the most elegant affair Afton had ever attended. When she and Lienor were younger Endeline had allowed them to watch dances from the pantler's tiny room off the hall, but now they were actually allowed to dance! There was no shortage of men who asked for their hands, either. Afton twirled and stepped and curtsied gracefully to the dainty music from the reeds and pipes of the musicians. Though Calhoun did not ask her to dance, she was aware of his gaze upon her.

Endeline watched the dance with speculative eyes. Calhoun was standing against the wall quietly, as well he should. She noticed that the hulking figure of Fulk was nearby; he had already assumed his position as Calhoun's mentor and guardian. Perhaps Perceval had made a good choice, but Endeline was frankly frightened by the man. He looked like he would not fear death—or even God.

Lienor was dancing gracefully and gently, but without animation or a smile. The knights did not leave her sitting idle, but Endeline knew their attention sprang from their regard for Perceval rather than love for his dark-haired daughter. Afton, on the other hand, danced lightly and with the glee of a young girl. As she twirled in the gauzy cotton dress, her golden hair flowing freely behind her, she looked like a heavenly spirit dropped down to earth. The roses in her hair matched those in her cheeks, and her smile lit up her face. Men lined up for her dances, Endeline noted . . . silly men who made no effort to hide their fascination with the girl.

"My lord, I would dance with you," Endeline said, placing her hand on Perceval's arm.

"It would give me pleasure," Perceval answered, standing to his feet. The crowd parted as Endeline and Perceval joined into the dance.

The musicians were allowed a few moment's rest, and Endeline made her way to Afton. Two knights stood in front of the girl, backing her up against the wall. "Kind sirs, I need to talk to this maiden," Endeline said, nodding regally. The knights bowed and left the women alone.

"Afton," Endeline said gently, "you are quite lovely tonight. Have you not noticed how desirable these brave warriors find you?"

Afton blushed. "No, my lady. I was only enjoying the dance."

Endeline nodded again. "I am concerned about my son. He is nearly of marriageable age—"

Afton's heart skipped a beat. Was this part of Endeline's "plan" for her?

"—but he is much too shy and has nothing to do with girls. I wonder if I could persuade you to dance with him."

Dance with Calhoun? "I'd be happy to, my lady," Afton answered. She looked down at the floor and folded her hands, remembering well her lessons in decorum. "If that were proper. Shouldn't a man speak to a maiden first?"

"I will see to it," Endeline said, taking Afton's hand. The musicians were resuming their places, and Endeline pulled Afton through the crowd. She whispered in the girl's ear: "And if all goes well, would you let him kiss you?"

The question caught Afton off-guard, and she felt her cheeks redden. Did Endeline know Calhoun had kissed her already? "If it pleases you, my lady," she murmured automatically.

"He needs to become self-assured in the ways of women," Endeline continued, whispering in Afton's ear as they made their way over to where Calhoun lounged against the wall. "I cannot ask him to marry if he has never even spoken to a maiden, can I?"

Afton was so embarrassed she didn't realize what Endeline had done until they stopped and Afton found herself in front of Charles.

"Charles," Endeline said, placing Afton's hand in his, "dance with this young lady. She is my maid, and I give her to you. Perhaps you will learn that maidens are not two-headed dragons." Endeline walked away, her head high, and Afton suddenly realized how the hare feels when the hawk descends upon it from the sky.

Endeline watched her older son dance with Afton and her hope turned into anger and frustration. The boy was hopeless when it came to women! He wouldn't look at Afton, wouldn't even raise his head except when he faced the wall of waiting knights. He was dancing with the most beautiful maiden in the room, and the boy looked as though he was being punished!

As for Endeline's other son, he never took his eyes off the girl. He had not approached her to dance, as Endeline had known he would not. She and Perceval had spoken to him about his inappropriate behavior after Jarvis told them about seeing Calhoun and Afton ride in one night after dark. Endeline didn't mind Calhoun taking his pleasure from the maids, but he certainly couldn't become attached to one of them.

"It is a good thing our son leaves tomorrow," Endeline said, tapping her husband's arm. "See how he watches the villein Afton."

"I have noticed," Perceval answered agreeably. "And I have noticed that our eldest son ignores her. Perhaps I should give him a lesson in how to appreciate the girl."

"That won't be necessary." Endeline's tone was sharper than she intended and it annoyed her that she should let her displeasure show. It was a wife's duty to overlook the dalliances of her husband, and a faithful wife did not scold or complain.

Perceval turned to her and winked. "I'm only teasing you, my flower. The girl is but a child's toy, more suitable for my sons than for the master."

"And yet you would give her to—"

"That is no matter of consequence, only a well-deserved reward. You said yourself you were tired of the girl. It is time she left."

Endeline did not answer, but she tapped her foot impatiently. If only Perceval would get things over and done with.

"Valiant knights and guests!"

The music stopped abruptly, and Afton was glad to release Charles' hand. Even though he hadn't even looked at her since they began to dance, he had doggedly kept anyone else from dancing with her, and she found his persistence endlessly frustrating. Would she never dance with Calhoun?

"According to the blessings of God, our family has grown and prospered," Perceval said, holding his hand out to his chaplain in acknowledgment. "And we are here to announce tonight that tomorrow our beloved son Calhoun

111

will leave for Warwick Castle to be trained for knighthood by the honorable Fulk."

Calhoun and Fulk were surrounded by those giving them celebratory pats on the back, and the crowd cheered.

"Tomorrow morning we will also welcome the arrival of Abbot Hugh, who will soon escort our beloved daughter Lienor to a nunnery at the abbey," Perceval continued. "We are honored to give our only daughter to God."

The crowd raised another cheer and salute to Perceval, and he held up his hand. "And it may interest you to know that for some time we have acted as a loving father to a child left here, the maid Afton. We have decided to give her as wife to the honored Hubert, upon whom we have also bestowed a fief of the mill in the village."

The crowd cheered as Afton's ears rang. She was being given to whom? Hubert? The old man who would run the mill in the village? As a *wife*?

"Thank you, my lord!" The balding man in the rough tunic raised his hand in salute to Perceval. His voice was heavy and slurred, and he rocked on his feet. "Can the wedding take place tonight?"

The men roared lusty approval, and Afton felt faint. She looked up at Endeline and saw that the lady wore a satisfied smile. Suddenly Abbot Hugh's words from long ago rang in her memory: "You, child of the earth, cannot be what you are not."

She was a villein, not free; she could be used by the lord and lady as they chose. Suddenly she understood that wishing for Calhoun's love was like wishing for the stars in the sky. *She* was not worthy of *him*. Despite the mantle of gentility that surrounded her, she was only a villein, worthy of slavery, work, companionship, but never love! Worst of all, Calhoun knew this! He had kissed her, but he would not dance with her, and he would never love her. He admired her beauty and spirit as he admired the garden roses, but the thorniness of her poverty prevented him from drawing her close.

Hubert, a wide smile on his red face, staggered through the crowd toward her, reaching out with fat, dirty fingers. Afton screamed like a trapped animal and ran, her sleeve ripping off in Hubert's hands. She left the great hall and flew down the stone staircase, running out of the castle into the night.

HUBERT
1123-1125

There is no fear of God before his eyes.
For in his own eyes he flatters himself
too much to detect or hate his sin.
The words of his mouth are wicked and deceitful;
he has ceased to be wise and to do good.
Even on his bed he plots evil;
he commits himself to a sinful course
and does not reject what is wrong.

PSALM 36:1-4, NIV

NINE

"The guests thought it an interesting comic escapade, but running away did nothing to raise your esteem in your future husband's eyes," Endeline said sharply to Afton in her chamber. "Nor did the knights enjoy searching for you throughout the night. Your behavior belies your previous words of gratitude to Lord Perceval. You have been given a glorious home, an excellent upbringing, and in Perceval you have a powerful patron. How could you run and defy his wishes?"

Afton lifted her tear-streaked face to her mistress's, but Endeline merely turned her back on the girl and fussed with the sleeves of her gown. "Marriage to a worthy man like Hubert is beyond the reach of a ploughman's daughter. He is a valiant man, prized by Perceval, and as his wife, you will remain in your lord's favor. Of course, any *grateful* girl would have consented to the marriage immediately out of respect for her mistress's wishes."

"He is so old!" Afton managed a strangled cry.

"My dear, the man is barely fifty, and his age is a benefit to you. You will be marrying a man wise in years, and if you serve him well, he will overlook the faults of your youth. Men often overlook the faults of immature girls because of the great love they hold toward them."

"I cannot love him," Afton sobbed. "Because—"

"Because you are inexperienced," Endeline interrupted. "My dear, the heart can love whomever it chooses. Loves

117

that fly into our hearts unbidden are best chased back out the door. The love that a wife holds for her husband must be cultivated as a delicate flower garden."

A rare aspect of tenderness played across Endeline's face, and she sank onto the feather mattress where Afton lay. "Do you think I loved Lord Perceval on the day I married him? Nay, I did not, but as I gave him gentle deference and humble service, my love for him grew as a well-nourished sapling. And when I gave him his firstborn son, that love grew into the confident strength of an oak. With each child I grew in his love and estimation."

Afton realized Endeline was revealing rare secrets from her heart, and she calmed her sobs to listen. In all her years at the castle, Endeline had never given lessons of love in marriage. She had taught Afton and Lienor how to walk, talk, dress, and entertain, but after that fateful day when Prince William's ship sank in the ocean, Endeline had not spoken of marriage.

"I thought you had taught me all a woman needs to know," Afton said softly. "But you have never spoken to me of these things."

"Nor shall I again," Endeline answered, standing up. The well of introspection closed up, and the lady's face hardened. "It is for your mother to teach you about a husband. I am not your mother."

The words stung like a slap, and Afton turned her face so Endeline would not see the hurt plainly revealed there. She took a deep breath to calm herself before asking one other question: "How can I marry Hubert if I love another?"

Endeline laughed. "You were not listening. All other loves will pass out of your heart when one man holds you as his wife. Past flirtations of the heart must be forgotten and, although your husband may parade you before other men so that they will fall in love with you, you must not return one glance or even a shade of affection." As Endeline paused and moved to the open window, Afton remembered the many occasions when Perceval had offered the favor of Endeline's smile or a dance as a trophy for the knights engaged in tournament. Had she felt affection for the young knights who vied desperately for her approval?

Given Endeline's reflective mood, Afton was about to ask, but the lady suddenly gathered her skirts and turned away from the window. "Hubert will be a fine husband for you," she said as if the matter were settled. "My son Charles will not marry a ploughman's daughter. Calhoun will not marry at all. You should thank God that a free man like Hubert seems willing to have you as his wife. You will give your consent to this marriage at dinner tomorrow."

Thus saying, she turned and left the room.

Lunette and Morgan dressed Afton the next morning in a new blue tunic and vibrant yellow surcoat. "You look lovely," Morgan said, braiding Afton's long tangle of hair. "This Hubert is a fortunate man."

Afton was trying not to think of Hubert. She would face the possibility of marriage to him later, perhaps tomorrow, but today was more important than a thousand tomorrows. It was the last morning she would see Calhoun. He and Fulk were leaving for Warwick Castle after dinner.

"Can you hurry?" she asked Morgan.

Morgan misunderstood Afton's reason for haste and chuckled. "Of course, any girl would be anxious to see her future groom. My fingers will fly for love, but you must be still, girl!" She tied the end of the braid with a long white ribbon. "There!"

Afton flew to the window, hoping to catch a glimpse of Calhoun or the knights who would escort him to Warwick Castle, but the courtyard was empty save for a ramshackle wagon driven by a villein and his wife. She would have given them but a cursory glance except for something familiar in the driver's form, and she groaned with the shock of recognition. Perceval had sent for Wido and Corba.

The midday dinner was a never-ending nightmare, where seconds stretched into minutes and minutes into hours.

Afton had looked forward to sitting across from Calhoun at their last dinner together, but she had been seated across from Wido and Corba at the first row of tables on the main floor. Hubert, red-nosed and simpering, sat at the lord's table with Perceval, Endeline, and Hector. Calhoun, Fulk, and other knights sat at the center table, where there was much noise and laughter, and Charles and Lienor were with other members of the household at the third table.

As the servants passed the ale, Perceval stood and raised his glass. "Honored guests, we drink today in celebration of the impending marriage of the miller Hubert to the maid Afton, whom we have raised from a child."

"Hear, hear!" the other dinner guests raised their glasses and drank. From the corner of her eye Afton saw Hubert raise his glass and felt his eyes upon her. The skin on the back of her neck crawled when he tossed back his drink, wiped his mouth on his sleeve, and smirked in her direction.

Afton was thankful for the habit of maidenly deference that forced her to keep her eyes downcast at the table in front of her, for she did not want to meet Hubert's look. But her eyes were torn from their habitual discipline when Perceval spoke again, his words slightly slurred: "And after dinner, our beloved son Calhoun leaves for Warwick Castle. Let us drink to the success, glory, and honor he will bring to our house and to the king!"

"Hear, hear!" The guests raised their glasses and drank again, more boisterously than before. Afton craned her neck to look for Calhoun in the crowd at the knight's table, but the stout form of Fulk blocked her view.

Perceval was unsteady on his feet as he raised his glass a third time. "And to my beloved son, Charles, who will inherit the castle and lands of Margate, provided he ever decides to choose a wife and bring forth a son." Perceval's eyes crossed, and he took a giddy step backward.

"Careful, my lord," Endeline cautioned, putting out a hand to steady him.

Hubert put a stout arm behind Perceval's back. "To

120

Charles!" Hubert roared, raising his tankard with his free hand, and the crowd replied, "To Charles!" They drank again, and Hubert coaxed Perceval back onto his seat.

Afton watched the scene with interest. Perhaps there was merit in this rough man, Hubert. Endeline could be right. Though she knew she would never love him as she loved Calhoun, perhaps she might like him. With liking might come respect, and with that, surely there could be a happy marriage.

Afton sighed and stirred her black pudding. Wido and Corba sat across from her, silent and obviously uncomfortable. Neither had said anything more to their daughter than "Good day." Well, soon she would be out of their lives, too, so there was no need to reestablish a relationship. Only one thing mattered—not letting Calhoun part without one last word, one last touch, and one last smile.

When Perceval was finally persuaded to stand and dismiss the diners, Afton sprang from her seat, intending to run for the courtyard, where Calhoun would prepare to leave. "Daughter, why don't ye sit with us a moment more," Corba said gently, her blue eyes wide with frank love and longing. "Lord Perceval has asked us to talk with ye."

"There's no need," Afton replied, smiling uneasily. "Lady Endeline has spoken to me of love and marriage."

The rustle of silk heralded Endeline's approach. The lady nodded regally to Wido and Corba and put her hand on Afton's arm. "I am sorry, but I have need of this girl," she said, her lips pressed together in a tight little smile. She turned her dark eyes to Afton. "Go upstairs with Lunette right away. I will meet you there in a moment."

Afton sighed in relief. How astute of Endeline to relieve her from a distressing situation! By sending her upstairs, Endeline had made certain Afton would not meet Wido and Corba again before they departed for the village. Lunette was waiting outside the hall, so Afton nodded politely to Wido and Corba and followed the maid to the chamber.

Lunette was unusually quiet as they climbed the stairs.

She held the door open as Afton passed into the chamber, then slammed it shut behind her. As Afton spun around, she heard the sound of the key turning in the lock.

"Lunette!" Afton shook the door. "Please, let me out!"

"I can't." There was genuine dismay in the maid's voice. "Lady Endeline said I should leave you here until she comes."

"Where is Endeline?"

"In the courtyard. Calhoun leaves immediately and she is saying her good-byes."

Afton turned and sank onto the floor in fury and frustration. Endeline wasn't being kind at all, she was simply trying to keep Afton away from Calhoun. It wasn't fair! Afton was willing to let Calhoun go, but to be deprived of one last good-bye—

She ran to the window and looked out into the courtyard. Fulk was mounted already, his sword and shield by his side. The ten knights who would escort Calhoun were mounted, too, each with a purple-and-white banner of Margate securely in his hands. Calhoun's horse alone was unmounted, for Endeline was embracing her son.

Afton rushed to the lavatory, Perceval's pride and joy. Frantic necessity overrode her common sense, and she sprang from the tub into the narrow window and studied the lavatory pipe. If she was quick and sure, she could climb down the pipe, edge her way along the skirt of the moat, and still catch the riders before they left.

She took a deep breath, kicked off her slippers, and placed the ball of her foot into a small crevice between the stones. Bits of gravel bit into the tender sole of her foot, but she ignored the pain and swung out onto the shaft, her fingers grasping for a handhold. Fortunately, her small hands and feet found gaps between the solid stones, and climbing down the shaft was no harder than shimmying down apple trees in the orchard.

Afton was at the bottom of the shaft before Endeline released her son. "Go with God," Endeline said, running her fingers through his sandy hair. "Farewell, my sweet son."

Afton easily stepped along the narrow skirt of stone at the interior edge of the moat, as Calhoun embraced his unsteady father. She was at the drawbridge as Calhoun quickly embraced Lienor and Charles, and by the time he turned to mount his horse, she had reached the courtyard. Calhoun saw her and his face twisted into a wry smile.

Why? Afton wondered, wringing her hands in despair. *Didn't he know I would come?*

With one agile leap Calhoun was in the saddle, and he saluted Afton with a flourish of his cap. *It can't end this way,* she thought, her heart racing. *I can't just let him ride away!* She raced toward his horse, her bare feet skimming the dusty ground, then fell to her knees, clutching his stirrup. "Please, Calhoun," she cried, her hand caressing the soft leather of his boot. "Do not go without giving me a parting word."

Afton felt Endeline's disapproving eyes upon her like pinpricks, but she didn't care. Calhoun reached down and lifted her chin with his hand. "A parting word?" he answered. His smile was bright, but his eyes were serious. "Perhaps it is this: we both undertake ventures *à grands frais,* at great expense. May God go with us."

He released her and gently kicked his horse. Fulk took the lead position, with Calhoun and the other knights behind, and Afton was left alone on her knees in the dust. She stood slowly, like an old woman, and when she finally tore her eyes away from the road she found that all had left save one: her future husband, who watched with amusement in his eyes.

"I can't do it! I won't do it!" Afton knew full well that ladies were never to raise their voices, but she was the daughter of a ploughman, so she screamed at the top of her lungs.

Lunette and Morgan were both pale with fear, but Endeline's face was set. "You can and you will marry Hubert," she answered. "The marriage will take place tomorrow."

Afton backed toward the fireplace and impulsively grabbed a burning log from the flames.

"*Mon dieu!* She's burning her hand!" Lunette cried, pointing in distress. "She'll mar her beautiful skin!"

The end of the log Afton held was hot, but the other end flamed as she swung it toward the women. "I'll burn off my hair and face, I will, and then Hubert won't want to marry me! If that doesn't work, I'll throw myself out of the window. I will do it!"

"She's gone mad," Endeline said, throwing up her hands as she marched toward the doorway. "I will have nothing to do with this girl. I don't know why I ever brought her here in the first place."

When she reached the door, Endeline motioned for her maids to follow her. "I leave you here to your thoughts," she said to Afton when Morgan and Lunette had left the room. She grasped the door, but paused before slamming it shut. Her eyes narrowed thoughtfully.

"Perhaps someone else can bring you to your senses," she said, then stepped out of the room, firmly closing the door behind her.

"Come now, daughter, and tell us what troubles you," Wido said, his cap in his hand. He seemed even stiffer and more uncomfortable in the lord's chamber than he had been in the lord's hall. Corba stood by his side, but she had lost all restraint and was gazing openly at the tapestries, the wardrobe, the riches.

Afton wearily lifted her head from the bed. Why had Endeline sent them? They did not know her, nor did they know whom she really loved. They were villeins, mere peasants, and it was impossible for them to understand what she was thinking and feeling.

"I do not want to marry Hubert," Afton said, consciously trying to keep her voice under control. "I would rather die than marry that man."

"Why?" Corba's eyes left the treasures of the chamber,

and she looked curiously at her daughter. "I can understand that ye would not want to leave all these riches, but Hubert is the miller now and a free man. His position will be great, and he is highly esteemed by Lord Perceval."

"Do ye not know that free man makes free wife?" Wido added. "Ye forget, I think, that ye are a villein, as we are. But if ye marry Hubert, ye and your children will be free."

Free. Afton had not thought much about the word. Long ago Abbot Hugh had told her that she could not be what she was not. But if she married Hubert, her status would change from that of slave to free woman. She would be freer than Wido and Corba, as free as Endeline and Perceval. And Calhoun.

"Free woman." She said the words thoughtfully.

"Ye could not be bought or traded with the land," Corba added. "Ye could inherit property. Ye could even appear in the royal court and plead your case before the king. Villeins do not possess these rights."

"A free woman." Afton said it again. The words were like a new garment; they had to be tried on for size and adjusted. "What would it mean, this freedom?"

"Ye would have your own home in the village, next to the mill," Wido said. "It is a fine mill, built by the miller who died last year, and the roof does not leak. There is a garden and livestock."

"Ye would have your own husband and babies," Corba added, her own hand resting protectively around her ever-bulging stomach. "If God so blesses ye."

Could this marriage be a blessing? If Calhoun could put her out of his mind and go away, possibly forever, couldn't she put him out of her mind and marry Hubert? Sudden anger overwhelmed her. How could Calhoun leave her without complaint or a second thought? He cared for her, she knew, but he cared more for glory and honor and adventure. How satisfying, how pleasing it would be if they should meet in the future and she could walk up to him as his equal and say, "Greetings, Calhoun.

See my children and my house. See my garden and my sheep. See my husband—"

No, she could never say that with pleasure.

"There is something else to consider," Corba began reluctantly. "If ye hold any regard for us, your parents, ye may consider that all has gone well for us since ye came to live in Perceval's castle. The steward has not demanded undue rents of us, and Wido has not had to perform more than his expected share of service in the lord's fields. But if we now incur the lord's displeasure . . . "

Afton understood immediately what Corba meant. If she disobeyed Perceval's wishes, all would not go well for her parents. Their rents could be increased, their work load doubled, their other children traded or sold.

"Besides, if ye do not marry Hubert, Perceval may marry ye to someone else, a villein or a scoundrel," Wido pointed out. "We should trust the lord's decision."

Afton got up from the bed and walked to the window. The road that had carried Calhoun away to his precious adventures and the pursuit of glory lay quiet in the gathering stillness of late afternoon. Perhaps it could carry her, too, to adventures and freedom.

She squared her slender shoulders and turned to face her parents. "There is wisdom in what you say," she said, raising her chin. "I will marry Hubert tomorrow, though I do not love him or even know him. And I shall be a free woman."

Endeline kept her vow that she would have nothing else to do with Afton, even after Wido told the lady that Afton had consented to the marriage. Rather than staying to prepare Afton for the wedding, Endeline rose early the next morning and left the chamber with Lienor. She did, however, allow Lunette and Morgan to dress Afton in the best clothes in the wardrobe, for Afton's wedding attire would testify to the entire village of Perceval's generosity. After a warm bath, Afton was dressed in a fine linen chemise, a silk tunic of royal blue trimmed with fur, and a red surcoat of velvet that had been embroidered with gold thread. Over her bridal costume she wore a blue mantle edged in gold lace.

Morgan braided Afton's hair and Lunette dressed it with a small lace veil held in place by a narrow gold band. *"Au revoir,* lamb, we will miss you." Lunette sniffed as she adjusted the veil.

"I will miss you," Afton replied, her heart heavy in her chest. "You must come and see me."

"In the village?" Morgan answered, her eyes growing wide. "I don't think so. But per'aps you will come to the castle with your 'usband on feast days. We'll see you then, dearie."

"Aye," Afton agreed.

Dressed for her bridegroom, Afton was led downstairs and out of the castle to a gaily decorated wagon. Wido and Corba sat among bundles of spring flowers in the back of the wagon, and Hubert stood at the castle doorway, his hat in his hand. He was wearing a fine tunic and surcoat, and Afton thought that he looked cleaner than usual. He held out his broad hand and assisted her into the wagon as Morgan and Lunette sniffed and waved good-bye.

As the wagon made its way from the castle to the village, Afton studied the pasture outside the castle walls and relived the time when she and Calhoun had ridden together in the twilight. Had an eternity passed since that night? Her fingers went absently to her lips as she remembered his kiss. There had been no promise in it, only affection and warmth. That was what he had had to give, no more.

But the man who now rode beside her could give freedom, security, and babies. Afton wasn't sure how babies came into the world, for there had been none born in Perceval's castle in years. But Corba knew, and she would share her knowledge, Afton was sure. And if she couldn't love the man she would call her husband, Afton was sure she could love a baby.

TEN

Wido breathed a sigh of relief when the wagon pulled up outside the village church. The girl hadn't bolted. Father Odoric and several villagers were waiting there, and the marriage might yet succeed. Lord Perceval would be pleased.

Hubert had already alighted from the wagon by the time Wido had helped Corba from the vehicle, so Wido jumped over the side and walked to where his daughter sat stiffly, a bouquet of flowers on her lap. He took her hand in his and was startled to find that it was cold, like a dead man's. "God help us," he muttered under his breath, but as tradition demanded, he led his daughter to the steps of the church and stood between the bride and bridegroom to answer the priest's questions.

Father Odoric cleared his throat and squinted at the assembled crowd. "Are these two persons who wish to be married of the proper age?" the priest asked, his hand quivering slightly as it held the book of sacraments.

"Yes," Wido answered. "My girl is nearly thirteen years and the groom is . . ." he faltered and looked at Hubert.

"I am of age," Hubert answered, his voice gruff. "Pray continue."

"Do you swear you are not within the forbidden degree of consanguinity?" the priest asked.

"We swear it," Hubert answered. "We are not related and have no common ancestors within five generations."

How does he come upon this information? Wido wondered. *I know of no one who has done the necessary study of my family tree*. But Wido remained silent.

"Do their parents consent to this union?" the priest asked.

"My parents are dead," Hubert barked.

Wido nodded toward Corba, who stood behind him. "Her mother and I consent," he replied.

"Do the bride and groom both freely consent to be married?"

"I do," Hubert answered.

Wido thought Afton went a shade paler than she had been, but through trembling lips she answered: "I do."

Wido took his daughter's right hand and placed it in Hubert's. The act was the common symbol of transferring a gift, but Wido was suddenly overcome by the old feeling that Afton was not his to give. This girl had been born to him, but he had not understood her then or known her. Now, after years away from her family, she was more of a stranger than ever. But when Wido looked at her face he was astonished to see her gray eyes upon his, frankly pleading for help he did not know how to give.

Wido stepped back, leaving his daughter alone beside Hubert. "Our Lord saved married creatures at the great Flood," Father Odoric continued, looking around at the assembled crowd. "And he allowed the Blessed Virgin to be married. It is his will that men and women marry and provide for domestic peace, mutual fidelity, and the religious education of children."

Father Odoric lowered his black book and looked at Hubert. "My son, you may now give the ring." Hubert withdrew a ring from his pocket, and he slipped it first onto Afton's index finger, then her middle finger, and finally on her fourth finger. Wido knew this act, a symbol of the trinity, was supposed to protect the couple from demons and evil, but he wished the priest could do something more.

For some reason Wido couldn't explain, he felt certain that this couple would need all the protection the saints could muster.

Tradition demanded that the bride should then prostrate herself at her spouse's feet, but Afton simply stood at Hubert's side. Wido wondered if she was merely ignorant or deliberately stubborn. Whatever the case, Hubert seemed willing to let the matter pass. He proceeded to the next order of business and withdrew a small pouch of jingling coins, which he gave to Afton. She then handed it to the priest as an offering for the poor. Father Odoric nodded to Hubert, who recited his vows: "With this ring, I thee wed. With this gold, I thee honor. With this dowry, I thee endow."

Father Odoric then kissed Hubert and Afton and opened the church doors for the couple to take Mass together. Corba and Wido followed, and Wido sighed in relief as he entered the church in front of the assembled villagers. The espousal was now official. Now they only had the wedding to get through.

In titled families the ceremony of espousal often occurred years before the actual wedding, but Afton had no title and Hubert had no room for patience. After Mass, the wedding party and interested onlookers trooped to the miller's house for the nuptial feast.

The walled home to which Hubert conveyed his bride consisted of a typical village house of wattle and daub with a timber framework, but it was larger than most, with a hall of its own and a separate bedchamber. Afton noticed that there were two large outbuildings: a large kitchen where smoke billowed from a central vent in the roof, and, situated next to the creek, what had to be the millhouse.

The hall was not nearly as grand or large as that of the castle, but it was clean and well aired. Pleasant-looking tapestries hung on two windowless walls, and the tables had been strewn with flowers. A small girl gave each of the guests chaplets of blossoms, and an older woman greeted the guests and ushered them to a seat. When the toothless old woman greeted Afton, she gave a small curtsy. "I met ye before in the castle yard, remember? I'm Wilda, and now I'm serving master Hubert here at his house, with Lady Endeline's permission, of course. I'm part of ye dowry, from the good lord Perceval."

Afton gave the woman a weary smile and followed Hubert to their table. Small candles, precious commodities even at the castle, burned at each table, and two minstrels had been engaged to play songs for the guests.

It was well known in the village that Hubert had lately been highly favored by Perceval for killing the rebellious Gerald, and the other villagers were quick to share their congratulations and their appetites. They gazed with envy at Hubert's beautiful bride, gorged themselves on his food, and loudly congratulated him on his upward progress.

Afton found it strange to sit at a raised table, and she had to remind herself that in this house, at least, she was the lady of the manor. The single servant was hers to command; the chairs, furnishings, and tapestries were hers to arrange. Tomorrow she would order the food that passed before her, but for today she was glad that Wilda had arranged everything.

Afton sat between her father and her espoused husband and watched both men eat as though the meal were to be their last. She had no appetite, so she merely picked at the pottages and pastries set before her. The people who surrounded her were rough and coarse, with bawdy laughter and dirt under their fingernails, but Afton sternly told herself that she was one of them. Endeline had brutally reminded her that she was only the daughter of a ploughman, and if this was to be her life, she could tolerate these new circumstances. Perhaps she could find friends among the women in town.

But why? her heart cried out. Why had she worked so hard and long to be a gentle lady? Why had she striven to please Lady Endeline? What was the use, here in the village, of reading Latin and French? Who here would appreciate her songs and poetry? Which of these peasants could make sense of the mathematical riddles she and Lienor had devised? None of these people would even have time to consider her talent for small talk and gossip, for they were too concerned with the daily toil of staying alive and serving the master.

Afton bit her lip. She had learned her past lessons to please Endeline and in the hope of loving Calhoun. Now she would have to learn to please Hubert. Perhaps love could be found in the miller's house as well.

As the sun set in the afternoon sky, Wido grew impatient. His daughter was pale, the food was nearly gone, and the groom was more than a little drunk. "What say ye, Hubert, are ye to be married today or not?" Wido asked, trying to be pleasant.

"By all the saints, I am!" Hubert stood and thrust his cup toward the crowd in an unswerving punch. "Who gives this woman to be married?" he called, motioning to the priest.

Father Odoric took his cue and fumbled for his black book. He rose from the feast table and repeated the question.

Wido glanced at his daughter and tenderly took her hand. He stood up. "I am her father, and I give her to you," he said, and he placed Afton's small hand in Hubert's.

The guests stood in anticipation, and Hubert put his broad hands on Afton's shoulders and helped her rise from her seat. The priest led the way out of the room, reciting prayers for the couple's happiness together, and Afton and Hubert followed him out of the hall and into the bedchamber.

Wido watched in fascination as Afton awkwardly climbed onto the flower-bedecked bridal bed and Hubert took his place beside her. The priest mumbled a benediction of blessing, but all Wido could think was that his wedding had been nothing like this. He and Corba had been awash in joy, carried away by love, and the quiet giggles of their friends had only added to their merriment as Corba covered him in kisses on their nuptial bed.

There was none of that joy in the scene before him now. Afton lay, still and white, on the bed, her arms thrown protectively across her chest. Hubert leered at her as he stroked her hair while the priest chanted his blessing. Wido closed his eyes; the wedding of beauty and death was too much for him to bear.

"Tell me something more about yourself, Fulk," Calhoun urged as they rode toward Warwick.

"How you do love chatter." Fulk frowned at his charge. "You will learn immediately that a squire does not speak unless spoken to. A knight must control his tongue, for even a fool is thought wise if he remains silent."

Calhoun laughed. Fulk was a dangerous man, a huge man, but Calhoun instinctively knew that gentleness existed somewhere inside the knight's spirit. The others did not see it, for Fulk never smiled and rarely spoke when in the presence of other warriors, but with Calhoun he seemed more relaxed, even convivial.

"The best warrior I ever knew," Fulk said, his dark eyes wide open as if to capture the memory, "was a holy man. A Benedictine monk."

"That's impossible," Calhoun answered, shifting in his saddle. "You jest. Benedictines do not fight. Those who follow the holy teachings are taught to turn the other cheek. Raimondin told me so."

"That is true," Fulk replied, "And it was a hard lesson for my friend to learn, so fierce was his heart and temper. He gave his heart to God when he accepted the call of a holy life, but his temper he kept about him."

"A fighting monk?" Calhoun crinkled his brow. "I still say it is unnatural."

"The brothers of his order assured him a monk might defend himself on one occasion," Fulk answered, speaking in a low voice so the other knights would not hear. "He was allowed to defend his breeches if attacked."

133

Fulk paused and Calhoun considered this new information. Yes, that made sense. Even his uncle the abbot would fight in such a situation. "So? When would a monk meet the sort of vile men who would attack a man's breeches?"

Fulk smiled, and the muscles in his jaw flexed under his wiry beard. "My friend the holy man met them often, for when he traveled he exchanged his monk's robe for traveling breeches and wore a valuable brooch pinned at the front. Every thief on the roadside tried for the brooch, and the holy man slew at least five thieves on every pilgrimage to Canterbury. He considered it a valuable part of his service to God, this cleansing of robbers and thieves from the highways."

Calhoun threw back his head and roared with laughter. A fighting holy man! Only Fulk would know such a creature.

"Was your friend a Knight Templar?" Calhoun asked, when his laughter had passed. "Such a man would do well in that sect of holy men. In fact, Fulk, I am surprised you have not taken the oath of a Templar. It is well known that you are a devout man."

"What?" Fulk's voice was sharp, and for the first time Calhoun sensed danger beneath the smooth expression on Fulk's face. The cross-shaped scar upon his cheek, shining naked through the beard, twitched slightly. "I am not a devout man. God and I have nothing to do with each other."

Calhoun felt his cheeks reddening. "I am sorry, but since you bear the mark of the cross, I assumed—"

"Never assume," Fulk snapped, gathering his reins. "And for the remainder of the day, young squire, do not talk. You have said enough." Fulk spurred his horse ahead, and Calhoun was left alone to ponder the offense he had given to his new master.

They bedded down that night under a sky filled with stars. Fulk built a fire and charged the other knights with the duty of keeping it well lit, for the woods that surrounded them were filled with bears and wolves. After posting a guard at each end of their encampment, Fulk drew near to Calhoun and sat on the ground.

"We will arrive at Warwick tomorrow," Fulk said, resting his back against the trunk of an oak. He pulled a dagger from its sheath at his side and began to strip the bark from a fallen branch. "It is an old castle, older even than your Margate, fortified by William the Conqueror and updated. Lord Thomas of Warwick is more a military man than an estate holder, and you will find that your situation will be much different there."

"I am ready for a change," Calhoun answered easily, not threatened by the challenge in Fulk's words. "Lord Thomas and his knights hold no fears for me."

"Then sleep," Fulk said, grinning, the busy blade of his dagger shining golden in the firelight. "Tomorrow is our last hard ride."

Calhoun breathed a silent sigh of relief as he spread his mantle on the ground. They had been in the saddle for three straight days and, though he would not admit it, he was beginning to feel stiff.

He lay down, but sleep would not come. An owl hooted in the darkness, and far away, an animal roared. He felt alive in every nerve of his body, tense and hopeful that somehow through the company of these men—and those he would meet at Warwick—he would become a man and, finally, a knight.

One of Perceval's knights tramped into the clearing and held up a stalk of berries. "Look what I found in the forest," he said, holding a clump of berries before Fulk. "Blueberries. They'll do for supper, won't they?"

"You eat those and you're a dead man," Fulk answered calmly, still whittling on the oak branch. "That's baneberry, not blueberry. You'll be dead within two days if you take a single bite."

The startled knight tossed the berries into the fire and closed his mouth in disappointment. "Better to be hungry than dead," he muttered.

"Aye," Calhoun agreed. He shivered and drew his sur-coat about him. The sight of the berries brought back the sharp memory of a girl collecting berries and flowers in the sun-drenched field outside Margate Castle. On that day Afton had come into his life, and yesterday she had passed out of it, as was the way of childhood toys and playmates.

But yesterday there had not been much of a child about Afton. She had knelt in the dust at his feet as a young woman, and her eyes had been filled with a haunting, lost look . . . a look that had embarrassed him and caused him to curse his own impotence, for what could he do about her pain?

Yet, as he closed his eyes to sleep, he seemed to feel her touch on his foot and hear the pleading in her voice. She had asked only for a parting word, and he had given her the truest and most terrible words he knew: at great expense. She would never know how much it cost him to turn away from her, for she reminded him of home, and childhood, and security. Now he was to become a man, and it was time to put away all those things.

Afton lay in the dark, trying to breathe in regular, deep breaths so the man who was her husband would think she was asleep. From the courtyard outside she could hear the singing and dancing of revelers who were enjoying them-selves at her wedding feast. Was a wedding a time of joy? She bit her lip to repress a shudder. Her union with this man had been too repulsive, too brutish for words.

The priest had scarcely gone when Hubert had turned to her and ripped her mantle and surcoat from her. The lovely garments she had been so pleased to wear were now scattered in ragged heaps around the room, and she felt shamed and unclean. Was it for Hubert's act of savagery that God designed marriage? Surely not! As a child she had slept in the same room with her mother and father, and she had never heard her father roar drunkenly or her mother cry aloud in humiliation.

She longed to get under the linen sheet on the bed, but

Hubert had passed out in stupor or exhaustion, and his arm and shoulder lay across her bare chest. He was too heavy to move, and she would willingly have died rather than wake him and risk beginning the nightmare anew.

So she lay in the darkness and wept.

The mountain did move from her, ere morning, and she slipped beneath the sheet and turned her back on her husband. He lay flat on his back, snoring, until the rooster in the yard crowed and brought Hubert slowly back to life. Afton heard him smack his lips, felt the twitching of his arms, and heard their hay mattress creak as he lifted one hairy leg and absently rubbed it against the other. His consciousness returned then and he rolled over on his side. Afton felt a stubby finger poke her on the shoulder.

"Wake up, my bride," Hubert growled in her ear. "Let me get a good look at you in the day's light."

She felt him crawl under the sheets next to her and she closed her eyes in disgust and loathing. But, she told herself, this man was her husband and master. Surely he would be in a reasonable mind now that he was not drunk. What would Endeline do? She would be pleasing and gentle and always give her husband undivided attention.

With a mighty effort, she cleared her face of all expression and pretended to yawn. "Good morning, husband," Afton said gently, turning onto her back. She struggled to keep her voice from breaking. "Did you sleep well?"

Hubert didn't reply. Instead he laid his index finger on the top of her head and gently ran it down her forehead, her nose, over her lips, down her throat, and down her body until she involuntarily cringed and lurched away from him.

He laughed, then one hand closed around her upper arm in an iron grip and the other fell across her mouth and nose, scarcely allowing her to breathe. "My proud little wife," he said, his voice rough. "Given to me as a favor from Perceval for killing a man. If I had known there were such rewards for killing, I'd have done it long ago."

Her eyes widened in terror, and Hubert laughed again.

It was much later when Hubert decided to get out of bed and begin his day's chores. As he dressed, he gave Afton explicit directions for her life henceforth. She was never to leave the house without Wilda, the maid, nor to talk to anyone unless Wilda was present. She was never to talk to another man, except to greet Lord Perceval if he should visit. She was not to go out of the house without her head properly covered. She was to be beautifully dressed for his friends at dinner and supper, and never dressed when Hubert came to bed. She was never to go into the millhouse or the kitchen, for neither of those were her place. If she remembered these things, she would be happy and do well. If she did not do these things, Hubert would kill her, as was his right.

Afton lay in dazed silence on the bed as Hubert gave his directions. She was no coward, but the heretofore unimagined brutality of the previous hours had stunned her into stillness. She had never dreamed such malignity could exist; for Hubert's deeds were more invasive and inconceivable than even King Henry's mutilation of his grandchildren. That had been a fierce act of war, however senseless, but this was life! How was she to endure it?

"May I—" her voice faltered. "May I get dressed?"

"Of course," Hubert answered, buckling his mantle around him. He stood up and smoothed his hair in the washbasin. "There is one more thing. You need not pretend with me. I know you fancy yourself too good to be my wife. I know you love Perceval's younger son. I read it plainly on your face. But I also know you sprang from a ploughman and a common woman, and as such will I treat you, now that you are my wife."

He adjusted his tunic and admired his reflection in a small mirror. "Wilda will show you around the house, and you may order what you wish for dinner. The house will be your responsibility, and I expect you to run it well."

"As you wish." Her voice was steady, but it was good Hubert did not turn to look at his bride, for even he might have been startled by the burning hatred on her face.

ELEVEN

Trumpeters blared a greeting to Calhoun and his entourage as they came within sight of Warwick Castle. Fulk urged the horses into an easy canter, and they were welcomed with an open gate and lowered drawbridge. Fulk's description was accurate: the castle was an old motte and bailey that had been fortified. Warwick Castle lacked the modern luxuries of which Perceval was so fond, but it rose strong and compact from the hill on which it was situated, and a trio of knights in full shining armor stood on the battlement to salute those who arrived.

Calhoun tried not to gape like a villein as he and his company entered the castle walls, but he wanted to see everything at once. A knight dressed in the red and gold of Warwick directed them to the magnificent stables, and as the horses walked slowly through the courtyard, Calhoun noticed an excellent mews filled with roosting falcons, a large kitchen, and a smithy. There was no women's area and no garden, Calhoun noted, and it was probably a good thing. With so many knights about, the ladies of the castle were undoubtedly kept inside under guard.

Calhoun and his men dismounted outside the stables, and a flourish of trumpets from a second-story window in the castle directed their eyes upward. Next to the trumpeter stood a stalwart-looking man and a golden-haired girl. "Lord Thomas of Warwick," the trumpeter announced formally.

"Welcome to Warwick Castle," the man said, smiling down and extending his hand toward the visitors. Calhoun instinctively liked the master of his new home. Lord Thomas was older than Perceval, Calhoun guessed, for there were streaks of gray around his temples and in his thick beard. But his frame was solid and straight, and the hand he extended was broad and unwavering. "We recognize Perceval's colors and know one of you to be his beloved son, Calhoun."

"I am he," Calhoun answered, stepping forward. He bowed. "I am privileged to serve as a squire in your court, Lord Thomas."

"We are honored to have you," Thomas answered. He directed his gaze toward Fulk. "And I seem to recognize the valiant knight who accompanies you. How goes it with you, Fulk?"

Fulk smiled carelessly and bowed. "It goes well, my lord."

Thomas gathered the hand of the young girl next to him and clasped it to his breast. "This, of course, is Lady Clarissant, my wife, who I imagine will be the center of your universe from this time forward." He nodded gallantly toward the beauty at his side. "I trust her comeliness and favor will inspire you to commit noble deeds in the name of your lord and king."

Calhoun was surprised, for he had thought the girl to be Thomas's daughter, but he caught himself and bowed. "It cannot be otherwise," he answered, smiling up at Lady Clarissant. She was young and fair, probably not much older than Calhoun, with golden hair that spilled over her shoulders and sparkled in the sunlight. Her eyes were surprisingly blue; Calhoun could see even from a distance that they were the color of an untroubled summer sky.

"We will leave you now," Thomas said, pulling his wife to his side. "You will dine with us at dinner and supper from this time on." Calhoun barely heard the welcoming words, so intent was he upon staring at the Lady Clarissant, but he felt Thomas' gaze upon him and reluctantly looked toward his host. Thomas gave him a wry smile. "Welcome to our castle, Squire Calhoun of Margate. May your time here be worthwhile."

In the master's chamber at Margate Castle, Morgan saw Lunette approaching and laid a finger across her lips. Lunette nodded, understanding. The sign could only mean that Lady Endeline was in a bit of a temper.

The lady lay on the bed in a fitful sleep, and the maids moved carefully toward the girls' dormitory lest they disturb her. The small bag they had packed for Lienor lay at the foot of Endeline's bed. *Was it the sight of that pitifully small bag that sent our lady to bed with a headache?* Morgan wondered.

Lunette had her own opinion. "I think a guilty conscience troubles her," she whispered in the small dormitory that had once been home to Afton and Lienor. "She sent ze child away with zat horrible old man. Wouldn't zat give a decent person nightmares?"

"It was a terrible thing to do, but it was 'er right to do it," Morgan answered. "The girl was a villein, after all. She should be grateful she was sheltered in the castle for so many years."

"Such a sweet girl," Lunette sighed. "Always so eager to please. Not at all like zat Lienor."

"Such a lucky girl," Morgan inserted. "A free woman now, and married to the miller! That's a prosperous position if there ever was one. Our Lienor won't fare nearly so well, starving at the nunnery."

"I won't starve." Lienor stepped soundlessly into the dormitory and Morgan blushed.

"Excuse me, miss, but we didn't mean any harm," Morgan explained.

"No harm was given," Lienor answered quietly. She nodded toward the bag on the floor in the chamber. "That is for me?"

"Yes," Lunette answered. "We packed your new habit

141

and your mattress. Lord Perceval said he would bring ze bag of gold for your entrance fee later."

"Good," Lienor answered, folding her hands into the long sleeves of her tunic. "Now come with me, I need an escort to the village and I do not want a knight for company."

"To ze village?" Lunette's eyes opened wide in surprise. "Whatever will we do in ze village?"

"It is not your affair," Lienor said, leading the way. "Just come with me."

Endeline's head was still throbbing when she awoke, so she lay back down on the bed, a pillow over her head. What demon made her head pound so dreadfully? Wasn't she doing all in her power to be the proper mother and wife?

Her own daughter was set to leave for the nunnery, a proper and respectable sacrifice in the eyes of God and man. Lienor, who could and should have married the son of the king, would now serve the family by offering prayers and praise to God for the rest of her life. The convent was a noble calling, and most noble families sent at least one child into the religious life. Yes, Endeline would be praised for Lienor's decision to follow God.

Her son Charles would continue the Margate family line. He would marry . . . Endeline compressed her lips into a tight line. Yes, he would marry, if she had to choose the girl and oversee them on the nuptial bed! He was born to be a landowner and, while he lacked Perceval's ambition and Calhoun's recklessness, he would be the solid, steadying influence the family needed to bring prosperity and heirs into the next generation.

Even Calhoun had been swept into his proper place. Despite the pounding in her head, she smiled at the thought of him, the improper boy who had caused her more than one headache. He had flirted so openly with the common girl, Afton, but now he had undertaken his rightful role. After two years in hard and humble training as a knight, he would return to the family and spend his life either at Margate or on the battlefield in service to the king. In either case, his sacrifice would bring glory to the family and would be written in the history of England and its kings.

Endeline's hands wandered over her barren belly, and she groaned as a familiar twinge struck her lower back. Soon the time of women would be upon her, and once again her body would issue bloody proof of its rebellion at the prospect of carrying a baby. Her mind flitted, unbidden, to the memory of the peasant Corba at the recent feast. Why should a work-worn peasant woman's face shine with the blessing of yet another impending birth? Why did God allow that peasant woman to reproduce as regularly as livestock while she, noble Endeline, did not bear another child?

Endeline's attempts at foster parenting had brought her satisfaction for a time, but her experiences had become unsettling when it became necessary for the children to leave. The small boy she had taken to raise had become willful and resentful, and Endeline had been more than happy to give him as a servant to Abbot Hugh on his last visit.

It galled Endeline to admit that Afton had been her most successful undertaking. The girl's gentle manners and beauty had reflected well on Endeline while she lived at the castle, and her presentation to the miller had ably demonstrated to the vassals the worthiness of service for Perceval. In all respects, the girl had done them credit.

So why did Endeline's heart feel so empty? Why did her head pound without ceasing?

Because I have fostered unworthy children, Endeline muttered under her pillow. *They were villeins, inferior, unworthy of membership in Perceval's family. I must be patient,* Endeline resolved. *It is better to find a perfect pearl than a dozen grainy substitutes. If it takes ten years, I will find a child without the flaws of my previous wards. Surely I can find a child whose noble heart is like my own.*

Endeline did not know where such a child would be found, but she was sure Perceval would. Once he understood the strength of her resolution, he would have to help her.

Rising from her nuptial bed, Afton moved like a weary old woman. She splashed water on her face and neck, washing Hubert's kisses from her body, wishing she could also wash their memory from her mind. The small mirror above the washbasin revealed bruises on her arms and neck from Hubert's rough handling. She dressed as best she could, but her chemise was torn beyond repair, and the tunic could be worn only as long as she kept her surcoat over it.

The fragrant blossoms that had adorned the room last night were bruised and brown now, and Afton gathered an armful of them, but their sickly sweet smell struck her and made her nauseous. She fell on the floor at the foot of the bed and waited for the sick feeling to pass, grateful for the coolness of the earthen floor. She would never willingly seek that bed again.

She was just beginning to feel stronger when there was a knock on the door. "Mistress," Wilda's crackly voice called. "You have a visitor."

A visitor? Could she speak to anyone without fear of Hubert's reprisals?

"Who is this visitor?" Afton whispered.

"The Lady Lienor," Wilda answered. "She wants a word with you."

Lienor! Afton struggled to her feet and hurried out of the room, her weariness forgotten. Was there news of Calhoun? Had Perceval recanted his gift to Hubert?

Lienor waited inside the courtyard, still mounted upon her horse, and Afton saw Morgan and Lunette outside the miller's gate. They waved timidly as she stepped out into the courtyard and shaded her eyes from the sun. "Lienor? Won't you come in?"

"I can't," Lienor answered, her voice void of all emotion. "I am entering the abbey today and wanted to make my peace with you before I go."

Afton stepped up to Lienor's side and put a tentative hand on the horse's bridle. "There is no bitterness between us," she said quietly.

"I did not welcome you into our household," Lienor answered, loosening the reins in her grip. "Charles and I were often cruel. And I harbored ill will in my heart toward you, and jealousy, because I was to marry a man with a king's certain cruelty, and you were free to marry a common man."

Afton closed her eyes and turned her face away lest Lienor should see the pain and shame upon it. "You had no reason to be jealous," she answered, shaking her head.

"You were beautiful and I was not," Lienor went on. "And my mother wanted me to be like you. I resented you terribly, but in the end I am glad that I was not born fair. Now I can live my life within the safety of the church instead of fulfilling the plans my mother had for me. I will not see my children blinded, or watch my husband strike them down. Once I prayed that God would take Prince William away—"

"Hush, Lienor," Afton interrupted, burying her face in the horse's neck. "You should not say these things. All things happen as God wills. . . . " She said the words automatically, but she did not believe them. Was it God's will that she be imprisoned by marriage to Hubert?

"You are my only friend," Lienor answered, a sudden trace of sadness in her voice. She gathered the horse's reins. "I shall pray for your happiness."

Afton's throat closed as her emotions welled up and she put her hand over the bruises on her neck. She managed to whisper, "And I for yours," then Lienor kicked her horse and turned back toward the castle road.

Afton watched the three women ride away in silence. *It is inconceivable that Lienor should have passed years in secret envy,* she thought, *for now I envy her. Her family is wealthy enough to pay the entrance fee to the abbey, and as a bride of Christ, Lienor will never have to give herself to any man. What better life than that could there be?*

The days settled into a routine in which Afton found herself driven to extremes of boredom and terror. Nighttime brought nightmares, but every morning Wilda knocked on her door with a cheery call of "How's our new bride today?" and helped her dress. On some mornings, the rough woman's touch seemed unusually tender, but she kept to her place and never offered comments on the evidence of Hubert's rough handling. Hubert had generously supplied Afton with clothing, so she had several fine tunics and richly embroidered surcoats. After dressing, she and Wilda sat by the fire in her chamber and planned the dinner menu.

After her meeting with Wilda, Afton usually wandered outside behind the house to enjoy the sunshine and fresh air. The house itself was in the center of a large courtyard, with the kitchen on the right and the mill house on the left. Behind the kitchen was a pen for livestock and a vegetable garden where Afton and Wilda worked in the afternoons.

The millhouse perched precariously on the bank of the creek; indeed, the water-facing side of the millhouse was supported by beams driven deep into the creek bed. It was the water that powered the huge stones that even now ground grain into flour, Wilda explained, and Afton accepted her explanation without question. She would have loved to see the mill, swim in the creek, or even walk along the bank, but she dared not for fear of Hubert's reprisals. Many villagers fished there regularly, and one might speak to her.

She was also told to avoid the front of the house, for Hubert's customers brought their sacks of grain to the mill by way of the front gate. She was not even allowed into Wilda's kitchen, for Hubert did not want his wife to sully her hands with menial labor.

The only person Hubert allowed her to address freely was Wilda, and Afton suspected that it was not by accident that one day Wilda brought her a kitten and complained that she did not have time to care for the creature. Would Afton like to care for it, or should she throw it in the river? Afton wept in gratitude as she held the purring creature against her cheek, and her face reddened in embarrassment because the older woman had obviously recognized her terrible loneliness. Afton had hoped to act the part of a great and capable lady, but Wilda had obviously recognized a scared girl in need of something soft, warm, and loving.

Afton had hoped that her husband would one day love her. Now she knew this was never to be. He would never care for her, but he did value her. Indeed, she was a rare prize, one to be paraded in front of the villagers as often as possible. He only reminded his wife of her humble birth in their most private moments; in public, he doted on her upbringing in Perceval's castle. Often at meals he commanded her to sing for his guests, and she would have to stop eating, swallow her food hastily, and stand and sing a song, preferably in French, for Hubert liked anything that smacked of nobility.

She knew better than to hesitate at any of his commands. Once he had asked her to sing at dinner and she had paused to pass a dish. Afterwards he had taken her to their chamber, stripped her of her clothing and dignity, and forced her to sing for an hour. She would have refused, but a harsh gleam in Hubert's eye promised worse if she did not obey, so she sang until her voice rasped. As he left, Hubert threw her clothes at her and warned her never to hesitate to follow his commands again.

If all went well at dinner, she spent her afternoons doing needlepoint or embroidery with Wilda, for Hubert wanted the tapestries in his hall to be as elegant as those hanging in Perceval's hall. He knew Afton could do such fine work, he told her, and if her tapestries failed to outshine those at the castle, she would pay the penalty. So Afton worked hard, her fingers trembling, and sternly reproved Wilda for the slightest irregularity in the older woman's stitching. Wilda said nothing in return, but occasionally smiled at the gamboling antics of the kitten that played at Afton's feet. The cat was their secret, and Afton's only source of pleasure.

At supper, any feelings of life or hope or happiness Afton had felt during the day were carefully quelled, for Hubert

came to sit by the hearth in their chamber. Afton brought
his slippers, washed his feet, and directed Wilda to bring him
supper. Afton was not allowed to eat at this meal, but
instead she was instructed to sit on a stool at his feet and
hear the things her master would teach her. Every night
brought a new variation on Hubert's philosophy of men and
women.

Women were tools of the devil, Hubert told her, and
their loveliness was the key to Adam's fall in the Garden.
That was why she was not to leave the house, and that was
why Hubert would burn her alive if she ever brought him
dishonor.

"Men are women's beginning," Hubert told her one
night as he munched on a chicken's leg. "Without man,
they have no purpose. And just as a dog licks his master's
hand even after he has been beaten for a fault, so a wife
ought to follow her husband after correction. A dog does
not upbraid its master, or scold, or question, but follows submissively, until the death, if necessary." Hubert's dark eyes
narrowed. "Do you understand, young wife?"

Afton gave the words that had become her reflexive,
automatic answer to everything. "Yes, my lord."

One night Hubert came in early and found Afton standing at the window combing her hair. He screamed in fury,
closed the shutters, and threw Afton onto the bed. Then,
though she sputtered in confusion, he was on top of her,
and his fist came down onto her face with such force the
room darkened.

Later, after she had regained consciousness and called
for Hubert's supper, he explained his position: "Sin arises
from a fondness for grooming," he said gruffly, dipping his
bread into the thick gravy that covered his venison. "If a
woman takes pride in her beautiful hair or her beautiful skin,
numerous evils arise. Every woman should groom and dress
in secret, not in an open window. You should not show your
beautiful hair in public, but keep it under a cap. Your hair,
your throat, your bosom, are only for your husband to see."

Afton's eye was so badly swollen that she could barely see at all, but she nodded. "Yes, my lord," she whispered, trying to keep her voice level. Hubert would not tolerate any sign of vacillation or weakness.

"I cannot believe Lady Endeline did not teach you these things," Hubert went on, "therefore I believe you must be deliberately ignoring the morals and manners with which you were raised. And that dress—" he pointed to the gown Afton wore, stained now with blood from her nose.

"This dress?" Afton looked down and smoothed the dress with trembling fingers. "Does it not please you?"

"It is cut tight," Hubert answered. "Women wear such dresses only so men will say, 'Look at that woman's fine body, worthy of being loved by a good man such as I!'"

Afton shook her head in confusion. "My lord, I have grown—"

"Does it fill your heart with joy to know men will say that if they see you in such a dress?"

"No, my lord." Afton shook her head again and stood up. "I will take it off."

"Leave it on." Hubert looked up at her and smiled. "I am your husband and I will enjoy it. But you are never to wear it outside this room."

"Yes, my lord."

Then, after dinner, came bed. And after bed, came sleep—the only means of escape that Afton found open to her.

Twelve

While Afton learned her lessons as a dutiful wife, Calhoun learned lessons of a different sort. As a squire, he was not a child of nobility or the son of a great lord, but Fulk's personal servant. Squires were taught service, loyalty, and the skills that would bring honor and the glory of victory in battle.

There were twelve squires, all in various stages of training, at Warwick Castle, and each squire had a knight whom he served. Smaller boys also darted through the castle courtyard, much like curious mice. The younger boys, sons of knights without estates, served as pages in Thomas's court, scurrying from place to place on various errands as they learned the manners of nobility and the politics and policies of castle life.

Calhoun found the children amusing. Most of them looked upon the squires and knights with faintly veiled admiration; a few were frankly ambitious and longed aloud for the day when they would be in command of themselves and others. But one boy in particular caught Calhoun's eye. He was called Gislebert and he chose to walk alone, never with the pack of pages who periodically pestered the squires. His eyes were large and wide like Afton's, but they never shone with defiance or longing as Afton's had. As the other boys roughhoused and wrestled in the dust, Gislebert hung in the shadows, his auburn head bent over a parchment. Calhoun knew instinctively that Gislebert would never be a knight.

He was surprised when his feeling of interest in the boy was apparently returned. As Calhoun dutifully followed the fearless Fulk, his teacher and master, Gislebert began to shadow Calhoun, his freckled face appearing behind every post, corner, and tree.

Fulk had immediately intimidated the vaunted knights of Lord Thomas, and he and Calhoun were given the choicest bunks in the tower garrison. One morning Calhoun awoke and was surprised to see Gislebert sleeping in the straw beneath their wooden bunks. From that night on, the straw beneath Calhoun's bunk became the boy's accustomed place, and Calhoun came to accept him as easily as he accepted the night terrors that routinely troubled Gislebert while he slept.

In the warm light of morning, neither of them ever spoke of the trauma of nighttime—but then, they seldom had time, for the days at Warwick offered enough activity to keep all three busy. Lord Thomas led frequent hunting expeditions into the forests, not only to feed the army in training at the Warwick garrison, but also to hone the boys' riding and hunting skills. In addition, the knights led the squires in team drills to teach them to act as a unit, and Lady Clarissant often asked an audience with the young men to enlighten them in the important social skills of dancing and composing verse.

When not participating in group activities, each squire endured private training from his master. Fulk directed that Calhoun's mornings should be reserved for sword practice. On these mornings, Calhoun helped Fulk into his forty-pound armor, then, while Fulk sharpened his sword and dagger, Gislebert climbed onto Fulk's upper bunk and dropped the hauberk over Calhoun's head. The hauberk, a shirt of tightly woven mail, weighed nearly twenty pounds and covered Calhoun from neck to knees. At first Calhoun complained that the sleeves of his hauberk were too long, but Fulk only laughed and admonished Calhoun to grow faster.

Sword practice was exhausting. Before Fulk would allow

Calhoun to engage an opponent, the boy had to stand in front of a tree stump and slash at it from the right, from the left, from above, from below, and from behind. Once his right arm was thoroughly exhausted, Fulk ordered that he repeat the exercise with the sword in his left hand.

"I can't do this anymore," Calhoun complained one day, dropping his heavy sword in the dust. "There's no sport in striking a tree stump."

"Your muscles are weak, particularly those in your left arm," Fulk answered, the corner of his mouth drooping in derision, "or you would not be tired. But perhaps a little motivation would help." Fulk walked over to the charred remains of the previous night's fire and picked up a blackened coal. On the bald tree stump he drew two eyes, a nose, and a mouth.

Calhoun laughed. "Who is that? An infidel, or you, mighty Fulk?"

Fulk's eyes glinted in appreciation of his student's wit, but he did not allow himself to smile. He merely walked back to Calhoun and crossed his arms. "I think . . . " he said slowly, regarding his artwork, "I think it bears a resemblance to the miller in Margate. What is the man's name?"

Calhoun straightened and looked into Fulk's snapping eyes. "His name is Hubert," he answered.

"Ah, yes, and isn't he now married to the lovely Afton?" Fulk raised an eyebrow as he spoke, then spat into the dust and looked back at his young charge. "Are you still tired, Squire Calhoun?"

Calhoun bent and picked up his sword. He steadied it in the sunlight and watched the blade gleam. "I think not," he answered. And he charged the stump again.

The squires and pages did not eat with the nobility, but in the kitchen after serving the knights, the lord, and his lady at dinner. Calhoun did not mind carrying a jug of ale and filling the cups of the thirsty knights, for dinner at Warwick meant two things to Calhoun, and both were dear to his heart: the sight of Lady Clarissant and talk of battle.

The loud knights loved nothing better than to talk of recent and historical battles. Calhoun heard names he had known from his history lessons with Raimondin, but here in this living tableau the images of men who lived only in war stories became as sharp as the swords that hung from every knight's belt. In every tale, blood flowed freely, courage ran high, and the glory of a righteous cause always brought certain victory. The gory narratives did not disturb Calhoun in the least. Indeed, the only night he felt any discomfort at all was the night he fought to hide his pride when his grandfather, Lionel, was praised as a sterling warrior.

At Warwick's table he heard again the stories of King Arthur. Endeline had loved to tell these stories to her children, but her tales of the Round Table and Camelot had been laced with romance. Here at Warwick Castle, where femininity and romance were allowed only for adornment, the tales were more bloody, the villains more fiendish, and the victors more courageous.

The knights also told stories of recent history, tales of the Holy Land, reports of skirmishes with infidels, and the exploits of Knights Templar, who gave their lives in the defense of holy pilgrims. Occasionally an older knight would stand and ask Lord Thomas's permission to tell a true tale. Calhoun was surprised one day when Fulk requested such permission.

"My father was one who heard Pope Urban speak of the necessity of an expedition to reach Jerusalem," Fulk began his chronicle. "The pope spoke of how the infidels had destroyed the altars of God after polluting them with barbaric practices. The infidels had circumcised Christians, spreading blood on Christian altars and pouring it on the holy fonts. They cut open the bellies of those whom they chose to torment with a loathsome death, tying them to a stake before tearing out their bowels, dragging them, and flogging them. Finally, merciful death took these Christians as they lay on the ground with their entrails hanging out."

The sounds of eating and drinking stilled as Fulk paused.

"It was an eloquent cry, and the promise of complete absolution of sins and certain salvation was enough to send thousands into battle to redeem the Holy Land. The knights sewed crosses on their garments, and many swore never to return to their homes, but to live and die in pilgrimage. I was two when my father left on the business of Christ."

Calhoun leaned against the wall, his water jug on his hip. He had known that Fulk had spent time in the Holy Land, but he had never heard the story of Fulk's father.

"It was a dangerous journey, fraught with battles on the way," Fulk continued, his hair shining darkly in the dim torchlight. "The infidels could not understand our rules of warfare, but they were tenacious. On a hot day in July, innumerable Turks swirled forward to surround the forces of God. The Christian knights formed a battle line around their camp, against which the Turks fought fiercely, expecting to gain the victory. The Christians were cut off and unable to maneuver.

"Through the heat of the day, however, the line of God held. A second part of our army marched to the rescue of the valiant defenders, and they fell on the Turks like the wrath of God. Soon the Turks were ensnared, and their camp, with a wealth of gold, silver, horses, camels, and sheep, fell like bounty into the hands of God's people.

"That was the beginning of the end. A year later, the spirit of Bishop Adhemar appeared to one of the holy knights and promised victory after nine days if the army of God would fast and make a barefoot procession around Jerusalem. The army obeyed, and a great column wound its way across the rocky slopes of the Holy City, holding crosses and chanting psalms.

"Nine days later, the army of God marched into the city, killing every infidel in its path. The horses waded in blood up to their knees, nay, some say it was up to the beasts' bridles. They say, my brothers, that it was a just and wonderful judgment of God."

Fulk's face was as smooth as marble as he sat down, and

Calhoun felt oddly cheated, as if Fulk had posed a question without giving an answer. Lord Thomas must have felt the same way, for he leaned forward and asked: "And what do *you* say, Fulk?"

The corner of Fulk's mouth lifted in a half smile, and he stood again and bowed to Lord Thomas. "Begging your pardon, my lord, it is not my place to sanction the judgments of God. I am a man of the sword. I live by it and I shall undoubtedly die by it, as did my father. Such a man as I cannot presume to speak for God."

Lord Thomas clapped his hands together in appreciation. "There, my fellow knights, you see the proper heart of a warrior. His is not to question or presume, but to follow orders into battle and the glory that follows victory."

"After such a story, I fear we need a song to lighten our hearts," Lady Clarissant said, lightly tapping her husband's arm. She smiled at a waiting troubadour who had recently arrived at the castle. "Sing to us of faraway kings and lands," she told him, the pearls in her hair gleaming like tears upon silk. "A sweet tale of love, not of battle."

The traveling minstrel bowed toward the lady and began his story in song, but Calhoun did not listen. His head was filled instead with visions of the future glory he would win in battle, and of the enemy blood he would spill to avenge Fulk's father and the thousands of men who had died before him.

There was only one cloud in Calhoun's bright horizon at Warwick Castle: Squire Arnoul, the self-proclaimed leader of the band of squires by virtue of his uncommon size and his distant relation to King Henry. Sixteen years old and already as heavy as Fulk, Arnoul had set his small probing eyes upon Calhoun's slender frame from the moment the entourage from Margate Castle arrived at Warwick. And once Arnoul's eagle stare was fixed on something—or someone—it was not easily distracted, no matter how oblivious Calhoun was to it.

"You should watch Arnoul," Gislebert warned his new-found friend as they returned to the garrison after supper one evening. "He hates you, we can all see it."

"He hates me?" Calhoun frowned, then shrugged. "What have I done to injure him?"

"Nothing. Still, he dislikes you," Gislebert insisted, his face reddening to the point that his freckles were nearly obliterated. "He was the leader here before you came."

"He can be leader still, for I direct no one," was Calhoun's reply. Gislebert looked at the ground in silence. Calhoun's easygoing attitude was precisely what drew the other boys' loyalty, but a carefree warrior did not last long in a contest.

The news was directed into the stream of consciousness one hot afternoon, and just as ants know when a meaty morsel has been dropped under the table, so the pages and squires knew that a contest between Calhoun and Arnoul had been arranged. Fulk and Jerome, Arnoul's master, had agreed that the squires were ready for a wrestling match. It would take place after dinner.

"Watch your back, for Arnoul is as strong as a lion," Fulk warned Calhoun as he lifted off the boy's heavy hauberk. "Fortunately, he is slow as a bear, so you must be quick. Let him see what you are made of, and then let him win."

"Let him win?" Calhoun's mouth opened in disbelief.

"Yes," Fulk answered. There was no teasing gleam in his dark eyes.

"But why? Just because he's the king's cousin? That means nothing to me, and I can beat him easily."

"If Arnoul means nothing to you, as you have said, then it will cost you nothing to allow his victory," Fulk answered, slapping Calhoun on the back. "You have two glaring weaknesses, young squire, and neither will be overcome without practice. So do as I say, and allow him the victory."

"What weaknesses?" Calhoun growled.

Fulk smiled. "Don't you know?"

"My left arm is weak," Calhoun admitted grudgingly. "But what else? I can think of nothing else, for I can best any squire here in hunting, riding, jousting—"

Fulk held up a hand. "Enough. We will see today how you fare against Squire Arnoul. Prepare yourself, for he approaches."

Arnoul stepped inside the wrestling circle that was drawn in the dust and scowled at Calhoun. Sweat glistened from his heavy chest even though they had not yet begun the match, and the boys who watched from outside the circle drew expectant breaths. Gislebert chewed on his thumbnail, but Calhoun knew that behind him, Fulk watched with a calm smile and sharp eyes.

Calhoun crouched lower than Arnoul so that the bigger boy's form blocked the sun from his eyes. He circled with the confidence of a stalking cat, his hands loose and open at his sides, and watched and waited for Arnoul to make the first move. It was so unfair of Fulk to ask him to lose the fight! He could beat Arnoul, he was sure of it—and wasn't victory always better than defeat?

The pages and squires around the circle had been joined by the knights of Warwick, their interest piqued by the stature of the contestants. Above him, Calhoun heard a shuttered window creak open. That meant that either Lord Thomas or Lady Clarissant was watching, too. Lord Thomas would undoubtedly favor Arnoul because of his relation to the king, but Calhoun felt unusual confidence in his strength. Today, in this hour, he could willingly defeat even the king himself.

Gislebert broke the unbearable silence: "Pin him, Calhoun! You can do it!" The sound stopped Arnoul's suspenseful circling and he lunged for Calhoun's leg. Calhoun spun quickly, as nimble as a squirrel, and Arnoul landed in the dust. Above him, Calhoun heard a gentle laugh—so it was Lady Clarissant who was watching. Her gentle laughter only propelled his determination to win. He would not only beat

Arnoul, he would pound him into the dirt. Today was marked for Arnoul's total humiliation.

But pinning the bulky boy would be a challenge. Calhoun knew that even if he threw himself directly on top of Arnoul's shoulders, his weight would not be enough to bring the bigger boy down. He circled, his hands dancing like taunting puppets, and waited.

Streaked with dirt and perspiration, Arnoul regained his feet and immediately lunged toward Calhoun again. Calhoun allowed his opponent to grasp his right leg, then he swung his left leg over Arnoul's body and sat firmly on the boy's back, grinning down at his quarry. Arnoul's eyes bulged in frustrated anger and he flipped Calhoun onto his back, but Calhoun wriggled out from underneath the more awkward boy and darted away, dancing on the edge of the circle just out of Arnoul's reach.

Arnoul staggered to his feet and caught Calhoun's left arm. Calhoun countered by grabbing Arnoul's outstretched arm with his right hand, then twisting his body around so he was underneath Arnoul's bulk. By jerking Arnoul's arm and heaving the boy's body across his back, Calhoun flipped Arnoul head over heels into the dirt. Arnoul, the bully of Warwick Castle, lay in the dust and gasped for breath.

In one movement, Calhoun pressed Arnoul's shoulders onto the ground and held them there. "The victor!" Gislebert shouted, running into the ring and clapping Calhoun on the back. Calhoun waved his arms in jubilation while the male chorus cheered his victory. A quick glance to the castle window assured him the Lady Clarissant had also seen and approved.

Only Fulk did not smile. No expression crossed his face. He simply withdrew into the garrison and left Calhoun alone to claim his conquest.

"I ought to send you home right this minute," Fulk snarled in the privacy of their chamber. His hot breath blew into Calhoun's face, and he spoke through clenched teeth. "You disobeyed an order! Squires have been hung by their heels for less."

Calhoun tried to smile at his master. "I could not see the advantage in losing," he answered, waving his hands, "when there was so much to gain in winning."

"And what did you gain?" Fulk retorted, his huge hand grasping Calhoun's neck. "You have gained a bitter enemy in Arnoul, when by losing you might have gained a friend. You have gained a smile from Lady Clarissant, who would have given you the same smile in pity had you lost. You have gained suspicion from your master, because I will not be quick to trust you again. Oh, you won one contest, true enough, but you lost a greater battle because you were not able to control your own spirit in obedience. The weakness I spoke of earlier, young Calhoun, has grown wider and deeper today than I imagined it ever could."

Fulk released Calhoun abruptly and stalked away. In the semidarkness of the garrison, the younger man rubbed his throat and blinked back tears from his eyes. He did not understand all that Fulk had said, but perhaps he had made a mistake in winning. . . .

"Calhoun?" Gislebert appeared from the shadows. "Don't feel bad. Your master will only be angry for a little while."

By the sword of St. Denis, the wide-eyed mouse had heard everything! "Get away from me, you little rat!" Calhoun screamed, balling his hands into fists. "Stay away from me!"

Gislebert turned and fled while Calhoun sank to the floor and buried his face in his hands.

THIRTEEN

Fulk was more reserved in the weeks that followed, and Calhoun missed the easy camaraderie they had shared at the beginning of their time together. Fulk had always been a tough taskmaster, but now he allowed Calhoun to take the full brunt of his mistakes, never softening either his words or his blows as they trained.

And, though Calhoun later apologized for the outburst that had hurt Gislebert's feelings, he regretfully noticed that his relationship with the younger boy had changed, too. The open admiration that had shone forth from Gislebert's eyes was muted into wary respect. The lad still slept in the straw beneath Calhoun's bunk, but he no longer accompanied the young squire throughout the day and was less quick to offer his thoughts.

As for Fulk's prediction about Arnoul, it was realized in full force. The vanquished squire befriended every knight, squire, and page in the castle—except for Calhoun, whom he despised. Though the larger boy lagged behind Calhoun in physical skills, he excelled in cunning and conversation. Soon he had wooed the others to his side, and Calhoun noticed that many of those around him seemed to distance themselves from him. Every night after supper, when Calhoun retired to his solitary garrison room to sleep, Arnoul entertained the other men around the open fire in the courtyard. Their ribald laughter echoed throughout the night and stirred Calhoun in restless sleep.

So be it, Calhoun thought one night as loneliness washed over him. *I live alone, but they can keep their jokes and foolishness to themselves. I need no one else.*

After a full year of training, Calhoun grew into his hauberk. It no longer hung loosely on the slender frame of a boy, but clung to muscles grown hard and sinewy. His face, which had held an aspect of softness and pampered nobility, was now bronzed and lean. More of a transformation than his physical growth, however, was his manner. The laughing boy had become a solitary knight, and Fulk thought one day that even Lady Endeline would have difficulty recognizing her son.

Calhoun was surprisingly agile in his heavy armor. Over his heavy shirt of mail, he now wore a white tunic, which would be exchanged for one in his family colors after he was officially dubbed a knight. On his legs he wore chausses, coverings of mail, and a conical helmet of steel covered his head. Calhoun did not leave his chamber without a dagger sheathed at his calf and a sword strapped to his side. When mounted, he carried a shield and a twelve-foot lance—his favorite weapon—unless Fulk had instructed him to practice with the mace or battle-ax. In Calhoun's hands, all were deadly weapons.

He no longer struck at tree stumps, but dueled with Fulk himself, trading blow for blow. Both warriors frequently drew blood; the heavy suit of mail protected its wearer from slashes and glancing cuts, but a direct hit from sword or lance would invariably part the woven metal rings and strike home. Keeping this in mind, Fulk and Calhoun fought carefully and with discipline. Soon Calhoun grew accustomed to bruises on his ribs and back from Fulk's heavy sword, but he bore his pain stoically and resolved to be quicker on the morrow.

From his first contest, Calhoun was Warwick's champion jouster, but he modestly attributed his skill to days spent tilting at the quintain at Margate when he was a boy. He and Charles had spent hours rushing the dummy quintain with long poles, and more than once he had missed the target or hit it and forgot to duck, so that the moving weight swung toward him and knocked him from his horse. He still remembered the humiliation of landing in the dirt and resolved never to be knocked from his horse at Warwick. As a squire, he no longer rushed at a dummy quintain, but at other squires who aimed long, padded poles at his chest as they charged toward him on their horses.

In his year at Warwick, Calhoun had quickly become the squire exemplar, first among his peers in fighting, wrestling, jousting, hunting, and even dancing—but he was not accorded this rank with Lord Thomas. As far as Lord Thomas was concerned, it was Squire Arnoul who was the best and finest boy in training, and it was Arnoul, cousin of the king, who was awarded honor, praise, and a seat at the lord's table. Calhoun, whom Arnoul now openly despised, received no attention and little praise from the lord of Warwick Castle.

Calhoun bore the injustice with as much dignity as he could muster, finding no comfort even in the surreptitious pitying smiles of Lady Clarissant, whose blue eyes seemed to understand the truth of the situation. Calhoun knew he could not even complain to Fulk, for his master had tried to remedy the situation long before. *Perhaps if I had let Arnoul win on that day, things would be better,* Calhoun thought. *But what honor lies in failure?*

Finally, an opportunity to right matters presented itself during the holidays of Christmastide. Lord Thomas announced a three-event tournament for the squires, consisting of jousting, swordplay, and a wrestling match. The winners of those three events would then compose and read a poem to Lady Clarissant, for a knight's social skills were as valued as his physical abilities. The lady would then select the winner of the tournament.

Calhoun threw himself into practice for the tournament. He would win all three events, surely, and thus he would be the only squire eligible to stand before Clarissant and read his poem of love to her.

It was vitally important that he win, for the days and nights at Warwick had wrought another change in him, too . . . a transformation he had not expected. Emotions and inexplicable urges stirred his days and nights, and often, in restless sleep, he was awakened by Fulk, who roughly commanded him to go outside and chop wood. Calhoun obeyed without protest, bewildered by the feelings that swayed his body and mind.

His emotions were a whirlwind, but anchored firmly in the center of his attention was Clarissant. Her voice, her form, her laugh—all had the power to send him reeling across the room in delightful delirium. She was the most lovely, most serene, most gentle woman he had ever known. It mattered not that she belonged to Lord Thomas, for Calhoun could not conceive of marrying—or even kissing—such a creature. It was enough merely to stand and gaze at her, and love chastely from a distance.

As a child, Calhoun had tolerated the visiting troubadours and their songs of love, but now he found himself drawn to both the pain and pleasure in their music. He wrote poetry to give to Clarissant, as did the other squires, but the most personal of his thoughts he hid from her, passionately scrawling them on snatches of parchment and later tossing them into the fire where they flamed with the intensity of his heart.

Sometimes after supper the squires were allowed to dance with Clarissant and her maids. At these times, Calhoun hung by the walls as he had at Margate. In earlier days he had not been interested in dancing; now he was vitally interested, but frozen with fear. If Clarissant should so much as touch him, he knew his heart would burst through his chest and she would be horrified by what she saw there.

But the Christmastide tournament offered a noble way for him to prove his love and devotion. He would outride, outfight, and outwrestle every other squire. His poetry would shine forth with the purity of his love, and her beauty would fire the words until they sang forth from his lips.

Then Clarissant, Thomas, and all the assembled host would recognize that Calhoun was a squire of the first order.

Calhoun of Margate would make a knight worthy to carry the king's own banner.

The day of the tournament dawned bright and clear, and Calhoun jerked Gislebert awake from a sound sleep. "Wake up, little mouse," Calhoun called, prodding the boy. "I need help with this armor, and my master Fulk awaits my arrival at the stables."

"So soon?" Gislebert mumbled, wiping sleep from his eyes. He blinked and stared fixedly at Calhoun's hauberk. "Does it begin today?"

"It begins today," Calhoun snapped, placing his cold hands under the boy's arms and lifting him to his feet. "Hurry up and help me get dressed."

The first event was jousting, and Calhoun thought his aim had never been more clear nor his hands more steady. He had dispatched his first four opponents with ease, knocking them from their horses as if they were made of nothing but straw and mud.

Now he faced Arnoul, who weighed considerably more than the young men who had nervously charged him before. Calhoun knew the key to unseating Arnoul lay in enticing the larger boy to let himself get off-balance. Then a mere prod with the lance would tilt Arnoul off his horse as easily as a turtle is tipped onto its back.

Calhoun lowered his visor, gripped his padded lance, and spurred his horse. This day would end in victory.

"How does it feel to be the first day's winner?"

Calhoun recognized Fulk's voice and he smiled slowly, bringing his thoughts from love to victory. He had been lying on his bunk trying to find the words for his poem to Clarissant.

"Victory is agreeable," Calhoun admitted, "but my next challenge is intimidating, Fulk. I cannot find the words for what I want to say in my poem. As the jousting winner I will certainly have to read a poem to Lady Clarissant, and though the words are here," he laid his hand over his heart, "they will not spring onto the paper."

Fulk grunted and pulled off his boots. Gislebert hopped up from his straw bed and ran to clean the dusty footwear, and Fulk stretched out on his bunk. "I cannot help you," he grunted. "I know little of love."

"I know so much," Calhoun sighed. "My heart is full of it when I gaze at the lady, but—"

"You know less than I," Fulk retorted. "Your heart is full of giddiness, but it knows nothing of true love."

"My love is true," Calhoun answered indignantly, pushing himself upright. "Love drives me to distraction. I can't think, I can't eat—"

"True love drives a man to destruction," Fulk answered, closing his eyes. "But you will not believe me now. So dream on, young squire, dream on."

Calhoun settled back on his bunk, more than a little upset that Fulk considered his devotion so insignificant. If this affection was not love, what was it? Calhoun shook his head. It did not matter. Whatever one called it, Calhoun decided with a scowl at the empty page in front of him, his passion was indescribable.

He fought the next day in the contest of swordsmanship and was so charged by his passion and the previous day's victory that his opponents scarcely managed to land a blow on him. He had to curb his impulses, so high was his energy, lest he turn his sword and run his blade through his fellow squires. The noble Arnoul did not even face him in the final contest; the royal cousin had been defeated two rounds earlier.

That night, though, Calhoun's victory felt hollow. The prize, so near for the taking, was still miles out of reach. He had no words for the Lady Clarissant, no adequate descriptions of her beauty, no praises eloquent enough to compliment her goodness.

The next morning Calhoun scowled at each of his wrestling opponents and dispatched them with such rapidity that
the spectator knights declared the contest boring. "Such a
one should be tempered in his skill to make the contests
more equal. Why don't we tie his feet together?" one knight
suggested, and they laughed until Fulk countered their rec-
ommendation with a glare. No one dared say anything after
that, especially since it appeared that Fulk's young charge
now possessed a scowl as threatening as his master's.

By midafternoon Calhoun was the victor in all three contests and the certain winner of Clarissant's favor. He alone
would stand before her tonight and recite a poem, but to
fully commend her beauty, the poem must be no less than
an epic, a timeless piece of workmanship.

The task was too great; Calhoun could feel his brain turning to mush. The distraction he had felt upon his first attempt
at writing had evolved into frenzy, and he paced through the
garrison until he finally collapsed upon his bunk in defeat.

"I'm not worthy to be a knight," Calhoun moaned to
Gislebert, who watched in bewildered silence. "I can face
any enemy who charges me on horseback with a sword or
with his bare hands, but at the sight of a beautiful woman I
am turned to jelly."

"You're working too hard," Gislebert said, shrugging.
"You're trying to produce something equal to your feelings,
and that's probably impossible."

Calhoun considered Gislebert's words. "What you say is
true. But it won't help me produce the poem my lady Clarissant expects."

"Write about someone else," Gislebert suggested.
"Someone else you have loved. Your mother or your sister."

"But I have never loved anyone like this!"

Gislebert sighed in exasperation. "Love is love, regardless of the degree. Write sanely about someone you once
loved, and let the purity of your thoughts guide you clearly.
After the poem is written you can just adjust the words to
reflect the lady Clarissant."

Calhoun stared at his young friend for a moment, then reached out and rumpled the boy's hair. He was a mouse, always underfoot, but he made sense. Calhoun thought a moment, then began to write.

That evening at supper, as the bowls were passed, Lord Thomas bestowed a rare smile on Calhoun. "Congratulations are due to you, Calhoun of Margate," he said, "for winning three contests in as many days. But to be declared winner of the tournament, you must read a poem for Lady Clarissant and find favor in her eyes."

Calhoun wiped his mouth and stood. His mouth felt dry and he was sure his hands were shaking, but he smiled as he boldly dared: "To find favor in my lady's eyes is prize enough," he said, "but to please her with a poem would bring joy beyond measure."

Clarissant leaned forward at her table, her eyes shining with expectation. She raised delicate eyebrows in Calhoun's direction, and he was momentarily distracted by the sight of her crimson lips and white throat.

"Read, young squire," she said at last, a teasing note in her gentle voice.

The clatter and clamor of a hundred feasting men ceased as Calhoun picked up his parchment, cleared his throat, and read:

> *When the flowers appear in the earthen green fields*
> *Along with the bitter baneberry,*
> *Then I must consider you, my lady,*
> *And the burden of love that I carry.*
>
> *My love for you cannot rightly be borne;*
> *It is not my place to declare it.*
> *Though my heart is heavy with longing each day*
> *I will never be able to share it.*
>
> *I will fight for the honor and glory due you,*
> *And deny what I ought not to say,*

But my heart is engraved with your image so fair,
Golden hair and love's sweet eyes of gray.

As Calhoun lowered his parchment, a visiting troubadour sprang to his feet and applauded. "It is magnificent!" he cried, rushing to Calhoun's table. "I must have a copy, please."

Lady Clarissant smiled and stood. "It is a wonderful tribute," she said, extending her hand. "I am pleased."

Calhoun came forward, took her cool hand in his sweaty palm, and bent from the waist to kiss it. There was an audible hush over the room as jealous squires and knights united in an envious intake of breath.

Calhoun straightened awkwardly and took a step back. "There's only one thing," Clarissant said, smiling. She tilted her head toward him, gently teasing. "I'm not sure whose image is truly engraved on your heart, young Calhoun. My eyes are blue, not gray."

FOURTEEN

When Hubert was willing and pleased with himself, Afton was allowed out of the house once a week, in Wilda's company, to attend church. That hour was the only spiritual nourishment her soul received, for while Hubert believed that a dutiful wife was religious and devoted to prayers, he himself consigned religion to fools and madmen.

Afton found the act of prayer more natural in the small village church than she had under Raimondin's strict instruction. While the nearsighted Father Odoric recited prayers, Afton let her eyes rise to the highest point of the vaulted ceiling. *God, do you remember me?* she prayed. *Or are your protection and blessings only for the powerful few who dwell in stone castles?* Though God did not answer verbally, Afton always left the church feeling that God would not forget her. Though he was very busy ruling the universe and guiding kings, still she felt his thoughts turned toward her in her misery. And she knew, somehow, someday, she would be delivered.

Afton's spirits were almost light one summer afternoon when she and Wilda walked home from church. Father Odoric had spoken kindly to her and had asked how her marriage was faring. "It's been nearly two years since I united you with the miller, hasn't it, my child?" the priest had asked, squinting at her. "Is all well with you?"

Afton had replied that, yes, all was well. In her heart she had excused the falsehood by reminding herself that things had not lately been as bad as they once were. She had learned Hubert's peculiarities and she knew now to avoid triggering them. And no matter how bad things became, she could always find some measure of joy in holding and playing with her beloved cat. Afton smiled to herself as she remembered the little animal's most recent habit—that of sleeping on her feet as she embroidered or sewed.

She was startled out of her pleasant thoughts when a dark-haired boy stepped across her path. "Please let us pass," Wilda barked vigilantly. Afton immediately cast her eyes down at the ground and prayed that the stranger would move without incident. Hubert was waiting for her at home.

"Afton, do you not know me? I'm your brother," the young man said in the deepening voice of youth. He bent to look into her eyes. "Jacopo, do you remember? I'm a year younger than you."

Sudden joy flooded Afton's heart, and her eyes rose to eagerly memorize the details of his face. She was not alone! She had not thought of her brothers in years, but here was one brother, and there were others, too.

"Jacopo? Of course I remember you! And there was Marco, and Matthew—"

"Matthew was killed," Jacopo interrupted.

"I knew that," Afton recalled, her face twisting in sadness. "But there is still Kier and Gerald."

"And William, who died while a baby, and Galbert," Jacopo finished for her. "I was hoping I'd see you in the village. Mama says we're not to bother you at the miller's house."

"Oh, but you can," Afton said, reaching out for his hands. "Please come to dinner! My husband has guests for dinner all the time, and I'm sure you'd be welcome. Tell Mama and Papa to come, too. I'd love to see them."

Jacopo backed away awkwardly and released her hands, but he smiled. "I will," he promised.

The veil on her head had slipped when she reached for Jacopo's hands, so Afton pulled it tighter around her head and resumed her walk home with Wilda. For the first time in months, she felt happy. At her marriage, when she had ridden with Corba and Wido in the wagon to the church, she had gazed upon their poor clothing and rough hands with disdain. Now the sight of their faces, no matter how unrefined, would be welcome at her house!

She was smiling when she entered the hall, and Hubert's narrow eyes flitted over her face. "What made church such a happy occasion?" he asked.

"The peace of God," Afton replied easily, moving past him into the chamber. Surprisingly, he did not follow her, but went out of the house, and Afton breathed a sigh of relief.

He did not come home for dinner or supper and, after waiting until her stomach growled and her legs grew weak, Afton directed Wilda to bring her dinner into the chamber. She did not care where Hubert was. In fact, she half hoped he had found something or someone to take his attention away from her. The only way she could survive life with Hubert was to enjoy the hours she spent without him.

Wilda seemed to take forever with her dinner, and when Afton finally heard a knock on the door she felt lightheaded with hunger. "Come in," she called brightly, putting her embroidery away, but Wilda did not open the door. The chamber door swung open and revealed Hubert, who carried a tray laden with two steaming bowls of meat.

The sight was so unusual that Afton gaped in astonishment. Hubert raised his bushy black brows and a corner of his mouth twitched upward. "You haven't had your dinner," he said smoothly. "Come, sit at my feet, and we'll eat together."

His voice was pleasant, almost soothing, but something in his unflinching stare made Afton shiver. The hair on her arms rose, and some primal instinct raged at her to flee. Forcing those feelings down, she smoothed her skirt, wiped her face, and walked to her low footstool while her husband took his place in his chair by the fire.

When she was seated, Hubert handed her a heaping bowl of meat and a knife. He took the bowl with the smaller portion and began cutting his food. "I heard a story in town," he said, placing a hunk of meat in his mouth, "about a woman who was unfaithful to her husband. Have you heard the story?"

Afton's hand shook as she cut her meat, but she steadied her voice. "Why, no, my lord," she answered. "Here in the village?"

"It doesn't matter where," Hubert answered. He stopped and stared at her bowl. "You aren't eating, my dear, and this meat is especially tender."

Afton put the meat into her mouth and chewed obediently. Hubert nodded in satisfaction and continued: "The husband found the lover, killed him, and cut out his heart. The unfaithful wife was then forced to eat the heart of her lover."

Afton had to clench her teeth together to keep from gagging. She kept her eyes downcast, though, and after pausing for a moment, she forced herself to swallow. "That seems an unusual punishment, my lord."

"But a worthy one," Hubert answered. They ate for a while in silence, and Afton noticed that Hubert was especially attentive. Once the bowl in her lap slipped, and he caught it quickly and returned it to her, smiling at her thanks.

His peculiar actions and manner terrified her. After they had eaten, he took her bowl, placed it on the tray, and reached for her hands. "I've a little gift for you," he said, gripping her hands firmly.

"For me, my lord?"

"Yes. I went to the village to inquire about the source of your smile today, and a brave soul told me you were holding hands with a young man, just as I hold your hands now. I knew you'd want to look your best for the lad, so I had an animal skinned for your pleasure. You have eaten the meat, and I believe the fur will make a nice collar for your new mantle."

He released one of her hands and reached into his tunic. With a flourish he produced a small, still-damp animal skin, white, with touches of orange fur. Afton stared at it in silence, a cold wave of realization washing over her.

She had just eaten her little cat.

Hubert gripped her hands again and watched in fascination as she trembled in terror, then he began to laugh, and drew her to him so tightly that she could not speak, could not breathe without smelling him. He jerked her upright, threw her on the bed, and reached for his leather whip. With the sneering smile she knew well, he motioned for her to remove her gown.

She wanted to die. After he had beaten her and bedded her, she vomited, but he only laughed and made her clean up the mess. As she cleaned, she tried to tell him that the young man in the village was her own brother, but Hubert glared at her with such ferocity that she closed her lips and did not utter another word.

When she was done cleaning, he bade her dress again. Now he sat in his chair and she on the floor at his feet. His hand rested on the top of her head; occasionally his fingers ran through her hair or pressed to her lips for a kiss. And kiss him she must, or the nightmare would begin again.

Afton slowly dressed herself in long sleeves the next morning, embarrassed lest Wilda see the marks from the lash on her body. For many months she had borne Hubert's public flaunting of her and his private humiliations, and now she was sure she was dying. She had been ill for several weeks, but she had not dared to let Hubert see her weakness, for fear he would laugh or find some new way to teach her his "lessons."

In the beginning of their marriage she had prayed that he would die, but he seemed to feed on his malignity, growing stronger and more cruel each time he belittled her. Now he was a giant, a shadow over her life, and no light could pass through him.

173

Once Wilda had learned about the little cat, it became obvious to Afton that Hubert had even cowed her into submission. She wondered what Hubert had done to the old woman . . . had he beaten her? Threatened to kill her? Nothing less would have made the woman give up Afton's pet, her only source of daily joy. Afton knew, too, that Wilda would no longer dare to show any kindness to her mistress. Nor was it likely that Wilda would be allowed to serve as a chaperon, which meant Afton could not go out of the house unless it was on her husband's arm.

She was sitting alone in her chamber, miserable and ill, when someone knocked on the door. Afton rose and peered into the hall. "Mama!" she whispered, overcome with surprise at receiving an afternoon visitor. She opened the doorway to her chamber. "Please come in."

"Your cook said I should come straight in through the hall," Corba said, looking around the room. "Jacopo said ye wanted to see me."

Afton closed the door and collapsed at her mother's feet. "I'm dying, Mama," she wailed. "I'm so sick and I'm dying!"

Corba gathered Afton into her arms and listened to her daughter's sobs. Afton did not dare tell of Hubert's brutality, but she poured out her symptoms and her desire to die. Corba listened intently, then a deep chuckle rose from her generous throat.

Afton pulled away and looked into her mother's face. "How can you laugh?" she sobbed. "I want to die!"

"No, ye don't," her mother said, hugging her again. "You're going to be a mother. Ye are with child." Corba smiled and then added proudly, "I know about these things. I've carried eight babes."

Afton froze in disbelief. A baby? Could Hubert's monstrous acts have created a baby?

"It can't be," Afton protested weakly. "Hubert—"

"He will be so happy," Corba assured her. "Why, a man of his age fathering a baby! He'll be so proud. The whole village talks of his pride in you, and this will increase his joy a thousandfold."

Increase his joy? His only joy lay in mortifying her. Her mother's words rang in Afton's ears as she fainted.

Afton did not have to tell her husband the news; Corba told him, pulling him close in her excitement and shaking his hand enthusiastically. "Congratulations to you," Corba said, her face beaming. "My own daughter will soon bear ye a child."

Hubert's face was inscrutable. From where she lay on the bed Afton could not tell if he was truly glad, but he smiled at Corba and graciously led her out of the house.

When Corba had gone, Hubert came into the chamber and closed the door behind him. He gazed at Afton for a long time in silence, and Afton closed her eyes and wished that death would come. Finally he spoke, and it was as if he read her mind: "Ye wish to die? If this child ye carry is not mine, ye shall."

"It is your child. My mother told me how the seed of a child is planted, and the child can only be yours." Afton answered flatly. She was too tired and too ready for death to cower before him.

Hubert crossed over to the bed and placed his rough hand over her stomach. "When will this child be born?"

"My mother says it will be February," Afton answered. "If all goes well."

"That will depend upon you, little wife," Hubert said, turning his back. "I have warned your mother to not speak of this, and we will tell no one of this impending birth. When the child is born, we will see who it favors. Your life depends upon the child ye carry within you."

For the next two months Hubert did not strike her. He watched her even more closely than before and, as she sat at dinner, he watched his guests to see which of them sent admiring glances toward Afton. Before her announcement he had been pleased to exhibit his wife as a treasure, but now he cast suspicious glances toward any man who even glanced in her direction.

Afton didn't care what he thought of his guests; she was only relieved that his humiliations now did not include his horsewhip. He still bade her perform for his guests, he still bade her kiss his hands and wash his feet, and he watched her with the sharp, swiveling eyes of an eagle. Still, Afton felt relief.

She wondered why Hubert found it difficult to believe she carried his child. Was it his age? Or did he honestly believe she had a lover? Common sense dictated that the latter was impossible, for she had been a prisoner in her own home for two years.

She found her answer unexpectedly when she overheard a conversation in the courtyard between Wilda and a village woman. The woman told Wilda of a girl who had been attacked by a man in the fields. Her father had planned to press charges before Lord Perceval, but then the girl was found to be with child.

"Ah," Wilda cackled, giving the woman a sly wink, "then the maid took pleasure from their chance meeting. Her father will have no suit to bring before Perceval."

The women went on with their conversation, but inside the house, Afton ducked behind the window and sank to the floor in sudden understanding. If conception could not take place without pleasure, then it was no wonder Hubert did not believe the child was his! She had shown no pleasure in his time with her—indeed, had felt none! All she had ever felt were disgust and mortification. She shook her head. This idea could not be true, but if it was commonly believed, her life hung by a thread more slender than she had realized.

As the days passed and Hubert continued to spy on her, Afton became more and more frightened. After the baby was born, what then? Hubert would look at the child and declare privately that it was not his, and he would kill her, as

was his right. He would have his heir and his pleasure in killing her, and her baby would be left in the hands of a monster. Her hands went protectively to her gently bulging stomach. Never. She would never leave her child unprotected.

One night as Hubert snored beside her, Afton raised up on her elbows and looked down at him. She could kill him as he slept. She could go into the kitchen for a knife and plunge it into his heart, for he was a sound sleeper and slow to wake. But she would be discovered, brought before Perceval, and, in all probability, hung.

Her fingers played with the edges of the wool blanket that covered them. Still, the venture might be worth the price she would have to pay. But at that moment, a fluttering in her stomach caught her by surprise and she drew in her breath. The life in her womb was moving!

She lay back and caressed her belly, considering her choices. If she killed Hubert, her own life would be forfeit, as well as the life of her unborn child. If she continued as she was, Hubert would undoubtedly kill her after his child was born. She could not run away, for she was never alone or unwatched. There was only one option remaining, and her soul shrank from it in disgust. But it was her only choice: she would have to convince Hubert that she took pleasure in him.

She awoke before he did, as always, and when she heard him stir she turned and put her arm around him. She snuggled against his chest and felt him recoil in surprise. With his free hand he grabbed her hair and pulled her head off his chest. "What is this?" he growled.

"I'm caressing my husband and the father of my child," she said sweetly, smiling at him. "Release my head, my lord."

Surprisingly, he did as she asked, and she snuggled a few minutes more and playfully ran her fingers over his chest.

"What has bewitched you?" he asked, his eyes narrowing in suspicion.

"Life and love," she answered, lifting her head to look at him. She ran a finger across the top of his balding head and traced the outline of his ear. "When we married, my lord, I did not suppose I would have the honor of carrying a child in your name. Even these past weeks I thought it a dream, but last night I felt your child move in my womb, my lord, and I suppose I am overcome with pleasure from the child within me."

He did not believe her, she could read it in his eyes, but he flipped her over and put his hand on her belly. "I feel nothing," he muttered. Afton fought not to cringe at the feel of his hand, which he suddenly removed as if he'd been burned. "I did feel it," he said, staring at her belly. "It did move."

"Our child," whispered Afton, praying that he would believe her charade. "The child of the valiant and worthy Hubert."

"So ye thought me an old man," he growled, smirking down at her. "Ye thought these loins unable to perform their duty?"

He did not wait for her reply, but fell on her, eager to prove himself yet again. Afton closed her eyes—not in pleasure, but in simple relief.

Afton continued her pretense diligently, for she knew her life depended on it. In the months that followed she kissed Hubert often and willingly; she asked, "What shall I wear for you today, my lord?" and she raised her eyes from the ground for him alone. She danced for him in the privacy of their chamber and sang him to sleep with his head in her lap. His suspicion gradually evaporated, and hard resolve and the growing hardness of her belly enabled Afton to continue doing things she despised for a man she detested.

She found an unexpected benefit in her new situation when she and Hubert were invited to Margate Castle for a feast on the eve of St. Agnes' Day. Ordinarily Hubert would not have allowed her to go, but now he was thrilled for the

opportunity, for only free men and the lesser lords of Perceval and their wives were to attend. He bragged openly before the villagers of his exalted position in Perceval's estimation, and pointed proudly to Afton as proof of Perceval's high esteem and his virility.

Afton looked forward to the feast as well. It had been over two years since she had last seen Endeline and Perceval, and she looked forward to seeing Morgan and Lunette as well. She was but fifteen, but she felt she had aged twenty years since leaving the castle in the bridal wagon.

Wilda helped Afton dress in a lovely gown of scarlet with a warm matching mantle edged with beaver fur. She was eight months with child, and very large, but she would be able to disguise her figure under the generous mantle.

Corba often joked about Afton's size, saying she was eating too much, but Afton didn't mind not being able to see the floor. She was even able to bear Hubert's fascination with her belly: he slept with his hands upon her and often pulled her to him so he could remark on the strength of his unborn child's movements. All these things could be borne, because Afton had fallen in love with the child who depended upon her for life and love.

Nothing would make Afton fail her baby.

Her distasteful deception had worked. Hubert had publicly acknowledged that his wife carried his child, and every man in the village had raised a tankard to Hubert's great virility.

The castle seemed smaller than Afton recalled, the courtyard more confining. As they drove through the massive barbican in Hubert's wagon, Afton saw Perceval and Endeline standing near the castle gate, braving the winter winds to welcome visitors as they alighted. Jarvis, Perceval's sergeant at arms, was there, too, and Hector, the steward, stood at Endeline's side.

Afton's own trials had eclipsed the bitter feelings she once harbored for Endeline, and she was eager to greet her former mistress as one mature woman greets another. Hubert gave the reins of the wagon to a servant and extended his hand to help Afton down. As she struggled out of the wagon, the edges of her mantle parted and revealed her pregnancy, though she quickly pulled the edges together and awkwardly curtseyed before Perceval and Endeline.

Endeline stared at her in stony silence, then remarked casually to Perceval: "I am chilled, husband. I will see you inside."

Afton stood in confused silence while Hubert greeted Perceval, Hector, and Jarvis. The other guests were proceeding into the great hall for dinner, but Hubert grabbed Afton's arm and pulled her away from the crowd and into a corner of the stable.

"What did ye do to offend Lady Endeline?" he snapped, his eyes dark and threatening. He raised his hand as if to slap her. "Tell me now, so I can apologize to the lord!"

"I did nothing," Afton stammered, searching for a reason to explain Endeline's behavior. Then it came to her and she forced a teasing smile. "Do you not know, my dear lord, that the lady is jealous of me, for I carry your child?" Afton whispered. She reached for Hubert's outstretched hand and pulled it down underneath her mantle and onto her belly. "Endeline wants a baby badly and she cannot bear to see a woman in this blessed condition. Her behavior is a compliment to you, dear husband, because you and I have accomplished what our lord and lady cannot."

The notion appealed to Hubert's vanity, as Afton had known it would, and his stormy expression broke into a smile. Afton linked her arm through his and laid her head on his shoulder. "Now can we go in and eat, please? Your child and I are famished."

The meal was excellent, and Endeline noted that the guests seemed suitably impressed. Her good mood had returned—once she managed to put aside the destructive feelings of jealousy that had struck her when she saw the very pregnant

Afton—and now she concentrated on her other guests. The servants had done well, and the tablecloths, silver spoons, salt dishes, and steel knives were shining in their abundance. As usual, today's guests would go home and tell stories of the opulence and generosity of Perceval's castle.

Endeline nodded to the troubadour she had engaged for the feast, and he sang as they ate. He sang lovely dawn songs, bawdy spinning songs, and a song of political satire that made Perceval squirm in his seat. Endeline smothered a smile. Perceval need not worry about this crowd; none of these people had the ear of the king or the power to do Perceval harm.

"Sing us a love song," Endeline commanded as the servants cleared away the dishes. She raised an eyebrow and glanced in Afton's direction. "Something fitting for young lovers."

The troubadour bowed. "I do have a special treat for you, my lady, a poem composed by a young squire of Warwick, quite stricken with love for his lady. It is a lovely piece, and I would be honored to sing it for you."

Lady Endeline leaned forward. "A young squire? Pray, what was his name?"

The troubadour bowed low. "Your honorable son, my lady. Squire Calhoun of Margate, a valiant and most excellent young man."

The crowd stirred in pleasure, and Endeline smiled and held up her hand for silence. Calhoun was in love! And obviously with a lady at Warwick Castle. She glanced at Afton and purred with pleasure: "Please, we would hear this song."

The troubadour bowed again, then clasped his hand over his heart and began to sing:

> *When the flowers appear in the earthen green fields*
> *Along with the bitter baneberry,*
> *Then I must consider you, my lady,*
> *And the burden of love that I carry.*
>
> *My love for you cannot rightly be borne;*
> *It is not my place to declare it.*

Though my heart is heavy with longing each day
I will never be able to share it.

I will fight for the honor and glory due you,
And deny what I ought not to say,
But my heart is engraved with your image so fair,
Golden hair and love's sweet eyes of gray.

The crowd burst into applause at the end of the song, and Charles, laughing, called out: "Who was the maiden for whom the song was written?"

"Now there's another story," the troubadour said, pleased with his reception. He lowered his voice to a stage whisper: "The poem was directed to the Lady Clarissant of Warwick, but later a page in Squire Calhoun's confidence told me the eyes of gray belong to another maiden, for the Lady Clarissant's eyes are blue."

Endeline clenched her fists under the table. From the corner of her eye she could see Perceval laughing at her.

She ordered the troubadour away.

FIFTEEN

Afton's skin prickled into gooseflesh when the troubadour finished his song, but Hubert seemed to make no note of what was surely a terrible coincidence. She sat still and solemn as the servants cleared the table and prepared for the dancing to follow. When Hubert did finally turn to her, it was merely to ask if she was ready to return home. Timidly placing her hand on his arm, she whispered, "Yes, my lord. I am tired."

She clung to him on the ride home, and he helped her out of the wagon with unusual tenderness. "Go rest in our chamber," he told her as he led the horses away. "I will join ye shortly."

She had just crawled under the warm fur on their bed when Hubert came into the chamber with a log for the fire. Afton managed a smile. "Thank you, dear husband," she said, struggling to lift her head to see over her bulk. "It will be wonderful to have a warm fire."

Hubert eased himself down on the bed next to her and his fingers found their way to her throat, where he pulled the string that held her cap on her head. Her eyes flew open in surprise, but he soothed her: "Lie back. Ye must be tired."

She obeyed, confident in his gentleness. He pulled the cap off her head and unbraided her hair, spreading it out on the pillow behind her. For a moment she was a child again, back in her cottage, with Corba dressing her hair. Sleep beckoned her, and she was about to obey when a sharp pain in her back brought her fully awake.

Hubert was no longer at her side. She raised her head and saw him sitting at the foot of the bed, watching her with eyes grown speculative and hard. Her pulse quickened and the old fear rose in her heart. What was this?

She smiled, even though her lips quivered, and held out her hand to him. "Dear husband, lie here with me and rest," she said, patting the fur on the bed.

"No," he answered, his voice clipped. "I have lain beside ye for the last time. Ye have made me feel proud in my manhood, proud of the thing ye carry in your womb, and ye have deceived me. Do ye not know that I realize the child in your womb was conceived as ye thought of the noble Calhoun? Ye have never ceased to love him, and together ye have made a mockery of me! He writes love poetry for ye and the entire world hears it, while ye carry the child conceived in his honor!"

"It is your child, dear husband," Afton said, struggling to sit up. "I have not thought of the master's son in these past two years. My only thoughts have been of you!" The bitter truth of her words rang freely from her soul, for what comfort was a childhood love when confronted with the daily terror of Hubert?

"He writes poetry for you!"

"I do not care what he does!" she screamed. She pushed herself forward and crawled to Hubert's lap. Placing her head against his chest, she calmed her voice and spoke clearly: "I am married to you, dear husband."

Another sharp pain crossed her back, and she cried out in agony. The sound broke the spell she had been trying to cast, and the rough hands that had been about to caress her head gathered her hair instead and dragged her off the bed. She fell, belly first, onto the floor.

"Hair of gold!" he roared, still holding her hair. "Eyes of gray! He writes of my wife!"

Afton clutched her belly and moaned. Something wet was coming forth from her; something had happened to the baby. Perhaps she could still save it. She reached for Hubert with her free hand: "My husband, kiss me. Give me your hand, and I will kiss it. Your feet, my lord, I will kiss your feet—"

Hubert dropped her head and kicked her, the sole of his rough boots cutting into the skin of her neck. It was the only blow she felt clearly, for the others came like thundering raindrops, one after the other in an unceasing storm. He seemed to dance to fiendish music that only he could hear, pounding the rhythms upon her head, back, legs, and arms as she curled into a ball.

When her mind and voice had stilled into oblivion, Hubert stopped his awful assault. She felt herself being lifted into his arms, then the softness of the bed was beneath her. She sighed and relaxed even as his hands removed the elegant gown from her. Pain stirred again in her womb, but she gave it no outlet. If she lay still, Hubert would stop, for she knew he found no pleasure in his acts unless she protested.

The room was silent. Had Hubert gone? She could not raise her eyes to look, for if he waited, he would know she was awake and capable of feeling his savagery. She forced herself to breathe deeply and, upon her third breath, an agonizing pain tore at her womb and forced her eyes open.

Hubert was waiting. At the sound of her muted cry, his lips parted in a smile and he uncoiled the whip in his hand.

Corba had seen Hubert's wagon return from the castle and was anxious to gossip about the goings-on of the nobles. She allowed Hubert and Afton a little time, then she threw on her shawl and set out for the miller's house.

All was quiet in the miller's courtyard when she arrived, and Wilda was nowhere in sight. Because she had often been welcomed of late, Corba confidently entered and walked through the hall to the door of Afton's chamber. A rhythmic snapping sound came from the chamber, a sound strangely out of place, but Corba only shrugged and knocked. The sound quieted and, after a moment, Hubert opened the door.

She had never seen his eyes so stony, devoid of all expression save a certain grim pleasure. His brows lifted when he recognized her, and he took her hand and drew her into the chamber. "It is good ye have come," he said, taking the rough shawl from her shoulders. "I believe your daughter is about to give birth."

Corba smiled and pushed past Hubert to the bed where Afton lay, then stopped in shocked horror. The wounded creature upon the bed could not be her daughter. The girl who lay there, clad only in a chemise, looked as though she had been painted with long scarlet stripes. Her face, her arms, her legs were a mass of tender bleeding skin and ruby-colored welts. Corba could even see red stripes bleeding through the chemise.

"I have whipped her," Hubert said simply, gesturing to the horsewhip that lay on the floor. "As her husband, it is my right. Now it is my right to witness the birth of this child."

As a villein, it was not the first time Corba had been in a situation that called upon her instincts of self-preservation. After a brief moment of hesitation, she casually smoothed her skirt as though this were an ordinary visit and she an ordinary midwife. "It is not customary for the father to be present," she said, calmly washing her hands in the washbasin. "Wouldn't ye rather wait outside?"

Hubert's eyes narrowed and he smiled bitterly. "No. I will wait right here."

Corba soaked a cloth in water and began to wash her unconscious daughter's wounds. The baby was indeed coming—Corba knew the signs well—but it could be hours yet, possibly even days if Afton did not have the strength to deliver the child. Corba heard Hubert settle into the fireplace chair, and she silently prayed for her daughter's soul.

Pain. Afton did not know that such pain could exist without bringing merciful death. Her skin stung, a sharp pain in her side stabbed with each breath, and her womb felt ravaged, as

186

though a monster struggled to break free of her. The blanket she lay on was bloody, she was drenched in sweat, and she could feel Hubert's malevolent presence in the corner of the room. Every humiliation she had borne was for nothing. He would kill her after the child was born.

Corba was doing her best to ease her daughter's pain. She rubbed Afton's belly with oil, unknotted her tangled hair, and wondered aloud how she would get Afton off the bed and onto the floor into the usual crouching position for birth.

"Leave her where she is," Hubert said, watching the scene through half-closed lids.

Afton dropped her guard and her pretense, for neither were of any use. As she lay on the bed, her body torn by pain, she struggled for breath and flung hoarse words at her husband: "I spit on you! I hate you! You may kill me, for I do not care!"

Corba's eyes went wide in horror, but Hubert merely sat in his chair, his eyes upon her belly as if his purpose for living was contained there. Once he smiled at Afton, and the malice in his eyes stirred Afton to find new strength. She could hate, too! She would never, ever again be passive before him. In her remaining weeks, days, or hours, she would never willingly submit to him.

"Sit up now," Corba commanded her, lifting Afton's shoulders. "Push!" Afton pushed with every ounce of energy and hate in her soul. She felt a tremendous, ripping pain, and then release.

Afton sank back onto the bed in relief, and Corba held up the baby, the bloody cord still dangling. "It's a beautiful boy," Corba cried, clearing the baby's nose with a cloth.

At the sound of the baby's cry, Hubert sprang up and pulled a dagger from his boot. Afton weakly thrust her hand toward him to save her child, but Hubert only sliced the cord with one quick movement, then took the baby from Corba. "My son," he said, his voice filled with pride.

Afton could not believe her ears. He still acknowledged

187

the child? Hubert laid the baby on the bed, wrapped it in a wool blanket, and placed it in Corba's outstretched arms.

"Ye must take the child immediately to the church and have him christened," he told her. "I will tend to my wife."

"What is his name?" Corba asked, cuddling the baby. "What do I tell the priest?"

Hubert did not pause. "Ambrose," he answered. "For now that I have a son, I am immortal. Ambrose, son of Hubert, will bear sons as well, and I shall forever be on the earth."

"Please," Afton whispered, waving a feeble hand in Hubert's direction. "I want to see the baby."

"No," Hubert answered. He turned back to Corba, who hesitated by the door. "Hurry, woman. Don't let the babe catch cold. And send word for a wet nurse. We will need one." Still uncertain, but too afraid to disobey, Corba left with the baby.

Afton was about to steel herself for a final confrontation with Hubert when another ripping pain made her scream. She pressed her hand on her belly and felt movement again. "I think there's another baby," she whispered hoarsely. "You must stop my mother."

Afton had seen Hubert roar in anger and seethe in silence, but now his face flushed red and his breath rasped in his throat. "Another child?" he said, clutching the wall for support. "Ye *have* been with another man!"

"No," Afton shook her head in her pain.

"If a woman has two babies, she has been with two men, any fool knows that," Hubert whispered, sinking to his knees beside the bed. His eyes were level with Afton's, and his hand brought forth his bloody dagger. Afton closed her eyes, expecting to feel the blade in her heart, but instead she heard the sound of ripping fabric. When she opened her eyes, Hubert had slashed her mantle and was ripping it into strips. "I will bind your legs together," he muttered. "This babe will die with you. It will not be born."

"No," Afton screamed, kicking as the urge to push overcame her. "The baby must be born!" She screamed as another pain tore at her, and the noise seemed to drive Hubert into a frenzy. He put his hands on his head, and his face purpled even as the baby he sought to kill arrived into the world.

The child lay between Afton's legs for only a moment. Hubert scooped it up, cut the cord, and headed for the door. "It is a girl child," he said, smiling at Afton in satisfaction. "And God has given me a sign, for the child is marked as the offspring of an adulteress. I read your sin in the child's face."

Exhausted, filled with despair, Afton sank into blessed darkness.

Afton did not know how long Hubert was gone; she only knew she was going to die when he returned. He came back into the chamber, without either baby, and methodically lifted the edge of the blanket she lay on and draped it over her body. "This will be your shroud, for I will burn ye on a pyre out back," he said, walking around the room to lift the other side of the blanket. "I will find another wife to raise my son, and a wet nurse to suckle him. But you, unfaithful wife, shall die the death ye deserve."

"My daughter?" she whispered.

"The child of sin is dead," he snapped.

She had been defeated. Though she had borne humiliations too great to fathom and flattered the man least deserving of praise, she was now vanquished, by his whip and his cruelty. Her daughter was dead. Her son would be raised by another. She had neither the energy nor the will to protest when Hubert lifted her into his arms.

She smelled rather than saw him; his rancid sweat seemed to fall upon the blanket that enveloped her. He faltered for a moment as he carried her, as though he were failing in his resolve, but Afton knew Hubert was a single-minded man. He had determined that she was worthy of death, and nothing short of that goal would please him.

When they were outside the house, Afton felt the freezing wind wrap her in a chilly cocoon. She felt strangely detached. Her arms and legs were numb, as unfeeling as they had been when, as a child, she had stayed too long in the cool waters of the forest pool at the twin trees.

She smiled. *Have I been away from the twin trees for so long?*

Twigs crackled beneath her and Afton was dimly aware that she was lying upon a bed of leaves and brush. *It's all right,* she told herself. *I'm in the forest and I'm safe. No one else knows about this place—except Calhoun.* Her eyes opened and, for a moment, she thought she saw Calhoun standing beside her. He smiled at her, clutched his heart in a farewell gesture, and fell down at her side.

She heard the wind whistle coldly, felt the cool numbness of death, and thought again, *Have I been away from the twin trees for so long?* And then she thought nothing more.

AMBROSE
1125-1126

Many waters cannot quench love;
rivers cannot wash it away.
If one were to give all the wealth
of his house for love,
it would be utterly scorned.

SONG OF SOLOMON 8:7, NIV

Sixteen

The bitter cold of the January night stung Wilda's eyes, so she drew her shawl closer about her head and muttered to herself. The biting wind whipped at her cloak as she walked on the long road that led out of town, and she shouted curses into it.

"Drown the babe! Indeed I *won't* do it!" she screamed, her crackly voice breaking as the wind carried it away. "Ye can lash me a thousand times like ye done the mistress, but I won't give in to ye. It's a mortal sin to even think of such a thing!"

Wilda suddenly became aware that the sun had set, and dark night surrounded her. It was dangerous for a woman to be out alone after curfew . . . but the infant in her arms mewed softly through the blankets, and Wilda clutched her burden more firmly and set her cracked lips together. "Don't ye worry," she croaked, hobbling down the road with greater speed. "God will be with ye. And I won't worry about the master, because I just won't go back there, that's all. I'm an old woman, with not many days left, and I'll not work myself into my grave in that devil's service. Sure as I'm here, the young mistress has met her end at his hands—"

The old woman's tortured words broke off as tears choked her. She shook her head in grief, almost overcome. She darted behind the shelter of a tree and peered into the blanket. At the sight of the baby, her broken lips parted in a smile, and she rebundled the baby and redoubled her efforts on the road. "God will watch over both of us, little one, ye wait and see."

From the distance, a light gleamed from the convent outside the village, and the bell tolled for vespers. "No one will know us at the nunnery," Wilda whispered under her breath. "The good women of this place don't come into the village."

The moon had risen high into the dark sky when Wilda made her way to the gate and pulled on the bell rope. A tiny peephole in the wooden gate opened, and a pair of wide eyes peered out at her.

"Please, missy, I've a present for ye," Wilda whispered, glancing nervously around her. "Please open the gate. A more God-fearin' and harmless old woman as me you canna' find anywhere."

The novice opened the gate and put her finger across her lips. "I understand ye canna' talk," Wilda said, shifting the bundle in her arms to the arms of the young nun. "But here. Take this to your abbess right quick, and God bless ye for your trouble."

The novice nodded, and the gate closed again. Wilda turned away and chuckled to herself. "Won't my lord Hubert be surprised if he ever finds out that part of 'imself's gone to God?" She laughed aloud. "That's the only part of 'im that will ever come close to God, that's for sure. The man's a devil in the flesh, 'e is."

She waddled on down the road in the darkness, laughing to herself.

Corba paced in the stillness of the church, the baby in her arms growing louder and more insistent by the minute. "Can't ye get the child to hush?" Wido asked her, wiping sleep from his eyes. "Isn't it enough ye woke everyone in our house? Do we have to wake the whole village, too?"

"Don't ye even care that this babe is bone of your bones?" Corba retorted. She made gentle shushing noises to the baby, who continued his squalling. "What is keeping Father Odoric?"

"He's probably still in bed," Wido answered, yawning.

"Well, he's got to get out here and tend to this baby. Wido, I fear for the child. I fear for our daughter. Though the babe seems healthy and strong, the man Afton married is not—"

The sound of Father Odoric's shuffling footsteps silenced Corba. The priest entered the church, carrying his candle and stifling a yawn. "What is it that couldn't wait until morning?" he asked.

"A baptism, father," Corba answered. "We did not think it wise to wait until morning."

"Bring me the baby, then," the priest grunted, gesturing.

Madame Hildegard, the abbess of the nunnery, sat up with a start when she heard the rap on her door. It had to be an emergency, for her nuns knew better than to wake her before Matins. She pulled her tunic around her and opened the door.

The young novice Lienor stood there with a bundle in her arms. She remained silent, obeying the rule of grand silence, so Hildegard took the squirming bundle without a word and placed it on her bed. She unwrapped the rough wool, and both she and the novice gasped at the sight of the baby lying there.

Hildegard had received babies at the nunnery before. Often she had found suitable positions for infants of young mothers who had died in childbirth; and on three occasions she had prayed over the forms of monstrous children destined for early deaths: one born without limbs, another with an open wound, and the third with a swollen head. Hildegard had the priest baptize the deformed babies, and she prayed for their souls up to the hour they died and for three days afterward, for she earnestly believed they bore the mark of some gross sin in their bodies.

But the child that lay before her now would not die. Even though the unwashed infant girl still bore the blood of childbirth, Hildegard could see that she was perfect and complete. She lacked neither fingers nor toes, nor did she exhibit the weakness or wheezing of impending death. She was a tiny child, probably born too soon, and would have been a beauty save for a scarlet birthmark across her face. Hildegard could not repress a shudder: it was as though a three-fingered beast had resolutely grasped the child's face with a bloody claw.

Hildegard tugged on Lienor's sleeve to draw the novice's attention, then nodded toward the door and made the sign of the cross. Lienor understood the older nun's sign language immediately, and went for the priest. Abbot Hugh was visiting in the abbey hostelry, and he would not mind rising at this late hour for this purpose.

Hildegard also rang the bell that would bring the housekeeper forth from her apartment. Trilby would know what to do with the tiny baby. She had borne ten children and buried four; she would know how to care for this little one.

While she waited for the housekeeper, Hildegard wrapped the baby warmly. Private moments like this were rare, and she lifted the baby to her face and inhaled deeply. There was no scent like a baby's: warm, earthy, and sweet! When Hildegard had been in the world, a married woman, how she had longed for a baby! But her impatient husband had cast her off and willingly paid her admission fee to the convent to free himself for a more fertile wife.

Hildegard lifted the baby to her barren breast. If only this little one could suckle there! Perhaps this infant had been sent to her from God, for no woman in the village would raise or endure this marked child. Hildegard knew instinctively by the way the baby energetically curled and flexed her long fingers that the child was strong and in no danger of an early death.

There in the midst of the grand silence, Hildegard heard the deep sleepy breathing of her sisters in God, and calmly resolved to accept this gift of God and raise the babe herself. Somehow the Almighty had seen fit to compensate her for her unfruitful womb; he had entrusted her not only with the rearing of nuns to spiritual maturity, but now with the rearing of a baby as well.

Hildegard placed her hand over the baby's downy head. *"Deus id vult,"* she whispered. "God wills it."

Father Odoric put his hand on the baby boy's head and blessed it. "Blessed art thou, young son of Hubert," he said, rubbing salt in the baby's mouth. He paused and looked at Corba. "What is the child's name?"

"Ambrose," she answered.

Abbot Hugh entered the convent chapel, where Madame Hildegard waited. "Greetings to you, Madame," he said, removing his dark cloak. "How can I be of service? You may speak freely, Madame Hildegard."

Hildegard smiled at the abbot and quietly jiggled the baby in her arms. "God, in his wisdom, has sent us a baby to be baptized. We wish to make a profession of faith for her."

She placed the baby in the crook of the abbot's arm and heard him draw in his breath when he lifted the blanket from the baby's face. "From where did this baby come?" he asked, his voice clipped.

"Is it not enough that God brought her to us?"

"Are we sure this is not a child of the devil?"

"If it is, can we not save its soul by baptizing it?"

Abbot Hugh hesitated, and Hildegard saw a flicker of confusion cross his strong features. "Your chapel has no baptismal font," he said, studying the baby.

Hildegard motioned toward a basin she had prepared. "We have a washbasin."

The abbot placed his hand on the baby's head and blessed her. "And what are we to call this baby, Madame?"

Hildegard toyed with the edge of her veil. The dawning day would be January 21, the day of the feast of St. Agnes, a day of rejoicing. "Agnes," she said, smiling at the infant. "For she is a lamb of God."

The priest looked down at the fragile baby in his arms. "She's just a lambkin," he corrected the abbess. "I baptize thee, Agnelet."

"I baptize thee, Ambrose, in the name of the Father, the Son, and the Holy Ghost," Father Odoric recited. He held the naked baby aloft over the baptismal font, then quickly immersed the baby in the water and brought it up again.

The baby squalled and shivered, and Corba wrapped it in a warm piece of wool. Wido had brought a worn christening garment, and she wrapped the baby securely while Father Odoric dipped his finger in holy oil and made the sign of the cross on the baby's forehead.

Abbot Hugh dipped the tiny girl quickly into the basin of warm water. The baby shivered, and then turned her head as if her nature compelled her to bear suffering without complaint. Madame Hildegard took the dripping baby and wrapped her in fine white linen, then held her up for the abbot's mark of blessing.

As he fastened the clasp of his mantle and prepared to leave, Abbot Hugh watched Madame Hildegard with concern. "You know there are some who will assume this child is from the devil," he said, his voice flat. "The mark on her face could represent an unholy trinity."

"We will prove them wrong," Hildegard answered, putting aside her usual dignity to smile wistfully at the baby. "For the face does not always reflect the heart."

"Can you be sure this child has an innocent heart?"

"Did you not just baptize her?" Hildegard answered, wrapping the baby tightly in a wool blanket. "Do not worry. We are cloistered women, and the world does not often enter here."

"For the child's sake, and your own, take care to keep the world out," Abbot Hugh answered. He nodded slightly to the abbess and slipped out of the chapel while she continued to stare in amazement at the gray-blue eyes of the infant.

"There has never been a night so long as this one," Wido grumbled as he and Corba trudged through the village, but Corba heard no genuine displeasure in his voice. Pale streaks of light had appeared in the east; the night had ended. "Do ye know how few men ever live to see the face of their children's children?" Wido continued as they walked. "I know of none who have."

"Nor do I," Corba echoed, looking down at the sleeping infant in her arms. "But we must hurry. This babe must be fed."

Wido's steps slowed behind her. "Woman, I leave ye to your task. Today I plow in Lord Perceval's fields, and the oxen await me."

"Take care, then." She smiled at him and waved him away, then clutched her bundle tightly in the stillness of dawn and hurried toward the miller's house. Her warm breath misted in the cold air, but she did not feel the chill, so eager was she to lay the child in her daughter's arms. Surely things would be better for Afton now that Hubert had a son. He had been so proud at the baby's birth! Perhaps now he could forgo his cruelty and be a gentler husband.

She slipped through the gate and knocked on the door of the house, but was not surprised when there was no answer. Surely Afton and Hubert were still sleeping. She crept quietly toward the bedchamber, but the hungry baby was squalling in earnest now, and Corba boldly pushed the chamber door open, expecting to find Afton awake and waiting. Instead, she found that the bed had been stripped of its covering, and the fire had gone out.

Corba frowned. Had something gone terribly wrong? She laid the baby on the bed and ran to the kitchen. That room was empty, too. Even Wilda's cot stood vacant, and the hearth fire had gone to ashes. Corba darted through the front courtyard, a light layer of frost clinging to her rough boots, but she could see that the trail down to the stream and the mill house lay undisturbed under a thin mantle of white.

Corba hesitated before venturing behind the house. The

back garden and woodpile were still enveloped in night's shadows, and two sheep in the back pen eyed Corba warily as she approached. The sun's struggling rays had not yet reached behind the house, and the cold ground under Corba's feet seemed to writhe under a thick white mist. Corba felt the skin on her arms prickle in fear, and she drew her tattered cloak more closely around her shoulders. Something moved in the distance, and she clapped her hand over her mouth—had she seen a ghost?

Of course not. She peered toward the back hedge, where Hubert kept the woodpile. A shroudlike bundle lay there, and another form jutted out from the mist as an island rises forth from the sea.

Corba ran toward the apparition. One glance assured her that Hubert was dead. His form was still, his features frozen in an agonized grimace, his fingers curled over his heart. Afton lay in her cocoon of bedcoverings, pale and silent, but a tinge of scarlet still lingered in her lips.

Corba threw her arms around her daughter and lifted with all her strength. The girl's body moved easily, as if her spirit, in the process of departing, had left a hollow shell. When Corba had brought Afton into the house, she laid the girl on the floor next to the fireplace and ran back to the woodpile for wood. Returning once again, she placed the wood on the fire and fanned the embers until the roaring flames brought a trickle of sweat to her own brow. When the fire burned steadily, and she had brought water to Afton's lips, Corba lifted the infant to her own breast and suckled her grandson, thankful again that God had blessed her with a fruitful womb and hungry children.

Later that afternoon, while Corba tended Afton and the baby, Wido dragged in Hubert's body. He laid the stiff miller on the table in the hall where Hubert had so often boasted of his greatness.

Father Odoric administered the rites of extreme unction, and Corba hired two village women to wash the body and wrap it in a linen shroud. She never wanted to think of Hubert again and would have happily left him outside to rot by the woodpile except for the shame such an act would have brought to her daughter. To further avoid dishonor, Corba and Wido told the villagers that Hubert's delight in his son had been too much for him to bear and he had died peacefully at home.

The proud miller's funeral was attended only by Wido, Father Odoric, and Josson, Hector's representative from the castle. "It breaks my heart to see that Hubert, the great friend of Perceval, has only the steward's steward to bid him farewell," Wido said, clapping young Josson's back with undisguised delight. "The depth of Perceval's true love for Hubert is finally revealed."

Josson smiled uneasily. "My lord Hector is busy with the accounts and unable to come," he explained. "But he does send his esteem."

Wido's face sobered. "There is no esteem for Hubert here," he answered. "The man was a thief, substituting bad flour for good grain and taking more than his due. Ye will find little love for him in the village."

"But much envy," Josson answered, looking down at the ground. "For he had a beautiful wife, the favor of Perceval—"

"That favor does him little good now, eh?" Wido answered. He nodded toward the priest. "And the beautiful wife, my daughter, is better off now. Her husband will do her more good dead than alive."

"He was not worthy of her," Josson whispered, his eyes fixed on the shrouded form in the pine coffin. "But yet she gave him a son. It is more than he deserved."

"Aye," Wido agreed. His eyes shone with curiosity. "Did ye know my daughter, young Josson? She lived at the castle many years, ye know."

Josson shook his head. "I saw her from a distance," he said, his voice edged with regret. "And I felt her pain when she was given in marriage to this brutish man."

Wido grunted agreeably, then glanced toward the priest. "I suppose it isn't very Christian to speak ill of the dead, is it, Father?"

Father Odoric smiled. "I heard a riddle the other day: What's the boldest thing in the world?"

"I don't know, Father," Josson answered. "Tell us."

The priest smiled. "The miller's shirt, for it clasps a thief by the throat daily."

Wido roared with laughter and slapped his leg while the priest looked serenely toward heaven and Josson tried not to smile. When their merriment had passed, Father Odoric pulled forth his prayer book. "Let us bury this man," he said. "And be done with this business."

SEVENTEEN

Afton remembered little of Ambrose's birth save that there had been two babes, and Hubert had killed one. When Corba told her that Wilda was nowhere to be found, Afton became convinced that Hubert had killed Wilda, just as he would have slain her had God not struck him down.

But she kept these dark deeds hidden in her heart, not daring to tell even her mother for fear of spoiling the genuine joy Corba found in her grandson and in Afton's new situation. Hubert's death left Afton as manager and co-owner of the mill, a valuable property.

One morning when Corba brought Ambrose to Afton, she looked up at her mother and shook her head. "I cannot believe I am finally free," she whispered, thinking that at last she was rid of Hubert's brutality and humiliation.

Corba misunderstood, but nodded happily. "Aye, dear daughter. Ye will owe Lord Perceval one-fifth of your living here, but ye do not owe him your life. Such is the blessing of freedom."

When Afton had fully recovered her strength, she donned her black mourning costume with gratitude, for the simple black tunic represented her emancipation. On the morning of her childbirth purification ritual, she went to the church door and lifted her heart to God with joyful appreciation, understanding for the first time the relief Lienor had felt when Prince William drowned in the sea.

But I'll not be troubled by guilt, as was Lienor, she told herself as the priest met her outside the church and made the sign of the cross above her head. *And I'll not spend my life regretting the comfort of widowhood, for I did not wish Hubert dead.* She closed her eyes submissively while the priest sprinkled her with holy water and recited a psalm. *I was willing to die myself, if that was God's will. But for your sake, little one, God has kept me alive.* She lifted out her hand, caught the end of the priest's stole, and followed him into the church.

"Enter the temple of God; adore the Son of the holy Virgin Mary, who has given you the blessing of motherhood," Father Odoric chanted as he walked before her. *Motherhood and widowhood,* Afton thought, *twin blessings marred only by the knowledge that Hubert took the life of my daughter before God took him.*

As Father Odoric's prayers wafted to heaven with the sweet smell of incense, Afton looked upon the baby in her arms and whispered a solemn promise: "For the sake of my child, never again will I give myself to a man in love with his own power. Never again will I be beaten or bullied or owned by any man."

Hildegard was ordinarily in strict control of her eyes, but she couldn't resist careful scrutiny of the village girl that Trilby had engaged as a wet nurse for the infant, Agnelet. The girl was broad, big-boned, and rough-mannered, but she held the hungry Agnelet to one plentiful breast while her own baby suckled on the other. "Elfgiva is a healthy girl," Trilby assured her privately, "and truthful. Ye won't have to worry about any undesirable traits being passed on through her milk, Madame."

Elfgiva seemed perfectly content in her role, happily nursing the children wherever she pleased while she watched the nuns with a mixture of awe and curiosity. Hildegard felt a strange stirring of envy when she saw the girl with the babies pressed to her breasts, and she quickly averted her glance. "From now on," Hildegard instructed Trilby, "have her nurse the babies in a private room. The sight of her might distract our sisters from their purpose in prayer."

Yet it was she, mistress of the convent, who was most distracted. It seemed odd to her that this most innocent of babies could cause her to struggle spiritually, yet daily in her prayers Hildegard fought with the fleshly tendency to adore this child above the One of the Virgin Mary. By a sheer force of will and spiritual strength she resolved that Agnelet's care would not interfere with or weaken her own spiritual life and, after a month of struggle, Hildegard began keeping the baby at arm's length. She regularly checked on Agnelet's progress, but, aware of the baby's draw, she put her nuns on a rotation schedule so that each cared for the baby for only one day a month. The nuns soon discovered that excess devotion to the child had its penalty: anyone making a great fuss over Agnelet received kitchen duty.

Hildegard had Trilby make discreet inquiries in the village, but apparently no woman had recently given birth who did not have a baby either in her arms or in a hasty grave. Afton, wife of Hubert the miller, had recently borne a son, and the wife of a villein ploughman had borne a daughter who died. In the past two months, no woman had died in childbirth.

The novice Lienor could give no help in solving the mystery of Agnelet's appearance. Six months before the baby's arrival Lienor had asked the abbess for permission to maintain a vigil of silence until she took her final vows, as penance for a mortal sin committed long ago. Hildegard had given permission, and Lienor had not uttered a word since. If she had learned anything about the baby on the night she accepted it into the convent, she said nothing.

But all the nuns, trained to a life of frugality in words, alms, and effort, spoke volumes with their eyes. And Lienor's eyes were particularly revealing, magnified and deepened by the white guimpe that surrounded her face. Still new in the ways of the convent, she had not yet learned to keep them fully guarded and cast down. When Lienor looked at Agnelet, Hildegard was surprised to see more than concern in the novice's eyes—fascination and a faint longing were also revealed there.

Hildegard first attributed Lienor's unusual reaction to the fact that it had been the young nun who had taken the baby in; perhaps she felt a certain proprietary interest. Hildegard was going to rebuke the novice for this fault, understanding it completely, until she discovered that Lienor's attention to the baby was substantially different from that of the other nuns. They doted on the child, cuddled and cooed at her, but were quite willing to leave her when the bell chimed for prayers. Lienor, however, never willingly touched the child, even shrank from holding her, but was the first to tug on the sleeve of a sister nun when Agnelet cried or needed care.

One afternoon at recreation, Hildegard decided to explore Lienor's reaction to the child. She felt responsible not only for Agnelet, but for Lienor's spiritual struggles. She was confused by the girl's reaction to the babe.

It was a balmy spring day in the convent garden, and the nuns sat in a circle so none would feel left out. Each was occupied with something to mend, embroider, or weave. Speech was carefully regulated during the recreation, for conversation had to be of interest to all and maintained in the spirit of sisterly love. *Fortunately,* Hildegard mused, *Agnelet is a favorite topic.*

Hildegard smoothed the torn tunic in her lap and began to mend the tear with mathematically precise stitches. "Our little Agnelet can now sit up by herself," she spoke to the assembled nuns. "Have you noticed this, Lienor?"

The novice smiled and nodded, keeping her eyes on her stitching.

"I have often remarked upon the child's beauty. If it were not for the unfortunate deformity we all have chosen to ignore, she would be perfection itself, don't you agree, Ula?"

Ula, an older nun, nodded in agreement with the abbess.

"In fact, I've so fallen in love with the little angel's face that I confess I've concocted a little game with the women who occasionally visit the chapel. I find one woman with Agnelet's perfectly straight nose, another with her bright blue eyes—"

"Excuse me, Madame," Ula interrupted, timidly waving a thimbled finger. "But they have darkened. I believe they will be gray."

"Gray." Hildegard inclined her head thoughtfully. "Sometimes I even look for women with the shape of her fingers." Hildegard casually glanced toward Lienor and noted that the novice's hands trembled. "Sometimes I wonder if my game is wise."

Hildegard looked pointedly at Lienor, her question repeated in her glance, and Lienor's eyes met the abbess's and stirred in a sea of trouble. The novice shook her head almost imperceptibly before turning again to her work, but Hildegard saw the movement and knew she had stumbled onto fertile ground. The novice Lienor knew something about the infant, and whatever the knowledge was, it was too great or too heavy to be spoken.

Later that afternoon, Madame Hildegard heard a quiet tap on the door to her sparsely furnished office. "Come in," she called, folding her hands. She was not surprised when the novice Lienor came into the room and knelt before her desk.

"Rise, my child," Hildegard responded. "What is it you seek?"

Lienor tapped her chest with two fingers, the nun's sign for "excuse me," and Hildegard smoothed her face into a pleasant smile.

"You are no bother to me, daughter. How can I help you?"

Lienor pointed to her throat, then looked heavenward and made the sign of the cross. "Your vows?" Hildegard asked. "Do you still wish to take your vows?"

Lienor nodded, then pointed to her throat. Hildegard

nodded, understanding and feeling a strong regret. "You wish to continue your vow of silence after you have taken your vows," she said calmly. "Are you sure this is wise, my child? One of our purposes is to sing praise to God. Can you sing in silence?"

Lienor bowed her head and laid her hand upon her heart. "Of course you can sing in your heart," Hildegard answered, her voice softening. "Can you give me a reason for this request, my child? Surely the penance for your past sin has been paid."

Lienor looked up and Hildegard saw that the girl's dark eyes glistened with tears. Hildegard knew she should not ask, but she could not ignore the unerring instinct she had developed from years of searching women's hearts. Her hand closed around the cross that hung from her neck and she inclined her head gently. "Has this request something to do with the infant you brought to me?"

The dark circles in Lienor's eyes widened, but her face remained passive. She would not answer, and Hildegard understood. The cross slipped from her grasp and she folded her hands once again. "My child, this request is between you and God. I trust that when you are at liberty to speak, you will let me know."

Lienor nodded and closed her eyes. Hildegard stood and traced the sign of the cross on the girl's forehead, wishing as she did that she could read Lienor's mind as easily as she read her heart.

Afton smothered a laugh as Ambrose toddled three steps forward, then fell on his hands in the dust. The cool September breeze flipped her mourning veil off her head, and Afton snatched it from her hair and stuffed it into the belt at her waist. What did it matter if she did not dress like a proper widow? She was an independent woman, and she cared little for what the villeins said about her. The only people who mattered anymore were Ambrose and Corba.

Wido had died in the spring, a victim of pneumonia.

The doctors bled him in vain, for he tossed feverishly through four days and nights, mumbling about crops and sheep. On the fourth night, he died. Corba had been distraught, and Afton was grateful for a chance to comfort her mother as Corba had earlier comforted her.

Afton's mother was a fount of knowledge these days, one that Afton greatly appreciated, for there was much she needed to know. Especially about caring for Ambrose, who was Afton's reason for living. For the first time in her life she understood the motivation behind Endeline's passion for motherhood, and the love Afton bore toward Ambrose eclipsed every tender feeling she had ever known.

Corba found Afton's single-minded devotion to her child amusing, for her attention had always been divided between her duties as a villein and the needs of her husband and other children. But for Afton, Ambrose alone mattered, and he filled her days and nights with a reason for rising, working, and caring. In him she saw not a single trace of Hubert, but only a mirror image of herself: gray-blue eyes, golden hair, and rosy cheeks, usually smeared with mud or twice-chewed food.

Afton found great contentment in caring for her son and dreaming of the days to follow. As the son of a free woman, Ambrose would inherit the mill and its business when he was of age. Or he could sell the property and leave Margate for another village with a fairer lord. He could enter the service of the church, if he so desired, or sail the seas in the service of the king.

"I would even marry again, if doing so would free you to do as you pleased," Afton whispered to her son as he nursed in her arms. "I would die for you, Ambrose."

She kissed his forehead and smiled at his greedy suckling. Her son would not bear arms or enslave others. He would not toil in the fields of a master for little or no reward. He would never be sold, or traded, or offered in exchange for a sheep. Ambrose, son of Afton, would forever be a free man.

With the help of her mother and brothers, Afton turned her attention to running a prosperous mill. She soon found that she had a gift for working with people, and running the mill was a thousand times more gratifying than sewing or weaving tapestries.

A necessity of village life, the mill was a monopoly strictly enforced by Perceval. If the villagers wished to eat, they had to bring their grain to Afton to be ground into flour. The mill operated throughout the entire year, though the busiest months were after the harvest in August and September. In those months the villagers streamed through her gate with freshly harvested grain. But even in the winter there were small bags of hoarded rye or wheat to be ground into flour.

The lazy stream that trickled by the miller's property kept the millstones turning in all but the freezing winter months. When this happened, Afton knew she could borrow the village ox and lead him in a never-ending circle until the villagers' grain was ground.

The villagers were amazed at Afton's manner. "The girl from the castle complimented me on my fine wheat," one whiskered man told the village tanner. "She said it was obvious I had worked hard. Can ye imagine? Perceval's steward tells me I am the laziest man on earth!"

"She let me watch the grinding," the tanner's wife added. "I told her Hubert had given me bad flour from good rye, so she helped me pour my grain straight through the funnel meself. Old Hubert would never have done that!"

Afton made her biggest impression when it came time for the villagers to pay her. The payment for grinding, the *multure,* was one-sixteenth of the ground grain, but Hubert had frequently demanded one-eighth as payment. "I've been grinding wheat at 'ome to escape Hubert's cheating," one woman confided to Afton. "But my husband heard the penalty for even owning a grindstone was to lose a hand. So since you're being so fair and all, we're bringing our grain 'ere."

"Even the weights are true," Corba told the village smithy. "My daughter took care of things. All of Hubert's false weights are now at the bottom of the stream, rusting and rotting like he is, the cheat."

The villagers who had come grudgingly to Hubert's mill now came readily to Afton's, and she found that she was able to reap enough reward from her labor to provide for herself and Ambrose. So she was not much disturbed when Corba appeared at the mill house, a frown etched into her forehead. "I have been working at the castle today," Corba said, easing herself slowly onto a bench. "And there is news of trouble for you, my daughter."

"How so?" Afton asked, putting her scale under the rough-hewn worktable.

"The kitchen maid overheard Hector rebuke Josson because the revenues from the mill are down."

"That is impossible." Afton lifted Ambrose from the small cradle at her side. "I give Perceval one-fifth of my income, and that is his due. My one-fifth is larger than Hubert's tribute, so why is there cause for complaint?"

"Because Hubert always gave Hector an extra tribute," Corba said, sighing. "Such is the way of villeins and stewards, daughter. Ye do not understand. Perceval's stewards must be paid in addition to what Perceval is owed. If they are not—" She opened her hands helplessly.

"Perceval's steward will not be paid by me," Afton snapped. She softened her tone and looked into her mother's tired eyes. "All is well, Mother. We have been through the worst. You will see."

No one brought grain to the mill on Sunday, so Afton was startled to hear the creak of her gate. A horse whinnied outside, and she thrust a crust of day-old bread into Ambrose's hand and smoothed her tunic. "Someone's coming to visit your mama," she told her son, running her fingers through his light wisps of hair. "So you play here in mama's chamber and stay quiet."

The aged Hector, more stooped and gray than she remembered him, and his assistant stood at her door. "We bring greetings from your lord Perceval," Hector said, his voice quavering even as he cast furtive eyes around the hall as if searching for hoarded riches. "We have come to inquire about your rent."

The assistant cleared his throat awkwardly, and Afton studied him. She vaguely remembered his face from her days at the castle, but then he had been a boy. Now he was grown tall, but his skeletally thin frame seemed barely able to support his heavy cloak.

The young man noticed her curious glance. "I am Josson, my lady." Hector glared at the younger man, but Josson took a deep breath and continued. "It seems that the rent you have lately paid is less than the amount pledged by your husband."

Afton lifted her chin and stepped out of the house, closing the door firmly behind her. "I know not what my husband pledged, for he did not allow me into his affairs. But I run a fair mill and pay the lord his due rent of my earnings. One-fifth is all I intend to pay."

Hector's eyes narrowed in displeasure, and Afton returned his intense stare. Josson tried to lighten the atmosphere and waved a bony hand. "My lady—"

"She is not your lady!" Hector growled. "She is the child of a villein, and a stiff-headed child at that!"

"Stiff-headed enough not to bribe you as do the villeins," Afton replied icily. "I am no slave and no peasant. I have purchased my freedom through marriage and I will not feed your appetite for more than your due."

Hector's mouth snapped shut, and Josson smiled. "Perhaps our lord did not think this situation through to the end," he said, laughing lightly. "He should have thought better of giving the mill to an old man with an honest young wife."

Hector stomped toward his horse, muttering under his breath, and Josson nodded toward Afton. "We will speak to Perceval about this," he said agreeably.

"Josson!" Hector yelled, and the younger man hurried to help Hector mount his horse. Once in the saddle, Hector took the reins and pointed a yellow-nailed finger at Afton. "We will examine your mill at our leisure to see if your accounts agree with your practices," he said. "And we expect you to greet us with hospitality."

"You may come to the mill whenever you like," Afton replied, drawing her cloak about her. "You will find my words to be true."

Josson mounted his horse and tipped his cap to Afton in a gentle act of deference, but Hector turned his horse. "At our leisure, we will come," he called over his shoulder, and Afton took great pleasure in slamming her door as they rode away.

The steed that approached from the castle the next day bore not Hector, but Josson. The young clerk tied his horse to Afton's fence and seemed apologetic in his approach as he met her at the front door of her house. "My master, Hector, is ill and cannot be bothered with such a routine task," he explained, his brown eyes meeting Afton's almost bashfully. "So he sends me to oversee the mill's operation and certify that all is in order."

Afton lifted Ambrose onto her hip and led the way to the mill house. "Does he not expect the mill to be in order? Has a single villager complained?"

"No," Josson answered, following behind her. "But, after all, you are a woman alone and—"

"As a woman alone I have learned to do many things, sir," Afton told him, pulling open the heavy door to the mill house. "But I do not cheat the rich or the poor. Honor is not solely a trait of the nobility, if indeed the nobility can lay claim to it at all."

Josson had no answer, but quietly stood in a corner of the room as she pulled on her work apron and settled Ambrose to play with his straw dolls. A village woman waited outside the mill house already, her donkey loaded with two large sacks of grain.

By midday, Afton had to admit that having a man around the mill was helpful. At first Josson stayed out of her way, allowing her to greet her customers and tend to the mill. Then, when she had nearly forgotten about his intruding presence, he offered to help her lift a particularly heavy bag of wheat to the funnel in the upper millstone. His slender frame possessed more strength than she had guessed, and soon he was working silently behind her, doing whatever he could to make her work easier—entertaining Ambrose, scraping flour from the grinding stones, measuring or bagging the ground flour.

When the last villager's grain had been ground, Josson tabulated her income and profit and declared that he would probably have to come still another day or more. "My master Hector is a skeptical man, not given to easy assurances. As for me, I am certain that you are as honest as you are fair, mistress Afton."

After that day, he appeared at the mill two or three days a month and probably would have come more often, but he traveled now in Hector's stead to Perceval's outlying manors. Afton gradually overcame her resentment at the sight of his horse tethered outside her house, for when he visited the mill he seemed to care only for increasing Afton's profit and lessening her work load. He pretended that his concerns and suggestions were prompted only by his interest in Perceval's enrichment, but Afton saw through his pretense. How did Perceval benefit from Josson's suggestion that Ambrose have the toy wagon he had collected from the carpenter?

One slow spring morning, Josson pointed to the stream that bordered Afton's property. "You ought to augment your living by fishing," he said, walking to the bank and peering into the water. "In the winter months, people would pay dearly for fresh fish or eels. I could have a servant at the castle fashion fish traps for you. In all months you could harvest a goodly amount of fish."

Afton smiled up into his warm brown eyes. "Thank you," she murmured. "You are most kind."

Josson frowned. "Not at all. I'm only thinking of Perceval. Two of every ten fish caught here are Perceval's, and of course, a portion must be due for me, as well."

Afton scowled. "And what portion is that?"

"You shall feed me dinner when I am here," Josson returned, folding his arms in a poor imitation of Perceval's dignity.

Afton turned away so he would not see her smile. There was no anger in her voice, as hard as she might try to put it there as she answered, "So be it, sir."

Eighteen

"Get up," Calhoun demanded impatiently as Gislebert writhed on the ground under the quintain, struggling to catch his breath. "You didn't duck soon enough. Hit and duck in one motion. Next time you'll know better."

Calhoun whistled for the horse from which the boy had fallen and the animal trotted over for the carrot Calhoun always carried in his pocket. While the animal nuzzled Calhoun's hand, Gislebert sat up and glared at his older friend.

"I'll never be a knight," he said obstinately, through clenched teeth. "I'd rather be a troubadour."

"You live in a castle as the son of a knight, and a knight you'll become," Calhoun answered, laughing. He patted the horse's rear and held out his hand to Gislebert. "Come. Let's go see if dinner is ready."

"I think there is something else I might become," Gislebert said, clasping Calhoun's hand and pulling himself up. "Since my father died, I think Lord Thomas might be willing to let another assume the role of my guardian. Perhaps he would allow me to become the ward of Lord Perceval."

Calhoun's right eyebrow shot up. "You think so?" His eyes danced with mischief. "And why would Lord Perceval want you as a ward?"

"Because I bear great love and loyalty to the squire Calhoun," Gislebert said, counting on his fingers. "And I can tell stories that hold the other knights spellbound. And I can dress a knight faster than anyone, and sing so beautifully that the ladies swoon."

"There is only one lady remaining at Margate Castle," Calhoun said, a frown settling over his forehead. "My mother, Endeline. Lienor is gone to the nunnery, and Afton—"

"Who?"

"Never mind. You'll have to come up with better reasons than those if you want to go home with me." Calhoun paused and looked toward the southern horizon. "Fulk and I leave in two weeks, you know."

"I'll find better reasons," Gislebert said. "And you won't regret it."

Two weeks later, Fulk repressed a smile as he watched Calhoun and Gislebert at their farewell dinner in the hall of Warwick Castle. The younger boy had convinced Lord Thomas to allow him to go with Calhoun, and Fulk knew Thomas was probably glad to be relieved of responsibility for the boy. If Gislebert had held property or possessed great skill, Thomas would have been reluctant to free him, but Warwick had little need for small, dreamy, ten-year-olds who did little but tell stories. Yes, Thomas would be glad to see Gislebert go—and he would probably breathe easier when he was rid of Calhoun and Fulk, as well. The animosity between Calhoun and Arnoul had divided Warwick's knights for too long.

It had been over two years since Fulk had seen Margate, and he was not sure he wanted to take up residence in such a civilized and courtly castle. His tenure with Gerald had been satisfyingly rough, and training Calhoun at Warwick had been a worthy challenge. But at seventeen Calhoun was a grown man and as skilled in the knightly arts as Fulk. Responsibilities at Margate Castle now called them both southward, but Fulk was not sure he would find his next duty to his liking.

Lord Thomas raised his cup: "To squire Calhoun, who

now truly embodies the ideals of true knighthood. He is brave and loyal, faithful to his king, a defender of the Christian faith, and a protector of widows and orphans. Salute!"

The other knights raised their cups, and Calhoun nodded in appreciation. After they had drunk, he stood to his feet and raised his cup. "To Lord Thomas, who opened his home to welcome me as a son, and to the fair Clarissant, whose beauty has inspired countless acts of greatness."

Fulk covered his smile with his left hand as his right held his cup aloft. Over the course of the last year the boy's passion for the fair lady had burned from the flames of madness to the steady glow of infatuation. Love was one subject about which Fulk had little knowledge to impart—Calhoun would have to learn its lessons for himself, as all men did. At least the boy could now speak Clarissant's name without sweating away ten pounds.

Fulk stood and raised his cup. "To squire Calhoun," he called, his voice echoing through the hall. "A knight is not fit for battle until he has seen his own blood flow, heard his teeth crunch under the blow of an opponent, and felt the full weight of an adversary upon him." Fulk paused and the corner of his mouth raised in a wry half-smile. "My master is truly fit for battle, having endured all, and more, from me and you, my comrades."

The hall erupted into noisy laughter, and Fulk noticed that Calhoun joined in with the rest. Across the hall, Arnoul rose to his feet, his face scarlet in his eagerness. "To my most worthy adversary," he roared, and the crowd grew quiet. "Whom I saw thrown from his horse twenty times, yet twenty times he rose up to fight again."

Arnoul stared intensely at Calhoun, and the knights present drew an expectant breath. There was no teasing in Arnoul's voice, and his eyes fastened upon Calhoun as a hawk spies its prey. "You have bested me in every contest this past year, but I have not finished with you. I, too, shall rise again to fight when next we meet."

Arnoul raised his glass, and every eye shifted toward Cal-

houn, who raised his glass in frosty agreement. Lord
Thomas broke the tension by proclaiming, "May these two
always fight on the same side!" and the knights roared their
approval. The entire company raised their glasses and drank.

Gislebert and Calhoun knelt in front of their horses at the
priest's feet, but Fulk was strangely absent. "Go ahead," Calhoun told the priest impatiently. "We are anxious to be off."

The priest traced the sign of the cross above their heads
and recited a benediction of peace. When the holy father
had turned and went back into the castle, Fulk approached
from out of the stable and mounted his horse. "What?" he
snapped, catching Calhoun's eyes upon him. "I had fare-
wells to say, young squire. Do not question me further."

Calhoun did not answer, but spurred his horse and led
the way out of Warwick Castle. Perceval's chaplain had once
told him that some men held to a private form of religion,
and while that theology bordered on heresy, still it existed.
Surely Fulk was such a man, else why would he have
branded his own cheek with the sign of the cross?

He had no time for further reflections upon Fulk's religion, for other thoughts demanded his attention. The day
marked an ending and a beginning. It was the ending of his
childhood, his training, and his time under the sublime influence of Clarissant; it was the beginning of his manhood, his
service to God and king, and the assumption of his proper
role in the family of Perceval.

The three of them traveled without escort, for no sane
thief or highway brigand would dare attack two armed warriors and a boy on horseback. The three-day journey passed
pleasantly for Calhoun, who now found the saddle as comfortable as his bed. Fulk seemed lost in thought on much of
the trip, but Gislebert peppered Calhoun with questions.

"Is Margate a large estate?"

"One of the largest in England. My grandfather, Lionel,
was awarded it from William."

"Is your mother as beautiful as Clarissant?"

Calhoun frowned. It seemed indecent to compare his mother with his love, for they fulfilled two completely different roles in his life. "They are as night and day," he answered. "Clarissant is day, golden and sweet, while my mother is night. Her hair and eyes are dark."

"And your father? Is he like Lord Thomas?"

"In some ways. My father is closer to King Henry, and the short distance from the crown influences all he does."

"And there's a village? Fulk said there's a village nearby."

"Aye. For the villeins who work on the main estate." Calhoun cast a critical eye at his young friend. "You ask too many questions. A knight must know how to control his tongue."

Gislebert shook his head. "I told you, I'm not going to be a knight; I'm going to be a troubadour and tell tales. What else am I to learn? I have been at Warwick for too many years. I know of nothing else."

"Then learn quickly, my friend, because we are nearly there," Fulk interrupted. The forest thinned beside the road ahead of them, and on the horizon smoke poured from a village chimney. Calhoun touched his spur to his horse's side and raced away from his companions.

"Lady Endeline!" Morgan ran up the stairs, her cheeks rosy and her breath coming in gasps. "The lookouts have seen three riders coming up the road from the village. One of them carries Perceval's standard."

"Calhoun!" Endeline dropped her sewing and flew to the window. Her beloved son, the most perfect of all her offspring, was coming home. She hesitated only a moment at the window, then sped down the stairs and out into the courtyard.

Perceval flew out of the garrison, alerted by the tower guard, and Endeline took her place by his side as three riders galloped through the castle barbican. Endeline scanned their faces quickly. The nearest dust-streaked rider was an unfamiliar boy, the second was Fulk, as impassive as ever, and the third was her dearest son.

How Calhoun had changed! He slipped from his saddle, a tall stranger, and embraced Perceval. Endeline's knees turned to water beneath her; only her skirts held her up. She had sent a smooth-faced boy with knobby knees to Warwick, but now a muscular, mail-covered warrior whirled around to embrace her. The freckles of the boy had disappeared beneath the swarthy tan and bearded stubble of the man, and the knobby knees had long been overgrown by muscle.

"Mother." Calhoun spoke softly and held out his arms to her.

"Calhoun." She extended her arm, stiffly, and saw puzzlement in his eyes, but he took her hand, bowed, and kissed it with great ceremony. The growth of beard on his face raked across her hand, and she shuddered.

"We are glad you have come home," Perceval said, beaming at his son. "King Henry plans to join us for your dubbing next month, as well as your uncle the abbot. We have made a room ready for you in the castle, of course, and your companions may lodge in the tower garrison."

"Thank you, Father, but my place is in the garrison," Calhoun answered. He reached out a hand toward the urchin-faced boy on the horse, who awkwardly dismounted and stood shyly next to Calhoun. "This is Gislebert," Calhoun explained, putting his hands on the boy's slender shoulders. "He is a former ward of Lord Thomas. He has served me well, Father, and appeals to be placed under your guardianship."

"We are always pleased to show generosity," Perceval replied, placing his hand on Gislebert's dusty head. "Come, I'll show you to the garrison."

Endeline stood in silence and watched the four men go, a strange pain twisting in her heart. Her son was now a man, and no one remained to take his place in her heart except an uncivilized and cast-off boy from another castle. She turned her head so that the assembled household staff could not see the turmoil reflected upon her face. Calhoun's manhood had suddenly signaled one unavoidable fact: at thirty-three, she had no more children to rear. Soon she would be past the age of childbearing.

I will have another child! she thought, curling her hands into fists at her side. *I will have the child I long for.* She would mention the matter to Perceval again at dinner, and at supper, and at bedtime, till he grew weary of the subject.

Then he would find her a child, and Endeline would be young again.

Matins and Lauds in the middle of the night, Prime, breakfast, and Terce: when the villagers began their daily labor, the nuns had already eaten one meal and said four of the seven daily offices. With her arms crossed and hidden in her voluminous sleeves, Hildegard inspected her community of nuns during morning prayers. As the nuns knelt in private meditation, Hildegard walked smoothly up and down the chapel aisles and, though her eyes were downcast, she missed nothing.

Without wasting a particle of effort, Hildegard's glance read the very souls of her nuns. A nun with bitten fingernails was guilty of a lack of faith and self-control. The frayed edges of another sister's tunic displayed her wastefulness, a lack of the spirit of poverty. A sister who frowned at another lacked charity or battled secret pride. A nun who passed the porridge bowl without partaking so as to starve her soul into obedience needed to learn moderation in all things. By such telltale signs, Hildegard inspected the heart as well as the body and knew full well what struggles each of her nuns faced.

After gleaning in her field of nuns, Hildegard stood in the front of the chapel and spoke in a voice measured to reach only the ears of her audience, and not an inch beyond. "Today our sister Lienor will take her final vows and join us in our service to God," she announced, smiling serenely. "Lift her to our Blessed Lord in prayer, as she dedicates her life to him."

There was no noise or visible movement, but Hildegard felt approval radiating from the eyes and hearts of the women before her. "Let us attune our hearts to God's voice," she said, turning toward the altar, "and anticipate receiving the kiss of peace from our new sister after her investiture."

Endeline stood between Perceval and Calhoun in the guest section of the nuns' chapel and pretended to be joyous for having given her only daughter to God. But under her clear countenance and upslanting brows, her eyes were hard. The nunnery had succeeded where she had failed, for they had managed to strip her daughter of the athletic walk and refine Lienor's mannish ways into gentility. As the veiled forms in black moved past the benches toward the altar, it was impossible to tell which of them was Lienor. All moved with grace and composure.

When the entire family of nuns had taken their places in a long row at the altar, Madame Hildegard lifted a circlet of blossoms and laid it on the veil of one slender nun. She bowed to the abbess, then genuflected before the altar. Her small white hand appeared from under her dark cape and she signed the parchment on the altar: the order's vows of chastity, poverty, and obedience. The young nun then turned to face her sisters and pressed her cheek into their veils.

Finally the new nun, Madame Lienor, stood before her earthly family. Endeline tried to mask her surprise, for surely this refined-looking personage could not be her rough-and-ready daughter! Lienor hugged Calhoun and Charles, her eyes misting over with tears, and embraced her father. She paused before Endeline, though, and folded her arms into her voluminous sleeves. Endeline stiffened. What reaction was this?

"You are looking thinner," Perceval said, oblivious to the slight Endeline had received. He rocked back and forth on his heels. "I trust the feast I've prepared will help you plump up a bit."

Lienor smiled demurely but did not answer, and Endeline felt her anger rise. "You ought to speak to your father," Endeline said sharply, raising her voice.

Madame Hildegard stepped into the family circle. "Our sister Lienor has taken a vow of silence," she explained, her voice perfectly modulated in an even whisper. "She had originally intended to end her silence today, but apparently she does not feel at liberty to do so. I know she would ask you to respect her vow."

Lienor's eyes shone in gratitude toward the abbess, and Endeline closed her eyes in resignation. She had done nothing to deserve such an unsociable and unnatural child, but she would endure it. If Lienor preferred the mothering of the smugly spiritual abbess to her own careful guidance, so be it.

Perceval's servants had arranged a vast celebratory feast, and the other nuns filed out of the chapel to the refectory, forming a neat row of black-robed supplicants edging the hall like orderly ants. Calhoun led Lienor out to the garden, filling her ears with tales of his trials and triumphs at Warwick Castle. Perceval and Charles followed, but Endeline hung back, still feeling the smart of her daughter's cool rejection. Had she been such a terrible mother that Lienor preferred black robes, silence, and prayer to life with her family?

Endeline spied her brother, Abbot Hugh, across the room in conference with the abbess. She gathered her skirts and moved gracefully toward him, hoping that he could explain the reason for Lienor's apparent coldness and the senseless vow of silence. Endeline suspected the girl wanted nothing more than to insult her, for since her childhood days Lienor had never willingly done anything that would have brought Endeline pleasure. "Why should she begin pleasing me now?" Endeline whispered under her breath.

As she moved, she was startled by the abrupt appearance of a small blond head. From under a rough pew in the spectator's section, a small boy raised his head and broke into a giggle. Endeline froze in her place and slowly drew in her breath, lest she frighten the child. In all her dreams, she had never imagined a child as beautiful as this! Dancing blue eyes reminiscent of Calhoun's, milky skin, rosy cheeks, golden wisps of silken hair . . . and he was yet a toddler, probably no older than a year. The boy grinned at her with a mouthful of dainty baby teeth and laughed aloud again, a startlingly deep and utterly charming belly laugh. "I'm going to get you," a woman called from the back of the chapel, and the boy laughed again and ducked under the pew.

"Ambrose! Where are you?" The woman's voice was familiar, and Endeline whirled around. For a moment she was confused, for there stood Afton in a common mourning dress. But Afton had no children! As quickly as Endeline thought this, the memory came to her that Afton had been with child and was now a widow. So this perfect child was the fruit of Afton's womb?

"Afton?" Endeline whispered.

Afton nodded with grave dignity. "Lady Endeline."

Endeline stared with fascination at the young woman before her. The natural beauty she had admired in Afton had been altered somehow. While Lienor's features had grown more refined in this holy place, it seemed that Afton's fragile beauty had become more earthy. Her figure was full and womanly; her eyes shone with confidence and a certain wariness.

The corner of Afton's red mouth drooped, and Endeline realized the girl had noted she was under scrutiny. Afton held out her hand to the baby, who staggered toward her on strong, chubby legs. "Good day, my lady," Afton said formally, lifting the child onto her hip. "Give my regards to your family."

Endeline put out her hand. "Tarry a moment, Afton, it's been too long since we've seen you. Did you greet the others? Who brings you here today?"

Afton turned slowly. "I sat in the back and saw no one, Lady Endeline. Lienor herself sent word to invite me."

"How delightful," Endeline purred. "Will you join us at the feast?"

"No. Ambrose and I must go home."

"Wait!" Endeline made an effort to keep her voice calm. She was nearly frantic with curiosity about and desire for the baby in Afton's arms, but Afton must not know. She raised an eyebrow and asked casually, "This child is yours? He is a charming boy."

Afton's eyes narrowed for a moment, but motherly pride seemed to overcome her reserve. "Yes. Did you not know Hubert had a son?"

Endeline shook her head, but she could not take her eyes off the baby. "I may have heard something of it," she finally answered. "You must bring him to the castle. Surely he would like to see the place where you grew up?"

Afton's eyes gleamed in the cool shadows of the chapel. "I think not, my lady," she answered. "This is Hubert's son, the son of a free man, and no villein to you." She lifted her head defiantly as she carried her baby away.

Endeline's hand flew to her throat as the mother and child left the chapel. The courageous spirit of the mother would surely be reflected in the child—an unexpected benefit. Endeline forgot about talking to Abbot Hugh and hurried to the garden to find Perceval.

Later that night Endeline rubbed Perceval's back with perfumed oil as he lay across her knees. "I have found the child I seek," she said smoothly, caressing her husband's back. "He is a free child, perfect in every way. We could rear him here in the castle, my lord, and he would bring honor to you and delight to my weary heart."

Perceval sighed. "Your heart should not be weary, my love. You have raised three noble children."

"Charles does nothing but watch the fields grow," Endeline answered, keeping her voice calm as she poured more of the sweetly-scented oil into her hands. "Lienor never once attempted to please me by winning a suitable husband, and we agreed with reluctance to allow her entrance to the nunnery. Calhoun alone has accomplished the goals we set for him, and I worry about him. I fear that bringing him home may remind him of the girl he pined for in his youth."

She pressed her hands on her husband's skin and Perceval shuddered at the first cool sting of the oil. Endeline went on. "Both he and she were at the chapel today, but fortunately, our son did not see her. She has grown to be a lovely young woman."

"Afton?" Perceval turned his head toward his wife. "Surely he does not still think of her."

"Remember the troubadour's poem? Calhoun has not forgotten the girl, and a knight who pines for love is useless," Endeline replied, warming the oil into Perceval's skin. He settled into her lap again and hugged her knees, and she pressed her point: "What villein would fear a knight who yearns for the daughter of a ploughman?"

"We could let him marry the girl," Perceval mumbled. "She's a free woman now, with property. Where's the harm? As long as it is understood that Charles's children will inherit Margate lands—"

"Charles has no children." Endeline rolled her eyes in frustration, grateful that Perceval could not see her. She forced herself to remain calm and kept her touch gentle, though she wanted to slap his balding head in frustration. "And if Charles does not marry, Margate lands would go to Calhoun's children. And, of course, that would never do." She laughed gently, as though Perceval had suggested a tremendous joke. "Would you give your father's holdings to the children of your ploughman? Would you share your grandchildren with the peasant woman who weaves for you?"

Perceval grunted in appreciation of her words, then moaned in pleasure as his wife stroked his back. "You're right, of course."

"I am always right," she purred. She bent for a moment and pressed a kiss against the smooth skin of his back. "And I know what we need here in the castle—the laughter of a small child. As I told you, my lord, the child I have found is charming and perfectly formed, and intelligence shines in his eyes. He would do you honor, my lord, and serve admirably as a knight or even a steward. He is Afton's child."

Perceval's head lifted and turned toward her again. "I suppose you have a plan for securing this child?" he asked. "The child is born free; he cannot be substituted for tribute. The king himself would not understand if I took the child without provocation."

Endeline stroked her husband's hair. "Afton bears us no love, my lord, I am sure of it. Her haughty manner and words this morning assured me that she will place her loyalties elsewhere, and time will reveal her disloyalty to you. We must have Hector watch her, and her fault and treachery will reveal itself."

Perceval turned onto his back and drew his wife's head down for a kiss. "As you say, my dearest love," he replied.

NINETEEN

The village buzzed with the news of Calhoun's homecoming, and Afton could not help but overhear it. She'd had few thoughts of him while Hubert lived, save for the night Hubert died and she thought Calhoun stood by her side. But now she found herself wondering about him almost daily. Had he changed? Would he remember her? Had he really written the poem the troubadour sang?

Corba came to her house one night, breathless with news. "Perceval's holding a fair in honor of Calhoun's dubbing," she said, collapsing on the edge of Afton's bed. "Merchants from all over the country are coming to show their goods. They'll be camped around the walls of the castle for miles."

"Why should people from all over the country come here?" Afton said, rocking Ambrose to sleep in her arms.

"Because King Henry himself will dub Calhoun," Corba went on, waving her hands in her excitement. "People for miles around will come to catch even a glimpse of the king."

"Murderers and pickpockets will come, too," Afton said, shaking her head. "Trouble follows in the king's footsteps."

"Ye are too bitter," Corba answered. She retied her shawl around her shoulders and looked curiously at her daughter. "Have ye seen young Calhoun since his homecoming?"

Afton didn't lift her eyes from the baby, but shook her head. "No," she answered.

The rough bag of grain was worn, and Afton had trouble covering a hole with one hand while she poured with the other. So intent was she on her task that she didn't hear footsteps behind her.

"He injures a fair lady, that beholds her not."

Afton whirled around and smiled in relief when she saw Josson leaning against the door frame behind her. "Oh, Josson!" she said, catching her breath. "You startled me. I thought you might be someone of importance."

He frowned as if upset. "I am not of importance? You insult me, madame."

"You know what I mean. Here, help me with this bag, will you? It leaks."

Josson held his large, bony hands over the hole in the bag as he explained his visit. "Hector has given me strict instructions for you on how to handle the new business from merchants at the fair," he said. "Some will barter with flour and grain, and you are to be sure Perceval's portions are free of weevils and bugs."

"I don't grind grain with weevils or bugs," Afton answered, lowering the now empty bag onto the floor. She reached for another bag of grain that stood against the door. "And it would please me, sir, if you would continue to help or move out of my way."

Josson moved back so Afton could proceed toward the millstone, and his strong arms encircled her as he helped her open the mouth of the sack over the upper stone. She was startled by the touch of his flesh upon hers, and she lowered her hands quickly once the bag was opened. Josson, however, didn't move away from her.

"Hector, um, is also concerned that your house is near the main road," Josson added quietly as the grain poured from the bag into the funnel. "He worries about your—the mill's—safety. The fair crowd will doubtless attract thieves, and if it is known that a woman lives here alone—"

"I can take care of myself," Afton answered, pulling away from him. She stepped toward the door and smiled at him, trying not to appear nervous. "I have my husband's dagger, which has done damage before."

Josson held up his hands and backed away. "Hector only seeks to preserve your safety. If you want to go to the fair and desire an escort, why—"

"I'll go alone if I choose to go at all," Afton replied. "My son is fine company." She wiped a trickle of perspiration from her forehead. "Thank you, Josson, but you can tell Hector that my mill and my safekeeping are in good hands. My own."

"Calhoun, why didn't you tell me about the joys of a fair?" Gislebert's exclamation could barely be heard above the caterwauling and hawking of the merchants, but Calhoun smiled indulgently at the boy's enthusiasm and tossed him another pomegranate. It had been many years since there had been a fair in Margate, and Calhoun himself was enthralled with the strange and eclectic mix of merchants, merchandise, and medicine.

In the hubbub of voices Calhoun could hear the strange accents of merchants from Saxony and Frisia, Spain and Ireland, Rouen and Lombardy. Walking through the myriad of booths, Calhoun breathed in the tang of salted fish, the sweetness of perfumes, and the rancid odor of sweaty peasants who had traveled miles to see the unique and tantalizing items never before seen in Margate: purple and silken robes with bright orange borders, stamped leather jerkins, peacocks' feathers, and the scarlet plumage of flamingos. One stall displayed scents, spices, and pearls from the Orient; its neighbor offered almonds and raisins.

"I see by your dress that you are a brave knight," a darkskinned merchant called to Calhoun. "How would your lady like a new pet? Ladies dote on such creatures as this." An excitable monkey perched on the man's shoulder and blinked golden eyes at Calhoun. The merchant waved the end of the monkey's leash in Calhoun's direction. "A baby monkey would certainly warm her heart."

"No, thank you," Calhoun answered, moving on. "I have no lady's heart to warm."

"Why haven't you a lady?" Gislebert asked, hurrying to catch up. He turned to gawk at a pretty peasant girl in a colorful tunic. "There are many fair maidens in this place."

"You talk too much," Calhoun replied, watching the crowd. He knew the people of the land well enough to recognize the villeins from Perceval's manor almost by instinct, and the merchants shared a certain largeness of mouth and brashness of manner. But one man in the crowd belonged to neither group. Dressed too richly for a villein and too simply for nobility, the man wore only a long white robe under a dark cloak.

"Do you see that short man with dark hair?" Calhoun whispered in Gislebert's ear. "The one in the long cloak?"

"The one whose eyes dart from booth to booth?" Gislebert answered. "What of him?"

"I cannot place him," Calhoun said, shifting his weight uneasily. His hand went immediately to the hilt of his sword. "He reminds me of a weasel—slippery and sly. He is not a villein, nor does he dress like the nobility, yet he is too quiet to be a merchant."

"Perhaps he is a knight," Gislebert suggested.

"He wears no armor," Calhoun inserted.

"Perhaps a religious brother, then."

"He walks too boldly."

The man in the long cloak darted away through the crowd, and Calhoun stalked after him. "Find Fulk," Calhoun called to Gislebert. "We may need his assistance."

After an hour of searching, Gislebert kicked the ground in frustration. How was he supposed to find Fulk? And why should Fulk, captain of the knights, listen to him? "What a bother you are," Fulk would say when Gislebert squeaked his request. "Can't Calhoun take care of himself?"

Gislebert wandered among the merchant booths, hoping for a glimpse of either Calhoun or Fulk, and the sight of a familiar face made him stop in mid-step. Was that woman truly Clarissant? Calhoun would thank him for finding her! But as Gislebert pressed through the crowd, he realized the woman at whom he stared was younger than Clarissant and somehow more appealing. She stood at a booth of fabrics, her head enveloped in a length of purple silk. Laughing, she unwrapped her head and returned the silk to the merchant, her long golden hair falling from her face in tendrils of gold. "I'm afraid this won't do," the woman told the merchant, blushing. She murmured something in fluent French; the merchant replied sympathetically.

"Now this is a woman my master could love!" Gislebert whispered, ducking behind a tall pile of woven baskets. He appraised her face and form, noting every detail, but as she turned away from the silk merchant he spied the burden on her back.

She had a baby.

She was married.

Gislebert sighed and resumed his search for Calhoun.

Calhoun had just sunk his teeth into a strip of salted beef when Gislebert burst forth from the crowd. "Calhoun! I've looked everywhere for you."

Calhoun glanced down at the younger boy, annoyed. "I've lost the man, Gislebert. By all the saints, there's not a fox in the forest that could hide from me, but today I've lost my quarry." He chewed thoughtfully on the beef. "I know the man intends evil . . . but where? When?"

Gislebert shrugged. "I don't know. But I know something that will take your mind off this man. While I searched for Fulk, I saw a woman like Clarissant, with long golden hair, fair skin, and—"

"Gislebert, you are too much a romantic," Calhoun muttered, spitting out the remainder of his beef. "This is not the time to think of women." He pulled on his helmet, then tramped off through the crowd with Gislebert at his heels.

A short time later, the curfew warning bell chimed from the tower at Margate Castle and the crowd at the fair dispersed quickly. Calhoun and Gislebert hung back in the shadows, watching for lurking figures, but there was no sign of the man in the long cloak. Driven by an unsettling certainty, Calhoun sprinted to the castle stables and saddled his horse.

"Are we going out?" Gislebert asked, his voice quivering. "The curfew bell—"

"I'm going out to look for violators of the curfew," Calhoun answered, testing the strength of his stirrup. "You don't have to come."

"But there are people everywhere, crowds of them—"

"A knight is to preserve the peace," Calhoun replied. "And peace is more easily disturbed in a crowd." He swung into the saddle and extended his hand to his young friend. "Are you coming?" Despite his reluctance, Gislebert took Calhoun's hand and pulled himself into the saddle. Calhoun turned the horse out of the stable, and together they rode out into the night.

Quiet lay upon the road like a thick blanket, for most of the villagers had returned home before the curfew bell sounded. The merchants had settled into their campsites outside the castle walls, and their campfires were steady beacons in the castle pasture. Calhoun let the horse walk slowly down the road, giving him his head in the darkness. Once they had passed the pasture, Calhoun peered into the thickening forest with his hand firmly upon the hilt of his sword.

"No mischief here," Gislebert said when they made it to the village hedge without incident. The boy's voice was heavy with relief, and Calhoun smiled. Perhaps he had been too vigilant. "Can we go back now?" Gislebert asked, the saddle creaking as he relaxed behind Calhoun. "There's no trouble afoot here. No one would dare make trouble when King Henry is expected any day."

"Don't you know the crown attracts trouble?" Calhoun asked cryptically. He turned the horse toward the road that led out of the village to the next manor.

"I thought we were going home," Gislebert said, his voice still full of hope. "There's nothing out here but the mill, and then nothing but miles and miles of road, remember?"

Calhoun held up his hand and stopped his horse. The miller's house lay ahead, quiet in the rising moon's light, but something alerted his senses. The stream rushed steadily in the distance, a wolf cried in the far-off forest, but there were no footsteps, no human sounds. He surveyed the miller's house with a coolly appraising eye and saw nothing unusual. The house, the kitchen, and the mill house gleamed in the moonlight, and the gate creaked lazily on its hinges as the wind blew. Calhoun turned the horse. Perhaps he was mistaken. . . .

He turned back sharply, his eyes narrowing. Why did the gate creak? Who left a gate open after dark?

He examined the gate again and heard a sudden cry of surprise and pain. Calhoun stood in his saddle. Scuffling noises came from the miller's courtyard, and somewhere in the darkness, a baby cried.

"Off!" Calhoun told Gislebert, drawing his sword, but the boy had already slid off the back of the horse. Calhoun spurred the horse's side and galloped through the open gate. A woman hunched on the ground in the courtyard, robed in black, and a baby sat wailing in the dirt. A man lay on the ground, a stain spreading darkly across his white tunic.

At the sound of Calhoun's approach, the woman whirled toward him, the flash of a silver dagger shining in the night. "Stay away!" she screamed, waving the dagger in front of him. "I've killed one man, and I'll kill another if I must."

Calhoun waved his sword and reined in his horse in response. What was this? Had the man fallen upon the woman or the woman upon the man?

"Is that the miller you have killed?" he asked, his voice booming through the darkness. "Speak now, woman, for I come in the name of Perceval and seek the lord's justice."

He could not see the woman's face, for it lay in the recess of her hood, but he could hear her sudden laughter. Surely he had come upon a madwoman.

"The miller has been dead for over a year," she finally answered, controlling her mirth. The hand that held her dagger fell limply to her side. "This man—" she pointed off-handedly with the dagger to the man on the ground— "thought I would be an easy prey for his villainy. But I am not an easy bird to snare."

Her words and voice had the ring of familiarity, and Calhoun leaned forward in his saddle to get a better look at her. Surely this bloodthirsty creature had nothing to do with his childhood, but with a jolt Calhoun realized she had the manner and voice of Afton. "Pull back your hood, that I may recognize you," he commanded, his voice hoarse with checked emotion.

She did not acquiesce easily, but stared steadily at him, her eyes glowing from the darkness of her hood like the eyes of a hungry, wary dog. "Who is this that commands me?" she asked. "If you would recognize me, you must live in these parts. But if you live in these parts, you would have known that the scoundrel who lies here is not the miller. I would have your name, sir, before you have my obedience."

Calhoun found himself dismounting. He walked toward her, even as she cautiously backed away.

"I am Calhoun," he said simply. He reached up and removed his helmet—a gesture that startled her, for none of Perceval's proud knights ever removed their helmets unless they stood in the presence of the lord or the king himself. But the words he spoke startled her even more. "One who once called you friend."

"Calhoun." The dagger fell from her hand onto the ground, and her head reeled back as if he had struck her. The hood slipped back a few inches, revealing enough of her face that Calhoun could see a smile flit briefly across her lips when she looked at him again. "You saved me with your sword once, in the barn—do you remember? And now you come again with your sword." Suddenly the wistfulness in her voice disappeared, to be replaced by a cold hardness. "But this time your help is not needed."

How she had changed! She had always been beautiful, but never more so than now, when she stood pale and trembling in the moonlight. Calhoun noted the strength in her arms where once there had been only grace, and the pride in her voice where once there had been only entreaty.

"I would give my help to you," he finally managed to say. "I did not know you were a widow. Are you in any difficulty?"

She closed her eyes and a sound rose from deep within her; Calhoun could not tell if she laughed or cried. "No," she said finally, wiping a tear from the corner of her eye. "I am not now in difficulty. But I thank you for your concern, sir. It is most unusual for a knight to be troubled with the concerns of a woman such as I."

He did not understand the anger that bubbled beneath her words. What had happened to her? "I am not yet a knight," he said softly, sheathing his sword. "I am to be dubbed when King Henry arrives."

She lifted her chin. "A knight in King Henry's service. So you always wanted to be, Calhoun."

"Aye."

Just then the child, who had been sitting silent in the dirt, toddled over to her and hid his face in her skirt. Calhoun tore his eyes from her face and gave the boy a cursory appraisal. "Your child is very handsome."

"Aye," she echoed.

He wanted to add, *He looks very much like you,* but did not know how she would react to words of flattery, sincere though they would have been. This woman was not Clarissant, who lapped up flattery as eagerly as a cat before a bowl of milk.

He turned away, but remembered something. "You promised your obedience if I gave you my name," he said, turning back to watch her eyes carefully. "I asked you to pull back your hood." She did not move, so he gently added: "Will you?"

Her eyes remained obstinate, not once leaving his face, but her hand moved as though it possessed a life of its own and pulled the dark hood from her head. Her golden hair shone as he remembered it, hanging long and loose as it had been on the night she had danced before him in the castle. Her lips were full and as dark as the bloodstains on the villain's shirt, and her eyes—wide and dark, they seemed both to accuse and entreat him.

"Thank you," he answered hoarsely, calling upon every reserve of discipline as he pulled himself away from the sight of her. He mounted his horse and pointed at the body in the shadows. "I'll send a sergeant to remove the scoundrel's body shortly. I'll take care of everything." Then he rode through her gate and vanished into the night.

She couldn't believe she had removed her hood for him. It was a simple thing, but she had yielded to him without protest—and for what reason? So he could *look* at her? So he could prove his power over her and lord his exalted position?

She placed Ambrose in his bed and fumed in the darkness. She had vowed never again to submit to a man, but she had done it without thinking because it was Calhoun who had asked a simple thing of her. His voice had grown deeper and more powerful, and his face had not lost its attraction for her. Under the firm set of his chin there still remained something of the sweet nature she had loved as a child, and at the sight of his sword she had been flooded with memories of the time he had tried to catch her in the hay.

And yet . . . Calhoun had not recognized her. He had not crashed through her gate to rescue his old friend, he had come riding to the aid of Perceval's miller. She told herself she was being unreasonable to expect him to know or care about her situation, but still she felt bitterly disappointed. In these past few weeks Calhoun had ridden by her house and stood in her courtyard, yet he had known nothing about her, not even that she had a child and a dead husband. In the weeks he had been home, he had asked no one of her whereabouts. He had not even been sure of her face.

Her disappointment flamed to furious resentment when the sergeant at arms and his men arrived the next morning to remove the body from her courtyard, and she overheard their conversation. "Yes, Lord Calhoun himself killed the fellow when he attacked the woman," the sergeant said, pride dripping from his voice. "It is the man he suspected and trailed all afternoon. By all the saints, Perceval's son may grow to be a mightier warrior than his father or grandfather before him."

She withdrew from her window and seethed in silence. Did men of Calhoun's breed keep score of the souls they dispatched to heaven or hell? Was this the first, or second, or hundredth soul Calhoun had claimed in order to boost his fame as a mighty knight? She had killed the intruder herself, and quite easily, for the man had not expected her to be carrying a dagger inside her sleeve. She had even been aware of his presence on the road behind her and in the courtyard, as he carelessly advanced his attack. And she had not been afraid when he struck.

She would never be afraid of anything again.

The killing of the prowler would have ordinarily provided the villagers with gossip for months, but the arrival of King Henry and his entourage doubled the peasants' work load and left no time for idle chatter. The villein women baked mountains of bread, and the men slaughtered and salted a small herd of cattle, sheep, and deer in anticipation of the king's varied appetite.

In return for their efforts, every villager was invited to attend the great feast and tournament that would follow the dubbing ceremony, and Perceval declared that no work would be done in the week that followed the king's departure. The work necessary in the week before the king's arrival had exhausted nobles and villeins alike.

Afton herself had worked in the mill from sunrise to sunset. Perceval had sent Josson daily to the mill with a substantial amount of wheat, and Afton's arms and back ached from lifting and hauling wheat and flour to and from the grindstone. The night before Calhoun's dubbing she lay on her bed and debated aloud whether or not she should attend the festivities. Surely staying home with Ambrose would be more satisfying than watching Calhoun pledge his life and sword to King Henry.

Corba would not hear of Afton remaining behind. "Ye must go," she declared with unusual fervor. She stopped rocking Ambrose and shook a finger at her daughter. "Ye will offend the lord and lady, and, mark my words, Hector will know if ye do not attend. It will mean trouble for all of us if ye do not go to the castle."

To calm her mother, Afton agreed to attend the ceremony. She would just have to steel herself for the task of watching her childhood friend take up arms in the service of a brutal king.

TWENTY

Endeline had spared no expense in preparation for her guests at the king's banquet, and the tables were bountifully arrayed with silver salt cellars, gilded goblets, silver spoons, elegant ewers, and fragrant sweetmeat dishes. But King Henry had changed little during the years of Calhoun's training, and the knight-to-be found it hard to enjoy himself at the king's table. The royal eye turned often in his direction, and Calhoun found himself glancing awkwardly at his lap in a most cowardly fashion. Perhaps it was the setting. Only five feet in front of Calhoun and his king lay the space of bloodstained floor where the king had once brutalized his grandchildren.

So Calhoun ate much and talked little, remembering too well how the king's eye could gleam violently at the least sign of treachery. For the first time he realized the wisdom in Fulk's persistent admonishment to keep a tight rein on one's mouth. It was obvious that Perceval had never received such training, for he fawned over the king, constantly praising, flattering, and giving homage. In the midst of the barrage of adulation, Calhoun sensed that King Henry did not love Perceval better for it.

The next two days held many challenges for Calhoun. Not only did he have to watch his actions, gestures, words, and facial expressions while in the presence of the king, but he knew the eyes of other knights rested upon him, eager to test the mettle of the young man who wished to join their ranks. The report of his having killed the intruder in the village had added favorably to his reputation, but it also had fueled the jealousy of knights who envied Calhoun's position as Perceval's son.

Fulk warned Calhoun of this danger, and Calhoun had felt the sting of it in the past week. One knight tripped Calhoun in the courtyard in front of the servants. Calhoun sprang to his feet, eager to fight, but one glance from Fulk halted his hand before he reached for his sword. Drawing a deep breath, Calhoun forgot his embarrassment and smoothed his features, then continued as if nothing had happened.

The taunting and testing had only just begun. In the darkness of the garrison as he tried to sleep, anonymous voices called out insults to his manhood, his parentage, and even his mother. These remarks he bore in silence, gritting his teeth, keenly aware of Fulk's warning presence on the bunk across from him.

But the week was now past, and all had gone well. Calhoun had borne his testing without once losing control of his temper; now he had only to endure the day of feasting and the day of dubbing.

After Endeline's sumptuous dinner, Perceval summoned musicians for dancing. As the servants cleared the tables from the hall, several young servant girls shyly entered. "Have you no other maidens than these?" the king asked, his wide hand sweeping toward the servant girls disdainfully.

Calhoun scanned the row of maidens and noted that Afton was not among them. "We have other maidens in the village, sire," he said, bowing his head respectfully. "But not many are up to the honor of dancing before Your Majesty."

Henry chuckled appreciatively, and Calhoun bowed again and left the table. As he approached the girls, he wished for a moment that Afton had been present; now that he knew how to dance he would serve as her willing partner. But he bowed before the first young girl he met and, as she twittered in pleasure, he took her hand and opened the dancing, thus fulfilling his proper role as a knight. He saw his mother smile in approval.

The dancing continued throughout the afternoon. A supper table was brought into the back of the room, where those who had developed an appetite could eat their fill, and the musicians continued playing as the sun set. When the late afternoon sun lowered the first shadows of evening into the hall, Perceval clapped his hands, King Henry took his leave, and the musicians and guests cleared the hall.

Calhoun was left alone with his father and his master, Fulk. Together the three men went upstairs to the lord's chamber, where Perceval and Fulk dressed Calhoun in a white robe. His father embraced him, Fulk clapped him vigorously on the shoulder, then they escorted him to the chapel, where Charles and Endeline waited. Abbot Hugh led the family as they partook of the body and blood of Christ.

Calhoun found it difficult to concentrate on Mass, for on a purple satin pillow before the altar lay his new sword, a weapon of unusual beauty. When all had partaken of Mass, Abbot Hugh sprinkled the sword with holy water and murmured a prayer of blessing over it, then Calhoun prostrated himself on the floor before the altar. His family slipped out of the chapel, but Calhoun spent the night on the hard wooden floor.

"Our Father who art in heaven," he prayed, hesitating, searching for the right words. "Hallowed be thy name and my sword. Use both my sword and my heart, my Father, for your kingdom and your eternal glory."

Calhoun did not dare stir from his position until daybreak, when the king appeared in the chapel doorway. Henry offered his hand to Calhoun, who accepted it and knelt at the king's feet, then Henry bid him rise and affectionately embraced him. In triumph the king led Calhoun to his table in the hall, where they breakfasted with Perceval and Fulk.

After breakfast, the maids Morgan and Lunette prepared

a ritual bath in Perceval's chamber so Calhoun might cleanse his body as he had cleansed his soul. After he had bathed, Fulk and his father helped him dress in fine linen undergarments, a tunic of white, a purple robe, silk stockings, and shoes ornamented with violet eagles. "Eagles are birds of strength," Perceval said, gazing wistfully at the symbol of his family, "and violet is the color of humility, which we bear before the throne of England."

A glimmer of pride shone even from Fulk's dark eyes, and under his mustache his lips quivered with suppressed emotion as he looked at Calhoun arrayed in the full costume of a royal knight. "You have done well, Squire Calhoun," he said, his voice husky.

"No longer squire," Calhoun answered, clasping Fulk's shoulder. He smiled at his friend and master. "After this hour, my training is complete."

"Training is never complete," Fulk corrected him, turning away to open the chamber door. "But after this hour, you have earned the sword of a knight."

Under the eyes of hundreds of spectators gathered into the castle courtyard, Calhoun knelt on a carpet of violet before the king and heard approval in Henry's words: "Rise, noble Calhoun, a knight in King Henry's service. Your father and I have provided for your arms in service to your lord and king."

The trumpeters sounded a musical flourish, and the crowd cheered. Calhoun stood, and Fulk approached with a new shirt of double-woven mail, which no lance or javelin could pierce. Perceval aided Fulk as they removed Calhoun's purple robe and slipped the shirt of mail over his tunic; then they helped him slip into iron boots of the same double mesh. Endeline approached with a white surcoat, which bore the violet eagle of Perceval's household. This Perceval slipped over Calhoun's head.

New spurs, gilded in gold, were strapped to his heels, and a shield with a violet eagle was hung around his neck.

On the young knight's head, Fulk placed a new helmet that gleamed with precious stones set into the headband, and Perceval set into his hand a spear of ash, tipped with iron.

Finally Henry motioned to a nearby page, and the boy approached with Calhoun's new sword, still lying upon its satin pillow. The silver blade gleamed in the sunlight. "Let the words engraved upon this sword, *Homo Dei*, forever remind you that from this day until your last you are to be the perfect image of a man of God, young Calhoun," Henry charged.

Calhoun removed his helmet and knelt again at the feet of the king and his father. Perceval stretched out his hands, and Calhoun curled his hands submissively into his father's open palms. As Perceval's hands closed over his son's, he recited the traditional vow: "Do you wish, without reservation, to become my man?"

"I wish it," Calhoun replied clearly.

Perceval leaned forward and kissed Calhoun lightly on the lips. Then he dropped his son's hands and motioned to Gislebert, who stood nearby with a casket of holy relics from the abbey church. Gislebert approached, and Calhoun laid his hands on the casket.

"Do you promise by your faith that from this time forward you will be faithful to your lord Perceval and your king, and that you will maintain toward them your homage entirely against any man, in good faith and without any deception?" Perceval asked.

"I swear it."

The crowd cheered, and Henry reached for Calhoun's sword and regally touched it to Calhoun's shoulder—with that gesture forging the bond of service—and then placed the sword in Calhoun's hand. Calhoun kissed its hilt, then stood and sheathed it at his side.

The crowd drew in a collective breath for what was to come: Perceval drew back his hand and struck Calhoun in the face. The traditional *coleé*, a strong slap, would serve to remind the young knight of his oath, and though Calhoun had been expecting it, the force of the blow nearly knocked him from his feet.

"Go now, fair son, and be a true knight and courageous in the face of your enemies," Perceval charged his son. "Be brave and upright, that God may love thee better for it, and always remember that you spring from a race that can never be false. Spare the vanquished enemy who asks for your grace, assist those in distress, and give of your love and strength to God. If you will do these things, you cannot fail to please your lord and your king."

"So I shall!" Calhoun replied. He turned to face the cheering crowd, which parted as the final gift from his father was led into the courtyard: a magnificent war-horse, the knight's destrier, a stallion especially bred for strength in battle.

Calhoun sprinted to the horse and swung into the saddle. He stood in the stirrups, his legs taut and straight, and waved his sword in triumph at the jubilant crowd. As the other knights mounted their horses behind him, he turned the animal and lifted his lance with a mock battle cry. One touch of the spur sent the beast galloping out the castle gate toward the field of contest, and the crowd parted as the other knights streamed after him.

As the hooves of Calhoun's mount tore the tender grass in the field of contest, the other knights stampeded behind him for an exhibition of their talents and skills. Calhoun of Margate, a noble knight in the service of the Earl of Margate and King Henry of England, had completed his ceremony and begun his celebration. Yet one voice was silent in the boisterous crowd, and one pair of gray eyes did not follow the knights from the courtyard to the tournament field. Afton, her eyes downcast upon the golden head of her son, patted Ambrose absently and nodded to her mother. "We have seen what we came to see," Afton said, lifting the child into her arms. "Can we go home now without offending Lord Perceval?"

Corba nodded, her eyes wide with understanding and, Afton thought, the tiniest trace of pity.

For seven days the castle household and the king's entourage feasted in the celebration of Calhoun's knighthood. Endeline felt herself begin to relax as the days passed, for Calhoun had accomplished all and more than she and Perceval had planned for him. King Henry took obvious pleasure in Calhoun's considerable skills as a fighter, hunter, and diplomat, and the royal tiger showed no sign of turning on his hosts.

When the celebration had ended and the royal guests had left, Endeline could not help noticing that Calhoun seemed detached from the daily routine at Margate. At meals he seemed distracted and aloof, and when she forced him to sit and talk with her, his replies were monosyllabic and his eyes no longer snapped with boyish abandon. It was as though the essence of her son had vanished, or wandered alone to a faraway place.

She asked the sergeant at arms how Calhoun was performing in his duties. Jarvis reported that Calhoun was proficient, but lacked zeal in his work. "He knows what he must do," Jarvis explained to Endeline one afternoon in the garden, "and he does it well. But the other knights delight in gaming and tournaments, and Calhoun participates only if required, and then he wins and seems to find no glory or joy in winning."

"With whom does he spend his free time?" Endeline asked, leaning forward in the garden swing.

Jarvis shrugged. "He spends a great deal of time alone with Gislebert, and even more time riding through the countryside. He is often with Fulk, but they do not speak often. Both are men of few words." Jarvis wiped a trickle of perspiration from his forehead. "I do not know what to tell you, my lady. Perhaps your son is bored. Perhaps," he laughed, "perhaps he is in love. I hear he was devoted to the lady at Warwick Castle."

Endeline smiled at Jarvis's joke and dismissed him, but a nagging certainty rose in her heart—a suspicion that she dared not voice to anyone. She was sure her son did not love

Clarissant, for he had been happy to be home up until recently. Surely if he pined for the lady of Warwick, he would have been miserable from the day he arrived home! No, if it was love, he had found a woman here. And if he had not confided in her, his mother, he had lost his heart to the one woman she despised.

She could not explain her thoughts to Perceval, for surely he would tell her again that no harm lay in Calhoun's marriage to Afton. But perhaps she was mistaken—perhaps there was another reason for her son's melancholy indifference.

"Why isn't Calhoun home more often?" Endeline cautiously asked Perceval as they lay near sleep in their chamber. "He has not even been at dinner in the last three days. What distracts our son from his purpose here with us?"

"It is nothing but youthful enthusiasm," Perceval said, his eyes closing in sleep. "He has a new horse, new armor . . . why shouldn't his life be an endless cavalcade?"

"But he is not enthusiastic." Endeline folded her arms and stared at the ceiling. "If anything, our son is melancholy."

"Then it is the inevitable sagging of the spirit that follows dubbing," Perceval mumbled, his voice heavy with sleep. "I remember the feeling well. The excitement flees, the routine begins, and a young knight wonders what is to come of the rest of his life. It will pass, my dear, the feeling will pass."

Endeline stared into the darkness for a moment. "Whatever it is that occupies our son," she finally whispered to her sleeping husband, "I will understand it and correct it."

Calhoun's horse snorted impatiently in the darkness. "Silence, my friend," Calhoun whispered, "or you will reveal our presence."

He and his mount stood in shadows outside the miller's gate, his self-assigned post. Every night for the past fortnight he had come here, waiting in the darkness for terrors that had not yet come. *The girl may think herself invincible,*

Calhoun told himself, *but it is not seemly or safe for a woman to live alone. Only hermits and the madwomen who roam the woods seek such solitude.*

He could smell the hickory logs on her fire and guessed that she sat before a late supper after putting the baby to bed. What did she feel for him, this child of Hubert's? Did she love him as a mother loves a son, or as a wife loves the child of her husband? What tender mercies rose in her heart when she looked into her child's face? Were they the same emotions that had risen, night after night, within his own breast as he thought of her?

The crunch of hooves upon gravel warned Calhoun that other knights approached from the castle, probably the regular patrol, and he reined in his horse so that the shadows of the forest trees concealed him completely. No one knew of his nocturnal visits here; he did not want to arouse speculation or gossip by being discovered. Fulk would only laugh at his devotion. As for Gislebert, the young man might understand even better than Calhoun why he rode to the spot night after night.

The patrol passed, four noisy riders more interested in the bawdy joke one of them told than in promoting peace on Perceval's road. When they had gone by, the quiet of night descended again, but a movement from the house caught Calhoun's eye. Afton had moved to the solitary window in her chamber, and she stood before the window combing her golden hair. Calhoun caught his breath, for she stared boldly out into the darkness as if she knew he waited there. She raised her chin in resolute defiance as she pulled the comb through her long locks, and he wondered again what had happened to the soft, trusting girl who had once ridden on the back of his horse.

Afton put down her comb and blew out her candle. Calhoun was left alone in the darkness with his questions.

Endeline rubbed her older son's shoulders playfully as he sat at supper. "I would know what keeps your brother from us at dinner," she said, keeping her voice light. "For a fortnight now, he's been absent from our table."

Charles shrugged. "He's sleeping. He rides out each night in the darkness and doesn't return until morning. He sleeps through dinner and eats later in the garrison."

Endeline frowned. "Does Fulk know of this?" she asked, sinking onto a bench next to Charles. "What sort of assignment has he given our son?"

Charles shrugged. "I assume it is the nightly patrol through the village."

Endeline's gown rustled as she stood and moved away. "We shall see."

Fulk bowed slightly and smiled at Endeline when she summoned him to the hall, but she had the distinct feeling the man did not trust her, nor ever would. "Your son rides at night by his own request," he said simply.

Endeline sensed that he measured his words carefully, and his caution annoyed her. "You have not assigned him to this onerous duty? My son was away nearly three years, noble Fulk, and I would like to see his face before me at dinner. Entreat Jarvis to assign him to castle duty, please, for I have sorely missed his company."

Fulk bowed again, but his dark eyes seemed to be gauging the truth of her words. "As you wish, my lady," he replied.

Calhoun kicked a stool across the room, and the tower rang with his cry. "No! I am not a child! What right has she to ask this of me?"

"Then do not act like a child," Fulk replied smoothly. "She is your lady and your mother and she desires the pleasure of your company."

"She wants to tie me ever more tightly to her side," Calhoun lamented. "She is not happy unless she is smothering someone."

"That may be," Fulk answered, twirling the corner of

his mustache. "But I think she is more concerned with keeping you from the village."

Calhoun turned and looked sharply at Fulk. Did he know where Calhoun had spent his nights? He had not asked, but Fulk possessed unerring instincts.

Calhoun knelt by his friend's side on the garrison's stone floor to confess all. "I watch her every night, Fulk, for she is not safe, living alone in the miller's house. It has been less than a month since one villain attempted to harm her. What danger will next month bring?"

Fulk's somber eyes searched Calhoun's face. "Tell me the truth—did you really kill the man who attacked her?"

"No." Calhoun looked down at the floor. "She killed the man herself. I let the others believe I had done it to spare her from inquisition."

The corner of Fulk's mouth rose in a half-smile. "I thought so. A dagger in the heart is not your style. You would have slit his throat."

"I would have cut out his heart if he had touched her!" Calhoun's hands closed into fists. "But what if she is not prepared next time? How can I protect her if I am tied to the castle?"

Fulk opened his hands in a submissive gesture. "My young friend, consider your position. You have servants, do you not?"

"None that I trust. All that serve me serve my mother and father also."

"Do you have friends?"

Calhoun thought a moment. "I trust only you and Gislebert."

"Then enlist the aid of your friends, young knight, and avoid arousing your mother's ire, lest you be sent away again."

Beginning the next day, Calhoun presented himself at dinner and made a great display of kissing his mother's hand. He ate at Perceval's table and showed himself conspicuously at the castle in the afternoons when Endeline sat with her ladies in the gardens or the orchard. All of this greatly encouraged the lady Endeline.

She would not have been so comforted, however, had she known that her son rose every morning before daybreak and rode through the village until smoke coming through the hearth chimney of the miller's house assured him that all was well. In the evening, Fulk took the same route and did not return to the castle until the miller's widow had extinguished her candle.

The villagers did not notice anything out of the ordinary, for Perceval's knights often rode through the village on their way to the outlying manors or simply for the purpose of intimidation. Besides, in their shirts of mail, surcoats, and helmets, one knight looked much like another, and rarely did the knights speak to the villeins except to harass them.

Afton paid no attention to the knights on the road, but she did meet an unusual new customer who began to appear regularly at the door of the mill house: a thin boy with wide brown eyes, who told her his name was Gislebert. He would not say where he lived, only that he was an orphan under the care of a free man. Her heart went out to him, and she always ground his small bag of rye without charging him the multure.

He loved to talk, though—as much as any woman she ever knew—and often he did not leave after she had ground his grain. Instead, he would stay by her side and tell her riddles, or sing silly songs of love, or jest while he checked her fish traps. His gossip involved not only the villeins, but men and women in the king's court itself, and he invented riddles that stumped her.

"If I didn't know better," she said one afternoon as he helped her set traps in the stream, "I'd think you grew up in the court of a lord."

Gislebert grinned slyly. *"Oui, madame,"* he answered. "I cannot fool you."

"And you speak French, too?" Afton was astonished.

"Doesn't everyone in a castle? My father was a knight, and my mother a ladies' maid . . . and both are now dead. The subject is painful for me."

A quick wave of sympathy swept over her, and Afton decided to let the matter drop. She put her last trap into the water and tied it securely to a stake on the bank. "Well, the grain you bring is finer than that grown by the villeins," she said, raising an eyebrow. "Are you certain you didn't steal it from someone's house? Perceval would have your hand cut off if you were found to be a thief."

Gislebert leapt to his feet and raised his hand. "By all the saints, I swear I do not steal," he answered. "And I give my thanks to you, good lady."

Before she could beg his pardon, he sprinted away through her gate.

"How is she today?" Calhoun asked Gislebert in the orchard. "What does she say? How does she fare?"

Gislebert frowned in annoyance. "She is well. She warned me not to steal grain. She sang while the grain was ground."

"Did she say anything—" Calhoun hesitated and looked toward the ground. "Does she ever speak of me?"

"Nay."

"Does she have other visitors?"

"Many. She does run the mill, and everyone visits her."

"Do people come to talk? Anyone?"

"Her mother has come two or three times in the last week. And Josson."

"Hector's man? For what reason does he visit the mill?"

Gislebert shrugged. "Once he came while I was there, and I barely got away without being seen. But I watched him through the hedge around her house."

"What does he do?" Calhoun snapped, his patience ebbing away.

"He marks in his ledger and watches her grind the grain.

On occasion he helps her lift the heavy bags. He plays with the boy."

"The child?"

"Yes. Ambrose."

Calhoun turned away from Gislebert and pretended to study the branch of an old apple tree. It would not be unusual for Josson to go periodically to check on the running of the mill, but it was highly out of character for the steward's assistant to play with a vassal's child.

Calhoun sighed. "Gislebert, I am so torn!"

"How so?" Gislebert jumped up, swiped an apple from the tree, and wiped it on his tunic. Calhoun saw the blank innocence of childhood on his young friend's face. How could Gislebert understand the burden of a hidden love?

"I love the lady, yet my heart trembles at the thought of speaking to her."

Gislebert bit into the apple and muttered with his mouth full: "This woman is far below the rank of Clarissant, yet you spoke to her."

Calhoun waved his hand helplessly, trying to find the words to explain his feelings. "I did not know Clarissant. This woman knows me like no other."

"You are a brave knight. You can do anything." Gislebert grinned like a little monkey, and if Calhoun hadn't been so tormented, he would have boxed the boy's ears for his impertinence.

TWENTY-ONE

Afton had just finished sweeping the rough stone floor of her hall when she heard hoofbeats. She peered through the door. A knight dismounted at her gate, one clothed in the violet-and-white surcoat of Perceval's garrison.

She took a deep breath and laid her broom aside. Had Josson found some irregularity in her bookkeeping? Or perchance this knight was sent to investigate the killing of the man in her courtyard.

She left Abmbrose to amuse himself on the floor and stepped out into the sunshine of her courtyard. The knight's horse blinked its eyes at her as it stood at her gate, watching as the knight approached and removed his helmet. Her eyes took in the man's strong frame and his confident step, and wandered to his face. Calhoun! She found herself leaning against her door for support.

"Good day to you," he called pleasantly, then he cleared his throat. "I hope you and your child are well."

She shook her head in gentle confusion. What brought him here? "We are well, as you are," she finally answered. "What brings you here?"

"I wish to speak to you, Afton." The sound of her name on his lips made her dizzy, and she fought to keep her voice under control. His voice had deepened, but it still rang with the friendly and familiar tone he had always used with her. It was as if he had only yesterday ridden away to Warwick and had now returned to pick up the heart she had left at his feet.

"Then speak, sir," she answered, more harshly than she intended.

"Mayhap we could sit somewhere?" He motioned toward the door of the house as if he would go into the hall, but Afton couldn't bear to have him stand in the place where Hubert had paraded her as a trophy.

"No . . . the mill house," she suggested, leading the way down the worn path. The babble of the stream seemed to come from far away, and for a moment she was sure she would turn and find him gone, that his approach had been a dream. But his heavy footsteps pounded the earth behind her, his shadow mingled with hers on the path, and the chink of metal from his spurs on the stone floor of the mill house assured her that he was real.

She motioned toward a wooden bench, but Calhoun waited for her to be seated. When she had taken a seat, he sank onto his knees before her. "My heart is too full to begin," he said, his voice husky, his blue eyes searching her face. He reached for her hand, and she gave it in surprise, amazed at his gentleness. How tender his touch was! How could this hand wield a lance and sword?

"I have loved you for years," Calhoun said, pressing her palm to his cheek, "and that love has grown to maturity. I must ask my father for permission to marry, of course, but I will ask him immediately if I know my plans meet with your approval. I cannot bear to see you alone and would put you under my wing, for protection—"

She gasped in dismay and wrenched her hand from his as if snatching it from a hot flame. "You would have me *under your wing?*" Quick, painful memories of Hubert flew through her mind. She had been under a man's "protection" once before. She would never be so used again! "Under your foot, you mean!" she whispered intensely, her eyes blazing. "You say you offer protection? Nay, for power like yours corrupts, Calhoun! It has torn my soul to see you carry a sword—"

She broke off. She could see honest hurt—and offense—

256

in his eyes. He pulled back from her, and the softness left his voice. "Obviously you do not value the mettle of a man who has undergone much to prove himself."

"What have you undergone?" She spat the words contemptuously. "A jousting match or two? Wrestling tournaments? The trials of courtly dancing?" In one fluid motion she stood and turned away from him. "Keep your protection and your fine mettle, sir, for I will not have them thrown over me."

She heard the creaking metal of his armor as he stood behind her. "Your behavior is not like you, Afton. It is quite unmaidenly."

She turned then and laughed at him. "I suppose killing the man in my courtyard was unmaidenly, too, so you had to cover my error. Or did it hurt your pride that I killed him before he attacked me and gave you opportunity for revenge? Is that why you let the sergeant attribute his death to your sword? Did it assuage your pride, noble Calhoun?"

He reached for her shoulders and pulled her to him so tightly that her elbows were pinned against his chest. "No, you little fool, I let them believe the kill was mine to spare you! Do you not know that my father and Hector would do anything to wrest the mill away from you? I talked to the servants, who overheard my father charge Hector to watch you carefully and find you in a fault. They covet your income and your property; that is why Josson comes here to spy upon your weakness. He would seize any excuse to remove you."

"Josson is not a spy!"

"He is!"

"I don't believe you," she whispered angrily, lifting her face to his. As their eyes met, though, her breath caught in her throat. They stood thus, caught in each other's gaze, for what seemed to be endless moments, and then his lips were upon hers. Her fury dissolved as Calhoun claimed the kiss she would have given a thousand times in her youth. She stood transfixed, locked in his embrace, and her reason

257

swirled in a wild cyclonic rush. Hubert had subdued her, but never had his kisses been like this. Never had Hubert's embrace tempted her to surrender, nor had it ever hinted that joy and wonder might be found in submission to the wondrous force that bore down upon her.

A maddening desire for Calhoun raged through her. Emotions she had thought dead quickly sprang back to life. She felt his lips upon her throat, his hands in her hair, and she heard him groan. The sound awakened something vital within her, and she felt her resolve slipping away.

"Mama?" Ambrose's shrill voice outside the mill house was like cold water in her face. Afton frantically shoved Calhoun away, and he fell back, panting, while his bewildered eyes searched hers. She closed her eyes and shuddered. A few moments more, and he would have had her under his control—as Hubert had.

She turned from Calhoun and pointedly wiped her mouth with the back of her sleeve. "Leave my home," she commanded.

"You would send me away?" he rasped, and the pain in his voice tore at her. "I'll not come back if I'm not wanted."

"You're not wanted," she replied, even though the words threatened to catch in her throat as a monstrous lie. Holding desperately to her resolve, she turned and left him in the mill house.

Her hand at her throat, she ran up the path, struggling to hold back the tears that threatened to overtake her, to quell the confusion and contradicting emotions that washed over her. She could not chance surrendering—and thus, losing—herself to Calhoun, and yet she longed for him with a fierceness that threatened to tear her apart. *Oh God!* her heart cried out in despair. *What am I doing? How can I turn away from the one I have loved for so long . . . ?*

She started to turn, to rush back into the mill house, into Calhoun's arms—and then she saw Ambrose wandering on the path, his forehead creased with worry.

Suddenly her confusion was gone. The child was her

love, her life now. Here was the only one to whom she would give herself—the only one she knew would never hurt or betray her. "Don't fret, sweetheart," Afton said, scooping him up into her arms. "Mama was only gone a moment. But I'm here now, and all is well."

Calhoun's heart was heavy, but resigned, as he knocked on his parents' chamber door. When it swung open, he saw Endeline and Perceval at their table, enjoying a quiet supper. "Excuse me," Calhoun said, coming into the room. "But I must ask a boon of thee, my lord."

"What is it?" Perceval asked, smiling at his son.

"My daily routine here chafes on me, Father. Fulk and I would like to join an expedition on the business of Christ in the Holy Land. We would welcome the chance to bring honor and glory to you and our king."

Calhoun saw his parents look at each other, then Perceval cleared his throat. "We will discuss it, my son," he said, "and give you our answer at dinner tomorrow."

"I will eagerly await your decision," Calhoun answered.

Endeline did not know what brought about Calhoun's sudden fervent desire to travel to the Holy Land, but his change in attitude delighted her. It would be good for Perceval's castle to send a contingent on the business of Christ. The king would appreciate Perceval's effort, Calhoun would be away from Margate Castle and whatever haunted him, and perhaps the still unmarried Charles could be goaded by competition into doing something about his calling in life. She did not once consider that her son's life might be in jeopardy. Jerusalem had been held by the Christians for nearly thirty years, and Endeline did not think it possible that Calhoun would be in any real danger from infidels.

At dinner the next day, Perceval stood and held up his hand for attention. When all had quieted, he spoke clearly: "Our beloved son Calhoun has been led of God to journey on the business of Christ to the East. We have granted him our permission, along with any knights in our service who wish to join him on this expedition. You will remember that the pope has promised complete absolution and certain salvation for any who die while engaged in this venture, and we trust that your efforts will continue to keep the Holy City safe from infidels."

Perceval paused and looked out across the tables of knights. "If you would join him, would you please stand now by his side?"

Calhoun dropped his napkin and stood to his feet. The other knights looked at each other, and several dropped their napkins enthusiastically and sprang to their feet. Endeline noticed that Fulk stood slowly and, as he rose, he raised an eyebrow in Calhoun's direction as if he would ask a question. Endeline wondered why the elder knight had hesitated.

The next month was spent in preparation. Fulk led the small contingent of knights in training exercises and cautioned them of the heat they would experience in the harsh deserts. Every night the knights sat around the hearth in the tower and listened to Fulk's tales of the Saracens' bravery and cunning. "They are worthy opponents," he summarized. "He who underestimates them will die."

Calhoun went about his preparation with a sense of resignation. At Warwick he had dreamed of the glory of going into battle for the king, and going into battle for God certainly would bring even greater glory. But the only image in his mind when he closed his eyes at night was that of Afton, her eyes blazing as she pushed him away.

She had changed from the girl he had known into a woman. Calhoun could not deny that he found her infinitely more desirable, but now he also wrestled with her mysterious reluctance to love him. And he had failed in his best attempt to win her.

Very well. It would be better to fight for God in the heat of the desert than to fight against Afton in the cool of England.

Perceval allowed the villeins to come in from the fields to see the knights off on their journey. The parade of knights promised to be splendid, with men and horses alike fully dressed in the best armor Perceval could procure.

Before mounting his horse, Calhoun found Gislebert outside the stable and drew him close. "I charge you," Calhoun whispered roughly, "as long as I live, you must continue to check on her and do what you must to meet her needs. Swear it!"

Gislebert blinked and threw up his hand. "I swear it."

Calhoun released him and gently smoothed the boy's tunic. "Go in peace, my friend. I hope all is well with you."

"You talk as one who rides into death," Gislebert answered as Calhoun swung himself into his saddle. The boy's eyes were wide with fear, and Calhoun knew he thought of the bloody tales from Warwick's campfires. Gislebert gulped. "You will be back."

"Perhaps." Calhoun stood in his stirrups, and Fulk pulled up alongside him. They raised their swords in salute to Perceval as the trumpeters blew a resounding flourish, then the company of knights spurred their horses and rode out of Margate Castle.

The procession of twenty knights traveled slowly along the castle road as the villeins and villagers cheered them on. They paused at the village church for Father Odoric to offer a prayer of blessing for their journey. Then, with drops of holy water cool upon his face, Calhoun directed his company to mount up for the long ride ahead.

He could see the miller's house as they approached the edge of the village, but no one stood in the courtyard to note their passing. Calhoun knew Fulk's somber eyes were upon him as he struggled to keep from frankly staring into the windows of the house, and he made a poor show of nonchalance as they slowly passed. Calhoun laughed loudly and called out to his fellows, but the noise roused no one in the miller's house; no woman appeared, no girl ran out to beg from him a parting word.

Why should she come? he rebuked himself. *She told you to leave. She does not want you.*

Calhoun turned to his companion and teacher. "Fulk, today we undertake ventures at great expense," he said, reciting from a well-worn memory.

"Aye, that we do," Fulk agreed. Fulk held the horses to a slow walk until they had passed the miller's house, then he signaled the riders to spur their mounts and make haste on their journey.

FULK
1126-1130

Like an earring of gold
or an ornament of fine gold
is a wise man's rebuke
to a listening ear.
PROVERBS 25:12, NIV

TWENTY-TWO

Calhoun's company of knights grew with every passing day. Whether they journeyed or rested in a roadside hospice, invariably other travelers were drawn to their formidable company. Though Calhoun would have chosen not to be slowed by so many pilgrims—many of whom traveled on foot—when he heard their earnest entreaties and looked into their faces, he could not refuse them.

In their eyes Calhoun read one of three reasons for their flight—religious fanaticism, unspoken dreams of life in a better place, or naked fear. One of the first to approach him was a dignified nobleman who might have been a contemporary of his father. The reason for his travel from England was apparent in his humble manner and slightly frayed dress. "I would welcome you to my home in return for your kindness," the man told Calhoun, bowing low, "but of late I have been dispossessed. Somehow my actions have displeased the king and my lands seized by another lord. I find I must leave England at once, for I know not how the royal wind blows. . . ."

A group of nuns joined his party at the English coast, the glow of religious devotion burning bright in their eyes. Calhoun wondered if he might find Lienor on such a journey, perhaps on this very road.

Two of the most recent travelers to ask his protection were a free man and his wife, who journeyed to the Holy Land in search of open trade and the hope of prosperity.

The couple traveled with a blonde daughter who reminded Calhoun of Afton. He granted his protection to the concerned father, grimaced at the sight of the daughter (*By all the saints,* he thought, *the girl even laughs as Afton once laughed*), and bore without comment the embarrassment of having the grateful wife kiss the stirrup of his saddle.

In return for his protection, his fellow travelers granted him their loyalty and respect, bowing low and calling him "My lord Calhoun," whenever he happened to come upon them. On the treacherous journey ahead, they would be a small country unto themselves, for in the foreign lands where they would travel, the names of England's lessor lords were not known and loyalty to King Henry would not be honored.

The band of travelers crossed the English channel and rode to Cologne, where they rested for a few days, then progressed to the Danube River, which led them south through Vienna, Budapest, and Belgrade.

After three months on the road, the earl of Margate's contingent to Jerusalem was considerable and well prepared. Calhoun's party continued to grow in strength and number as the journey continued. Knights joined his caravan and pledged their service to Calhoun for a period of forty days once they had reached Jerusalem. A few of these were eager sons of English and French lords, but others were fighting men who had been admonished by war-weary lords to turn their weapons toward the infidel instead of against their fellow countrymen.

"Do not be too companionable with these new knights," Fulk warned Calhoun one evening as they camped under the stars. "Maintain your distance. The rogue knight is usually one who does not easily submit to a master; that is why he is seeking adventure alone or in a small company. Despite their valiant pledge to you, these men are unpredictable in battle."

Calhoun nodded gravely at Fulk's warning, recognizing the truth in the older man's words. The bearded and scarred knights who had lately joined their group seemed coarse, bawdy, and undeniably bloodthirsty. They were not the sons of gentlemen, nor were they familiar with notions of chivalry and gallantry. Many had served in the expedition of Christ before, and having returned to England only to find no use for their swords there, they ventured again to the new frontier and vowed to spend their life's blood in the sands of the Holy Land.

Outside the larger cities, the roads were a gulf of merry chaos. In his impatience, Calhoun would often ride ahead of his own party and scout out a location for them to camp. While he waited for the others, representatives from every imaginable situation passed him on the road. Great lords traveled in caravans with their wives and a full contingent of the necessary serving women, cooks, musicians, scribes, pages, and servants. Priests walked the road to Jerusalem, many of them aged, a few young and impatient.

One afternoon Calhoun watched a group of priests wheel a wealthy elderly patron in a two-wheeled cart over the pocked and rugged road. The priest in front of this caravan recited prayers for the elderly man's health; the priest at the rear prayed just as fervently that the man would die in peace.

Alongside the religious pilgrims and the warriors traveled simple tradespeople who had heard of the glorious and privileged life in Outremer, the four crusader states established by the soldiers of Christ after Jerusalem was retaken. Hope shone in their eyes as they walked in search of a better life than the one they had known on the feudal estates.

"It is a marvelous and laughable sight," Fulk remarked one afternoon as they watched the parade of pilgrims on the road. "These poor men who bear their earthly possessions in a single wagon ask at every walled town if they have reached Jerusalem."

Calhoun only grunted in reply. He understood their reasons for leaving home, but he did not yet understand his own. It was not religious devotion that drove him to Outremer, nor was it the desire for prosperity. Perhaps he was among those motivated by fear, for wasn't he afraid to live in England—near Afton yet unable to have her?

No, he told himself firmly. *I am here to do a knight's job. If in that job I find forgetfulness, then I shall count it as God's blessing.*

It would not, however, be easy to forget. Whenever he saw a solitary woman on the road, his heart leapt, thinking that perhaps for some inexplicable reason Afton had left Margate lands and stood before him, just within arm's reach. But reality invariably descended, and Calhoun realized that Afton would never follow these dream-seekers to Outremer, for she had a child, and property, and every aspect of self-sufficiency. She did not need him, or—what was it she said?—*his protection.* More than that, she did not want him.

There came one moment every night, though, when Calhoun was grateful that Afton was not at his side. For every night as the sun set, Calhoun joined Fulk by the side of the road, each man with his shovel. Laboring together with other knights, they dug graves for children and old people, many of whom died in hospices or simply fell over on the sides of the road. Always on the road there were pilgrims who sat stupidly in a sick daze, too exhausted, hungry, or confused to continue their journey.

No, this was not the life he would have chosen for Afton.

One night, Calhoun sat near the fire, the flames crackling and snapping at his feet. Far in the distance, he heard the tailor's baby crying. As he stuffed the last of the goat cheese into his mouth, Calhoun nodded to Fulk, who stared into the fire. "Are they all bedded and settled?" he asked, wiping his mouth on his sleeve. "The families? And are the knights ringed 'round the camp?"

"They are," Fulk replied, never lifting his eyes from the flames. "You should take your rest, young knight. Tomorrow the sun will climb high and hot."

"I am not tired." Calhoun glanced at the other men

who had camped around his fire. "Be there anyone here who can give us a song? Surely one of you fellows has spent time with a troubadour?"

A tall, lanky knight with a grizzled beard stood and brushed dirt from his tunic. "Aye, good lord," he said, his smile showing a mouthful of blackened teeth. "I served at Lord Edmund's house as troubadour for three years in my youth. I fancy I can still sing a song."

"Sing it, then," Calhoun answered, reclining on his mantle in the sand. "Take our minds from this dust and sand."

The knight cleared his throat and began to sing. His voice was surprisingly sweet and clear, and the sounds of the camp stilled as his words floated through the night in a ballad of love and chivalry.

"'Tis a pity there are no fair maidens in this circle," Fulk remarked dryly when the knight had finished his song. He waved a languid hand at the men gathered around the fire. "I would do much for a fair and soft maiden right now."

The men laughed in appreciation of Fulk's rough observation, then settled back for the night. When all was quiet, Calhoun put out his hand and tugged at Fulk's sleeve.

"What?" Fulk lay on his mantle, his eyes closed.

"Are you asleep?"

"No."

Calhoun paused, rising up on his elbow. "I went to see Afton, you know. Before we left Margate, I declared my love and devotion to her, but she flung my words back in my face."

A log snapped in the stillness, and Fulk opened one eye. "I guessed that it was so."

"I cannot understand why she turned me away, Fulk. She loved me once, I know it. I loved her, as a boy, and when I return with a man's love for her, she will not have it. Can it be that she loves her husband and son too much to leave room in her heart for me?"

Fulk snorted. "I have known little of women, Calhoun, but I know your lady Afton bore no love for the miller. Her son she loves, truly. And the day of your dubbing, I saw her face alight with love for you, but fear and trouble clouded her eyes."

"She need not fear for me," Calhoun answered, waving his hand. "I can handle myself."

"I do not think she fears *for* you," Fulk answered, both eyes open now. He scanned Calhoun's face with an impenetrable gaze. Calhoun looked away and studied the stars above him. Surely Fulk did not mean Afton was afraid *of* him! Though he wore a sword and carried a lance, he would never do anything to hurt her!

"They say," Fulk spoke in a low voice, his eyes closed again, "that God sends to each of us one refining moment of painful experience, in which we see with the sight of God. In this moment we look either outward and see the world anew, or we look inward and see ourselves as we really are. I think your lady has been through such an experience, Calhoun, and she does not see the world as she did long ago. Even you are different in her eyes."

Calhoun snorted in impatience. "Have we not all suffered? Were the trials I endured at Warwick merely for sport?"

Fulk waved his hand as if brushing away Calhoun's protest. "God has been merciful to you, young knight, for you have not yet suffered. When you do, perchance you will see the world in which your lady dwells. Perhaps then you will find each other."

"And if we do not?"

Fulk shrugged. "If your eyes are turned inward, young knight, as mine were, you will see yourself. Then you will be alone as I am, with your faults and your fate."

Calhoun picked up a stick and stirred the fire impatiently. How like Fulk to wax philosophical after hearing the young man's deepest secret! Calhoun could not find one bit of help or comfort in his words.

"You continually upbraid me for my faults," Calhoun remarked to his teacher. "I know my left hand is weak, for so you have proved to me time and again. But I keep waiting for you to explain where my other faults lie, for I would banish them as easily as I vanquished my foes at Warwick. Where, noble Fulk, am I remiss?"

His only answer was Fulk's gentle snoring.

Calhoun had first noticed the knights in white tunics with bold red crosses on them at Belgrade. A company of the uniformed knights stood in a single line outside the city, and he felt their sharp eyes on his company as he approached.

A husky knight held up his hand as they drew near, and Calhoun signaled his company to halt. "We do not recognize your colors or ensign," the knight said, his words heavy with a French accent. "From where do you come and what is your destination?"

Fulk shifted in his saddle, but Calhoun put his hand out and took control, as was his right. "We bear the colors of Perceval, earl of Margate, servant to King Henry of England," he said. "We seek service in the Holy Land, to honor God and our king."

The knight nodded without expression. "We are ze holy Knights Templar," he answered, "perpetually vowed to aid ze peace of pilgrims on ze holy road and fight those who would disturb zat peace. I am called Reynard."

"I am Calhoun, son of the earl of Margate," Calhoun answered. "Perhaps we will be able to wield our swords to preserve the same peace. I come with thirty dedicated knights and a host of people who wish safe passage to Jerusalem."

"So I see." Reynard did not smile, but his eyes gleamed in approval. "We will offer you safe journey to Jerusalem. The Saracens will be at our backs as soon as we reach Constantinople, and ze larger our company, ze greater our chance for survival."

"We welcome your company," Calhoun answered, nodding. "And now we would seek our rest for the night."

They camped outside of the walls of Belgrade. The place had an exotic air of intrigue about it. Calhoun breathed deeply—the very atmosphere tasted different here: hot, dry, and scorching, even in the dark of night.

He hesitantly approached a group of knights seated around a fire. They were all older than he and more seasoned in battle, and for the first time he felt uncomfortably aware of his youth and his titled position. The men parted wordlessly for him, leaving him a seat by the fire, and he crouched in the dirt without saying a word.

Garwood, a gray-haired knight who had joined them in Vienna, squatted nearby, lazily poking at the burning coals with a green branch, and began to tell a tale. "I was one of those who first took Jerusalem," he said, his eyes shining in the firelight. "I have not seen a sight like it in the twenty-seven years since."

"Tell us," another knight spoke up. Calhoun recognized Parnell, a young French knight who had joined them in Budapest. "I have never met anyone who was there on that fateful day."

A strong emotion crossed Garwood's face, and Calhoun could not tell what it was. Pride? Sorrow? Regret? All three?

"Forty thousand defended the city," Garwood said, stirring the fire. "For days they hurled hot oil, stones, arrows, and Greek fire at us. Our priests led us to fast for three days, then we walked around the city, hoping the walls would fall down."

His eyes grew dark. "They did not. While the infidels in the Holy City jeered at us from the walls, we positioned three siege towers on Mount Zion. Fire and a rain of arrows fell upon us, but we pushed the towers against the wall and the next morning, the tower manned by Godfrey de Bouillon breached the wall.

"We tore into the city, which was rightfully won. We dragged men, women, and children from their homes and killed them even as they cried for mercy. Many people swallowed their gold and jewels, and once we realized this, the corpses of the infidels were slit open to retrieve the treasure, for it had been promised to us.

"Every street and alley ran red, and in some places the blood flowed so high it washed over our ankles. We were free to claim houses for ourselves, and I placed my shield on the door of a small house just outside what was known as the Temple Mount."

Garwood's eyes closed and he shook his head slowly. "But it was impossible to look upon the vast number of slain without horror." His voice quivered as he spoke. "Everywhere lay the fragments of human bodies, and yet it was not the spectacle of the headless bodies strewn in all directions that roused horror in us at the end of the day—it was the sight of ourselves, the victors, who stood dripping with blood from head to foot—" Garwood broke off, his voice choked with emotion.

Not a knight dared interrupt, and there was only silence for a few moments. When he had gained control of himself, Garwood spoke briskly: "We put it behind us. The few we had allowed to live as prisoners were made to clean the streets and burn the bodies. We dressed in fresh clothing and walked barefoot in reverence to the Holy Sepulchre, where we prostrated ourselves upon the ground and thanked God for our victory."

He paused and stirred the fire again. "In the end, I could not stay. I left my house and returned to my lord's castle in England and served him faithfully until last year, when he died. Now I seek to go back and see what has become of the land bought at so great a price."

"May it be a land full of the mercy of God," Calhoun spoke from his heart. "For surely we have brought the light of God to the land."

"If we have not, we shall!" Parnell said, striking his breast. "By all the saints, we shall!"

Garwood looked down into the fire again. "I can only hope the land is better now than when I left it," he answered. "For in that bloody time, the light of God was eclipsed by the swords we wielded in his name."

Twenty-Three

Hildegard tried to keep the frown from her face as she folded the bishop's letter. She had been instructed to open the hostelry of the convent to a Lady Harriette, who requested refuge from Normandy. Lord Rainger, wrote the bishop, had died, and his brother had inherited the estate. The widowed Lady Harriette sought shelter within the confines of a nunnery, not to take vows, but to find a place of refuge from a hostile brother-in-law.

Hildegard knew she had no choice but to welcome the lady, who would doubtless come with an entourage of ladies-in-waiting and servants. Her own nuns would be hard-pressed to care for these women, and Hildegard knew full well how the inclusion of women of the world affected women of the convent. She pursed her lips and began to write a letter in return.

A tap on her door interrupted her thoughts, and Hildegard smiled, momentarily forgetting her troubles with the bishop. Only Agnelet tapped so gently, and Hildegard lightened her voice: "Come in, dear."

The little girl glided into the room with the motionless step of the nuns. She wore a white tunic and white veil, cut exactly like the nuns' black habits. Hildegard thought black was not appropriate for a young girl. Such things should be reserved for the time when a child had recognized the presence of evil in the world and, thank God, Agnelet, at four, had not yet seen it.

"Madame Hildegard," Agnelet spoke clearly and distinctly, her eyes cast down at the ground, "our sister the sacristan wishes to know if the chapel should be dusted today or tomorrow."

"Tomorrow will do," Hildegard said, smothering the smile that wanted to creep onto her lips. "Is there anything else, Agnelet?"

"Madame Luna wishes to know if she has your permission to give five loaves to the poor today."

"She does."

Agnelet walked to Hildegard's side and removed her dainty hands from beneath the short cape that served as her scapular. She climbed into Hildegard's lap with the natural abandon of any four-year-old, then turned her dark eyes toward the abbess. With her tiny thumb she traced the sign of the cross on the band of cloth that covered Hildegard's forehead, then sighed. "Grace and peace be unto you, Madame," she said, snuggling against Hildegard.

Hildegard did not answer, but hugged the little girl tightly. *For the child's sake,* she told her strict conscience, *not for personal pleasure or fulfillment.*

Thus received, Agnelet struggled out of the nun's grasp and skipped out the door. Hildegard stared after her for a moment, then pursed her lips again and picked up her pen to write the bishop.

When Lady Harriette finally arrived with her retinue, Hildegard burned with secret anger, for she had discovered the situation was not at all as the bishop had described it. Lady Harriette was indeed the widow of Rainger, but that noble lord had died ten years earlier. She was not choosing sanctuary in an English convent to escape a brother-in-law; rather, she was obeying the wishes of King Henry, who had made the noble lady of Normandy his mistress.

Hildegard fasted for three days to cleanse her soul of the bitter anger that threatened to poison her. *Perhaps the bishop himself did not know the full extent of the situation,* she surmised, *and it is not my place to judge, for Christ loved the woman caught in adultery, did he not?*

Still, she resented having to give shelter to the women from Normandy. These worldly women were not allowed in the nuns' private cloister, nor did they eat with the nuns. Even so, they were free to use the chapel, the very heart of the convent. The sounds of their revelry in music and dance carried over even as the nuns recited their daily offices and prayers and, for the first time, Hildegard felt that the world had entered mightily into the convent she guarded.

"The three Ds," she muttered one day as a lady's maid dashed through the back of the chapel, gleefully chasing an escaped pet. "Dances, dresses, and dogs. They are all of the devil."

The ladies had brought plenty of all three with them. Hildegard noticed without pleasure that her nuns had already fallen prey to the rather womanly tendency to ape whatever was fashionable. More than one nun had already raised the headband that was supposed to come down to the eyebrows, because the ladies from Normandy had high, wide foreheads. *Of what value is it for us to live in a mirror-less world when my nuns gaze daily at women of the world?* Hildegard fretted in prayer. *Viewing these women feeds vanity more than any mirror.*

In recreation, Madame Ula had actually suggested that they wear tunics of a "more soothing color . . . blue, per-haps?" and Luna asked for permission to keep a puppy in the cloister.

"We are here for one purpose," Hildegard reminded her nuns. "To raise prayers and praise to God on behalf of our-selves and the people we serve. We are not called to be fash-ionable or in the world, but we have left it and its pleasure behind." She cast reproving eyes upon Luna. "We do not keep pets."

Ula raised her eyes from her sewing. "The ladies, Madame Abbess, have asked why we keep the child Agnelet. One asked if she was our pet."

Hildegard took a deep breath. "Agnelet is a child of God," she answered smoothly. "And just as Saint Agnes dedicated herself to Christ, so we have dedicated Agnelet. She is certainly not a pet."

"That is how I replied," Ula answered, not looking up from her work.

"And from this day on," Hildegard said, as if she had been considering the matter for some time, when in fact, she had just made the decision, "let Agnelet be kept from the women in the hostelry. She shall be as one of us, confined to the cloister."

A bell rang at the convent gate, and a young novice hurried to answer the summons. When she returned, her arms were burdened with two turkeys, which Hildegard noted and motioned for the novice to send to the kitchen.

Hildegard kept her face smooth and expressionless as she continued to work, but her thoughts were troubled. Such gifts had been coming regularly since Lady Harriette's installation at the nunnery, and Hildegard worried that accepting them violated her vows of poverty and obedience. She knew, of course, that the food and other gifts were compensation from the king for accepting his mistress, and she grudgingly received them, for the year had been hard and the tithes and offerings of the villagers had been few. A drought had hurt all the villagers, and the nuns' own garden had yielded little to augment their store of provisions.

Though it rankled her soul to receive these gifts, Father Odoric had told her to quiet her fears and receive them as the provision of God himself. So Hildegard bore all in silence.

She did, however, unburden her heart to the bishop when he came for his regular visit to oversee the operation of the nunnery. During these annual visits, each nun sat with the bishop in private and made complaints not allowed in the fabric of everyday life. Hildegard relished the occasion and complained freely about Lady Harriette and the worldly pleasures she brought into the cloister.

"Her ladies wear gowns with low necks and costly furs," Hildegard said in a calm voice as the bishop's scribe recorded every word. "They procure dogs, monkeys, rabbits, and birds, all of which too often escape into the chapel and distract our worship. Moreover, the reason that she is here concerns me most. The church supports the holy institution of marriage, and yet this woman is not the king's wife. And she is quite proud of her calling as his mistress."

The bishop pressed his lips together and laid his finger upon his nose as if he were thinking. Madame Hildegard waved her hands. "Apart from this situation, all is well here. We strive to remember that we are dead to the world and alive to God. We seek in all things to give him praise and prayer."

The bishop paused until he was sure she had finished speaking, then he folded his arms. "I have spoken to each of your nuns, Madame, and find that the more mature nuns share your concerns. They, too, worry about the worldliness of your paying visitors, and have prayed that God would send a messenger to call Lady Harriette and her retinue away."

His hand circled the crucifix that hung from his neck. "But, Madame Hildegard, is it possible God has sent Lady Harriette to you as an exercise in the heavenly virtues of patience, forbearance, and true charity? Might you lead these women by your virtuous and holy example? Who knows but that they will amend their ways and even consider a vocation of the religious life as a result of their stay here."

Hildegard controlled the muscles in her face so the bishop would not see how her heart rebelled at his words. She had tried to show charity. Indeed, had she not borne their foolishness with a serene and gracious air as her Holy Rule demanded?

The bishop leaned forward and lowered his voice so that his scribe would not hear. "We are not in a position to give affront to the king. He has recently levied a scutage against the clergy in England, and this new taxation is being appealed even now. If we protest his actions on so personal a matter, he might see fit to raise our rate of taxation."

The bishop leaned back and resumed speaking normally, and Hildegard knew the matter was closed. She would be hostess to Henry's mistress for as long as the king saw fit.

"Your sisters also speak of your harshness," the bishop went on. "Two or three described your nature as 'scolding.'"

"I rebuke them when necessary," Hildegard said, stiffening in her chair.

"Another sister mentioned the appearance of favoritism. She said you bear an obvious love for the child called Agnelet."

The river of emotion in Hildegard's heart burst its strict boundary; tears sprang to her eyes. How could it be? She had made every effort to assign Agnelet's care to several nuns, and she had forcibly stifled every maternal instinct that threatened to elevate her love for the child above love for Christ.

"I love her, as do we all," Hildegard said, her voice quivering. "I love all the souls placed within my care with the tender love of Christ."

"What is to be done with the child?" the bishop asked, his dark eyes piercing Hildegard's calm. "What place does a four-year-old child have in a nunnery? More than that," the bishop went on delicately, "she has no father to give her a dowry and, whether she is married to a man or to Christ, what bride goes empty-handed to her marriage feast?"

Hildegard folded her hands beneath her scapular and knotted them into fists. "She may reside in the nunnery as a servant and a companion to the nuns. She is most useful and will grow to be even more so."

"Can you not return her to some family in the village?"

"No." Hildegard shook her head resolutely. "The mark on Agnelet's face would invite speculation and fear. Father Odoric agrees with me: to send Agnelet to the village would be a mistake."

279

The bishop nodded slowly and brought his hands together as if for prayer. "Then I shall abide by your wisdom. On my next visit here, we shall see what good or evil has come of this decision, and we pray that only good will come from it."

He traced the sign of the cross in the air before her, and Hildegard breathed a gentle sigh of relief.

Madame Lienor was chosen to serve as Hildegard's chaplain for the coming year and, though she still did not speak, Hildegard found the girl to be thorough, well-educated, and an excellent worker. One afternoon, after dictating several letters, Hildegard paused and looked carefully at the young nun who assisted her. Maturity had been kind to Lienor. Her skin sparkled clear and smooth, her spare figure complimented her height, and her manners had been refined by the austere training of the Holy Rule. She had full black brows that spoke eloquently in place of her words, and her forehead, Hildegard noted with approval, was modestly concealed by the veil and headbands she had never attempted to raise.

"I read an interesting comment from a fellow nun the other day," Hildegard remarked, picking up a letter from the abbess at a neighboring convent. "I'd like to know your opinion, Madame Lienor."

Lienor looked up from her parchment, her eyes eager and trusting. Hildegard smoothed the letter on her desk and read: "Anyone who has received the gift of knowledge and eloquence from God should not remain silent or conceal it willingly."

Hildegard glanced quickly at Lienor's face, which had fallen.

"Do you agree that knowledge from God should be shared?" Hildegard asked.

Lienor did not look up, but nodded hesitantly.

"I have asked you before, Lienor, but I will ask again. Do you have some knowledge from God about the child

Agnelet who has been with us all these years? I have often read something in your eyes, some knowledge you possess but are not free to reveal. Could you reveal it now?"

Lienor shook her head, then reached for a quill pen on the desk. On the parchment in front of her she scratched a message and pushed the paper toward the abbess. Hildegard glanced at the page and read aloud: "Who is to say whether the knowledge we possess is from God?"

Hildegard nodded slowly, the nun in her overruling the curious imp in her brain that demanded to know more. "Who, indeed?" she answered. She folded her hands under her sleeves. "When you feel at liberty to disclose this knowledge, I trust you will," she answered gently. "Until then, daughter, I will trust your judgment."

TWENTY-FOUR

Calhoun breathed a sigh of relief. They had reached Antioch, the northernmost outpost of Outremer, and in a few
days they would be in the sacred city of Jerusalem. Now, at
last, they were safe within a city controlled by Frankish
Christians, not by the dark-skinned Saracens whom Calhoun
had not learned to trust.

No house or hostelry in Antioch would take so large a
company, so Calhoun's contingent pitched camp in an open
field. Calhoun directed the knights to posts around the
camp, aware that Fulk carefully inspected his management.
"Do you think this a good arrangement?" he asked Fulk privately when the other knights had gone. "I know nothing of
this land or its people, and I shall defer to your judgment, if
necessary."

A corner of Fulk's mouth dipped in a wry smile, and Calhoun felt slightly offended. "I am not so proud as to be foolish," he added. "Have I not listened to the good advice of
Reynard of the Knights Templar?"

"You amuse me, my young friend," Fulk answered, his
teeth gleaming in a dark smile. "You find pride even in your
humility!" Fulk gathered his belongings and moved toward
the outskirts of camp. He waved the back of his hand in Calhoun's direction. "Good night, my lord. Sleep well in Outremer."

The wish went unfulfilled, for Calhoun had not slept
well since they had left Constantinople. The night air bit

into his lungs, waking him with dry coughing attacks, and even the creatures in the sand on which he slept were sharp and venomous. Twice Calhoun had wakened in the night to find horrible spiders on him—*tarrents,* Reynard called them, terrible creatures that wounded a man and tortured him with pain. The desert sands sheltered other detestable creatures, all of which inflicted pain-filled stings: small, scaly reptiles that crawled out at night and stunned innocent men as they lay on the ground. No, Calhoun did not sleep well in the desert sands of Outremer.

As if the pests were not enough, disease also had plagued the knight and his company since they had left Constantinople. At a small outpost outside that city, several families had eaten eels from a small stream and had become terribly sick. Within days the flesh on their legs dried up and their skin seemed to grow black spots. "Leave them behind," Fulk told Calhoun, his eyes hard. "They will not survive the month."

It had been difficult to leave the affected families behind and, for miles afterward, Calhoun had the impression that their eyes followed him on the road. More than once, the skin on the back of his neck prickled as if he were being watched by a number of eyes from close by. Once he *knew* he was being watched from behind a great dune, and he spurred his mighty war-horse and charged over the sand only to find a solitary dark-skinned bedouin there, a skinny lamb over his shoulders. Calhoun nodded sheepishly at the man and turned back to his company.

Yet the feeling did not leave him at night. Though the fire raged in the center of camp and thirty valiant knights surrounded the edges of their circle, still Calhoun felt as though the stars themselves watched him. And waited.

He had just saddled his horse the next morning when Reynard rode up beside him. "We are short one knight today," Reynard announced, his eyes glancing warily at the sand dunes that surrounded them. "Saracens came into camp last night. Parnell's body rests on his carpet, but the Saracens have his head zis morning."

Calhoun felt his empty stomach heave, and he hid his face against the strong shoulder of his horse. When his stomach and nerves had quieted, he looked into Reynard's impassive eyes. "Is there anything to do?" he asked.

"We bury ze body, of course, or ze cannibal Saracens will return for it," Reynard said, turning his horse. "I will handle ze rites of ze church. We will be free to proceed in an hour."

Reynard disappeared in a cloud of dust, and Calhoun squinted around the circle of their camp, trying to remember at which point the eager young Parnell had slept. Was it northward or eastward? From where had the enemy come?

A heavy hand clasped his shoulder, and Calhoun whirled around, drawing his dagger instinctively. Fulk leaned back and raised an eyebrow at the sight of it. "Easy," he cautioned. "We cannot kill each other in our haste to rid ourselves of the enemy."

"How cowardly is this enemy, who kills under cover of night?" Calhoun whispered, watching the sand dunes around them. "He attacks a sleeping knight without warning or the challenge to a fair fight?"

"The days of fair fighting are past," Fulk replied, stooping to gather the remainder of Calhoun's belongings. "Now we are dealing with a bitter and conquered people who seek their lands and their honor. You forget, my friend, that we showed little honor or mercy when Jerusalem was captured, and we ask too much if we expect those virtues now from those we once conquered."

Calhoun frowned as he mounted his horse. "I care nothing about the past," he muttered. "My duty is to do right in the present."

Three others of Calhoun's company died before they reached Jerusalem, but none at the hands of the Saracens. One woman died in childbirth, moaning piteously for hours and then dying with the babe still unborn. Calhoun observed the spectacle with open and immodest curiosity. Had Afton undergone such pain? Was this the experience of suffering that had changed her so resolutely? Rather than finding any insight, though, his unanswered questions left him feeling confused and strangely disquieted.

Next the desert itself claimed two lives: first was a two-year-old boy who somehow stumbled into a nest of tarrents. Though Fulk ran to lift the boy's swollen body out of the nest, he continued to struggle for breath. Death followed soon after. Second, the desert sun claimed the life of an older man, who collapsed in the heat and died beside the road to Jerusalem.

Fulk, Calhoun, and Reynard buried the dead on the side of the road as quickly as possible, for the extreme heat made it impractical to transport anything more than life's necessities. And with each hurried ceremony, Calhoun struggled anew to understand what God's purpose could be in bringing him to such a barbarous land and people.

When they entered the walls of Jerusalem at last, the common people in their band fell to their faces in the dust and lifted their hands in rejoicing. Reynard and his Knights Templar reverently crossed themselves, and Calhoun repeated the action in gratitude and thanksgiving. Fulk alone sat unmoved upon his horse.

"*Allons, mes frères!* You and your knights may come weeth me," Reynard called to Calhoun, after the initial celebration. "I will show you a place where you can rest and drink. Zen we will discuss your plans."

Fulk nodded in agreement, and Calhoun nudged his horse to follow Reynard through the streets. How different Jerusalem was! It bore little resemblance to either the dry desert or cool, forested England! The houses sparkled bright in the sun like gleaming jewels, and through open doors Calhoun spied brightly patterned mosaic tiles covering walls and floors. The air was filled with the scent of spicy foods roasting on open braziers; women in gauzy veils lowered their eyes demurely while murmuring explicit invitations as he passed. Everywhere the evidence of wealth abounded: merchants and lords alike were adorned with gleaming bracelets of gold and silver and copper, all jangling together in a glorious witness of excessive wealth and prosperity.

Reynard took Calhoun and his men to a large house where a dark-skinned man bowed and greeted them. "Zis is Khalil," Reynard said, grasping the man's hand firmly. "He is a friend. Khalil, please attend to my companions. I will return for zem shortly."

Khalil clapped his hands and three black servants appeared to take their horses. Calhoun could not resist staring—he had seen the dark-skinned Saracens throughout the journey, but he had never seen a black person before.

Fulk caught Calhoun's stare. "Negroes," he explained quietly. "Slaves, probably purchased from Venetian shipmen."

The house of Khalil was unlike anything Calhoun had ever seen. Brightness and color gleamed from every surface; even the ceilings were painted with elaborate frescoes. Khalil motioned toward pillows and divans luxuriously stuffed with fine down, and Calhoun sank into their softness, sighing at the unexpected comfort.

The serving girls whom Khalil summoned to bring trays of pastries and preserved fruit wore no veils, and Calhoun was fascinated by their dark and enormous eyes. Their cheeks seemed to be continually flushed with secret emotion, and their lips were as slender threads of scarlet.

Fulk watched Calhoun with amusement and, when the girls had gone, he offered a one-word explanation: "Cosmetics."

Calhoun took a bite of a tantalizingly sweet pastry spread with almond paste. "Fulk, I thought Jerusalem an uncivilized place," he muttered as he chewed. "But no wonder they call it the Holy City. Surely this is like heaven!"

"This area is rich in things of the world," Fulk said, looking around. "Oil and wine flow from Sicily, honey from Corsica, and a wealth of treasures from other ports. But the land also abounds in the dangers of the world."

"With such rewards, I'll risk the dangers," Calhoun exclaimed, reaching for another pastry.

After Calhoun and his men had eaten their fill of the finest food Calhoun could remember, they bathed and donned cool silk robes. Calhoun felt almost naked without his heavy hauberk and somehow embarrassed at his lack of proper clothing. Without a word, Fulk handed him a hooded cloak of light wool. "This is a burnous," he said simply, slipping his own cloak over his head. "In the heat of the city you'll be glad to leave your armor behind."

When Reynard joined Calhoun and his knights later that afternoon, he offered each of them a white tunic emblazoned with a blue cross: the uniform of the knight on the business of Christ. "Ze tunic is much cooler to wear in ze desert sun," he explained, "and ze people know what ze insignia means. Of course, it is our hope that many of you will exchange ze blue cross for ze red cross of the Templars and join our Order."

Calhoun looked up from his robe as Reynard finished speaking. The invitation—and Reynard's glance—seemed to be pointed particularly at him.

"In time, my friend, God may call all of us to your vocation," Calhoun replied, placing the tunic on a bench with his armor. "But let us test ourselves for several months to see how we handle the Lord's work in Jerusalem. Then we will know if we be fit for the red cross of the Templars."

Calhoun turned back in time to see Fulk watching him, a curious expression on his face—almost like that of a cat watching a mouse. Calhoun raised an eyebrow as though asking "What?" but Fulk replied with only his sardonic half-smile and turned away.

Life in Outremer was both more and less than Calhoun had imagined. He had expected—and found—a land filled with barbarians. What he had not expected was Jerusalem's advanced level of civilization. Water flowed freely, despite the surrounding desert: cool water from underground springs splashed in public fountains and in many fabulous private homes. The ancient Roman sewers in Jerusalem still worked with amazing efficiency, and baths were an everyday luxury.

Calhoun could hardly believe his ears when Khalil's maid asked for his tunic at the end of the day. "You want what?" he asked, clutching his tunic to him.

"Give it to her," Fulk answered, jerking his head toward the door. "She will wash it for you."

"Wash it?" In England, where clothing consisted of woolen tunics and heavy fur-lined cloaks, the idea of submersing a garment was inconceivable. Of course, Calhoun's mother had often wiped away stains with verjuice or vinegar—but was it not mad to completely wash a garment after only one wearing?

He handed the silk tunic to the girl, thankful that at least she did not want to wash his burnous. These people in the land of bright sun were altogether obsessed with cleanliness.

They were also obsessed with open spaces. Calhoun felt a curious lack of privacy in the room he shared with Fulk, for a large open window looked down into the street. From the window Calhoun could see over the city and into the foothills of the mountains outside Jerusalem. Olive trees bent in the wind, and the same breeze that bowed them touched his cheek. What a change from the narrow, shuttered windows of the castle at Margate!

Here laurels and vines over brightly-colored awnings protected doors and windows from the hot midday sun. The houses stood close together in rows throughout the city, but each house had its own tiny courtyard covered with red cloth to keep the hot sun away. The heavy scent of sheep and goats permeated even the grandest houses and, to counter the smell, incense burned in every home, leaving the spicy sweet odors of sandalwood, musk, and pungent herbs to greet Calhoun everywhere he went.

At the end of the day, Calhoun and his company of knights sat at dinner with Khalil and Reynard. "Each lord does as he pleases here in ze kingdom of Jerusalem," Reynard explained as he peeled a sweet onion. "Though many have claimed to be king here, ultimately we owe our allegiance only to ze Holy Father in Rome."

Calhoun nodded, mesmerized by the delightful variety and abundance of the food that passed before him. Reynard smiled and waited for Calhoun to select his dinner, then he leaned across the table. "Why, young Calhoun, do you come to Outremer?"

Calhoun had a ready answer, for often on the journey he had asked himself the same question. "We come to help fight in the cause of our Lord," he said, peeling the skin from an unusual fruit.

Reynard nodded. "And how long did you intend to stay 'ere in Outremer? Is zere some obligation zat will draw you back to England in time?"

The image of Afton passed unbidden before Calhoun's mind, and he closed his eyes to wish her away. She did not need or want him.

"I have no further obligations," Calhoun finally answered steadily, meeting Reynard's penetrating eyes. "My brother is heir to the family estate, and my sister has taken the veil."

Reynard's eyes still did not waver. "No others?" he asked, prodding gently into Calhoun's soul. "Is zere no one else in England who waits for you?"

"No one," Calhoun muttered, his temper beginning to rise.

Reynard smiled. "*Bon.* Zen perhaps you will consider taking ze vow of a Templar," he said, lifting a bunch of grapes from the passing platter. "We vow ourselves to poverty and austerity in ze defense of God's pilgrims. We are warriors all, as you are, and many of our Order are from noble families."

289

"Such a vow would reduce your life to nothingness," Fulk interrupted, setting his cup down on the table. "Did your mother give you life so that you could spend it here among the heathen? Did I train you only to have you vow service to a vengeful God who demands the spilling of blood?"

Calhoun glanced sharply at Fulk, whose eyes gleamed darkly at Reynard. "Careful, Fulk," he began, "Our companion Reynard does not spill blood, he defends innocent pilgrims who are en route to the Holy Land. He is a knight, as are we."

"My God is not vengeful," Reynard answered, gazing steadily at Fulk. "And I took my vow of perpetuity only after serious consideration. I shall defend ze pilgrims of God, and no man shall pay for my life. If captured, I will take my own life rather than cause my brothers to ransom me. In battle, I will defend the people of God, but no Saracen need fear violence from me if he is peaceable."

"Yet your God has exacted everything from you and given you nothing!" Fulk answered, his voice grating roughly across the dinner table. "Your life, the children you might have had, the women you might have loved—"

"Nothing is too great a sacrifice for his service," Reynard answered smoothly. "I do not spend my days counting—or regretting—what might have been."

Calhoun looked from Fulk to Reynard, the one man's face dark and distrustful, the other's shining with unassuming honesty. Calhoun clasped his hands on the table in front of him. "I, too, resolve not to count the things that might have been," he said, nodding to Reynard. He looked toward Fulk with an easy smile. "And I shall not give my life to the church until I have tested my ability to assume such a vocation. I must see how God honors my efforts in Outremer. Then I will be better able to hear his voice if he calls me to a lifetime vocation."

"Zat is well spoken, *mon frère*," Reynard answered. He bowed to Khalil. "Let zese knights rest for a week within your gracious home, Khalil, zen I shall return to see if zey wish to join us on an expedition. If zey have any need, please let me know."

Khalil rose in respect to Reynard, who took his leave. Calhoun rested his elbows on the table in thoughtful consideration. Becoming a Knight Templar would more than fulfill his family's aspirations, for long ago they had instructed him that his way lay as either a man of God or a man of the sword. A Knight Templar was both.

His glance wandered across the table to where Fulk ate in silence while the other men jostled and joked around him. Fulk's outburst to Reynard was unusual, but Fulk was strangely irreligious. Calhoun stood up, his wooden stool scraping back across the floor.

Do not regret what might have been. Those had been Reynard's words, and Calhoun thought he could also abide by them. He might have had a life at home with Afton, serving his father and growing old as a father of sons himself . . . but what might have been no longer mattered. He stood now as a knight of Outremer in the service of God.

In the week that followed, Calhoun learned much from Khalil. The child of European parents, Khalil was born on a pilgrimage to Jerusalem and remained there when his parents died. "Khalil" was the first Arabic word his parents had learned, for it meant "friend," and the man had made it his personal goal to befriend the Saracens who now worked as tradespeople inside the city.

"Outside the city, war still rages," Khalil said over supper one evening as Calhoun and Fulk joined him on the covered terrace. "So, too, war continues inside the city, but in subtle ways."

"What do you mean?" Calhoun asked.

"The Assassins," Khalil whispered, looking around him with wide eyes. "They are a secret society sworn to kill the enemies of Muhammadanism."

"Why doesn't someone confront these people and destroy them?" Calhoun demanded.

Khalil smiled. "They are ghosts. No one knows where they meet or who they are. The beggar sleeping on the corner of the road might be hiding a dagger meant for your heart; the loyal servant who daily pours your wine might one day add the poison that will strike you down."

"Such actions are cowardly!" Calhoun ranted, the image of Parnell's headless corpse flitting through his memory. "What sort of coward does not confront his enemy?"

"A terribly clever one," Khalil answered. "And, in truth, my friend, they are not cowards. They will die in the commission of their sworn duty, if necessary, and will kill themselves should they fail. You may have noticed that I have no Muslim servants. I will buy from them, sell to them, and befriend them. But I will not have a Muslim working in my house. I simply do not trust them."

Khalil explained that the Muslims were divided amongst themselves, and that the Sunni Muslims believed the Frankish armies of the first expedition of God had been summoned by a rival Muslim group to destroy them. "It was a sad day when the Sunni Muslims realized the Franks had come to stay," Khalil said, sipping from a silver goblet. "And for years the warring factions of Muslims have been trying to put aside their differences for a *jihad*, a holy war against the infidels."

"The 'infidels'?" Calhoun asked. "But the heathen who have desecrated the Holy City are the infidels!"

Khalil shook his head. "You forget that Jerusalem is a most holy city for the Muslims, too. It is said that Muhammad was awakened by the angel Gabriel in Mecca and advised that he was to take a night journey to paradise. To prepare for the trip, Gabriel slit Muhammad's body open, removed and cleansed his heart, and, when it was returned to him, it was filled with faith and wisdom. Muhammad then mounted a magic mare which had a woman's face, a mule's body, and a peacock's tail. Accompanied by Gabriel, Muhammad was at the 'fartherest place' in a heartbeat."

"What is this 'fartherest place'?" Fulk muttered.

"Jerusalem," Khalil answered. "Though certainly Muhammad never visited here in the flesh, it is said he visited in spirit. He tethered his magic mare at the wailing wall, then went up to the Temple Mount. There he discovered the rock of Abraham's sacrifice and a ladder of light that led to paradise. This he climbed, meeting Abraham, Jesus, Moses, and Noah on the ladder. At the top of the ladder Muhammad saw Allah unmasked."

"Nonsense!" Calhoun snorted. "This is a crazy tale."

"It grows more interesting," Khalil answered. "Allah told Muhammad he wanted his subjects to pray to him thirty-five times a day, but Muhammad talked the deity into a more practical five-times-a-day ritual. After being filled with the wisdom of Solomon, Muhammad climbed down the ladder and rode back home to Mecca."

"I suppose there is a monument on the place now," Fulk remarked dryly.

"But of course," Khalil said, a sly smile lighting his eyes. "The Most Noble Sanctuary. The Knights Templar use it as their headquarters, and the Muslims would love to see their most holy place cleared of all Christian infidels. There is a regent in the north now, a man named Zengi, who is said to be amassing an army for this purpose."

"Why do we not ride out and stop him?" Calhoun asked, his eyes blazing.

Khalil shrugged. "Before Zengi, there was another. After Zengi, there will come yet another. The Saracens are always massing, always attempting to wage war. While they do prompt a man to sleep with his dagger at his side, they have not posed a severe threat."

Calhoun pondered the man's words, then nodded. Though Jerusalem was not the war-torn city he had envisioned, still it offered opportunities for service. He looked over at Fulk and smiled.

His dagger might taste of blood yet.

Twenty-Five

The next two years passed smoothly in the convent. Agnelet grew as long and slender as a reed, and there were times Hildegard completely forgot about the horrible bloodred mark on the girl's face. On those occasions Hildegard would notice the beauty of Agnelet's clear complexion and delicate features, and then, like a thunderclap, the reality of the crimson claw mark upon the girl's face would assert itself. In Hildegard's mind the mark was no longer a coincidental configuration, but the actual print of the devil's claw, a fiendish hand that had tried to snatch the babe from the land of the living.

But you failed, Hildegard told the ground beneath her feet. *The devil himself failed to take this child, and now she abides with God.* Indeed, Hildegard found Agnelet more dedicated to the holy rule of the nuns than many of the nuns themselves. Agnelet seemed to know instinctively how a nun should respond in any situation, and she read the nuns' delicate sign language easily, incorporating it often into her own spare conversation.

The girl slept in a curtained alcove in the cloister with the other nuns, and when the bells rang for the night office at two in the morning, she sprang from her straw mattress to go with the nuns to the dark, cold chapel. Along with the others, she recited Matins, followed immediately by Lauds. The nuns then went back to bed, Agnelet with them, though often the child lay awake until the bells rang at six o'clock for Prime.

After Prime the nuns ate a light breakfast of bread and beer (Agnelet, by special dispensation, drank milk), then went about their work, for the nunnery was affiliated with a working Order whose Holy Rule considered labor as important as piety and prayer. Agnelet's everyday chores were simple: she served as assistant to the gardening nuns and the cooking nuns. Occasionally she assisted the abbess.

At noon the community of nuns stopped work to eat a solid meal, at which no one spoke, for the meal they ate for their bodies was not as crucial as the meal they received for their souls through the dinnertime reading of the day's Epistle. All language having to do with the physical meal was secondary, and relegated to the hands: an upraised hand with a waggling index finger asked for water, a cutting motion of the back of one hand against the palm of the other told the server that bread was needed, and two humble taps on the breast eloquently asked excuse for the latecomer or the nun who had unceremoniously belched at the table.

Throughout the rest of the day the nuns dropped their work and retreated to the chapel to recite the other offices, Terce, Sext, None, and Vespers. Finally, after Compline— the last office of the day—they went, in an orderly row, straight to bed.

Such was the life of Hildegard, Lienor, and Agnelet. As Hildegard watched her flock struggle to perfect themselves in the heavenly graces, she thought she had never seen a more perfect nun's heart than that which resided in Agnelet. Never cross, never impatient, never jealous . . . the little girl was so unworldly that Hildegard began to wonder if Lienor had accepted the babe from the holy arms of Saint Agnes herself.

Afton smiled at Ambrose as he struggled to pull a fish trap from the stream. "I've got it, Mother," he called, struggling to raise the heavy trap. "I've almost got it!"

"Careful, or it will get you!" Afton teased, rising to stand behind her son. "It will pull you right into the river if you're not careful!"

She grabbed a section of the rope that held the trap and pulled steadily. It rose slowly, water flowing out of it. Inside three healthy trout flopped about, and an eel struggled to free himself. "Quick, cut off his head," Afton said, handing her dagger to Ambrose. "We'll have eel for dinner."

As he cut, Afton couldn't resist rumpling her son's golden hair, even though he pulled awkwardly away. At six, Ambrose was tall and fair, with dark blue eyes that sparkled wickedly when his thoughts turned to mischief. He was handsome, quite the most beautiful boy in the village. And he was Afton's primary reason for living.

Just then a shadow fell across Ambrose, and Afton turned to see Josson standing behind her, his ledger in his hand. "Hello, Josson," she replied casually, accustomed to his presence at the mill. "We're not grinding today, there's been no demand for it. More people are coming for fish this week than for grinding."

"I know. There has not been much harvest from Perceval's fields, either."

Josson knelt on the bank and inspected the fish trap. "But there are three fine fellows! And an eel! Ambrose, did you haul that trap up yourself?"

Ambrose scowled at Josson, and Afton felt her face flush with embarrassment. Lately the boy had been openly hostile to Josson, and she had not the vaguest idea what the lord's assistant steward had done to offend her young son.

"Yes, he pulled it up himself," she said quickly. She patted Ambrose on the back and took the dagger from his hand. "Take the eel to the kitchen, Son, and put it in a bowl for dinner. Run along now!"

As Ambrose held the eel by two fingers and sprinted across the courtyard to the kitchen, Afton wiped her hands on her apron and looked at her guest, where he knelt on the ground. "I suppose you'll want one of the fish for Perceval?"

"No, the tribute is only one fish out of five, not one of three," Josson answered, squinting up at her in the sun.

"But if you serve me dinner, I think that will meet the requirements for today's bounty."

"Come, then." Afton smiled at him and took the arm he gallantly offered, and together they went into the hall.

After dinner Afton sent Ambrose out to play and looked earnestly into Josson's eyes. "Sir, I would ask you an honest question," she said, tapping her finger lightly on her cup. "You have been coming here for several years. Your attitude is pleasant toward me, your talk is all of business . . . but you do not visit the tanner or the smith with such regularity, and they are free tradespeople such as I."

She paused and frowned slightly. "I would know the reason for your visits, sir. Why do you come so often?"

Josson smiled at her words and shifted in his seat. "It is no mystery," he said, spreading his hands wide. "Lord Perceval and my master Hector do not trust the operation of the mill by a woman. I am sent as overseer."

"No other reason? Have you been charged to find me in a fault?"

"What makes you ask?"

"Long ago, the idea was suggested to me. I thought it nonsense then, but lately your visits have become more regular, and I would know if I stand in jeopardy of losing my livelihood."

Josson cleared his throat and looked away for a moment. Afton knew him well enough to realize he was searching for a harmless means of subterfuge. "I am entrusted to ascertain that all is within the measure of the law," he said finally. "I am charged—"

"All is well," Afton finished for him. "I understand. You can be sure, Josson, that I have reasons of my own to continue in honest trade. My son and I have suffered much to acquire the mill, and I intend to run my business honestly so that we may keep it."

Josson spread his hands and smiled. "Then there is no problem, aye?" He grinned and leaned toward her on the table. "There is perhaps one other reason why I visit so often. Mayhap it is because I am so fond of eating in your house, mistress Afton."

He was teasing, and Afton knew it, but it had been so long since any man had teased her that the woman who prided herself on her independence blushed and hid her face.

The sun sank lazily in the west, and Afton put away the remains of the meager supper she and Ambrose had shared. The day had been long and full, and Afton congratulated herself. The mill had run well, there had been fish aplenty in her traps, and Ambrose had charmed every villager he had met with his quick smile and winning ways. The thought of her son's bright face and smile never failed to lift Afton's heart. And yet—

She frowned. Though she seldom let herself take note of it, she was hounded by the sense that there was something behind her little boy's smile . . . something reminiscent of another, more sinister smile . . . a smile that still haunted Afton's dreams.

"Stop it!" she said sternly to herself. "There is naught in the boy of his father." But no matter how confidently she assured herself of Ambrose's sweet nature, she could not still the small niggling voice of concern.

At a sudden commotion from the chickens in the courtyard, Afton thankfully turned her attention away from her thoughts. Draping a towel over the bowl where the dough for the morrow's breakfast rested, she hurried to open the kitchen door.

"Ambrose?" she called. "Are you all right?"

The sight that met her stopped her cold. There stood her small son, his dark eyes gleaming, his tiny right hand clenched around the neck of Afton's prize rooster. The creature struggled, scratching the boy frantically, but Ambrose seemed oblivious to the damage the rooster was inflicting on him. Instead, he was transfixed upon his task: yanking handfuls of the rooster's brilliant feathers from its body.

Something in her son's detached manner and posture sent a chill of horror through Afton—for she had seen Hubert stand thus many times as he took the whip up into his hands—and her hands flew to her throat as she screamed. At the unexpected sound, Ambrose turned in her direction, even as he nonchalantly tossed another handful of feathers over his shoulder.

"Do you want something, Mama?" he asked, his eyes wide and innocent.

Afton sank to her knees on the ground. "Ambrose, dear child," she said. "Release the rooster."

Ambrose tilted his head slightly. "Why? He ran from me when I called to him, so he deserves it." Then he smiled brightly. "Just listen to him scream, Mama."

"He's hurting you, son. Look . . . you're bleeding."

Ambrose did look down then and, when he saw the bloody scratches, his eyes narrowed and his grip tightened around the rooster's neck. As the poor animal's eyes bulged, Afton stood swiftly to her feet.

"Release him now!" she ordered. At her tone, Ambrose reluctantly let the dazed rooster drop to the ground, then wiped his hands on his tunic. "I wasn't going to kill him, Mama. I know we need him. I just wanted to teach him a lesson."

Her son's words echoed in Afton's mind, and she shuddered. *God, give me wisdom* . . . she prayed silently. "Ambrose," she said, placing a firm hand on his sturdy shoulder. "You must never harm anything or anyone weaker than yourself. God has appointed us to be masters over our animals, but we are to treat them with kindness, gentleness, and care."

Ambrose scowled as his mother drew him into the kitchen. "You're wrong, Mama," he said in a hard tone, glaring up at her. "The animals are stupid! And I can do to them whatever I want, whenever I want to. You can't tell me what to do!"

The hand that had been reaching for a cloth to wipe the

boy's cuts suddenly detoured and smacked him firmly across his bottom. Then Afton took hold of her son's shoulders and looked him squarely in the eyes. "You are the one who is wrong, my son," she said, enunciating each word carefully and firmly. "I am your mother and I will tell you what to do, and you *will* do it. You are not to behave like a lawless heathen. You are my son, and you will behave yourself."

Ambrose's eyes glistened with angry tears and his lips quivered, but he did not cry. Instead, he set his jaw firmly and crossed his arms defiantly before sitting down on the stool at their table. Afton closed her eyes in frustration. Most parents, she knew, would whip a child for such insolence—but she had long ago sworn she would never take a whip into her hands.

"All right then," she said, taking a deep breath, "you will stay here in the kitchen—all night, if necessary—until you apologize for your words and behavior. And then we will never, ever repeat this scene again!"

With that, she stormed out of the kitchen, slamming the door behind her, feeling more like the child than the parent.

Agnelet wandered about the convent, bored and uneasy with the unusual abundance of free time. Two new novices were being vested in the chapel and, because the chapel overflowed with visitors, Hildegard had asked Agnelet to stay out of sight and amuse herself until the vesture and feast were done.

Agnelet wandered for a while in the garden, her favorite spot in the convent, then lay on her back to watch the sky. The sun shone bright on her pale face, and she closed her eyes to enjoy its warmth. Soon its heat became uncomfortable, though, as it was drawn in through her tunic, veil, and cape.

She got up and crossed to the garden gate, peering outside at the grassy field where the world met the cloister. She had never been through the gate, for the outside world held no attraction for her, but on this day the sun beamed upon her from the direction of the field and the grass beckoned invitingly. How would it feel to scamper outside the walls? How would it feel to run in a straight line until her breath gave out, without having to turn to avoid either a wall or a black-robed nun?

Agnelet lifted the iron latch of the gate and scrunched up her face as it squeaked. Madame Hildegard had never told her *not* to go outside the gate, but Agnelet knew in her heart that nuns had no place in the world. Still, if it was not expressly forbidden . . .

She slipped through the gate and took a few tentative steps over the grass. A field of bluebells and buttercups nodded in the sunshine, and she made a dash, darting from flower to flower, delighting in each touch and smell of flowers and grasses. A flock of blackbirds roosting in a large bush took flight as she ran toward them, and Agnelet stopped in wonder as they filled the sky.

The sky was so wide! She had never dreamed it filled such a wide expanse, for she had never seen more of it than the narrow band visible in the nuns' high-walled courtyard. She stood quietly, breathing in the marvel of it, and wondered how Madame Hildegard and the other nuns could bear not to walk in the sunlight, breathe the sweet air of the outdoors, and dance in the flowers.

Beyond the next hill lay a stream, and Agnelet drew in her breath at the sight of it. The stream moved slowly, like a garden snake with its skin shining under the sun. In its liquid surface Agnelet could see the sky, the trees, even the birds reflected. It lay as a magic mirror in the stillness of the countryside.

The sound of childish voices surprised her, and Agnelet threw herself down in the grassy bank that overlooked the stream. She must not be seen! Cautiously, she peered over the bank. Two children played nearby: a boy about her age and a little girl. Both children played in their bare feet, throwing pebbles into the water and squealing with merriment at the resulting splash.

"Let me, Ambrose," the girl said, pulling on the boy's arm. "It's my turn and I want to throw that big rock in your hand!"

The boy acted as though he didn't hear and pitched the rock overhand into the water. The girl seemed to forget her disappointment when the rock thunked into the water. "That was a good one! But it's my turn!"

The guilt that had forced Agnelet down into the grass evaporated, and she found her feet skipping down the hill before she even had a chance to think about what she was doing. They were children, after all, like she was. Surely they would welcome her as the nuns always did.

She slowed her pace and crept up behind the pair with her silent tread, habitually tucking her hands under her cape. She sought for words, then finally blurted out: "Grace to you from our Lord Jesus Christ."

The children turned slowly. Then the boy's eyes met hers and he shrieked even as his hands covered his face. "Aruggggh!" he screamed, covering his eyes. "A witch! She bears the mark of the devil! Run, Laudine, run!"

The barefoot girl burst into tears and sprinted away, the boy running close behind her. Agnelet tried to speak, but words failed her, and she sank onto a rock by the water in confusion. Why had they run? Was it because she wore a robe like the nuns? Had she said something to frighten them?

Agnelet fought back the urge to cry and twisted her face into a crooked smile. She bent over the shining water to see her reflection, then gasped with horror at the image gazing back at her. A bloodied three-fingered hand had left its mark in a horrible handprint upon her face! Agnelet could not remember how it had happened. Had this scar come upon her as she slipped through the nunnery gate? Did this mark result from disobedience?

She slipped her cloak from her shoulders, dipped it in water, and began to wash her face energetically until the rough wool was red with blood from her frantic scrubbing.

Madame Hildegard must not see . . . Lienor must not see . . . the nuns must not know that she had been disobedient!

When it became obvious that the mark of disobedience could not be erased by her efforts, Agnelet prostrated herself in the mud-spattered grass to wait for the judgment of God. She had disobeyed an unspoken law of the convent, and surely she would be punished.

Trilby found the child later that night, after Vespers. She wrapped her in a warm cloak and brought her to Hildegard, much as Lienor had brought her as a newborn babe six years earlier. And, just as Hildegard had blanched when she saw the birthmark upon the infant's face, so she blanched now when she observed the raw places where Agnelet had tried to rub the offending mark from her face.

"We will wash her wounds and let her sleep," Hildegard said, calling for Lienor. "Let no one speak of this until the morning. I will talk to the child then." She paused and rubbed her crucifix as if for inspiration. "I think it necessary, as well, to have the vestiaire make a new veil for Agnelet, with a veiling for the face as well as for the head."

Trilby nodded, understanding, and went for warm water and clean cloths for cleaning the child's skin. Hildegard sank to her knees and prayed for wisdom.

Endeline paced impatiently in the hall and rang again for Hector. She had been out riding and had gone past the mill, where she had seen Ambrose playing in the yard. She could no longer bear the infernal waiting for the child. He had had years to catch Afton in a fault. Was that not long enough?

Over the past months Perceval had tried to dissuade her from taking Ambrose. In fact, he had brought her two other children from the village—villein's children—and Endeline had disdainfully cast them off and set them to work in the kitchen. She would not rear slaves! She had endured Afton only for Lienor's sake, and if she reared another child, it would be for her own pleasure. She wanted a child who would reflect upon her, and no child less beautiful than Ambrose would do.

Hector shuffled into the hall, his weak legs barely carrying the weight of his ponderous stomach, grown fat from years of gorging himself on the bribes of villeins. His face was drawn and pale, but Endeline—in her frustration—didn't even notice.

"Hector! Have you no reason yet to procure the child Ambrose for me? Surely there is something Afton has done to indicate her disloyalty to her lord Perceval."

Hector shook his head. "Nothing, my lady. My assistant Josson goes there as often as his schedule permits and watches her like an eagle, but he reports nothing amiss. If anything, the mill's revenues for Perceval have grown in the last two years—"

"Josson goes there? You do not go yourself?" Endeline sank onto a bench and snapped her riding whip against the edge of a table. "You fool! Josson is young and unattached, and you send him to the home of a widowed woman who seeks a husband! Can you not see that she has bewitched your assistant? He pines with love for her, that is why he reports nothing amiss!"

Hector stepped back in indignation. "Indeed, lady, you could not be more wrong. Josson is an equitable judge and he assures me—"

"Do not send him any longer," Endeline snapped, standing up. "Go to the mill yourself next week, and the next, if you have to, until you catch the widow of Hubert in some large or small act of treachery. Then run to me, that I may hear of it. Do you understand?"

"Yes, my lady," Hector answered, backing out of the room. "I will go myself."

The next afternoon Endeline heard a careful rap on her chamber door. "My lord and lady," Lunette said, pushing the door open, "Josson wishes to speak with you."

"Bid him come in," Endeline said, rising eagerly from

the bench where she had been halfheartedly embroidering. "Has he news for us?"

"Urgent news," Josson answered, coming in behind Lunette. He walked to the bed where Perceval reclined and respectfully bowed his head. "My lord, Hector is on his deathbed. He was suddenly taken ill, and the doctor has been summoned. The barber bled him last night, but it does not seem that Hector will recover."

Perceval nodded reflectively. "It is expected," he answered. "Hector is an old man. Well, Josson, his station is now yours. Upon Hector's death, you will become my chief steward. The house inside the courtyard is yours, as is the right and duty to collect tribute from the vassals on my estates."

Perceval reached for a stick and handed it to Josson, who knelt and received it. Endeline recognized the ceremonial gesture of receiving a fief, which Josson would now hold until his death. She and Lunette had witnessed the transfer of property. There was nothing else to be done.

"Do you wish to speak to Hector before—" Josson began, but Perceval waved him away.

"No, there is nothing to be said. Call Father Odoric, if you like, from the village. Make whatever arrangements you need to make. I leave him in your hands."

"Did Hector say anything about the mill?" Endeline interrupted, her hands tense and still in her lap. "Has he visited the mill as I requested?"

"I do not know, my lady," Josson said with a shake of his head. "Hector fell ill yesterday and took to his bed. He has not been to the village in over a month."

Endeline lowered her eyes back to her sewing, fuming in silence, as Lunette opened the door for Josson to leave. *Hector will soon be dead*, Endeline thought, *and that too-soft Josson will remain in his place.* She would have to find another way to discover Afton in a fault. If it took another five years, she would claim Ambrose as her own son.

Twenty-Six

For two years Calhoun and Fulk spent most of their days in the company of Reynard and the Knights Templar, escorting pilgrims through Outremer and always being on guard against the persistent bands of raiding Saracens. Calhoun was constantly frustrated in his search for meaning in the bloodshed, for he had yet to see or fight a fair battle. Either the Saracens crept upon his people in the dark, striking brutally, or he was ordered to run down desert dwellers who happened to be on the road at the wrong time.

Calhoun could not bring himself to kill the unarmed Arab men, women, and children who ran from his horse's thundering hooves, yet his brain hummed in fury when the enemy struck and killed those under his protection. The only moments in which he found rest from his frustration were those in which he rested at Khalil's house and thought of Margate . . . and Afton. He remembered how she had hated war, cruelty, and even his sword. Years ago, he had thought her foolish. Now he was beginning to think her wise.

The years in Jerusalem opened Calhoun's eyes to the ways of the world. Many of the Christians in Jerusalem came there originally to seek God, but had stayed for the comfortable climate and the promise of easily obtained wealth. The knights—who came, like Calhoun, for the glory of defending the Holy City—tarried in Jerusalem, lured by the promise of bloody battles, plunder, and rich booty.

Calhoun was not sure why he remained in Jerusalem. He supposed it was simply easier to stay than to go home. Yet an inner voice reminded him that he remained because he had not accomplished what he had set out to do: forget Afton.

One thing he knew: it was not the glory of battle that kept him in Outremer. The barbarism he discovered there turned his stomach and tortured his sensibilities—and it was not confined to the Saracens. Once Calhoun happened upon a victorious party of knights who had just raided a Saracen camp in the desert. There he was met with a gruesome sight that still haunted his dreams, for dangling from the saddles of the knights' horses were the heads of women and children. Calhoun had expected that battle would be honorable and victory untarnished. He soon discovered the reality: battle was often dishonest; victory, a one-sided slaughter.

One hot afternoon Reynard pulled Calhoun and Fulk aside in Khalil's house. *"Ecoutez!* It is rumored that Zengi marches on Antioch soon," he whispered gruffly. "We are to go at once to 'elp fortify ze city."

"At once?" Calhoun echoed, standing to his feet. "A real battle?"

"Oui, and perhaps more zan a battle," Reynard replied. "Zengi may attempt to besiege the city. Antioch cannot hold out indefinitely."

"I am ready," Calhoun replied without hesitation. He glanced at Fulk and smiled. "Finally, my teacher, an honest battle for honest men."

After two days in the saddle, Calhoun had no idea they were near Antioch until he mounted the crest of a hill and saw the battle lines drawn before him. A circle of knights, many emblazoned in the familiar uniform of the Knights Templar, surrounded the city walls. A line of Saracen warriors stood below the hill at a distance, watching warily.

"Bon, we're behind them," Reynard muttered. "Hold your position, brothers, until we see ze battle forming."

There were few trees to conceal their company of thirty knights, and Calhoun felt uncomfortably exposed in the desert. At any moment the Saracens would turn around, see them, and lead off in an outward charge to scatter them.

But the Saracens were intent on the battle before them. Somewhere in the distance a kettledrum beat insistently, and suddenly the flourish of trumpets split the air. From Calhoun's vantage point it seemed that unseen hands propelled the two lines of warriors toward each other as the Saracens and Christian knights furiously charged each other.

"*Allons-y!* For ze glory of God and ze defense of Antioch, we attack!" Reynard cried, waving his sword above his head. He spurred his mount and shot off into the fray. Calhoun followed almost without thinking, Fulk at his right hand.

He had never dreamed battle contained such noise. The kettledrums on a distant hill thrummed in an unceasing cadence, and trumpets squealed battle signals as horses screamed and swords and shields clanged in the melee. Calhoun galloped toward the fighting, his horse's hooves pounding over the dry ground. A turbaned Saracen warrior charged at his left side, his bloody scimitar flashing in the late afternoon sun.

Calhoun's shield rose from his left arm reflexively; he brought his sword down upon the man's neck without thinking. The blow took his opponent's head from his body, but Calhoun took little notice. His horse carried him further into the fray, where swords and axes rose and slashed in a reckless frenzy.

The Saracens had the advantage of flexibility. Without rigid armor, the barbaric warriors were lighter on their feet when felled from their horses, and they used their opportunities on the ground to fire arrows at riders and horses as they passed.

Calhoun drove his horse through the crowd, toward the city, hacking and slashing at every advancing form not attired in the uniform of the cross. His enemy was nimble;

more than once he drew back his sword to strike a blow and found that the Saracen simply whirled his mount about and disappeared.

His shield he kept firmly at his side, repelling blow after blow. *It will be battle-scarred after this day,* he thought as he turned his horse to face another aggressor. *Still, let them come!* His horse, eyes wild in fury and fear, trampled blindly through the men and carnage, not pausing even when wounded men lay underfoot.

A turbaned figure ahead of Calhoun whirled and rushed in his direction. Calhoun expertly lopped off the arm that brandished the scimitar, but before he could turn to finish the enemy, a shooting pain pierced his leg, and his horse fell beneath him.

Calhoun saw the ground coming to meet him and he made an effort to roll off the horse and remove himself from his vulnerable position, but his leg was firmly attached to his saddle. He felt his stomach churn as he noted for the first time that a long arrow had struck from the sky, pierced the armor on his right thigh, penetrated his saddle, and killed his horse.

His world began to go black, and Calhoun steeled himself. If he fainted now, he would never again see the light of day. Pinned to his horse, he was a helpless target. His life depended upon his quick escape. Quickly, dispassionately, he reviewed his options. He could cut off his leg at the thigh, but he knew he would bleed to death or be trampled underfoot in the battle.

Fumbling at the metal sheath surrounding his calf, he took a deep breath and pulled out his dagger. He hacked wildly at the portion of the arrow that protruded from the top of his leg, wincing as the shaft reverberated in his flesh and drove waves of pain through his leg and up his spine. When he had cut through the top of the arrow, he put his weight on his left leg and lifted his right leg from the arrow that had felled his war-horse.

"Young Calhoun!" Fulk's voice rang out from the din,

and Calhoun grabbed his sword and ducked under his shield until the elder knight galloped toward him. Fulk's strong arm was extended, and, struggling to his feet, Calhoun grasped it and swung himself onto Fulk's mount.

As they continued into the fray, the trumpets of the Saracens sounded a different note. Suddenly, the remaining warriors whirled on their mounts and galloped toward the eastern hills. A few knights of the Cross followed them, but Calhoun and Fulk stopped in the sandy field to survey the battle site.

It seemed to the young knight that all of creation had gone black with dust and trampled earth. The blue sky was now murky with an obscuring cloud of dust, and the field of brown grass now ran black and red with blood. Fragments of bodies lay scattered across the thirsty earth: arms, heads, and feet torn asunder by pike and ax and horse hoof. Men lay in the mud, gasping their last breath through the stench of death.

Calhoun surveyed the field and felt curiously empty. Where was the rush of glory he had expected to find? They had routed the enemy and saved the Christian city of Antioch—so why didn't he feel victorious?

Reynard rode toward them, looking curiously like a porcupine. Five or six arrows stuck out from his armor, but he appeared to be unhurt. *"Dieu merci!* A great victory, my friends," he said, nodding to Calhoun and Fulk. "You fought well. God 'as preserved our lives and his honor here this night."

"The young knight is injured," Fulk answered, pointing to Calhoun's leg. "Perhaps we should go into the city and see a physician."

Reynard did not answer at first; his eyes carefully scanned the skies. "They will send a messenger pigeon to Zengi," he said, explaining his action. "To tell of their defeat and suggest a counterattack, *certainement.* I 'ave to tell the falconers to prepare a falcon to bring ze pigeon down." He kept searching the sky. "Zese Saracens are like flies. If you swat zem and drive zem away, zey will go, but zey return. Always, zey return."

Reynard's eyes fell upon Calhoun for the first time. "You are injured," he said. "Antioch will be crowded with wounded tonight. If your wound is not serious, I suggest you go north to Aleppo and find a physician zere."

"We will do that, holy man," Fulk answered, turning his horse to the east. "If you need us, you will find us there."

Outremer's eastern frontier was defended by a line of castles from the northern city of Aleppo, south of Damascus. Aleppo itself was a small city with many Muslim inhabitants, and Calhoun felt curious eyes upon him as he and Fulk rode through the city gate. "A doctor," Fulk demanded of the first fair-skinned man they saw. "My friend is wounded."

"Ah." The man nodded. "Follow me."

Fulk dismounted and led the horse through the city streets as he followed the man. Each step of the horse's hooves jarred Calhoun's leg and brought a new wave of pain, but Calhoun gritted his teeth and tried to think of other things. The houses in Aleppo, he noted, were not as ornate or lavish as those in Jerusalem, but sleep in any one of them would be wonderful.

His leg was stiff and throbbing when Fulk handed the horse's reins to a servant at the doctor's house, and Calhoun nearly fainted when Fulk pulled him off the horse and led him inside. As they waited, Calhoun reclined on tapestry-covered cushions while Fulk removed his armor. Finally the doctor came in to see them, and Calhoun noticed that his mentor's eyes narrowed in distrust. The doctor was a Saracen.

"Is there not a Frankish doctor?" Fulk demanded, putting out his hand to stop the man's approach.

"For a Turkish wound, you need a Turkish doctor," the man replied, his bald head shining in the dim light of his quarters. "If you would rather your friend die, then I will not treat him."

"It's all right," Calhoun whispered through clenched teeth. "Let him see it."

When the doctor took hold of the bloody tunic, which had dried to the wound, and ripped it from the gaping hole, Calhoun cried out—then a dark veil came down and he relaxed into blessed unconsciousness.

The battle had wounded more than Calhoun's leg. For days he tossed on his mattress, dreaming of flying heads and smiling scimitars, which appeared in darkness and danced dangerously near to his throat. He would awaken for snatches of time, drink broth served by dark-skinned servants, and then doze uneasily again. During one of his periods of wakefulness he realized that Fulk lay silent on a mattress next to him.

Calhoun raised up on his elbows, determined not to sleep again until he had news of Fulk, who now shivered under a thin blanket. "It is the sickness," the doctor told Calhoun when he came in. The old man shook his head. "Possibly a tarrent bit him. Possibly he was scraped with a poisoned sword. I do not know if he will recover."

The doctor applied foul-smelling ointments to Calhoun's leg and kept a careful watch on Fulk for a stretch of days until the older man's fever finally broke. On that day he opened his eyes and saw Calhoun watching him.

"How long have we been here?" he whispered.

"I don't know," Calhoun answered, grinning. "First I was out, then you were. I suppose we can ask the doctor. I will tell you this, Fulk, I feared you were taking leave of your duty." He groaned as he lifted his wounded leg to turn toward Fulk. "But you wouldn't die and leave me here alone, would you, fearless Fulk?"

Fulk moistened his lips. "What of the attack on Antioch?"

"It's over." Calhoun sat up and stretched his arms, noting that his muscles felt incredibly weak. "We chased them away, remember?"

"No." Fulk swallowed. Each word was an effort, and Calhoun had to strain to hear him. "The counterattack. The fly, remember? Reynard said they always come back."

The dingy brown curtain that was stretched across the doorway of their room parted, and the doctor entered, bowing slightly to both men. "It is good you are both awake," he said, ringing a bell on a small table. "You must go now."

"I do not think my companion is able to travel," Calhoun said, gesturing toward Fulk. "If you will allow him to recover his strength, we will pay you for your trouble."

"I have been paid," the doctor said agreeably, nodding. "There is a bounty on the heads of all Christian knights. Zengi has rewarded me well, for I have promised him two Christians for his dungeons."

"Zengi?" Calhoun was startled.

"Lord of Aleppo." The doctor bowed again. "Four days ago, my lord Zengi annexed Aleppo as part of the Saracen kingdom. Tonight you both sleep in the lord's prison."

PERCEVAL
1130-1140

In his arrogance the wicked man
hunts down the weak,
who are caught in the schemes he devises. . . .
He says to himself, "Nothing will shake me;
I'll always be happy and never have trouble."
He lies in wait like a lion in cover;
he lies in wait to catch the helpless;
he catches the helpless and drags
them off in his net. . . .
He says to himself, "God has forgotten;
he covers his face and never sees." . . .
But you, O God, do see trouble and grief;
you consider it to take it in hand.

PSALM 10:2, 6, 9, 11, 14, NIV

TWENTY-SEVEN

A sag-bellied rat skittered across the worn path in Zengi's courtyard, and Calhoun thought tiredly that, over the last two years, the rat had grown fatter even as he and Fulk had grown thinner. He glanced at Fulk's chest as he walked: pale skin hung loosely over the older knight's ribs. *I wonder if I have lost as much weight,* he wondered, the chains between his feet clanking unevenly over the rough stones.

The dusty track upon which they were forced to walk every day had once been a garden pathway, but now that Zengi was master of this castle the garden had become an exercise yard for weary, underfed prisoners. The daily ritual of exercise was a feeble concession Zengi had allowed to keep his prisoners alive until their families paid the exorbitant ransoms he demanded.

As they had circled the garden for an hour each day during the past two years, Calhoun and Fulk had vowed to maintain their strength until Zengi decided upon their fate. But days and nights passed with no news. With every approaching footstep, Calhoun hoped for word that they were to be ransomed or released. Finally, as the days passed with no end in sight, Calhoun thought death would be a welcome change from his tired and meaningless existence.

When they had first been captured and arrested, Calhoun had feared for his life. Death in battle was honorable; dying as a helpless prisoner was not. Fulk had faced their Saracen captors without fear or resistance, but Calhoun had struggled and grappled with every restraining hand placed upon him.

At last, bound and subdued, they had been taken immediately from the doctor's house to the hall in the castle Zengi had appropriated. Calhoun recalled forcing himself to remain calm and copy Fulk's cool detachment, but fury had blazed within him when he saw the meek doctor who had attended them receive a handful of silver coins for his treachery.

His temper did not go unnoticed. "Does my hospitality displease you, Christian?" a sharp voice had cut through the murmur of voices in the crowd, and Calhoun had turned to face his captor. A dark-skinned man with a hawkish nose sat on a mound of furs among a group of Saracen warriors, and his eyes were fastened intently upon Calhoun. "Why do you not bear the situation with the steadfastness of your companion, young warrior? Is it the brashness of youth which fuels your anger, or have I offended in my duties as host?"

"If you be Zengi," Calhoun had said, struggling to keep his voice calm, "then I am disappointed in you. You have seized two warriors from their sickbeds without giving even a chance for resistance. Your actions are totally without honor."

The man had thrown back his head and laughed, and the other warriors smirked and murmured among themselves in Arabic. "So Zengi is without honor," the man had said, glancing to those who stood at his right hand. "The Christian infidel speaks of honor as if he would recognize it."

Zengi had turned his burning gaze back to Calhoun. "Do not fret, young knight," he said, smirking. "We will display every courtesy. My friend the doctor tells me you have been injured, and I know something of medicine. I would like to see the wound."

At Zengi's gesture, the doctor who had treated and surrendered them came forward and unwrapped the bandage from Calhoun's thigh. In his mind's eye, Calhoun watched again as Zengi approached, gently fingered the still-tender skin of Calhoun's wound, then thrust his dagger in and twisted it. Despite being weak from his sickness, Fulk scowled and strained at his bonds as Calhoun forgot every noble intention he had ever possessed. He had screamed in pain and terror.

"I will show you the same honor and courtesy your fellow Christians have shown to our people," Zengi had screamed, withdrawing the dagger from Calhoun's leg and gesturing to his warriors. "Take them to the dungeons below."

Thus ended the first of many sessions of Turkish torture. At least once a week Calhoun and Fulk found themselves standing before Zengi and his son, Nur al-din, to endure the pain of daggers, splinters of wood, and boiling oil until they were willing to agree that the Frankish nations had visited barbaric crimes upon the Islamic people.

"Bands of Christians have been routinely attacking trade caravans to the Turkish states," Zengi would tell them, "and other Christian infidels have burned villages, killing women and children. Admit it, young knight! Admit that you and yours are wrong!"

"These men are not like us," Calhoun once protested. "They are renegades. They are not honorable and noble knights."

"I have seen those who call themselves the noblest of knights," Zengi answered, his dark eyes narrowing in hate. "I have seen them run women and children through with the sword and then fall to their faces and give thanks to their God with blood still on their hands."

"I use my sword in defense only," Calhoun objected.

"You fought at the battle outside Antioch," Zengi snapped.

"To defend the city!"

"You defended the people who killed the inhabitants of Antioch one generation past!" Zengi howled, slapping Calhoun's face with the back side of his hand. "Would you, noble knight, have defended Antioch if its inhabitants were Turkish? Jewish? Or do you only fight for Franks?"

Calhoun's face burned where Zengi had struck him. He looked at the tile floor and chose his words carefully. "I am sworn to defend those of the true faith," he said. "Wherever they are. I cannot account for the actions of others."

"It is time you and those like you were called to account," Zengi said, turning and settling back on his chair. He pulled a scimitar from his belt and ran his index finger lightly across the blade, drawing a faint line of blood. "I shall send word to your king that you are my prisoner," Zengi said, eyeing the blood on his finger. "If he values your service, you will be ransomed. If he thinks little of you, it will be your blood that next satisfies my hungry scimitar, young Christian."

A shadow of a smile played across Zengi's face. "I hear this method of commerce is common in England. We Turks have little patience for trading with Franks, but I find you and your notions of nobility interesting, young knight. For the sake of my entertainment, I shall keep you and your brave companion alive . . . for now."

One day was very like another. Even the seasons varied little in this arid land, and Calhoun lost all track of time. Had he and Fulk been imprisoned for two years or twenty?

If it had not been for Fulk, Calhoun was sure he would have gone mad. Except for the hour or so each week that Zengi summoned them to berate them for the crimes of the "Christian infidels," and for the hour-long walk in the garden, Calhoun and Fulk lived in a small room with moldy stone walls, a dirt floor, and a bucket that served as a lavatory.

For men accustomed to open spaces and the sweet breath of the outdoors, the prison cell was a torture in itself. Fulk encouraged Calhoun to think of their confinement as an opportunity for further training. Thus they resumed their roles of teacher and pupil, exercising and conversing as much as possible. Calhoun felt his wiry muscles growing even more defined as his body fat melted away.

The tedium threatened to push Calhoun over the edge of his endurance, and he spent hours pacing back and forth in the room until Fulk commanded him to stop. "Sit down," Fulk would say, doing so himself. "They can cage your body but they cannot cage your spirit. Free yourself of this place. Close your eyes and use this time to sharpen your mind—for if it grows dull, we *will* well and truly be lost."

Fulk sat cross-legged for hours with his eyes closed, but Calhoun found that sitting still was contrary to his nature. Then, out of desperation, Calhoun tried to imitate Fulk's peace and calm. Day after day, he sat erect, closed his eyes, and forced the dank green walls of his prison to become the sandy road that led to Margate Castle. The road formed in his mind's eye, and he turned his back on the castle, walked through the meadow and into the forest. There he dodged through the greenery at his feet and followed deer trails until he found the place he sought.

The twin oak trees stood there still, twisted about each other and rising through the greenery until they brushed the blue of the sky. Calhoun put out his hand and felt the rough bark. He drew in a breath and found the air sweet and moist in his nostrils. A leafy fern obscured his vision, but he brushed it away and saw before him the pool he had not seen since his childhood. A smile flitted across his features, for now, as in his childhood, Afton swam in the pool.

She smiled at him—a smile that was at once unsure and enchanting. Her eyes filled with love and concern for him, and she swam to the edge of the pool, rose from the water, and took his hands.

As he took her soft hands in his, he gave in to the impulses that had long burned in his imagination and wrapped his arms around her soaked skin. He buried his head in her wet hair, felt the coolness of her damp cheek, and thrilled to the smoothness of her skin and the flutter of her breath in his ear. Her lips waited for his and his hungry mouth found them, drinking in all the love he had missed, gasping for air as a man who has never had enough—

"Calhoun."

The vision evaporated.

"What?" Calhoun snapped at Fulk, exasperated.

"Pardon the intrusion." Fulk grinned through his bushy beard. "But I think it is time we recognized that England has forgotten about us. Two years without a word is a long time."

"Perhaps the king is in Normandy. Travel is slow in the winter, and a messenger could take many months—"

"I rather doubt that the message will reach King Henry. I fear Zengi's letter lies in the purse of a man murdered for some bauble hanging about his neck. It is not very likely that the letter reached England at all."

Calhoun sighed. "Why do you tell me this?"

"You are growing weak. The tools I gave you to escape this prison must be used wisely. But you spend more and more time in your fantasies. You cannot sit and daydream forever, for your mind and body will become unfit for service if you use one more than the other. Reality lies here, my friend, and you must not leave it too often. We must remain strong if we are to survive captivity. A means for escape will one day come our way, and we must be up to the challenge."

"And if we cannot escape?"

"We must give attention to understanding Zengi. He knows as well as we that his message did not reach England. He keeps us alive because you interest and amuse him. If you grow predictable or dull, young knight, you will no longer be of value."

Calhoun reared back in indignation. "I *amuse* him? Fulk, he is our enemy. I am not his court jester."

"You amuse him with your anger and your sense of nobility." Fulk's dark eyes sparkled from behind the stringy hair that hung in his face. "He cannot understand how so seasoned a knight clings to an impractical and quite useless sense of honor and integrity." Fulk shook his head slowly. "The desire for glory and honor usually costs a knight his life, but in your case, it has preserved you."

"My life is in God's hands," Calhoun muttered, stretching out on the floor.

Fulk shook his head. "My life is not," he answered calmly. "And since my life is entwined with yours, I beg you not to throw our lives away."

Perceval threw off the fur covers of his bed and lumbered toward the fireplace. Endeline felt him go and warily raised her head to see if he was merely restless or genuinely worried. Perceval had been troubled by many things lately.

"Come to bed, my lord," she called, her voice husky with fatigue. "Tomorrow will come soon enough."

"Another day without a word from the king," Perceval fretted, clenching and unclenching his hands in front of the fire. "And without word of Calhoun. For months we received good reports, then my son fell into a dark hole. When our knights returned today without my son—" he broke off, unwilling to voice his fears.

Endeline closed her eyes; she did not like to think of Calhoun's bones bleaching in the hot eastern sun. "I'm sure he is fine, my lord," she said, pulling her bare arm out from under the furs on their bed. "He is a man grown, and perhaps he has found a life apart from England. A new enterprise, perchance."

"I spoke with Jarvis, who interviewed those who returned," Perceval went on, turning to his wife. "He said Calhoun and Fulk fought with a band of Knights Templar in a skirmish outside Antioch. They were victorious, and they rode safely away together." Perceval sank wearily onto the bed. "They were not seen again."

"Perhaps Calhoun is still exploring," Endeline said, struggling to keep her own feelings under control. "He was always riding off on his own. Remember how he wanted to ride with the knights as a very young boy?"

"Gislebert does not think Calhoun will return," Perceval remarked. "When he heard the news, he took leave of me and thanked me for my guardianship, saying that his allegiance to Calhoun was finished."

"The lad did not take Calhoun's absence well," Endeline remarked softly. "How like a boy. He has no patience to wait! But it is good that he goes, for he is seventeen and no longer in need of a guardian. Though I shall miss him, it is time he went out to seek his own fortune." She paused, weighing her words carefully. "Perhaps what we need is another young man in the castle—someone else to amuse and divert us."

She sat up so the bed covers fell away from her. Reaching out to her husband, she pulled his graying head down to rest against her and whispered, "You need a diversion, my lord, to take your mind from these troubling thoughts. Why don't you ride through the village tomorrow? The fields are ready to harvest, and your plentiful tribute to the king this year will place you ever more firmly in his good graces. Go out to the mill and prepare the miller for the bounty your estate will yield this year."

"The king has not called for me in months," Perceval mumbled, but his words were softer now. His hands clutched his wife.

"You are more than secure in the king's favor," Endeline assured him, stroking his hair. "Your name is mighty and honored in his majesty's court. Do not fear, my lord. Take your pleasure in life, wherever you find it. You are the master of all you survey, villein and free man alike."

Perceval lifted his eyes to hers, and Endeline delicately ran her finger over his brow. "Yes, my lord, you are master of all you survey."

The next morning, Endeline stretched luxuriously as Morgan and Lunette scurried about the room preparing her bath and clothing. She had given Perceval pleasure last night and relieved his mind from his troubles. She smiled. For the moment, at least, he was in her debt.

She heard his step outside the chamber door, and she modestly covered herself with the furs, pretending embarrassment when he burst into the chamber. "My lord! I am not yet dressed."

"Never mind," Perceval said, his eyes sparkling. "I have a gift for you, my dearest wife."

"For me?" She arched an eyebrow and sat up, keeping herself covered. "What is it?"

"Bert the tanner cannot pay his annual tribute. He has offered his young son, a one-year-old, as substitute instead." Perceval clapped his hands in delight. "Is this not the diversion you suggested last night? The son of a free man, a child you can raise as you will?"

Endeline sighed in exasperation, then smoothed her face. It would not do to put Perceval out of his good humor when he was finally willing to obtain what she wanted.

"Thank you, my good lord, but I have already chosen another boy," she said smoothly. "One that will reflect upon you much more graciously."

"How so?" Perceval asked, sinking onto the bed and reaching for her hand. "Bert's child is a handsome fellow. I saw him myself last week."

"I do not doubt your word, but, my lord, I have already invested a great deal of myself in the child Ambrose. You see, dear Perceval, I reared his mother, and I am confident my gracious training has been instilled in the son. Ambrose is already a little gentleman." She made an effort to keep her voice delicate and light. "It is Ambrose I want, and no other."

Perceval sighed and looked away, and Endeline lifted his hand to her cheek. "An opportunity will arise, dear husband, if you seek it. Visit the mill today and see what irregularities you find there. After all, she who holds the mill is your vassal, and is commanded to do . . . " Endeline paused and gently kissed Perceval's palm, " . . . *whatever* you bid."

Perceval withdrew his hand from his wife, then stood and squared his shoulders. "I shall think on it," he said, striding out the door, and Endeline knew Afton would have a visitor before the day had ended.

Josson stopped by the mill on his way to an outlying manor, and Afton halfheartedly listened to him ramble about things at the castle as she prepared dinner for herself and Ambrose. Castle gossip rarely interested her, for she had shelved her memories of the place and pushed them to a dark corner of her mind. It hurt too much to think of the castle, for every brick, tower, and corner held a memory connected with Calhoun.

"Calhoun's troop of knights to the Holy Land returned yesterday," Josson said, and Afton's attention jerked back to the steward.

"Oh?" she answered pleasantly, trying to disguise the fact that her heart had begun to race at the mention of Calhoun's name. She picked up a knife and began to cut the skin from a chicken. "I suppose they have tales enough to last ten years."

"Aye, the men who returned do," Josson said, shuffling his feet uneasily on the dirt floor of her kitchen. "No one knows what tales Fulk and Calhoun would have told. They alone have not returned. The news of their disappearance upset young Gislebert so much that he has left the castle to seek his livelihood elsewhere. I shall miss him."

The knife in Afton's hand slipped and she sliced her left hand instead of the chicken on the table. As though in a stupor, she watched a thin red line appear across her palm and, as it widened, her lips parted in a gasp.

"You've cut yourself," Josson cried, jumping to his feet. He reached for a basin of water. "Here, wash the wound and let me bind it."

"It's nothing," Afton said, feeling faint, but Josson had already grabbed a cloth and wound it around her hand.

"Sit here and rest a moment. You look pale," Josson said, fussing about her like a mother hen. He gently pushed her down onto a kitchen stool. "You really need a cook. I could arrange for one if you like. Perceval would agree, because it would free you to spend more time at the mill."

"No." Afton looked into his face and tried to smile.

"I'm not tired, it's just that I will miss Gislebert, too. He visited me often." She wrapped the cloth more tightly around her hand. "Sit down and finish your story. You said Fulk and Calhoun did not return? They have—disappeared?"

"Yes." Josson nodded. "The company had been in Outremer for two years when they fought together in a battle outside Antioch. Our knights were victorious, of course, but apparently Calhoun was wounded. He and Fulk rode off in search of a doctor, and no one has seen them since. The other knights searched for them for months, then decided to return home."

Afton spoke slowly. "So Calhoun died of his wound?"

"No. Denton told Lord Perceval that Calhoun's wound was not serious—an arrow through the leg. Denton himself took an arrow through the shoulder, and he said it wasn't bad, just—"

As Josson rambled on, Afton's thoughts wandered away. Calhoun had been wounded before riding off into oblivion. A wave of anger swept over her, and she had to close her eyes to keep it from erupting into a scream. By what right did Calhoun ride off and die?

The image of his face as he reached for her in love on that sunny afternoon years ago danced before her. Did he not know that she loved him desperately? If only she could have told him that it had been the brutish memories of Hubert which had kept her from surrendering to him, not that she didn't love him. *But time has erased the memories,* she thought, her brain swirling madly. *If you had only waited, Calhoun!*

But he had not. And because she had refused to become his wife, he had taken his sword into battle and become one of many who intimidated the poor and lowly through force. And, according to God's justice, he had surely been killed.

Oh, Calhoun, she moaned inwardly. *Why did you go? What glory lies on a field of battle that does not lie in the love of truth and honor at home? Is the honor of the battlefield greater than that a wife gives her husband?*

327

"Afton? Are you sure you are well?" Josson stared at her pale face in concern.

His voice reminded her where she was and that she was not alone. She managed a weak smile. "I suppose I don't handle the sight of blood very well," she said. "I think I'll just go lie down for a while. Have a good journey, Josson."

He stood awkwardly as she passed out of the room. When she reached her chamber and looked out into the courtyard, Josson's horse was gone.

TWENTY-EIGHT

Later that afternoon Afton pulled on her cloak and veil and left the security of her courtyard. Ambrose would be fine by himself for a few hours; he was already adept at overseeing the mill and the fish traps. A frantic urging pulled her down the road out of town and to the convent.

She rang the bell at the convent gate, and soon the unlined face of a novice appeared in the tiny window. "Please, I need to see Madame Lienor," Afton whispered. "May I come in?"

The nun smiled sweetly and opened the heavy door. Afton forced herself to take a deep breath and be still, though her heart was about to burst. She followed the silent novice to a small foyer off the chapel.

The sound of sweet voices rising in praise to the Virgin did nothing to soothe her, and she perched on the edge of a bench and tapped her toes, impatient for the nuns' prayers to cease. She knew she ought to pray for Calhoun, but her sense of guilt clouded her conscience so that she could not lift her thoughts toward heaven.

At last the chants from the chapel died away and a procession of dark-robed nuns filed past her. Afton lifted anguished eyes and studied them until she recognized Lienor's refined features, then she startled the entire procession by grabbing for Lienor's hands. "Lienor! I must speak with you!"

The stern abbess approached and peered curiously at

Afton. "I am afraid our sister Lienor will not talk to you," she said gently. "She has taken a vow of silence."

"Then I must talk to her," Afton cried, squeezing Lienor's hands tightly. "Please, Madame! I must!"

Lienor lifted an eyebrow in the abbess's direction, and the abbess nodded and indicated a small receiving room. Lienor bowed graciously and led Afton into the room. Once inside, she nodded toward two small benches.

When they were finally face-to-face, Afton lowered her head into her hands and let her pent-up tears flow. "Lienor," she cried, not even looking up. "Have you heard? Calhoun has been missing for two years. It is my fault, Lienor, for I sent him away. I fear that he is dead and I fear that God holds me guilty. What shall I do? If I repent, will God bring Calhoun back?"

When Afton lifted her face, she realized she had been selfish. Lienor's eyes were wide with fear and surprise and her mouth gaped open as if she would speak. But after a moment the stern discipline of the nuns descended like a veil, and Lienor's face settled into its customary expression of peaceful resignation. She folded her arms into her yawning sleeves and nodded gently. Though she uttered not a word, Afton knew she was saying, "If God wills it to be so . . ."

"Forgive me, Lienor." Afton leaned forward and rubbed her cold hands together. "I was thoughtless to spring that news upon you. But surely you know that I love Calhoun and I always have. Is that a crime so terrible that God must punish me for it? Is it a sin that the daughter of a villein loves the son of the lord?"

Lienor did not answer, and Afton licked her dry lips and continued. "I think . . . I think that if I promise God to love Calhoun always, he will send him back to me. Do you agree? Perhaps I should not test God in this way, but I must do something. Can you help me, Lienor?"

The nun offered no answer, but in her friend's dark eyes Afton saw understanding and a trace of pity. Lienor smiled and delicately traced the sign of the cross on Afton's forehead, then bowed her head for a moment of silent prayer. Afton sat quietly until Lienor had finished, then smoothed her tunic as Lienor stood and walked toward the window. With one smooth movement the nun pushed the wooden shutter open and directed her gaze outside.

Afton stood up behind her. "I know I should leave now, so I'll go. But I want you to know that if Calhoun comes home, I'll accept him. Maybe I don't deserve him after this, but if God sends him home, I'll not send him away again."

The sound of a child's laughter came drifting through the open window, and Lienor leaned out to wave in response. Afton sighed. Lienor had obviously dismissed her. She had no answers, for she had never loved a man, had never wanted to be married.

"Good-bye, Lienor." Afton glanced at her old friend one last time and saw that she had turned from the window. Her eyes were open wide and inviting, almost pleading, but Afton did not understand what she was expected to do. Did Lienor want an embrace? Did she want an assurance?

"I promise I'll send word to you if and when Calhoun comes home," Afton said, opening the door. "I'm sorry to bring you bad news, but I just needed someone to talk to."

The squealing laughter of a child rose through the open window again, and Lienor once again turned pleading eyes upon Afton. Her head tilted gently toward the window, as if inviting Afton to take a look outside, but Afton had no time for pleasantries. "If I hear good news, I'll send word," Afton promised again, and she left the room, closing the door behind her.

In the garden, Agnelet scampered around Madame Hildegard and Madame Luna, her apron full of daisies. The older nuns were trying to read from their prayer books, but as they recited, "Unto thee, O Lord, do I lift up mine eyes . . . ," each of them found themselves looking to the child instead of the hills.

"Madame Hildegard," Agnelet said as she stopped running and sat on the bench between the nuns. "I have a question to ask when your prayers are through."

Hildegard nodded slightly to acknowledge the request and continued her prayer until the end. Then she closed her prayer book and deposited it in her pocket with one smooth motion. "Ask," she told Agnelet, folding her hands out of sight.

"I've been thinking," Agnelet said, the wind catching the edges of her white veil. "Why am I the only child here at the convent?"

"You are the only child the Lord sent us," Madame Luna answered, leaning toward the girl affectionately.

"How did the Lord bring me?" Agnelet asked. "Where was I before I was here?"

Hildegard paused for thought and thanked God that Madame Luna kept silent. "As a very small baby you were brought to us," she answered truthfully.

Agnelet pursed her lips. "Where did I come from?"

Madame Luna turned her head slowly toward the abbess, and Hildegard knew her answer would make the rounds of the convent. "The Lord sends babies from the wombs of women," she said, weighing her words carefully. "Just as Jesus grew in the womb of the Virgin Mary. When it is time for the babies to be born—" she paused delicately and spread her hands in the air "—they come into the world."

Agnelet placed a trusting hand on the abbess's arm. "In what woman's womb did I grow?"

Hildegard patted the child's hand. "The Lord God knows, my child, but I do not."

Agnelet's chin quivered. "Does God know why I have this mark upon my face? Is it because the woman lost me? Did I disobey her?"

Hildegard placed her hand on the child's face. "Each of us disobeys, Agnelet, that is why we all stand in need of God's mercy. Most of us carry the marks of sin on our souls, and I tell you truly, I would rather have ten thousand marks like yours on my face and your sweet heart than the most perfect face in the world and a sin-scarred soul."

The chime of a bell echoed through the convent, cutting off all further conversation, and the three stood and strode in unison toward the chapel for prayers.

Perceval stalled his task as long as he could, then mounted his horse and rode alone toward the village, dismissing the knights who offered to accompany him. Keenly disappointed that Endeline had rejected his suggestion of the tanner's son, he resented the fact that he was on his wife's errand. "The woman is obsessed," he muttered as his horse carefully picked its way over the rough road. "I give her three honorable children, and still she pines for another. I would do well to shut her up in the tower."

The image of an imprisoned Endeline brought a smile to his lips, but he dismissed the idea immediately. Endeline was too powerful and too useful to put away. With every year she grew more cunning and, though she was not the beauty she had been in younger days, her loyalty and sharp intelligence served Perceval well. Her only flaw was her demented obsession with motherhood, but he had managed to distract her odd fixation for months. "Her madness will be stalled no longer," the earl mused aloud. "It is time to appease my lady, no matter what the cost."

He smiled and kicked his horse, urging the beast into a canter. Confronting Afton would not be entirely unpleasant. If she were removed from the mill, the property would go to her son and, as her son's guardian, Perceval would once again be in direct control of that fine establishment. His revenues would increase, and he could charge whatever he pleased for flour and the fish from the creek.

He tied his horse at the miller's gate and wiped his hands awkwardly on his tunic. The house and courtyard were clean and neatly swept, with nothing out of place, and Perceval recognized the ploughman coming from the mill house. Upon seeing the earl, the ploughman set down his bag of grain and bowed.

"Is all well at the mill?" Perceval asked, coming through the gate. "Does the woman Afton run a fair enterprise?"

"Aye, my lord," the ploughman replied, keeping his eyes on the ground. "Very fair."

"You have no cause for complaint, then? Has anyone in the village voiced a complaint?"

"Their complaints come against the wind and rain, not the woman at the mill," the man replied, ducking his head awkwardly. "She runs a fair mill."

Perceval grunted. If no one in the village would testify that Afton cheated in some way, large or small, it would be hard to prove her incompetence. He would have to find another way to gain control of the mill and gain the boy for Endeline.

"May I go now, my lord?" The ploughman looked up timidly, his cap in his hand. Perceval dismissed him with a wave of his hand and adjusted his tunic. Very well. He would interview Afton and see where her weaknesses lay.

He found her by the side of the creek and, for a moment, Perceval forgot that the shapely woman standing with her back to him had lived under his roof as a child. The thin girl-bride he had sent away years ago had grown into an enchantress! Her hair, still long and woven into a golden braid, adorned her more beautifully than any crown or veil. She had developed an enticing fullness to her figure, and her arms were slim and strong as she lifted a fish trap from the water.

Perceval's upper lip curled into a smile. Why, Endeline had known that he would find Afton pleasing! He knew his wife well, and her insistence that he visit the mill was but a gentle way of granting him a favor in return for her request. Years before, when she had wanted permission to travel to Canterbury, she had gently suggested that he interview her new maid in the privacy of the bedchamber. Afterward, he would have granted her permission to fly to the moon. What a clever woman Endeline was!

Perceval's pulse quickened in his confidence and desire. Yes, the scrawny child who had once slept outside his own bed had become most worthy now of sharing it. Of course, he could never take her to the castle, but he was lord of all he surveyed, even here at this rustic mill. He would sleep with her and, when he was done, she would be quiet and submissive like the others. It would be a simple matter to take the boy, and he could even leave Afton in possession of the mill.

He licked his lips in pleasant anticipation of many afternoon visits to the mill. "Afton of Margate, I would speak with you." He kept his tone low and soothing, the voice he had often used with the maids.

Afton whirled around and the fish trap tumbled from her hands. Her face was lovelier than ever, her dark eyes wide with surprise, and her cheeks flushed with the exertion of her labor. Perceval stepped toward her and bowed gallantly. "Shall we go inside?"

"Whatever you need to speak, my lord, can be spoken here." A light shone in her eyes . . . was it fear? He would soothe her as he had soothed the others; he would assure her that he would not humiliate her later or bring her pain.

"I am a man of power, but I will not do you harm," he said smoothly, taking her hand. "Our business here will concern only two."

Her eyelids fluttered, and he thought she might faint. By all the saints! Was his power over her as strong as that? This conquest would be easier than he had thought.

He slipped his arm around her slender waist and lowered his lips to her ear. "Of course, we can exchange our love here, but the house would be better, don't you think?"

She stiffened in his arms, then a resounding crack and the sting of pain thrust him back. The wench had slapped him! The lowly daughter of a ploughman had struck the earl of Margate, confederate of the king! Perceval stood in shock, his hand covering his face where her handprint burned his flesh.

"How dare you!" Her eyes burned in the late after-noon sunlight and her body trembled with suppressed anger. "You forget, my lord, that I am a free woman, not a villein to you. You do not own me and you shall not pos-sess me!"

"I shall do both if I choose," Perceval answered, slowly lowering his hand. He thought for a moment about wres-tling her to the ground, but she would undoubtedly scream, and the villagers were still moving about outside her gate. It would never do to have it said that the earl of Margate was given to grappling with peasant women in the dirt. "I hold this land and all that rests upon it," he said.

"My son and I hold it, as Hubert's heirs," she corrected. "According to the law of the king, and your own decree."

"I am lord here!" he bellowed, forgetting his dignity. "And you will be brought to realize it, Afton of Margate." His head throbbed in sudden pain, and he turned and stalked out through her gate.

Endeline knew from Perceval's countenance that all had not gone well for him at the mill. Troubled and discontent at dinner, he sent an undercooked chicken flying across the hall. So Afton still had her pride! Endeline silently cursed the days when she herself had taught Afton and Lienor to handle themselves. She had created in Afton a worthy match for any man, even Perceval himself.

"I know how to settle things at the mill, my lord."

"What?" Perceval turned startled eyes upon her. "I fol-lowed your instructions today, woman, and was—" He broke off, his eyes narrowing into slits. "Afton of Margate must pay for her wrongs," he finished darkly.

"And pay she will, for I have a plan," Endeline said smoothly. "If you approve it, the mill and the boy can be yours within the week."

Perceval smiled slowly. "Speak on, beloved wife," he said, placing his hand on hers. "I am eagerly waiting to hear."

Afton looked up from the grinding stone and her eyes widened in surprise. The girl who stood there was a stranger and too finely dressed to come from the village.

"Excuse me, madame, but I have some rye to grind," the girl said in a delicate French accent. "Have I come too early?"

"No," Afton answered, pulling out her scale. "I am ready." She looked curiously at the girl. "From where do you come? Surely you do not live in Margate village."

"No, I am with a traveling troupe," the girl replied, handing a rough woven bag to Afton. "You now hold, madame, my wages."

Afton smiled as she placed the small bag on her scale. "I didn't know a carnival had come to our village."

The girl paused a moment to look out the window. "It has not. Not yet, anyway. Oh my, what a darling boy!" The girl looked back at Afton and smiled. "He is your son? How old is he?"

Afton poured the rough rye kernels onto the grinding stone and smiled. "My son Ambrose is eight, but he considers himself a man already."

"Isn't that ze way with men?" The girl paused. "May I go speak to him?"

"Certainly," Afton said with a shrug, but the young woman had already stepped out of the millhouse and was on her way to Ambrose.

Later that afternoon Josson stopped by the mill as Afton ground a bag of grain for Father Odoric, who was now stooped with age and truly blind. Josson greeted Afton warmly as always, but he ignored the aged priest and did not offer to help her with the sack of flour she hoisted from the floor to the table in the mill house.

"Is your new position as steward too much to handle?" she teased, as she wiped the table clean. "Excuse his lack of greeting, Father. Josson is usually more civil than he is today." She stopped wiping and looked straight into Josson's eyes. "I would find it difficult to be near Perceval, much less govern his affairs."

"It is not too much," Josson answered, waving his hand casually, "except that I have much on my mind." His eyes twinkled. "Perhaps it comes from living in a house with no wife. My thoughts stay trapped inside my head; I have no one with whom to share them."

"Share them with God, my child," Father Odoric inserted. He pressed his palms together. "Prayer is a powerful purifier."

"I like living alone," Afton inserted, her voice light. "Except, of course, I'm not really alone. There's Ambrose. I couldn't imagine being without him."

Josson's brown eyes clouded a moment, but then he brightened. "At least I don't have to feel guilty about coming here today. Perceval himself asked me to spend the afternoon here."

"He did?" Afton turned sharply and her eyebrow shot up.

She lifted the sack of flour from the table and placed it in Father Odoric's arms. "Careful, now, Father. Is your assistant outside to guide you?"

As if by magic, the tonsured head of the priest's young assistant appeared in the doorway, and his hand reached out to the older priest. "God be with you," Father Odoric murmured in Afton's direction.

When the two men were on their way, Afton turned to Josson. "Do you know why Perceval wants you to be here?"

"No," Josson answered, turning his warm eyes from the priests to Afton. "It is enough that I can be here."

His easy confidence soothed her fears, and they chatted carelessly for some time before another shadow filled the doorway. Afton looked up. There stood the young French woman who had visited earlier in the morning.

"Another bag of grain?" Afton asked. "You should have brought it this morning and saved yourself a second trip."

"This time, my wages have improved," the girl answered with a sly smile. "I am bringing wheat."

The girl moved gracefully and placed the bag on the

counter and Afton noticed that Josson was carefully studying the girl. "You're Lizette, aren't you?" he asked, snapping his fingers. "The new girl, from—"

"I'm from France, *oui,*" the girl replied hastily. She
turned again to Afton. "Could you please hurry? I am
needed elsewhere."

Afton funneled the golden grain without comment.
Obviously uncomfortable, the girl went to the window and
tapped her foot impatiently, once waving to Ambrose, who
played by the creek. A few moments later Ambrose appeared
at the door of the mill house and he smiled up at Josson
with his hands behind his back.

"Watch out, he's likely to play another trick," Afton
warned Josson, keeping an eye on the grain as it tumbled
from the funnel onto the grinding stone. "Yesterday he told
me he found a diamond in the creek. When I put out my
hand, I found nothing there but a slimy toad."

"You could not trick me," Josson laughed, bending
down to Ambrose's level. "I've mined that creek for dia-
monds already, and there are none to be found."

Afton scooped up the ground wheat, weighed it, funneled it into an empty bag, and gave it to the girl. She
came out from behind her table to watch Ambrose play
with Josson, but her attention was diverted when the girl
gasped.

"What's wrong?" Afton said, turning around.

The girl peered into the bag of grain. *"Mon Dieu!* This is
coarse rye!" the girl cried, pulling out a handful of the dark
flour. "I gave you fine wheat! You are a cheater, madame!"

"That's impossible," Afton said, coming closer. "I see
that this is rye, but what happened to the bag of wheat
flour?"

"You substituted cheap flour for expensive!" the girl
cried, stamping her foot in anger. She pointed to Josson.
"You are an agent of the earl, monsieur, and you have seen
this trickery with your own eyes. Arrest this woman!"

Josson shook his head. "I have seen trickery, but I do

not know whose trickery I beheld. What do you mean by this, Lizette?"

"I mean to have this woman arrested, and if you don't do it, my mistress will have your head!" Lizette cried, her cheeks reddening.

Afton spoke slowly and clearly. "A carnival girl with a mistress? Who is your mistress, mademoiselle?"

Lizette lifted her chin. "I am maid to Lady Endeline of Margate Castle," she answered proudly. "I have never been with ze carnival. I am not a common gypsy."

Josson cleared his throat. "Afton, I'm afraid you'll have to come with me until this situation is resolved." He tenderly took her arm. "We'll talk to Perceval and explain—"

"But my son," Afton protested, pulling Ambrose to her. "I cannot—" A dark cloud of foreboding filled her heart, and she felt herself beginning to shake. She whispered hoarsely: "I cannot take him to the castle. I must leave him with my mother in the village."

"The boy will come wiz me," Lizette said, taking Ambrose's hand. "We have already become friends, 'aven't we, Ambrose?"

Ambrose smiled up at Lizette. "I'm going to become a knight, Mama," he called as Lizette led him away. "I'm going to live in the castle and eat meat every day and learn to ride a horse."

He skipped beside Lizette's hurrying steps, and Afton struggled briefly against Josson's grip, then surrendered and sagged against his shoulder. She should have known. She had experienced too much happiness, and Endeline had swooped in again to take it from her.

TWENTY-NINE

When she and Josson rode through the castle gates later that afternoon, Afton thought the castle had not changed much since she visited it with Hubert. Knights still lounged about the tower garrison, and the villein working-women still scurried in and out of the women's quarters. Afton knew she should have been taken to the castle garrison until Perceval had a moment to hear her case, so when the castle guard told Josson to escort her immediately to the great hall, she felt like a helpless rabbit in a cage. Endeline had laid a careful trap, and Afton had stumbled into it with both eyes open.

Perceval's court and counselors were already assembled inside the hall. Endeline and Perceval sat in chairs on the dais while the counselors waited on benches in a long row. It was an impressive tribunal, designed to intimidate, but Afton entered confidently on Josson's arm, her head held high. They stopped at the rear of the room while Josson bowed.

"Why, Afton," Perceval said, pretending amazement. "A surprise to see you again so soon. What is this all about, Josson?"

"What do you mean?" Afton demanded, shaking loose of Josson's grip. "Surely I was expected. I should ask you the purpose of our meeting."

"We are enjoying the quiet of the afternoon with our counselors and friends," Endeline purred. "We did not expect this intrusion."

Josson cleared his throat. "The woman, Lizette, brought wheat to be ground at the mill," he explained. "The bag she opened later contained rye flour. She accuses Afton of substituting common grain for fine."

Perceval shook his head. "A serious charge," he said. "The villagers will not stand for such a crime. Does your greed know no bounds, Afton?"

"It is a false charge," Afton answered. She raised her head and glared at the man who had dared to accost her. "It comes from my refusal of your inappropriate advances."

Endeline and several counselors gasped in horror, and even Josson stepped back in shock. Perceval gaped at her like an openmouthed fish. "Do you, the accused, accuse me?" he shouted, his face purpling in rage.

Afton stood firmly in front of him as his words rang in the hall. "I do," she answered.

Endeline stood up. "Josson, as witness to this case, did you see the woman Lizette bring two bags of grain to the mill?"

"No, my lady."

"Did you see the woman Lizette switch the bags of grain?"

"No, my lady."

"Did you see the woman Afton actually give ground wheat to Lizette?"

Josson shook his head. "I saw her give a bag, my lady, but I could not tell what was in the bag. Also, I was distracted."

"Distracted? Why?"

Josson blushed. "I was playing with Afton's son."

Perceval cast a disapproving glance at his steward, then waved his hand. "Apparently Afton engages the boy to distract people while she commits fraud," he said, throwing his hands into the air. "What can I say? We have taken this woman to our bosom, nourished her as a child, given her a husband and a fief, and now she rewards her lord and master by making profane accusations and cheating the populace. My counselors, what more can I say?"

One of the counselors, a thin man whom Afton vaguely

recognized, stood and nodded skeptically at Afton. "Does she have anything to say in her defense?" he asked.

"I do!" Afton answered, stepping forward. "The bags of grain were switched, but not by my hand. I have never cheated anyone."

"Who switched the bags?" the thin man asked. His eye twitched in his sallow face. "The woman Lizette?"

Afton shook her head. Lizette had had nothing in her hands. Only one person could have committed the switch: a little boy who had come into the room with his hands behind his back and a smile on his face.

Ambrose.

"Who switched the bags?" the man asked again, and Afton could not reply.

"Her guilt forbids her to answer," Perceval said. "It is my decision that this woman is guilty of a crime against the populace." Perceval slammed his hand down upon the table in front of him. "The ownership of the mill is taken from her immediately and transferred to her son. Because he is not yet of age, I will act as his guardian." He paused and looked at his counselors. "Is there anything to add?"

"Lord Perceval," the thin man stood again. "Such an offense in a man would result in the loss of his life or, at the least, his hands, so that he would cheat no more. Your sentence is unusually merciful."

Perceval bowed his head. "Let it be recorded that my fault is mercy, then," he said, waving to the guards in the back of the hall. Afton felt she would choke on her fury at his manner and his words as he continued, "I will show mercy to the free woman Afton of Margate by allowing her to live. But her property is hereby confiscated, and her son becomes my ward. She shall serve in the fields for three hundred sixty days. After that, it will be with her as God wills. So it shall be from this day forward."

The ox would not move. As Afton wrestled with the plow the binding around her palm slipped, and she yelped as the rough wood scraped across a ruptured blister. For six days she had grappled with the rough plow, and her skin had not yet grown tough.

The little girl whose job was to goad the ox stood still and looked wistfully at Afton. "It is not time to stop," Afton snapped, rewrapping the rag around her hand. "It will not be time to stop for many more days. But when it is time, I will stop. And I will take my revenge upon her."

The child's eyes went wide in fear. Afton smiled grimly; the child thought her mad. *Aye,* she thought, gripping the handles of the plow again. *Mad I am, and with good reason, I have a mortal enemy as cunning as the devil himself.*

Endeline was to blame for everything. Afton knew it. It had been Endeline who had sent Lizette to arrange a trap for her and bait for Ambrose, and both of them had fallen easily into her hands. Ambrose had been won with the promise of the fine things at the castle, but Afton knew corrupt ambition lay behind the finery, influencing all who lived there.

The villein child jabbed the ox again with the goad, and still the stubborn animal would not move. Afton screamed and furiously threw her entire weight against the plow to propel it through the impacted soil. "I know you, Endeline," she ranted, her bare feet sliding in the muddy furrow. "You cannot bear to let another woman have anything of worth! I saw your covetous glance toward my son when he was yet a baby, and I know you have stolen him from me!"

The girl scampered away from Afton, running as though the devil himself howled in the field, and Afton walked over to the ox and struck the animal's head with her fist. The creature bellowed and blinked uncertainly, then reluctantly moved forward. Afton sighed in relief and returned to the plow.

"She will wish Perceval had been less merciful to me," she muttered under her breath. "One day, I swear it, Endeline, you will regret your first sight of me."

Nighttime brought rest to Afton's tortured body, but not her soul. From Corba's tiny cottage she could see the mill, which bustled with activity in the day and stood still as a graveyard at night. Perceval instructed Josson to keep the mill in operation, and the drunk villein who now ran it raised the percentage of the multure, charging the villagers twice as much as Afton had. But he did not live in the house. The house that Afton had shared with Ambrose sat empty.

"Give up this sadness," Corba told Afton one night as she sat in the darkness by the window. "Ye are alive. Ye have a roof over your head. Your son is alive and well in the lord's house."

"But he is *my* son!" Afton cried, slamming her tender hand down on the table. "What right have they to take my only son?"

Corba stopped stirring her pot and Afton regretted her words. Her mother knew too well how it felt to lose a child to the castle.

"I know your anger," Corba answered, her face dimly lit by the glow of the coals from her hearth. "When they took ye away I wanted to run down the road and steal ye back. And when Endeline told me to strike ye—"

"I remember, Mama," Afton whispered. "It was horrible for both of us."

"Unbearable," Corba said. "But Afton, I knew ye were alive and well. I felt a worse grief when Matthew died. Death took him out of my reach forever. Even though I shall see him again in heaven, there is no grief like that of death."

I have felt that grief, Afton wanted to cry out. *I had another baby, a baby Hubert killed. And death has surely taken Calhoun from me.* But her mother knew nothing of either love, and Afton knew the knowledge would only bring her pain.

So she answered simply, "Ambrose was all I had left."

THIRTY

"Do you sense it?" Calhoun asked Fulk as they sat on the floor of their prison. "Something unusual is afoot today."

"I have noticed it since this morning," Fulk answered, not even opening his eyes. "A different jailer left our food this morning, a man that did not walk with a limp. The guards have not changed since before sunrise, we have not been allowed out of the cell to excercise, and I have not heard the sound of horses tethered in the courtyard."

"Has the garrison been emptied?" Calhoun asked, standing up. "Could we escape?"

"The door is still locked and the window still barred," Fulk answered. "Wait, young friend, until the day is past. Then we will see what the winds of change have brought."

The winds of change did sweep through the palace after dark, bringing more than Calhoun had imagined. He and Fulk had just settled on their dirty cloaks to sleep when the door to their cell opened and three other men were roughly pushed inside. In the darkness, Calhoun could not make out who or what these men were, but they smelled of blood and death. One of them moaned through the night and tossed with pain in his sleep; the other two lay still.

As the rays of morning light came through the high narrow window, Calhoun rose on his elbow and studied the men who lay in the cell. All three wore the white tunics of the Knights Templar. The first two men gazed at the ceiling with the glassy stares of the dead, but the third still tossed in delirium. Calhoun looked at the clean-shaven face and felt the shock of recognition.

"Reynard!"

Fulk jerked awake and they examined their old companion. Delirious in his pain and burning with a raging fever, Reynard stayed far from consciousness. Fulk rose and furiously kicked the heavy oak door. "Water!" he cried out, cursing every Saracen chief he could name. "Water, or the man will die!"

Fulk's rough cries brought a response from the lethargic guard, and soon a gourd of water was thrust through the opening in the door. Calhoun wiped Reynard's flushed face and dribbled water between his parched lips. The wounded man shook his head and grasped Calhoun's shoulder with an iron fist. *"Ne t'en fait pas,* my friend. Do not trouble yourself," he whispered hoarsely. "I am ready to meet God."

"Not yet, you're not," Fulk answered, dropping to one knee beside the knight. "We're not allowing you to escape us yet."

While Calhoun bathed and cooled Reynard, Fulk found the oozing wound in Reynard's stomach and cleaned it as best he could. He ripped Reynard's surcoat into shreds and bound the wound, laughing as he did so. "I hate to tear the cloak of a holy man, Reynard," he said, wrapping the strips around Reynard's belly. "But our own cloaks have several years' worth of dirt on them."

Reynard opened his eyes and managed a weak smile. "Fulk, you insolent devil, it is good to see you," he croaked. "I scarcely recognized you behind zat beard. Could it be zat this ragged specimen with you is Calhoun of Margate?"

"It is," Fulk answered, knotting the ends of the make-shift bandage.

"Dieu merci! Praise God for his goodness," Reynard whispered, wincing as he struggled to sit up. "I 'ave been praying for your departed souls for zese many years and now I find you 'aven't departed at all."

The cell door was opened again that night and the two

dead bodies taken away. Fulk propped Reynard up against the wall, and Calhoun fed him a generous portion of their daily meal: gruel and hard black bread. Reynard was not a good patient. "It is my place to suffer as a servant of the Lord," he said, weakly gnawing on the crusty bread. "I ought to be giving you my portion."

"We wouldn't take it," Calhoun retorted. "And wasting it would violate your vow of poverty, would it not?"

As he ate, Reynard related the story of his capture. He had been riding with a small party of pilgrims on the road to Nazareth when Zengi and his war party had swept over the sand dunes and attacked. "Ze bloody Saracens killed ze men, women, and children," Reynard muttered, wincing in pain. "And we fought until we could fight no more. My two brothers fought more valiantly than I, and zey have paid ze price with their lives."

"You fought smarter," Fulk said, lifting the water gourd to Reynard's lips. "Drink."

Reynard drank noisily, then turned his head from the gourd. "Zey 'oped to ransom us, of course," Reynard said, as Fulk laid the gourd aside. "But zose of my Order 'ave vowed to give our lives, not trade them. And so zis is where I will die." He smiled weakly at Calhoun and Fulk. "I had supposed you both long dead. When you did not return to Jerusalem, I surmised you had met with bandits or murderers on ze way. Many of my brothers and your fellow knights searched for some sign of you on the road."

"We were surrendered to Zengi by a physician," Calhoun grumbled. "We were not even granted a fair fight."

"Zen why are you not ransomed?" Reynard asked, lifting an eyebrow. "Surely ze king or ze earl of Margate would pay any price to have you released."

"We fear the message was lost long before it reached England," Calhoun answered. "And I will not ask Zengi to send another. We stay alive here by taunting the Saracen prince."

"He enjoys our company," Fulk added dryly. "Every

week or so he calls us out to insult the entire Christian world to our faces. We return the insults, then we are beaten and spared for another week."

"You may not realize it, but Zengi does you honor by sparing your lives," Reynard answered. "He has killed others for no reason at all, and his name now carries great influence with the Saracens. His son, Nur al-din, follows in his footsteps to rouse and unite ze people. Many in Jerusalem fear zat our foothold zere may be weakening."

"Impossible!" Calhoun protested. "How could it be?"

"Ze world has changed since you left it," Reynard answered. "Some say England's King Henry is near death, and zere is already turmoil over who will claim ze throne. Zere is talk of anarchy and uprising among ze earls."

"Who contends for the crown?" Fulk asked quietly.

"Matilda, ze daughter of Henry, feels ze throne is her right, and many agree with her," Reynard said. "But Henry is disposed to look upon his nephew, Stephen of Blois. Zere are others who feel ze throne of England should go to Robert of Gloucester, Henry's illegitimate son."

"Never!" Calhoun shook his head.

"*D'accord*, I agree," Reynard nodded. "If ze throne is optioned to Henry's illegitimate offspring, half ze world would vie for ze crown."

"The rivers would run with blood," Fulk added, laughing, and Calhoun suddenly remembered the sickening sight of Henry's granddaughters, their faces running with blood in the hall of Margate Castle.

"I want no part of Henry's cruelty," Calhoun interjected, turning his face to the wall. "Though I have vowed to serve him ably, he is a hard man. I hope his successor renounces his bloody ways."

"We shall see," Reynard said, rising stiffly to his knees. "Now if you will excuse me, my brothers, it is time for prayer."

"You should rest, you have been ill," Fulk protested.

Reynard smiled and folded his hands together. "If I need strength, I shall find it in prayer."

The days and nights Fulk and Calhoun had spent together in solitude bound them in a knowledge of each other so complete that they found it odd to have a third man in the cell. Their conversations were often interrupted, their journeys of imagination curtailed by Reynard's insistence that unholy thoughts be banned from their minds.

Though Calhoun respected Reynard the knight, he found he did not always agree with Reynard the monk. Reynard served a strict God, one that demanded sacrifice and pain and led men to forswear every possible pleasure. Calhoun had always envisioned God as a beneficent giver of gifts and favors, a kindly parent one must be careful not to offend.

One night as they waited for sleep in silence, Reynard posed a simple question. "Would you, *mes frères,* rather have leprosy or commit a mortal sin?"

"That's easy," Calhoun answered, stretching his arms, then propping them behind his head. "I'd rather commit a mortal sin. Life with leprosy is not life at all, but slow death."

"And zere is your folly, young Calhoun," Reynard answered smoothly, "but I'll give my reasons in a moment. Fulk, what say you?"

Fulk exhaled a long, contemplative breath. "The question is not debatable, for a mortal sin already exists on my account. I cannot be forgiven, and the only mercy I have seen of God is that he allows me to continue in earth's misery instead of consigning me to hell."

Calhoun raised up on one elbow to examine Fulk's face for signs of pretense. Was he telling the truth? Did this confession explain Fulk's eternal skepticism? What had he done? Murder? Blasphemy?

"Confession is good for ze soul, brother," Reynard whispered in the dark. "Perhaps God will not deprive your soul of sanctifying grace if you confess and repent."

"I am already doomed to hell and no amount of repentance will change that," Fulk snapped. "So you have your answer, priest."

They lay in silence and finally Reynard spoke again. "I would rather have leprosy zan commit a mortal sin," he said slowly. "For when I stood before God at life's end, my leprous flesh would be cleansed, but what can cleanse a polluted soul? For zis reason I cannot take my own life, as my cowardly heart would like to do. Soon, though, I will stand before Zengi and die, and I hope you will pray for me on zat day."

His words proved prophetic. A few days later a guard beat on their door. "Priest Templar," the guard roared through the small window in the door, "Prince Zengi craves amusement. You die within the hour."

The guard moved away, and Reynard bowed his head in prayer. Calhoun stood in the corner of the room, cursing his impotence, and Fulk turned his back upon the monk.

After a few moments, Reynard stood and placed a hand on Calhoun's shoulder. *"Au revoir,* young friend," he said, smiling. "I am glad to see your courageous spirit has not been dimmed by zis captivity. Keep faith and you will yet again walk free in ze light of day."

"Argue with Zengi and stall for time," Calhoun said. "Suggest that my father will ransom you. He would, I know it! You don't have to die today, Reynard!"

"Eh bien? I am ready," Reynard answered. "It is my calling." He placed his hand on Fulk's shoulder. "Farewell, faithful Fulk," he said simply. "I give you one last chance to confess to me, for your sin may not be as grievous as you suppose."

"Go, Reynard," Fulk answered, shaking his head. "God go with you."

"He does," Reynard replied, his voice ringing with confidence. He moved to pound the door and call out.

"Guard! I am ready!"

THIRTY-ONE

March, April, May, and June were the plowing months, and during those months Afton reported to the fields every day but Sunday. The months of plowing toughened her: after the first season her hands developed deep calluses that did not wear away, and every time she took up the plow she strengthened her resolve to seek revenge upon Endeline and the house of Margate.

She despised all of them! Perceval, vile and lecherous; Endeline, cunning and cruel; Charles, weak and addled . . . even Lienor, who suffered silently in a house for religious fools. To think she had gone to Lienor, hoping that her confession and promise to love Calhoun again would somehow bring him back! Her love for Calhoun made no difference now. As she plowed the fields and wallowed in mud or dust, she grew ever more certain that Calhoun was in the earth, dead beneath some farmer's feet in an eastern land. Obviously God had not been pleased with her promise or her change of heart. Well, so be it. Afton was finished bargaining with him.

As her heart hardened, so did her appearance. The pleasing softness of her body disappeared as a result of malnutrition and hard labor, and her eyes grew wild and wary. She knew many in the village thought her mad; even Josson approached her gingerly when he happened to meet her in the fields.

After three annual seasons of plowing in Perceval's

fields, Josson came and told Afton she had completed her term of duty. She did not smile at the news, but set down her plow, wiped her hands on her dress, and walked stiffly to Corba's house.

She was twenty-five years old, a free woman, and never again would she willingly work for Perceval.

"Messengers from the king are approaching!" eleven-year-old Ambrose shouted as he burst in upon Perceval and Endeline at supper. Perceval stood so quickly he overturned his chair, but Endeline caught her husband's hand. "Calmly now," she said smoothly. "It is not the king, just his messengers." She smiled at Ambrose. "Show them in, dear."

Ambrose returned a few moments later with two knights, both of whom wore tunics richly embroidered with the king's herald. One knight unfurled a parchment and proclaimed: "King Henry is dead. Long live King Stephen!"

"So he has done it," Endeline murmured under her breath. "Henry named Stephen as his successor."

"Can it be?" Perceval whispered back, but then he stood and lifted his cup in tribute. "Long live Stephen! I will send the appropriate tribute at his coronation."

The messengers nodded and withdrew to speed their message to the next manor, and Perceval sank back into his chair. "Shouldn't you have offered them lodging?" Endeline said, looking out the door after the messengers.

"I don't think so," Perceval answered, his chin in his hand. "I am in a precarious place, my love, torn between two thrones. The forces of Matilda are even now aligning themselves with Robert of Gloucester. Matilda will oppose Stephen, and who can tell who the victor will be?"

"No one can tell," Endeline replied, straightening her shoulders. "And we have no blood ties to either side. Gather your tribute for Stephen, my lord, and make the same tribute for Matilda. Send them in separate convoys on the same day, and instruct your knights to say nothing ill of one side or the other."

Perceval smiled at her, and his eyes sparkled in appreciation. "The castle will have to produce more to maintain double tributes," he remarked offhandedly.

"The villeins will produce the extra work with pleasure,
my lord," Endeline answered, "and your family will stand
behind you in all that you do."

"We will," a young voice echoed, from a dark corner of
the room.

"Come out from there, my Ambrose," Endeline said,
beckoning the boy with her hand. "You are a little mouse,
always hiding in shadows."

"A cunning mouse," Perceval added. "Will you drink to
our new king?"

Ambrose nodded and reached for a goblet on the table.
He lifted his glass. Endeline smiled and touched the rim of
her golden goblet to his. "To Sir Ambrose," Perceval said,
nodding gravely. "Who is certain to do justice to the name
of Margate."

"I will do my best, sir," Ambrose answered, his eyes
shining darkly in the torchlight.

Calhoun shivered in the cool wind that blew through the
barred window, grateful for the partial warmth of the cast-
off cloaks Zengi had allowed him and Fulk to have. In the
corner of their cell, Fulk turned another sag-bellied rat on a
spit fashioned from a green branch. The roasting rodent was
the only meat they would eat today, but the rats had kept
them alive through years of captivity.

"Fulk," Calhoun asked, crinkling his nose in appreciation of the roasting meat. "Has it been ten or eleven winters
since we came here?"

"Twelve winters," Fulk answered, wiping his silver-
sprinkled beard with his right hand. "And in that time
we've single-handedly regulated the rodent population of
Aleppo."

"Why has Zengi not killed us?" Calhoun wondered
aloud, watching the glowing coals. "There have been occa-

sions when I know he thought about it. Just the sight of us makes him angry."

"Have you not yet divined the mind of our keeper, young knight?" Fulk asked with a wry smile. "Zengi keeps us as pets." Fulk lifted the impaled rodent from the coals. "We are his amusement. He could have ransomed us time and again, but we serve as a visible reminder that he is victorious over the Christian invaders. Besides, he loves to hear you talk of honor."

"It is only honor that has kept me sane," Calhoun said, looking at the hint of deepening evening sky through the high window. "I know that my king and my father would have ransomed me if they knew my situation. I know the cause for which I fought is right. And I am certain I have not raised my sword except in the cause of justice."

"Your talk of ideals grows more wearisome through the years," Fulk remarked lightly, nibbling at the rat. He meticulously ate half of the creature, much as a man might eat a chicken leg, then handed the spit to Calhoun. "What has honor brought you? Nothing. It has stolen your youth and granted me more than a few gray hairs."

Calhoun looked at Fulk. He spoke the truth—Fulk was very nearly gray. While Calhoun had matured into a man during the years in prison, Fulk had grown old, stooped, and wrinkled.

"How old are you?" Calhoun asked gently.

Fulk scowled at the compassion in Calhoun's voice. "Old enough to know life holds little more for me." He held his hands to the warming coals, then added, "And old enough to wonder if my life ever had purpose."

"You talk like a man who goes to his grave tomorrow," Calhoun chided him, nibbling at his dinner. "Come now, surely tomorrow will find us here together, as will the day after that. You will tell me again the stories of battle, and I will describe for you again the charms of my beloved Afton."

"Your beloved Afton is no longer a maiden," Fulk

groused. "She is surely married to some minor noble and is counting the gray strands in her own hair."

"Her golden hair will not go gray," Calhoun laughed. "My Afton will remain as fair as the morning. If I never see her again, why, that is better, for her memory will never fade from me. In my dreams she will always be beautiful, chaste, and brave. Do you not have a handsome woman in your memory, Fulk?"

"One," Fulk muttered.

A guard barked "Quiet!" at the door of their cell, and they were silent until his footsteps had passed out of range.

"Miranda," Fulk answered Calhoun's unspoken question. "On the day I feel death's grip I will tell you her story, but not before." He grinned at his young companion. "I will thus give you something to look forward to."

The next morning Calhoun awoke to unusual sounds. From the narrow peephole in his cell door he could see Zengi's warriors rushing by in full armor. The noise and commotion of battle began at daybreak and continued throughout the day and night.

"Are we still under attack?" Calhoun asked Fulk as the rosy pink of dawn began to appear in their small window. "What army keeps Zengi enclosed in his castle?"

"A clever one," Fulk answered. "I believe we are seeing the beginning of a siege, though I pray I am wrong. The populations of entire cities die in a siege, young friend, and prisoners are the first to go. If a fat rat crawls across your face tonight, do not spare him. The entire city may be feasting on rats before the siege is done."

Three days later Calhoun realized Fulk was right. They were summoned from their dark prison and brought before Zengi, who glared at them from his high seat. "The Christians are besieging the city," he stated flatly, his tone nasal and more clipped than usual. "I would like to ask advice of my two resident Christian prisoners. What tactics would you advise, gentlemen?"

"I will give no aid to you," Calhoun declared. "I will not raise my voice or my hand against my brothers."

Zengi scowled and turned toward Fulk. "Your friend's misguided notions do not amuse me today," Zengi snarled. "I need advice, old man, and you will give it."

"You might try Grecian fire," Fulk said quietly. "The mixture of oil and rock is a gruesome rain upon those at the base of the city walls."

Zengi waved his hand. "We know of Grecian fire," he said impatiently. "You have been in prison too long, Fulk."

"Be still!" Calhoun hissed at Fulk. "Have you no honor left in you?"

"All I have within me is a smattering of life," Fulk said. "I desire to live it in relative peace, not under siege."

"Wisely said, old man," Zengi answered. "What else is in your head?"

"Only this," Fulk answered. He closed his eyes. "If the wells run dry, have your men bury themselves in the dirt to conserve the moisture in their bodies. If food and water are scarce, equip each man with a dagger, that he might eat his own flesh until sustenance arrives."

Zengi's eyes gleamed. "By Allah, you are beginning to think like me," he crowed. "It shall be done."

The siege wore on for three more days. During that time the prisoners of Zengi received neither food nor water. "He didn't even give us a dagger," Fulk grumbled in their cell. "I thought perhaps he might."

"You are a madman," Calhoun whispered from his corner. "Zengi does not give daggers to prisoners."

He lay back on the cool stone and tried to collect his thoughts, but his body cried out for water. Strange visions churned in his brain, and he remembered two skeletons he once had found in the sand, both bleached by the sand and sun. One skeleton wore the tunic and armor of a Christian, the other the clothing of a Saracen. They had killed each other bravely, but their sacrifice had gone unnoticed in the madness of warfare. What difference did their sacrifices make?

"If I get home," Calhoun muttered, "I will find my Afton and marry her. I will lay down my sword and never pick it up again."

"You do not know yourself," Fulk answered from the darkness of his corner. "You are a knight and you will die by the sword as you have lived by it."

"No," Calhoun murmured weakly. "Fighting and death accomplish nothing. Only family matters. Husband. Wife. Mother. Father. Children." He smiled briefly, then rolled over to look at Fulk, his eyes burning in their intensity. "If we survive this siege, I will escape or die within the week. Zengi has taken twelve years of my life. He shall have no more."

"Zengi did not deserve to know you for even a day," Fulk whispered, then the old man slipped over onto the floor, unconscious.

CALHOUN
1140

A man's pride brings him low,
but a man of lowly spirit gains honor.

PROVERBS 29:23, NIV

THIRTY-TWO

A mob raged outside the strong walls of Margate Castle, but Calhoun felt himself endued with superhuman strength and agility. Lightly he leapt from tower to tower, raining arrows upon the dark-eyed assassins who screamed at him in fury; then he jumped into the thick of the fray and began to slash and hack his way through the mob. He was invincible, and even though battle cries and the clang of swords rang in his ear, he knew the day would have a victorious outcome. The sounds of battle grew louder, smoke burned his nostrils, and he gloried in the sheer gore and violence before him.

A Saracen warrior stood with his back to him, and Calhoun raised his sword to remove the man's head, but the warrior whirled around.

Zengi!

"By the strength of my God, I'll have your head now!" Calhoun roared, and his blade sliced cleanly through Zengi's neck. Blood spurted into Calhoun's face, and a wave of repulsion swept over him . . . then his parched lips opened in search of more life-giving liquid.

"Up, you sons of dogs!" a voice behind him spoke. "If you would live, get up and drink."

Calhoun opened his eyes, blinking in confusion. He was not in a battle at Margate, but on the floor of his cell in Zengi's prison. An earthen pot sat by the door, and in it was a gourd—and water. "Fulk, we are saved," Calhoun croaked, crawling toward the pot. "The siege is lifted."

The guard behind the door laughed. "Give thanks to Allah for Nur al-din," he said. "Zengi's son routed those who besieged us. You owe your lives to the mercy and strength of Nur al-din, Christian knights!"

Calhoun brought the gourd to Fulk and slowly poured a slow stream into the man's mouth. Fulk's eyes flickered, and his swollen tongue weakly licked his lips. "Easy, there is more," Calhoun said, crawling back for another dipper of water. "We have an entire jar of water to ourselves."

Fulk pressed his cracked lips together and tried to smile. "Never was water more precious," he croaked.

Calhoun sat up and lifted the jug with both hands, drinking deeply. The water seemed to sit upon his stomach and he felt nauseous. "Aye," he said, dragging the pot over to Fulk. "Water is precious, but freedom is infinitely more so. God has seen fit to let us live, and his mercy shall not be in vain. When you have regained your strength, Fulk, we shall escape this place or die trying."

They ate well that night, and through their solitary window Calhoun could hear sounds of celebration. "Zengi's city celebrates today," Fulk said, putting his ear to the outer wall. "And, knowing Zengi's pride, I believe he will launch a counterattack very soon. He will not suffer a near-defeat without a counterstrike."

"And?" Calhoun lowered his voice, mindful that the guard could be outside the door.

"We escape while the army is diverted," Fulk answered. "Never has Zengi been as angry or as weak as he is today. Tomorrow or the next day will bring our chance for freedom, for Zengi will not fail to act quickly."

That night when the guard slipped their bowl of gruel through the small opening in the door, Fulk rapped to get the man's attention. "Zengi rides tonight, does he not?"

The unseen guard paused and did not move away. His

muffled voice came through the door. "You know of this attack?"

"Certainly," Fulk answered confidently. "Zengi often consults me on his plans. He has asked for my advice about how to defeat the Christians who dared to besiege this city."

"Indeed?" the guard replied, and Calhoun could hear skepticism in his voice.

"Yes," Fulk answered. "And I have sketched a map of the Christian city of Damascus here in the floor. If Zengi rides for Damascus, you may look at this map, describe it to him, and earn yourself a place of honor far from these dread dungeons."

Calhoun held his breath. How ambitious was their unseen guard? The man knew Fulk's words contained more than a germ of truth—

A jangling noise reached them, then the door creaked, and the guard's dark head peered into the room. "Here," Fulk said, standing innocently against the far wall. He pointed to scratches on the floor. "This is the map of Damascus."

The guard hesitated and drew his scimitar, peering at the scratches on the floor. Calhoun and Fulk leaned against the wall of their cell, their hands casually behind their backs. The guard glanced warily about, then approached.

"You see," Fulk said, advancing toward the map and pointing down at the floor, "just inside the city gates you will find a stable." The guard peered more closely, and Calhoun reached silently for the water jug. With his remaining strength, he swept the jug into his hands and brought it down over the guard's head. The man staggered for a moment, then fell, and Fulk sprang to close the cell door.

"Why don't we leave?" Calhoun asked, his heart racing. "Why do we wait?"

"We wait for darkness," Fulk answered, tearing the guard's tunic into strips. "We keep the guard quiet and we leave after Zengi's troops have departed. If we go now, we would get no farther than the stairs." He quickly bound the unconscious man's hands and grinned up at Calhoun. "Obey me, zealous friend, and I will get you home safely."

Zengi's warriors rode for nearby Damascus as the sun set, and when the last horse had left the courtyard Fulk and Calhoun armed themselves with the guard's dagger and scimitar and crept from their prison cell. The castle was unusually quiet, for those who had not ridden off with Zengi had gone out in search of food and water to replenish the city's supply.

As they climbed the stairs from the dungeon to the courtyard, Calhoun nearly ran into a veiled serving woman, whose dark eyes widened in fear at the sight of him. Calhoun shook his head and put his finger across his lips, and the woman retreated silently, then turned to run down the hall.

"Quickly! She'll alert the remaining guards!" Fulk said, dashing down a long corridor. "Here! This will take us out of this accursed place."

Calhoun wished there were more guards in his path; his soul burned with the desire to exact vengeance for the beatings, bruises, and blood he had spilled in these halls of Zengi's. But the palace was nearly deserted. They ran through the open courtyard, toward the stables, where they surprised a young warrior napping by the door. Awakened by the sound of their running footsteps, he leapt to his feet and rattled a question in Arabic.

"What was that?" Calhoun asked, waving his scimitar.

The young man tensed and drew his dagger. "By all the gods, we don't have time for this," Fulk answered and rushed the warrior. Calhoun followed and, as steel bit steel, his scimitar knocked the dagger from the young man's hand. The startled guard struggled, but Calhoun and Fulk grabbed his arms, dragged him to the stable and left him unconscious in a pile of manure.

Fulk grinned at Calhoun. "Now we blend with the darkness," he said, his silver hair gleaming in the faint moonlight. "Like shadows, we fly out of this city and find shelter in the desert."

They gathered rough blankets from the stable and covered their thread-worn clothing. Thus arrayed, Calhoun and Fulk looked like the other bedraggled siege survivors, and so passed by the guards at the city gate without arousing suspicion.

Later, as they walked along the desert road, Calhoun felt the sting of disappointment because their escape had been too easily accomplished. *Do you not feel gratitude for God's favor and protection?* his conscience challenged him. But he just shook his head.

"Not a worthy opponent did we meet," he complained. "After twelve years of confinement, my blade thirsts for the blood of those who tormented us!"

Fulk kept his eyes steadily on the road ahead. "Turn your thoughts from vengeance to survival, young friend. Now we look for food, water, and clothing. We will rebuild our strength, then we shall journey home. Our work as soldiers of God is done."

"I cannot go home without vengeance upon Zengi!" Calhoun interrupted. "Turn and run from the man? How can you suggest it, Fulk? He has taken twelve years of our lives! I would kill twelve—no, twelve *dozen* Saracens to exact my revenge!"

"I promised your father that I would deliver you home safely and I intend to keep my word," Fulk answered, his eyes puffy and tired in the starlight. "I did not promise to kill Saracens for revenge. We are alive, young friend, and that is what matters. There is no dishonor in survival."

Just before daybreak, they came upon a small bedouin camp and waited behind the sand dunes until the men had taken the sheep and goats to graze. Calhoun would have descended upon the women and children and simply taken their food, but Fulk put out a hand to stop him. He waited for a long time, it seemed to Calhoun, until a boy of about eight or nine set out toward the fields with a large bundle.

"The dinner boy," Fulk whispered. "He carries food for the men." Fulk motioned to Calhoun, and they crept behind the dunes and intersected the boy's path. His dark eyes opened wide at the sight of the two men before him, but Fulk smiled and pointed carefully at the boy's bundle, then at his own mouth.

The boy paused, and Calhoun could see fear and uncertainty in his eyes. What was to stop him from screaming? The women would certainly hear him, and the men were probably not far away. Surely Fulk's insanity would result in their capture—or their deaths.

But the boy nodded and held out the bag of food with a shy smile. Fulk bowed graciously, took the bag, and sat upon the sand. He held out a loaf of flat white bread to Calhoun. "Eat this," he commanded gruffly, "and be pleasant about it. Smile."

The boy said something in Arabic, and Calhoun shook his head, not understanding. Fulk, however, smiled, and pointed to the rough horse blanket on his shoulders. He pulled it off and handed it to the boy, while gesturing that he now had nothing to wear over his robe.

The boy grinned and gathered up the blanket, then turned and scampered back in the direction of the camp.

"Let's be gone," Calhoun urged, grabbing another piece of bread from the boy's lunch. "He'll be back with the others."

"No, he won't," Fulk answered slowly, his eyes on the boy's footprints. "The men are in the fields, and the women are busy. The boy will be back. These people are natural traders."

Before long, the boy did return, and he was carrying two cloaks of rough wool. Fulk nodded in appreciation and accepted his cloak. Calhoun willingly removed the heavy horse blanket from his shoulders and presented it to the boy, who beamed and gave him the second cloak.

They might have bartered longer, but a man's sudden shout broke the stillness. Startled, Calhoun and Fulk looked up to see one of the men coming toward them. Spurred into action, they grabbed the food and the cloaks and ran over the dunes until they were sure no one followed.

"I can't go on getting our breakfast this way," Fulk said, gasping to catch his breath. "Soon some young girl will out-run me."

"You are right, old man," Calhoun answered, laughing. He bit a hunk of meat from a goat's leg in his hand. "But today we shall eat well."

As the sun rose higher in the sky, Fulk pointed toward a scrubby olive tree. "We should rest here during the day," he said. "We will move at night. We cannot have the sun steal our remaining energy."

Calhoun reluctantly agreed and, after glancing warily about for tarrents, whose bite might prove fatal in their weakened condition, the two men lay down under the olive tree. Fulk fell asleep immediately, but Calhoun tossed and turned restlessly. Images of home passed before his mind's eye, and he frowned. Did home still exist? Would he ever really make the journey back to Margate? Tormented by his thoughts, Calhoun tossed and turned until fatigue finally overcame him. Yet, as slumber at last claimed him, one final image flitted before him: one with laughing gray eyes and golden hair and a husky, dream-induced voice that called his name. . . .

He awoke instantly when Fulk's hand tapped his shoulder. "Time to rise," Fulk said, putting the dagger again at his belt. Calhoun looked around and saw that it was dusk. "We will find food, and we will walk southward, toward Jerusalem," Fulk continued. "Perhaps we can find a camp and secure horses."

The prospect of riding again stirred Calhoun, and he strapped the scimitar to his waist with relish. "Why do we linger, then?" he asked, but Fulk held up a warning hand.

"Zengi's battle at Damascus is done, or nearly so," he said. "The Saracen warriors will be scattered throughout the desert, either returning victorious or sorrowful in their defeat. We must stay off the road and be wary."

Calhoun nodded. "I am with you," he answered, and they set off.

They had not gone far when they saw firelight in the distance. Fulk and Calhoun crept toward the light, keeping low in the shadows, until they crouched behind a sand dune. From there they clearly saw what remained of Zengi's war party: less than two dozen warriors milled about or rested around the campfire while physicians tended their wounds. Five men stood outside the circle as lookouts; two others guarded a cluster of horses. Fulk pointed toward the animals, and Calhoun nodded.

Through gestures Fulk outlined his simple plan. He would seize one guard and Calhoun the other, then they would each mount a horse and ride swiftly away from the camp. Fulk laid his finger over his lips to emphasize the need for silence, and Calhoun nodded impatiently. He was not a child! He well knew Fulk's intent: with God's aid, they should be able to ride away without the men in camp even knowing they had come and gone.

The horses were some distance from the men at the campfire, and the two warriors who stood with the animals were intent upon their conversation. Before moving closer, Calhoun studied the horses with longing eyes. It had been so long since he had ridden! And these were magnificent beasts, the quick, surefooted stallions of the desert, known for endurance and agility.

He had already decided upon a black stallion with long legs when he and Fulk crept near in the shadows thrown by a clouded moon. With a wordless signal they ran toward the hapless guards, and Calhoun felt his scimitar pierce the guard's rib cage as his left hand stifled the man's cry. Within a moment the man crumpled to the ground, and Calhoun flung himself astride the black stallion.

Fulk struggled with his man but, as Calhoun watched, the dagger found its way home, the man fell, twitched, and lay still. Fulk ran for a horse, and Calhoun kicked the stallion's sides, turning the animal's head with a quick pull on his mane.

Calhoun knew he should ride away, but he could not.

Something within him demanded restitution, warring as it did so against the small inner voice that called him to follow his mentor, who silently mounted a horse and rode away. But the younger knight's anger at all he had endured suddenly exploded within him, silencing all but the cry for vengeance. Clenching the handle of his bloody scimitar, Calhoun thrust it above his head, then turned his horse toward the men in the camp.

"Cursed be Zengi of the Saracens!" he yelled, thundering past the startled warriors. "Praised be Jesus Christ!"

He whooped in glee as the Saracens stirred like angry bees in a hive. Defiantly, he circled once around the camp, then caught up with Fulk, who rode southward. "You fool!" Fulk roared as Calhoun galloped past, but Calhoun only grinned and clenched his scimitar more tightly. He would not only escape Zengi, he would cover the act in glory. *This* would be a tale fit for regaling a company of valiant knights.

Fulk's horse galloped only a few paces behind, and Calhoun's heart raced as their desert stallions pounded over the sand dunes, as swift as the wind. Behind them, Calhoun heard the sound of other hooves and knew that some of the warriors were in pursuit, but he urged his horse on in the mad rush of victory. He had escaped! He had killed an enemy! Even if one of the pursuing warriors' arrows found its way into his heart, nothing could steal his victory from him.

As they raced on, Calhoun knew he had chosen his horse well, for he and Fulk soon outdistanced their pursuers. When he was certain no warriors lingered in their trail, he slowed his mount to a canter, then to a trot. Fulk's horse still followed, and Calhoun glanced back, grinning gleefully. But the proud words he had been about to utter stilled in his throat when he saw that Fulk's head was down.

"What's wrong, old man?" Calhoun called, a vague unrest growing in his heart. "Don't tell me you wanted to leave without saying farewell."

Fulk made no reply. Instead, his horse slowed to a walk

and, as Calhoun watched, the large man slowly slid off the animal's broad back and landed in a heap in the sand.

Calhoun's smile froze when he saw the long arrow protruding from Fulk's back.

"Fulk!" Calhoun shrieked and he clumsily slid off his horse and ran to his teacher's side. The older knight's eyelids fluttered weakly as Calhoun sat him upright. "Should I pull the arrow out?" he asked frantically. "Tell me, Fulk! What should I do?"

"I want . . . to . . . lie . . . down," Fulk managed to whisper, and Calhoun knew the arrow would have to be removed. Biting his lip, he braced Fulk's back with his left hand and tugged on the arrow with his right. The bloody instrument came out in his hand with a hissing sound, the triangular arrowhead tearing the flesh more severely during its exit than it had in its entrance.

Fulk screamed in pain, and Calhoun fought down panic as he hastily tore a strip of wool from his tunic and stuffed it into the wound to staunch the bleeding. "Be still, Fulk, and I will take you to a doctor," Calhoun babbled, reclining his friend in the sand. "The sun is not yet up, so you will be cool. The doctor will make you well, you will see. Then we will be on our journey."

"Be still," Fulk whispered raggedly, grasping at Calhoun's cloak. "And help me!"

"What?" Calhoun asked, bewildered. His stoic teacher's eyes were filled with an emotion he had never seen there, not in all the years he had known and fought beside him: unmitigated terror.

"I am going to die," Fulk said, spitting his words out with effort. "And I am frightened!"

"You're not going to die," Calhoun said, tearing another strip of cloth from the edge of his tunic. "This is just an accident, and it's all my fault. If I had not been so intent on showing myself, we could have escaped with no trouble. I don't know what possessed me, Fulk, but I—"

His words died off under Fulk's wide, wild gaze. "Your

main fault has killed me," he wheezed. "All these years I tried to warn you against it, to make you turn your back on your damnable pride, and now I see that it has won. And, one day, it will kill you, too, young Calhoun."

"Forgive me," Calhoun whispered brokenly, ripping his cloak. "Just let me make another bandage."

"There is no need for a bandage," Fulk answered, spitting blood on the sand. His trembling hand sought Calhoun's and held it tightly. "What I need is a companion. I journey alone to death and I am frightened, young friend, for I go to everlasting hell."

Calhoun covered Fulk's trembling hand with his own. "Perhaps you do not go to hell," he said, trying to keep his voice calm. "Even if a man commits a mortal sin, is not God merciful?"

"Miranda," Fulk answered. The word gurgled in his throat, and he pulled his hand from Calhoun's grasp, struggling to sit upright. Calhoun supported him as he spat another mouthful of blood and drew a slow, shallow breath. "I loved Miranda. She was all to me and she was beautiful, much like your Afton. I was . . . jealous. So much so that I thought I would go mad."

A fit of coughing seized Fulk, and blood spewed out of his mouth. Calhoun wiped his friend's face with a shred of cloth, and the injured man inhaled slowly, painfully.

Oh, God! Calhoun screamed in his mind, pleading in desperation. *Spare him! Do not let me have killed him. . . .*

Fulk closed his eyes and continued speaking. "One day I accused her of loving another and I struck her. She fell against an oil lamp and the cottage caught fire. As I ran to help her, she fought me off, screaming, and a priest ran into the house to aid her."

He wheezed, frantically trying to draw in air, and Calhoun waited until Fulk got his breath and continued. "I pushed the priest out of the way, and he fell upon a chair I had broken in my anger. The splintered wood pierced his neck—" he broke off, his eyes filled with pain. Calhoun wondered if the cause was Fulk's injury, or his story. When he resumed, his voice was a flat, emotionless whisper. "As I watched him die, I knew God could never forgive that murder, or my jealous temper."

"You don't know that," Calhoun answered softly.

Fulk nodded impatiently and drew a quick breath. "Yes, I do. I had murdered a priest and set my house afire. And Miranda ran out through the flames, screaming that I was the devil himself. I dropped to my knees in the flames and threw my arms about the priest's burning body, thinking to burn myself alive, but villagers pulled me out of the house and preserved my wretched life."

Fulk struggled again to catch his breath, and Calhoun nodded slowly. "The scar upon your cheek . . ."

Fulk lifted his hand weakly to the cross-shaped area of dead flesh upon his face. "'Twas the imprint of the cross on the priest's rosary, which burned into me as I flung myself upon him. It was a sign from God, one that showed he had marked me forever as a man beyond redemption, beyond love."

Fulk erupted in another violent fit of coughing, and Calhoun lowered him gently to the ground. "Fulk, never have I had a better teacher or a more loyal friend. That priest's death was an accident! But even if it were not, if God is God and all-powerful, then surely he has the power to forgive even the greatest of sinners!"

Fulk could no longer speak, but he clasped Calhoun's tunic tightly. Desperation gleamed in his eyes. Searching for words, Calhoun pulled his friend upright again until they were face-to-face, master to pupil—but suddenly Calhoun felt their roles were reversed.

"Fulk," he said urgently, "can you forgive me for bringing you to this place? Can you forgive my damnable pride?"

The hand on his tunic relaxed somewhat, and Fulk slowly nodded.

"Then, if you can forgive me the act that has cost you your life, surely God can forgive any sinful act you have committed! You don't need a priest to make your case with God, for he is all-powerful and all-knowing, and he knows and forgives your repentant heart."

Fulk gasped in reply, a strange light coming to his eyes—and then they closed slowly. He placed his hand protectively on Calhoun's shoulder and, as the young man watched with tears streaming down his face, the mighty Fulk gasped three times in quick succession without exhaling . . . and then his hand fell limply to his side.

THIRTY-THREE

Afton straightened her back and groaned. Though Perceval's forest was cool and shady, berry-picking was backbreaking work. She and Corba worked to fill their empty stewpot, so anything edible Afton could find went into the pot for supper.

The past eight years in Corba's house had taught Afton how hard life as a villein could be. In the castle, Afton had been sheltered and pampered; at the mill, she had known the luxury of a steady income and a comfortable home. But in Corba's cottage there were no luxuries and few even of life's most basic necessities.

While her mother went to the castle to perform her boon work for the estate, Afton wove on the loom; toiled in their little garden plot of cabbage, lettuce, leeks, spinach, and parsley; or tended the chickens. Two or three times a week she ventured into the forest to look for berries or primrose.

It was in the dark of the forest that Afton could forget her situation and become a child again. She stretched her weary arms and put down her basket of berries, moving past the prickly bushes to a cascade of wild roses. She silently cursed the thorns that obstinately pricked her callused fingers and tucked several bright buds in her hair. Fingering the delicate petals, she laughed softly.

Corba would think her addled if she saw her thus, so it probably was just as well that Corba never followed her daughter into the forest.

Afton grabbed her basket and sprinted through the forest, heading by instinct to her favorite place. She saw the twin oaks from a distance, their green limbs reaching high above the other trees, and soon she stood in front of the massive trunks of the two entwined trees. Four years ago, in a fit of melancholy, she had carved names upon the trunks, and those names were there in the scarred wood still, having grown deeper and darker with time. Afton's fingers wandered tenderly over Calhoun's name, as they always did when she came to this place, and she whispered a prayer for his soul.

She moved quickly past the trees to the cool green pool. Leaning forward upon a rock, she examined her reflection in the still water. "Thirty years old and you still fancy yourself a maiden," she told her reflection, laughing. The water was kind to her, softening the tired creases around her eyes and the resolute line of her jaw. The rosebuds in her hair winked brightly back at her from the water, and Afton rose and imagined herself once again in front of a mirror, adorned in a lovely gown.

She hiked her skirts to a manageable length, curtsied gracefully to the oak trees, and began a slow and graceful dance to music that played from her memory. The soft, dead leaves on the forest floor made no sound as she danced lightly over them, and the pool did not protest when she fell breathless at its edge to splash water on her flushed face.

She reclined upon the rock near the lip of the pool until her gaiety had passed, then she straightened her tunic, released her skirt so that it fell once again to the ground, and took up her basket. She touched Calhoun's name again as she passed the tree trunk, a final offering to days long gone. She cast a last, wistful glance back at the pool of the twin trees—her only refuge, the one place where she could climb out of her protective shell—and then turned to leave the forest. When she stood on the road to Margate Castle, she let the walls come back into place, once again fortifying her soul.

She knew many of the villagers thought her mad or bewitched, and she did little to dispel the notion. With the village women and her brother's wives she was silent; though they knew little of life except its hardships, Afton often thought them more fortunate than she. They did not miss the comfort of a soft bed, nor did they curl their noses in distaste when their clothing smelled. Indeed, why should they? For they had never taken a bath nor known the sweet scent of perfume. Their tongues did not rebel against the taste of a bland soup of strawberry leaves, nor did they complain when their hair matted with dirt. They calmly accepted all life had to offer because they had never known anything better.

Corba seemed to be aware of Afton's discomfort and once suggested that she enter the convent. Afton did not have the heart to remind her mother that the nunnery was reserved for the daughters of rich men, those who could afford to pay the dowry the convent demanded. Even so, she could have entered the nunnery as a servant, except for two things: a most unchristian desire to take revenge upon Endeline, and the hope that Ambrose would one day choose to return to her.

She waited patiently for those two desires to be fulfilled. As she rocked her brothers' infant children, she remembered her own children and swore once again to avenge them. Slowly her hatred would burn within her, growing ever stronger as it focused upon the one Afton knew she would someday destroy . . . one enemy, one foul creature: the good lady Endeline. And the litany of sins would begin again in Afton's cold heart: Was it not Endeline who had married her to Hubert, father and murderer of Afton's daughter? Had Endeline not stolen Ambrose, Afton's beautiful son? Aye, Endeline had taken the mill, sent Calhoun away to his death, and stolen Afton's own childhood, making her ashamed and afraid of her rightful heritage.

"I will kill her with a wooden stake from the forest," Afton thought absently one afternoon as she rocked

Jacopo's infant daughter. "I will walk into the castle, go straight up the stairs and into her chamber, and kill her as she sleeps in her bed. Then I will be hung, of course, but I will have my revenge."

She only had to wait until Corba was safely in the grave and out of Perceval's reach, for she knew well that if she attempted anything rash her mother would surely be punished. So Afton stalled her anger, and worked, and watched over her aging mother as the days and months passed.

As he watched the sun set on yet another day, Calhoun felt as though he had aged more since beginning his solitary journey home than he had during his years of imprisonment. Fulk was gone, and the young knight had come to realize how much he had relied upon his master and friend.

"It is as you said, Fulk," he muttered aloud as he rode his black stallion northward from Damascus. "God sent my moment of revelation, and I saw myself for the prideful fool I am. May God have mercy on me for the pain I brought to you."

His eyes gleamed now with the dark knowledge that comes from introspection, and those who met him on the road smiled timidly and then stayed far out of his way. That night, as he sat near a campfire outside of Constantinople, he heard one knight tell another: "Calhoun of Margate is surely a tormented man. He speaks little, but it is rumored he killed a thousand Saracens in Outremer."

If they knew I killed my master, they would not welcome me at all, Calhoun thought bitterly. *But if God has any mercy, I will carry that dark secret to my grave.*

The next day, he entered Constantinople. There he fell in with a band of pilgrims returning to England and learned that King Henry had been dead for five years. Stephen of Blois now wore the crown, and "a more mild and genial king we've never known," the lord of Lydd told Calhoun. "He's a good man and gentle, but what England needs now is a rod of iron."

The lord looked carefully at Calhoun. "I see that you are a knight, and battle-scarred," he said, seeing the marks of Zengi's whips upon Calhoun's arms. "May I have the pleasure of knowing your name?"

"Calhoun. I have been away for many years."

"Do you return home or to service, noble Calhoun?"

"I return—" Calhoun faltered. Did he still have a home? "That remains to be seen," he finished, bowing politely.

"It is enough that you return," the lord nodded. He extended an arm to his campfire. "Come, join our feast. If you have been away, you will want to know of England."

"I do." Calhoun bowed to all assembled and settled himself comfortably around their campfire. He ate with relish, delighting in the familiar tastes of foods he had not seen in years. How wonderful the food was, how delightful the spices and honey-sweetened breads!

While they ate, the lord described the civil war that currently divided England. Robert of Gloucester, the illegitimate son of Henry, had joined forces with Matilda, Henry's daughter. Together they vied for the throne of England. Matilda had gone so far as to abandon the gentle ways of women and put on armor to lead an army against her cousin Stephen. "Things are at a strange pass when a woman wears armor and the king is clothed in mercy," the lord remarked. "But England runs with blood these days. Family wars against family, and neighbor against neighbor."

"Truly?" Calhoun asked, dipping his bread into a bowl of porridge.

"Indeed. John Marshall, a fierce and loyal ally of Matilda's, was forced to hand his son to Stephen as a hostage," the lord said, leaning forward with an air of confidentiality. "Then Marshall, who fought for Matilda, sent a message to the king that he didn't care if the boy was hung, for he had the anvils and hammer with which to forge still better sons. Well," the lord laughed, "the king set out to hang the boy for his father's treason, but at the sight of the poor lad upon the tree, Stephen couldn't do it. He cut the boy down, took him back to the castle, and spent the afternoon playing 'knight' with the child."

Calhoun shook his head in disbelief. "This man is descended from William the Conqueror?"

"You would never have known it, but he is the Conqueror's grandson," the lord said with a nod. "But he is too gentle for England's throne and he does no justice. My lord and I have allied our houses with Matilda's forces."

"And your lord is?" Calhoun asked.

The lord of Lydd puffed out his generous chest. "The earl of Margate, Lord Perceval," he exclaimed proudly.

Six months later, as his homeland gave up its harvest and prepared for the coming winter, Calhoun finally left the lord of Lydd and his party at their estate. For all the time they had traveled together, he had avoided revealing more of his identity. Now, as he took his leave, he thanked his host profusely, then mounted his stallion to ride for Margate. The stallion, who had spent all his days in the desert suns of the East, pulled restlessly at the bit. He was not accustomed to the chilly winds that assaulted him and his most recent master in this new land.

As he journeyed toward Margate, Calhoun wondered what changes lay in store at home. Why had his father turned against a longstanding loyalty to the throne and allied himself with Matilda? Did this mean that the knights of Margate now served in Matilda's army? Would his father expect him to disobey his vow of fealty to the throne of England?

On a deserted stretch of road, two mounted knights rode toward him, the royal ensign of England flying proudly. "Halt," one of them called through his iron visor. "Identify yourself, sir, and state your purpose for traveling on the king's highway."

Calhoun rested his right hand on the scimitar at his side, but forced himself to speak agreeably. "I am Calhoun, son of Perceval, earl of Margate," he said clearly. "I am journeying home."

The knight who had spoken raised his visor and peered uncertainly at Calhoun. "I know of Charles and Ambrose," he called, frowning. "But I do not know of Calhoun of Margate."

"I have been on the expedition of Christ for many years," Calhoun answered quietly. "I return now to show my father that I am alive and seek service in the name of my father and king."

"Swear your allegiance to Stephen, and you shall pass," the other knight barked. "For Perceval has allied himself with the forces of King Stephen."

Calhoun raised an eyebrow, then called out his answer: "Gentlemen, if God has ordained Stephen king, then I swear my allegiance without benefit of my father's alliance." He pulled the reins taut and his horse jolted forward. "Now, by your leave, sirs, I am going home."

Darkness lay over the village like a blanket as Calhoun's horse clip-clopped over the well-worn road. The knight guessed that, while candles were plentiful in Outremer, they were still a luxury for villeins.

It might as well be a town of ghosts, he thought, *much like the burned Saracen villages we saw on our way to Jerusalem.* Not a light flickered at a window; not a soul disturbed the stillness, save his own.

He looked about to see the mill that lay on his left. He frowned, for it, too, lay quiet and gloomy. Calhoun scrutinized the mill and house carefully as his horse walked past. Though the path to the mill house shone clear in the moonlight, the garden plot was overgrown with yellowed weeds, and tall grass blocked the entrance to the house. He sighed. Fulk was right. Afton had surely married and left this place; perhaps she lived in another village or even in a city.

He spurred the stallion, and the animal cantered smoothly down the castle road through the forest and past the open meadow, both stirring memories in Calhoun's mind as he passed them. Soon he glimpsed Margate Castle itself, its tall twin towers majestic against the purpling night sky. Calhoun noticed with approval that Perceval had updated the castle walls. The square towers had been rounded, leaving an enemy no place to hide. *Lessons from the East,* Calhoun thought to himself. *The Saracens' influence extends even here.*

"Who goes there?" Two guards called out their warning from the tower post as he approached, pointing the arrows in their bows at Calhoun's unshielded chest. *A trifle slow,* Calhoun thought, warily eyeing the men's weapons. *If I had intended damage, I could already have inflicted it.* He opened his mouth to speak, but a sudden surge of emotion threatened to block his words.

He was home.

He cleared his throat awkwardly, sounding much like a boy asking a maid for his first dance, and replied, "Calhoun, son of Perceval."

The two guards conferred for a moment, then a third guard in stout armor moved to the edge of the tower and peered down at Calhoun. "Prove yourself," the man commanded, his voice rough and familiar. "The night is thick with traitors."

"I know you, Sir Jarvis," Calhoun answered, shifting easily on his horse. "And I long to see my brother, Charles, and my sister, Lienor, who resides in the nunnery."

"And?" one of the young knights asked, keeping the line of his arrow upon Calhoun.

"And what?" Calhoun shrugged. "I have no other brothers or sisters. Would you have me name the servants as well?"

"You do not know Ambrose?" There was a faint trace of wonder in the young knight's voice, and Calhoun was irritated by it.

"No," Calhoun's voice sharpened. "But I know he is no son of my father's."

Jarvis smiled in satisfaction. "Praise be to God! Raise the gate!" he commanded. "It is Calhoun, returned from certain death. Let him pass!"

Calhoun heard the chink of the chains that operated the castle gate and he nudged his stallion forward.

The walls of Margate Castle had not heard such weeping and wailing since the day Henry smote his own grandchildren in the hall. Awakened from sleep, Lord Perceval bounded down the stairs, red-eyed, to embrace his son. Endeline wept and screamed hysterically that her son was back from the dead. Charles came from his bed, bewildered, and Calhoun noticed with surprise that the years had left his older brother nearly bald.

Morgan and Lunette, now middle-aged women, kissed Calhoun's hands and showered him with tears. A new maid hung back against the wall and smiled coyly in his direction, but Calhoun forgot about her when the knights entered the hall to welcome him home. The older knights in Perceval's service bowed stiffly in almost reverential respect, and the young knights saluted him in awe. All came forward to welcome the missing son home and pay him homage. All but one. One well-appointed young knight held back, regarding Calhoun coolly, as one would scrutinize an opponent.

"You are here. You are alive!" Perceval kept repeating, and Calhoun answered over and over that he had been a prisoner, but, with Fulk's help, had escaped. "The honorable Fulk endured until the end, Father," he said, grasping Perceval's hand as he led his father to a chair. "He kept his vow to you with his life."

"Bless Fulk," Endeline answered, her eyes spilling over with tears. Her long hair flowed down her back, and Calhoun was startled to see that the hair at the crown of her head was quite gray. "Sit, my son, and eat, and tell us of your journey."

The servants brought food and fresh clothing, but Calhoun waved them away. "I have come home to serve you, Father," he said, bowing to Perceval. "But first I need to sleep." The crowd laughed, and Calhoun patted his brother affectionately on the back. "After my tired body sleeps, I want to talk to each of you and discover what the years have brought to your lives. I'll visit Lienor at the nunnery and I'd like to visit Afton in the village, if she still resides there."

Endeline's smile froze. "Why would you wish to see her?" she said, her eyes faintly worried. "You need to spend your time in the bosom of your family, beloved son. And you should get to know our dear Ambrose." She gestured with a delicate hand to the young knight who had scrutinized Calhoun so carefully. He was adorned in a knight's hauberk and a tunic embroidered in Perceval's family colors and, at the mention of his name, he stepped forward and bowed stiffly.

"Who is this?" Calhoun asked softly, knowing full well who stood before him, for Ambrose was the very image of his mother.

"He is your father's ward," Endeline explained. "We supposed that you were dead, dear son, and so we brought Ambrose into our home. He has been of great joy to us for many years. He was dubbed a knight earlier this year—"

"This boy?" Calhoun asked, raising an eyebrow.

"He is sixteen," Endeline answered, her tone registering disapproval of her son's reaction. "You were but fifteen at your dubbing, Calhoun."

"That was different," Calhoun answered, studying the boy again. He seemed so young, so . . . delicate.

"I am pleased to meet you, Calhoun," Ambrose spoke, his words cutting sharply through the room. "It is not often that I meet a living legend."

Calhoun sputtered. "He speaks of me as if I am an ancient artifact," he said, scowling at his mother.

"You may still think of yourself as a young knight," Endeline replied, raising her chin. "But you are a man, my son. It has been thirty-two years since you sprang from my womb, and the house of Perceval has cried out for the freshness of youth."

Her words deflated Calhoun's joy at being home again, and he suddenly felt very old and very tired. "Aye, I am no longer young," he said, rising from his seat. "But I am glad to see you all. Now what I would like most is to sleep."

"By all means, take your leave of us," Ambrose nodded, bowing and extending a hand toward the door. "I am sure you need your rest, valiant knight."

Calhoun stood and walked out of the hall, but something about Ambrose irritated him dreadfully. Never had the words "valiant knight" sounded so insulting.

THIRTY-FOUR

The news of Calhoun's homecoming spread like wildfire, and Corba hurried home from the women's quarters to tell Afton. Afton's mind reeled in shock at the announcement, and her first reaction was an impulse to fall on her knees and thank God that Calhoun had been spared so that she might see him again. Overwhelming gratitude welled up in her heart, and she dropped her broom and instinctively lifted her hands to the sky in praise to God.

But when she opened her eyes and looked at her upturned hands, her gratitude turned to shame and revulsion. Calhoun had come back, but to what? She was now a peasant! He would reach for her hands and find calluses; he would put his face in her hair and gag from the stench of it. Her tunic was not silk or even linen, but rough workday wool; her skin was no longer smooth, but constantly reddened by the chafing rash caused by the rough clothing she wore.

She lowered her hands quickly and picked up her broom. He would come to see her, of that she was certain, so how could she escape? She could not hide; Margate was far too small a village. She could only let him find her and show herself as she was. If he turned from her in revulsion or pity, then that, too, was a fault to be laid at Endeline's feet.

Lunette and Morgan were at first reluctant to tell Calhoun about Afton. "I care not if she is married, or even dead! Only tell me, for I must know of her!" Calhoun demanded, cornering the maids in the hall. "And if she is alive, then tell me where I can find her."

"She is alive," Morgan spoke slowly, "but she is greatly changed, Calhoun. Some say she has grown mad, for she shies away from the villagers like a scared colt."

"It is said zat she talks to herself," Lunette added. "She will not go to church and she will not come to ze castle on feast days, not even to visit her son."

"He is her son no longer," Calhoun said, thinking of Ambrose and his confident position in the household. "He has found his way into my parents' hearts."

"Afton has no 'ome of her own, nor any means of support," Morgan said, wiping her hands on her skirt, "and she does not welcome visitors."

"I have heard zat Josson ze steward tried to visit her once," Lunette added, "and she threw herself in ze creek rather than face him."

Calhoun stared at the maids, disbelieving. The Afton he remembered was strong and stable. He knew she had met with sorrow, but surely, though she had lost the mill and her son, she had not gone mad!

"Where can I find her?" he asked gently.

"She lives with her mother in the village," Morgan whispered, peering around nervously. "Now go. And don't tell anyone we told you."

Calhoun smiled at the maids. "Thank you very much."

He chose to go to the village in the morning, when the men would be off to the fields and the women off to their work. The sun shone brightly on the colored trees in the forest, and dappled shadows danced on the road in front of him as lightly as Afton once had danced in the castle. "She cannot be much changed," he reassured himself. "She is, after all, the same person."

He stared for several minutes at the mud-walled cottages in the village, uncertain which was Corba's. He finally asked a group of children where Corba lived, and one of them, an urchin with red hair and a dirty face, pointed to a thatched roof near the center of the village. Calhoun nodded his thanks and nudged his horse forward.

The house sat behind a well-swept courtyard, and a thin thread of smoke rose from the opening in the roof. He dismounted, tied his horse to the sparse hedge that served as a fence, and called out a greeting. "Hello? Is anyone home?"

The wrinkled face of an elderly woman appeared in the doorway and, upon seeing him, the woman curtsied with grave dignity.

"I come seeking Afton of Margate Castle," Calhoun said, making an effort to keep his voice gentle. "Is she here?"

The woman shook her head and her hand flew to her throat as if she could not trust her voice. She cleared her throat nervously. "No, my lord, she is in the forest. She goes there often."

Calhoun grinned in spite of himself. She *was* the same person! He had known it would be so! And he would prove it by finding her in the forest, for he was certain he knew where she had gone. But could he still remember the way to the pool by the twin oak trees?

"Thank you," he called to Corba as he mounted his horse and left the village. He let the horse walk along the road that bordered the forest, and prayed that he would remember where Afton had found the path to the forest pool. She went there often, her mother said, so perhaps there was a well-defined trail. He searched for an opening off the road and found none.

He dismounted and tied the stallion to a tree at the point where the forest ended and the meadow began. Margate Castle, tall and imposing, loomed in the distance, but he paid it little heed as he stomped through the meadow, his boots crushing the few remaining flowers. His horse whinnied from the road, voicing his displeasure at being abandoned far from the comfort of the stable.

"It's no use," Calhoun muttered after he had gone a few hundred yards into the pale meadow. The forest was at his right hand, but it stood as a dense tangle of fading vegetation and broad tree trunks. If there was a trail, he could not see it.

But you've been here recently, the voice of a memory whispered. *You visited often while you were in Zengi's prison, don't you remember?*

Calhoun paused, closing his eyes and relaxing his tense muscles. He focused his thoughts inward as a distant memory beckoned, and then he stepped forward into the vividly colored foliage. His feet moved as if under their own power, his eyes were as wide and unseeing as a sleepwalker's. The sanctuary of the forest drew him in, and the overpowering majesty of creation erased his frustration.

After years of sun and sand, Calhoun found the forest a glorious cathedral. The Holy Land, for all its religious shrines and significance, did not have the power to move him as did the tabernacle in which he found himself at that moment. The trees seemed to lift his thoughts high above the earth and toward the heavens.

Surely God has led me here, he thought, watching overhead as the trees rustled in the early fall breeze. *He has brought me home and spared my life for some purpose.*

For the first time since his arrival in Margate, Calhoun felt as if he had come home. The memories and fantasies he had conjured in his captivity paled in contrast to the reality he experienced as his feet moved deeper and deeper into the forest. There was no trail, but with every step he felt less and less hesitation. And so he progressed further into the woods until he stood before the mammoth trees he remembered from his childhood. The twin oaks were broader now and more tightly woven together. As he stared, he noticed that someone had engraved a name into each of the trunks. He leaned forward and read "Calhoun" on the first tree, and "Afton" on the second.

He caught his breath. She had not changed. It mattered not when she had written this, whether it was last year or years before, she loved him still. He was as elemental to her soul as the right tree was to the left.

A sudden splash from beyond the twin trees interrupted his thoughts, and he ducked behind a leafy bush that had not yet lost its leaves. Cautiously he peered out, and the sight he beheld took his breath away.

A woman walked out of the pool, her bare feet stepping carelessly through the colorful leaves the oaks had thrown for her carpet. Her long hair hung in wet tendrils down her back and over her breasts, and she moved quickly to a bare sapling where her simple tunic dangled.

He averted his eyes in consideration for her modesty and, when he guessed she had had time to slip on her tunic, he stood and called her name.

"Afton."

Her eyes went wide at the sound and she flinched like a deer who has seen the hunter too late. He stepped into the clearing, embarrassed at his awkwardness, and walked nearer. Twenty feet from her, he faltered and stopped. Her eyes did not reflect the heart of a woman who gladly receives the man she loves. Instead, there was a remoteness in their dark gray depths.

"Calhoun." She pronounced his name calmly, without surprise.

He gazed at her in silence, drinking in her appearance. He wanted to laugh, for Fulk had been so wrong! Afton was not old and gray, or stooped from carrying another man's children. She was still beautiful, and yet she was different from the threadworn memory he had replayed over and over in his captivity. Her hair was still long and lush, her lips still full. The skin at her long neck was pale and smooth, disappearing into the simple dark tunic that made her seem thinner than he had remembered.

But the youthful curve of her cheek had been replaced by a square jaw that suggested resolute strength. In fact, her entire posture had changed, from that of a young girl to that of a woman more regal. He drew in his breath.

By all the saints, this woman could pass for a queen!

She inclined her head slowly in his direction. "Welcome

home," she called, then lifted her skirt and began to move away.

"Wait!"

He stepped toward her, and her hand flew up to block his approach. "Come no closer," she said, backing away.

"Do not do this," Calhoun answered, unable to tear his eyes from her. "Do you know how many nights your image kept me alive? In my dreams I came upon you, much like this, and held you in my arms—"

She closed her eyes and covered her ears with her hands. "Say no more!" she screamed, startling a flock of pigeons into flight.

"I must," Calhoun answered, covering the distance between them in frantic steps. She turned and ran, but he caught her in a moment and turned her to face him. She struggled, and he caught her flailing arms.

"God spared me to come home to you," he said, relishing the feel of her. "From this day forward, if you will have me, I am a warrior no longer."

She lifted her eyes to his, and he saw himself reflected there, an anguished man in love. "There was a day when I would have died of joy to hear those words," she whispered. "I promised God that if you would come home, I would receive you and be your wife. But that was before, and I can no longer keep that promise."

"In the name of God, why not?" Calhoun asked, his eyes sweeping over her. "I came home for you, Afton. Though I tried to forget you in Outremer, still each day brought nothing but a clearer vision of how dear you are to my soul."

He clasped her to him tightly, and she did not resist. "Fulk said God sends to each of us a moment of revelation," he whispered through her hair, "and in my moment, I saw myself as a prideful fool, just as you have seen me through the years. Please, dearest Afton, do not let me spend my days alone."

She did not answer, but he felt her hands slide from his

chest and run down his arms. He heard her gasp and, when he released her to look on her face, he saw that she stared at the welts on his arms—scars from Zengi's regular repeated whippings.

He took her hand from his arm and gently kissed the palm. As he did so, he felt the calluses of her labor beneath his lips, and she clenched her fist in embarrassment and looked away quickly.

"I see we have both suffered," he said gently. "Let us not suffer in our love as we have in our lives. Consent to be mine, Afton."

He bent his face to hers and sought her lips, which she gave slowly at first, then willingly. Her arms slipped around his neck and her body pressed into his, and he felt her yielding to the strength of his love, as she had so often in his dreams.

His lips left hers and he kissed the soft skin of her throat. "I will do anything for you," he whispered. "I will build a house for you, defy my father and mother if necessary, and—"

She gasped as if he had driven a dagger into her, then pushed him away with all the force she could muster. "No," she said, her voice quivering with emotion. "I will not love the son of my greatest enemy."

Calhoun gazed at her in confused frustration. "Your greatest enemy?" he repeated dumbly.

Her eyes grew cold and hard. "The Lady Endeline." She spat the name out as though it were poison.

"My mother is your enemy?"

"She has stolen my child!" Afton shrieked, striking out at the air as if battling an unseen foe. "She took the mill from me. She has snatched from my arms every joy I have ever known. Do you not know that my own son now despises me? I know it is so, for she made me despise my own father and mother."

"That is not so," Calhoun answered, stepping toward her. "She merely wants to give him every advantage—"

"She steals children's hearts!" Afton cried, covering her

face with her hands. She sank to her knees and began to sob. Calhoun put an arm around her, but she rose and turned on him in fury, beating his chest with her fists until he backed away and let her cry in silence.

She glared at Calhoun through her tears. "I will kill her before my life is over," she whispered. "Do not doubt it. My heart has always belonged to you, Calhoun, but until Endeline lies in her grave, it is directed toward another purpose. I cannot love you now."

"You could be arrested for this threat," Calhoun said, trying to discern if she spoke truly. "Have you spoken this intention in the village? Think, Afton, and be reasonable. Forswear this vow of yours and come with me. Let me love you . . . let us be together that we may forget the sorrow of the past. Do not hold to this path of vengeance, for I know in truth that it will destroy you!"

Afton turned calculating eyes upon him. "So you threaten me, son of Endeline," she said, holding her head regally. "So be it, then. Have me arrested, if you like, but know that my heart is fixed upon my determination."

He turned away in confusion. This could not be happening!

God! his heart cried out. *Why have you brought me home to find a lonely and bitter woman instead of the girl I loved? Have I been spared only to face a choice between my mother and my love?* Breathing heavily, Calhoun whirled around to argue with Afton again, but she had gone.

He stood alone with his reflection in the pool by the twin trees.

THIRTY-FIVE

Perceval's family shared a quiet supper that evening. Calhoun ate without speaking and reflected upon his visit with Afton. The forest of his memory had stood green and delightful in its vigor, but the forest of today was dyed a yellowish color and robbed of leaves. Autumn had brought decay to the forest, just as time had embittered Afton's heart.

There is nothing here but change and mutability, Calhoun thought, studying his parents at the supper table. He noticed for the first time the crescents of flesh below his father's eyes and the crinkled complexion of his mother's throat. His parents were aging and would not be many more years on the earth.

"So how fares the manor, Father?" Calhoun asked, breaking off a piece of fine wheat bread. "I met the lord of Lydd on my journey here, and he spoke highly of you."

"I know the estate," Charles interrupted eagerly. "A bountiful wheat crop they had last year. Their harvest put even ours to shame."

"As always, your brother's head lies in the fields," Endeline answered, smiling tenderly at Calhoun. "Tell us of this lord of Lydd. What did he say of us?"

"He did not know of my affiliation with this house," Calhoun answered carefully, dipping his bread into the pottage. "He told me Perceval's castle was aligned with Matilda's forces."

Ambrose snickered. Perceval smiled.

"Matilda's people have no reason to doubt our loyalty," Perceval said, leaning toward Calhoun. "And we remain loyal to Stephen as well."

"How is this feat accomplished?" Calhoun asked. "You cannot feed a two-headed snake equally, Father. Sooner or later, one of the heads will bite you."

"Bah!" Endeline pouted. "Those warring factions have no business with us, and we send each of them equal tribute. Are they not both descended from William the Conqueror? It was to him we pledged our allegiance, and now we honor both of his descendants."

"But it is Stephen who wears the crown," Calhoun pointed out gently. "And knights dubbed in this castle swear loyalty to the crown."

"I didn't," Ambrose interrupted. "I swore allegiance to my lord Perceval, and him alone."

Calhoun examined Ambrose carefully. Lean and handsome, his countenance presented a strong jaw and bold eyes, yet his demeanor hinted at some hidden devilish quality, something slippery and untrustworthy. For a moment Calhoun was reminded of Zengi's favorite executioner, the guard who regularly tortured the prisoners. "Judas," Fulk had christened the man, for when he had finished plying the whip and the prisoner had allowed himself to breathe freely, Judas would whirl around and begin again, more forcefully than before.

Calhoun gave Ambrose a careful smile. He felt sorry for the young knights who trained with this brash boy; Calhoun would bet his life that Ambrose did not fight fairly.

"What noble knight gave you training?" Calhoun asked pleasantly.

The corner of Ambrose's lips rose in a smirk. "The honorable and aged Jarvis was the only knight suited for my training. I bore every contest and vanquished every challenger without ever once feeling the scratch of a sword." He noted with a downward glance the scars upon Calhoun's forearms. "I can now best any knight in this castle in any event. I am the champion of Margate."

"An untried champion," Calhoun amended gently. "The practice tourneys of knighthood are nothing compared to the brutality of real battle."

"You think not?" Anger flared Ambrose's nostrils, and his eyes gleamed darkly. "Does not blood flow as freely when one is pierced with a noble tournament sword as with the cowardly dagger of the enemy? Who is more valiant, the knight who wields a lance in competition or one who sits in prison for over a decade and does nothing?"

Calhoun stood, his blood pounding in his veins. *He is an upstart, unworthy to wear the family herald!* Calhoun thought, his hand going automatically to the handle of the scimitar strapped to his side. *And he is far too much like Hubert, his father.*

"Sit down, Calhoun," Endeline said, her voice sharp. "Ambrose may not speak wisely, but he speaks the truth. He is a valiant knight, and you would do well not to doubt him." Her voice softened and she held out her hand to her son in supplication. Her slanting eyebrows lifted in her face, and Calhoun was struck by the abundance of fine lines upon her skin. "You must understand, my son, we thought you dead because we were sure no prison could hold you. Apparently we were mistaken."

At the barely veiled insult, Calhoun felt hot color rush into his face. Ambrose grinned from the end of the table, and Charles lowered his head in the awkwardness of the moment. Perceval said nothing, but gulped his ale.

"It is clear I have no business here," Calhoun said, still on his feet. He looked at Perceval. "I trust, Father, that I may have a suit of armor and a sword? I am yet a knight of this family."

"Of course," Perceval answered, waving his hand carelessly. "Whatever you need, my son. We are pleased to have you as a knight at Margate and welcome the sight of you again wearing the colors of our house."

"I do not wish for our colors, nor the role of Margate knight," Calhoun answered, eyeing his father steadily. "I will take the armor, but it is plain that I cannot remain here. And so, honored parents, I beg your leave and I will take my sword elsewhere."

As he turned to leave, he heard his mother's startled gasp: "Stop him, my lord!"

But Ambrose replied quickly and loudly enough for Calhoun to hear. "It is for the best, my lady. A knight with no spirit is of no use to Margate."

And, while the upstart's words stung, it was his parents' assenting silence that echoed in Calhoun's mind for a long, long time.

He rode for four days, stopping only to feed and water his stallion and sleep under the stars. He once again wore the hauberk and carried a proper sword, but over the suit of mail was a plain blue tunic instead of the white-and-purple uniform of Margate's knights. No longer would he wear the colors of Perceval's house, nor would he wear the cross of the knights of God. Like Fulk, he had become a solitary knight who sought life and an honorable cause with naught but a sword in hand.

"And like you, dear teacher, I carry the scar of revelation," Calhoun whispered one afternoon as his horse daintily picked its way through a stream. "You carried yours boldly upon your face, but I carry mine upon my heart. May God, who used you mightily in life, lead my sword to some equally useful purpose."

He rode toward London without consciously considering his destination, until he drew near to Stephen's camp. At the first sight of Stephen's royal banner and smoking campfires, Calhoun shook his head in confusion. Had he ridden to volunteer in Stephen's service merely to spite his father and Margate's divided loyalties? Or had his own loyalty to the crown led him to Stephen? Perhaps God would use him as an instrument to stop the bloodshed of this cursed civil war.

"Lofty thoughts," he murmured to his horse, pausing

on a hill overlooking Stephen's camp. He patted the beast's neck in affection. "Too lofty for truth. Perchance I come here merely to forget the life I would build with Afton, who now hungers for death and vengeance with more appetite than I have ever possessed. If she, the most gentle and innocent of souls, waits for violent opportunity, then surely the entire world wallows in the lust for blood."

He paused and put his hand upon the hilt of his sword. "If every man and woman, too, stands before God with bloodstained, murderous hearts, then one tool is much like another in his hands, no better and no worse, except that it be willing in service."

He lifted his eyes past Stephen's camp to the horizon, where the sun was slowly sinking in the west. Drawing his sword, he thrust it above his head. "Employ me, then, God," he cried, and the startled stallion reared up, pawing the air. Calhoun held firmly to the reins as he continued shouting to heaven: "My life is in your hands, for no one else claims it. Use me or kill me, God, as it suits your purpose!"

Two scouts found him outside the camp, and although he identified himself as loyal to Stephen, he was escorted immediately under guard to a captain's quarters. The burly captain who whirled around to question him was Thomas of Warwick, his old master from his training days.

"Calhoun of Margate! Can it be you?" Thomas asked, his dim eyes squinting in the darkness of the tent. "I heard you gave your life in Jerusalem."

"I gave twelve years," Calhoun replied, removing his helmet. "And now, upon returning home, I find there is a need for skilled swords in England. Before God I vowed my loyalty to the throne and I am here to prove it."

"Well said!" Thomas smiled and patted his now generous belly. "You are as skilled a man as I have ever known, and your rightful place is over a company of men. We have been recruiting peasants of late, but they are of little use except as foot soldiers and archers." He winked at Calhoun. "Even so, archers will win a battle, my friend, as we have learned from the expedition of God."

Calhoun cleared his throat. "I have not been engaged in battle in many years, Lord Thomas, and my skills may need improvement. I shall need some time to sharpen them."

Thomas puffed out his cheeks. "Nonsense, my boy, you were the most natural soldier I ever saw. When the enemy comes upon us, and you find yourself sword to sword with a man who wishes to slit your throat, your skills will reappear as if they had merely been asleep." He paused a moment and his eyes twinkled. "Whatever became of your master? A more fearless man than Fulk I have never known."

"Fulk is dead," Calhoun answered, his voice sounding oddly flat in his ears. "He died in the East."

"Ah, well." Thomas nodded agreeably. "He gave his life in a good cause, did he not? Come, my son, and let me assign you a tent and a servant." Thomas walked from behind his desk and put a stubby arm around Calhoun's shoulders. "You are needed now more than ever, good knight. I suppose you know who leads Matilda's forces?"

Calhoun shook his head.

Thomas rolled his eyes in disbelief. "Arnoul, your old rival. They call him the 'Limb of Hell,' and there is no greater root of evil alive, as surely as I stand before you now." Thomas chuckled as they walked toward the tent's opening. "How well I remember the contests you two had! But as I recall, you usually bested him, did you not?"

"That was a long time ago."

Calhoun felt his flagging spirits begin to rise as they walked out of the tent and through the camp. He had not thought of Arnoul in years, but perhaps they would soon meet. His fierce sense of competitiveness began to stir. Perhaps his sword would find a worthy opponent after all.

Four days later Calhoun knelt on the carpet in front of Stephen's chair and recited the traditional vow of a vassal to a lord: "Food and clothing both for my back and for my bed, and shoes, and thou shalt procure me, and all that I possess shall remain in thy power."

"Rise, Sir Calhoun," Stephen said, the point of his sword nudging Calhoun's shoulder. "As you have served God in the Holy Land, now serve your king in your fatherland."

"I shall," Calhoun answered, rising to his feet.

So began his journey into the bloody battlefields of Britain. Matilda and her half-brother Robert had succeeded in dividing the land and turning brother against brother in a bitter strife. Calhoun found that he was to join a company of knights who patrolled the countryside in search of Matilda's army or sympathizers. Though he fought valiantly when they had occasion to skirmish with the enemy, his spirit rebelled against the gruesome deeds accomplished in the names of both Stephen and Matilda.

At York, Calhoun watched the lady of the castle writhe in anguish between two guards as her husband was murdered. Her noble brother, who fought for Stephen, ran her husband through with a sword as penalty for his aid to Matilda. Though Calhoun tried in vain to dissuade him, the offended brother then cursed his sister and threw her two infant children from the castle tower in the king's name.

The countryside, now in the full throes of winter, reminded Calhoun of an old woman who was afflicted and decrepit with age, nearing death. After hours on his stumbling horse in the blowing wind and snow, Calhoun wished that he were anywhere but in a warrior's camp. Unfortunately, stern reality reminded him that he had no place in the world but this.

One cool, crisp winter day he led a small group of archers and foot soldiers on a purge of the country north of London. The scout he had sent ahead appeared from the bushes as they approached, breathless and red-faced. "Arnoul's company lies ahead, just off the road," the poor man gasped, his eyes wide with fright. "I saw 'im meself, I did. The Limb of Hell himself waits ahead for us."

Calhoun raised his head defiantly. "Then it is time we cut off this limb," he answered, "and send evil away from King Stephen's land. If Matilda relies on Arnoul as heavily as is reported, the end to this bloody war may lie within our grasp."

He divided his men—most of whom were runaway villeins from warring manors—into two lines, one of archers and one of foot soldiers. He then led his troops in an advance, pausing at the crest of a hill. Below him, Arnoul's men lounged around a stream, watering their horses and filling their gourds with fresh water. A small village church stood less than a stone's throw from the gathering.

"There," the scout whispered, pointing to a burly man standing next to a handsome red horse. "That's Arnoul. He's the biggest man I've ever seen."

Indeed, Arnoul stood taller than any man on the field and seemed as wide as his horse. With one huge hand he held his helmet, and Calhoun noticed that his old nemesis stood as proudly as he had in the days of Warwick Castle. Now they would see if he was still as easily defeated.

Silently, Calhoun motioned for his archers to surround the hill. Arnoul was too confident and unsuspecting. If the archers did their job well, it would be the last day the "Limb of Hell" championed forces for Matilda.

When the men were in place, Calhoun raised his sword and brought it down. A hailstorm of arrows fell upon the unsuspecting men below, and they scattered as ants when a mound is disturbed. Calhoun's eyes did not leave Arnoul's face, and he felt grim satisfaction when he saw the man raise his eyes to the crest of the hill and a spark of recognition flashed between them.

There was no time for further acknowledgement, for the battle was on. Calhoun motioned for his foot soldiers to advance even as the archers positioned arrows again into their bows, then sent another barrage raining down upon Matilda's men. Calhoun's soldiers surged forward, sweeping down upon the startled men in Matilda's camp.

It was not an easy battle, for Matilda's soldiers were well-trained. Those who survived the rain of arrows fought bravely, and a few fled to the nearby church and barricaded themselves inside.

"What do we do now?" a breathless archer asked Calhoun. "They are inside a holy place."

Calhoun managed a wry smile, seeing Fulk in his mind's eye. "They have defiled it," he said resolutely, knowing what Fulk would advise. "Burn it." Calhoun's men immediately sent flaming arrows into the church, then encircled the structure to prevent any escape.

Through the crackle and roar of the blaze, a voice from above Calhoun cried out, "Calhoun of Margate! We meet again! I have not yet had my vengeance!"

Looking up, Calhoun saw Arnoul in the bell tower, surrounded by dancing flames that seemed to lick his feet. He cursed Stephen and Calhoun repeatedly, his voice carrying over the sound of the blaze. Then, as Calhoun and his men watched, a river of melting lead from the tower roof splashed over Arnoul's face. Though Calhoun winced in imagined pain, Arnoul did not even pause in his streaming vituperation.

Several of Calhoun's men looked away as the flames rose and the tower crumbled, but Calhoun's eyes never left the burning church, though Arnoul disappeared from sight. Six hours later, Calhoun's men reported that no survivors were found in the burned-out shell that remained. Calhoun insisted they carry forth the charred bodies of the victims, throughout the night if necessary. Though the sight of so many twisted and blackened bodies was sickening, Calhoun examined all of them carefully to determine if Arnoul was indeed dead.

The next morning Calhoun concluded that none of the corpses could have been Arnoul.

"He was a big man, and none of these woefully departed knights were above average height," Calhoun told his men. "Check the church again, thoroughly, for that root

of hell must not be allowed to escape. When you have
brought me his sword or his body, then will I rest."

They did bring him a sword, but the twisted molten
lump could have belonged to any of Matilda's knights. "Perhaps the fire shrunk 'im," one soldier offered hopefully,
eager to be gone from the place. "We will never know for
sure what 'appened in that church."

Calhoun reluctantly agreed and led his men away, accepting at last that his foe was vanquished, and leaving the blackened church behind. *I wonder if Fulk would consider this a
mortal sin,* Calhoun thought idly as they rode. *I have burned
my enemy beyond recognition in a place of sanctuary. Can God
forgive such an act as this?*

Winter's cold and appalling misery brought sickness and
hunger to the battle camps. Matilda and her men scorched
the bare earth as they traveled, burning the dry fields and
storehouses of manors that were aligned with King Stephen,
further depleting the country's already lean resources.

In retaliation, Calhoun's men wanted to burn the manors in allegiance with Matilda, but he stopped them. "All of
England will be a burnt wasteland if this continues," he told
his men. "And who knows but that by sparing the manors
we shall not win hearts for our merciful king? Therefore we
will not burn any barn or house, nor will we be the cause of
any innocent man's death."

His fellow knights grumbled, and Calhoun knew they
thought him as "soft" as King Stephen, but he refused to
change his opinion. And so they continued throughout the
winter, chasing Matilda's and Robert's elusive armies and
trying to save England from self-inflicted starvation.

THIRTY-SIX

"Your son fights for Stephen."

Endeline's sharp words disturbed Perceval's game of chess, and he glared at her. He was aware of his knights' eyes upon him, and the last thing he wanted was a confrontation with his wife in the great hall for all to see.

"Later, woman."

"Your son is making quite a name for himself. His reputation has spread far and wide as the merciful leader of Stephen's army."

Perceval toyed with the ivory chess piece in his hand. "What would you have me do about my son, woman? He is a man grown and does what he pleases."

Endeline put her hand on her husband's arm and whispered intensely: "If Matilda's nobles hear these stories, they will be on us in an instant. They will burn the fields and the castle, and kill you, Perceval."

Perceval jerked his arm from her grasp. "Leave me, wife! My knights and I concentrate on amusement today."

Endeline gathered her skirts. "Play your games then, my lord, while there is yet time," she said clearly, striding out of the hall.

Nighttime found Perceval more willing to hear reason, as Endeline knew it would. His advancing age had left him a toothless lion, all bluster and bravado in front of his knights, and all fear and trepidation in the solitude of their chamber. As he climbed into bed beside his wife, he explained his reasons for the day's brusqueness: "I cannot stop Calhoun, nor can I stop his reputation," he said, slipping beneath the heavy furs on their bed. "So what am I to do? Surely his bold adventures for Stephen will be our undoing."

"You must bring Calhoun home," Endeline said, her dark eyes gleaming in the glow of their candle. "Write him a letter, promise him anything, just bring him home."

"What do I promise him? He wants nothing to do with us."

Endeline shook her head. "If I know my son, there is yet one thing he desires. He would have your blessing to marry Afton. For that, I believe he would come home."

"Afton?" Perceval scratched his head. "What leads you to believe this, woman? The girl has not been seen in years. Does she still live in the village?"

"Aye, with her mother. And I have it on good report that Calhoun visited her the very day after his return home."

Endeline slipped out of bed and took a sheet of parchment and a bottle of ink from the table in the room. She brought both to Perceval. "You must write and suggest that Afton is willing and able to marry. You must also tell our son that you have given your permission and your blessing to this marriage."

Perceval's hand shook as he took the parchment. He looked up again at Endeline, and the expression on his face was that of a confused child. "Do we really want them to marry?"

"Of course not!" Endeline snapped, then she forced herself to remain calm. "We will see to it that she is married before he arrives here, so you will not lie, my dear husband. You will say nothing in the letter that can be used against you, so write what I tell you."

"Yes, my love." Perceval took the quill, dipped it in ink, and began to write.

Calhoun broke the embossed seal and read the letter hastily, then read it again slowly, not believing what was written there. Was the message a trick? Or had God smiled upon him at last and provided deliverance from his life of blood and battle?

Still disbelieving, he read again: "I have decided that it is time for my vassal Afton to marry again," his father had written. "And knowing that she is the love of your life, I give my blessing and permission for this marriage. Come home, dear son, as soon as you can."

Marry Afton? What had changed in her situation? Why had she agreed to this marriage? He looked out the doorway of his tent, toward the distant horizon. Was it possible that God had worked a change in his lady's heart? Was God finally rewarding Calhoun for his years of service with the love he had always sought?

He refolded the letter and placed it inside his tunic, over his heart, as he paced up and down in his tent. Winter lay heavy and dead upon them, and there would be no more fighting until the spring. Stephen would allow him to go home, of that Calhoun was certain. He had served his king ably and well, and Stephen had no cause to doubt Calhoun's loyalty.

"I must go!" Calhoun muttered to himself. He stepped out of his tent and gave the order for his company to mount up. They would return to London immediately.

"My lady Afton." The man's hesitant voice came from beyond the doorway of Corba's cottage, and Afton looked up from her sewing with surprise. No male visitor had come to her house to call upon her in years.

"Josson!" She stood, her cheeks flushing in pleasure at the sight of him. He was still thin, but less so, and his fair hair was tinged with gray at his temples. But he was nicely dressed and handsome, and she was thrilled by the presence of an old friend and a reminder of happier days.

Afton let her sewing fall onto her stool and went to the gate to greet him. "It is good to see you!" she said sincerely, taking his hands in hers and leading him through the hedge. "Please come in."

"It is good of you to welcome me." His eyes shone at her greeting and he licked his lips nervously.

"Where have you been these many months, Josson? First you haunt my days for years, then you disappear entirely from my life. I was beginning to think you no longer enjoyed my companionship."

"That was not the situation, I assure you," Josson answered. He took off his hat and shuffled his feet in the dusty courtyard, looking around uncomfortably. "I did not come earlier because I have been busy, and—" his voice faltered. "I was sure you did not wish to see me."

Afton looked away as a group of laughing children ran by. "There was a time when I did not wish to see you," she said, her cheeks flushing as she remembered her days of forced labor. "But much time has passed since those days."

Josson nodded. "I come today with good news, Afton. I could scarcely believe it myself, but Lord Perceval has passed his fiftieth year, and sometimes people try to make amends for their past deeds—"

"What news do you bring?" Afton drew in her breath, hoping to hear that her prayers had been answered and Ambrose was to be restored to her. Perhaps regret and guilt had so plagued Perceval's heart that he had to give back her son.

"Only this." Josson led her to her sewing bench and motioned for her to sit. When she had seated herself, he put his hat across his heart and fell to one knee. "Afton, Lord Perceval has given me permission to ask for your hand. Marry me, Afton, and let me take you out of this place. You are a free woman, a woman of quality, and a woman I have loved for years. Come to my house, my dearest, and let us live and love together."

The eloquence of his speech touched her heart, but the only words that rang in her mind were "marry me" and "come to my house." Marry Josson? The idea seemed as absurd as marriage to one of her brothers! Josson had always been a friend and nothing more. Still . . . as his wife she would live in his house, the steward's sturdy stone house, which lay next to the castle keep.

If she lived in that house, she would be close to Ambrose, close enough to watch him and hear him and talk to him. She would be close to Endeline, too, near enough to slip hemlock into the lady's tea when the time came. And she would be close to Calhoun should he ever come home—though it seemed unlikely he ever would, unless it was in his coffin. But even then, she would be able to kneel by his side and touch his dear face one last time.

She looked right through Josson, smiling at the unspoken promises his words had suggested. Then her natural wariness surfaced—why had Perceval approved this plan? Josson's explanation did not suffice for such an extreme change of heart. Surely Endeline would not want Afton living on the castle grounds unless there was some deeper motivation, a darker plot.

"Does Lady Endeline know of Perceval's approval?" Afton asked, raising an eyebrow. "Tell me, Josson, and tell me quickly!"

"No," Josson said, and he shook his head and spread his hands in bewilderment. "In fact, Lord Perceval came to me privately and asked me to tell no one until I brought my bride home. Please, Afton, I have waited years for you. Be gentle, good lady, and do not make my heart suffer longer!"

His eyes gleamed with the pain of desperate love, and Afton felt a stab of pity for him. Had this secret love burned within him for as many years as she had loved Calhoun? She knew the pain of that suffering, and the anguish of that patience.

"Yes, Josson, I will marry you," she whispered.

Josson closed his eyes in relief and clasped her hands to his chest. "My precious lady, you have done me a great service," he whispered. His eyes opened, his lips curved into a smile, and ever so gently he leaned across the open space between them and placed his lips upon hers.

Afton allowed the kiss, recognizing that the feeling of

his lips upon hers did not evoke the passions that Calhoun's few kisses had unleashed in her soul. But neither was Josson's kiss hard and demeaning like Hubert's. *Yes,* she thought quickly, *I can marry Josson.*

"Thank you, Afton," Josson breathed, pulling away from her reluctantly. He held her hands tenderly, then placed them in her lap and stood to his feet. "Lord Perceval suggested that the marriage be performed quickly, so I will make the arrangements," Josson said, placing his hat on his head. He turned toward the gate, then returned to Afton again, his face brightening. "I would like to have some material sent over for your wedding dress," he said, wringing his hands in embarrassment. "Does that please you?"

"It pleases me," Afton answered, standing. She took his frantic hands and placed one upon her cheek. His eyes filled with unexpected tears, and she smiled. This man would never browbeat her into humiliation, and she would always be grateful for his goodness. "Thank you, Josson, for this great honor," she said quietly. "I promise I will make you a good wife."

Corba was ecstatic when she heard the news. Her daughter married to the steward! She might as well be marrying the lord himself, for Josson managed Perceval's entire estate.

"Remember, Mama, you are not to tell anyone," Afton reminded her. "We do not want the news to reach Lady Endeline. She would certainly find a way to spoil this happiness, as she has spoiled every other. And we must not give her that chance."

King Stephen relieved Calhoun of his command, complimented him on his brave performance in battle, and offered congratulations on his impending marriage. "Go in haste, for your bride grows old while you wait here," Stephen told Calhoun, his eyes twinkling. "You have our royal blessing."

Corba obviously did not keep the secret well, for on the wedding day more than twenty villagers appeared in Corba's small courtyard to escort the bride and groom to the church door. Afton dressed carefully in her new tunic of dark gray silk that matched her eyes, and saw admiration in her mother's eyes. "Ye look just as a widow bride should look," Corba said approvingly. "But never again shall ye wear such dark colors after today. As the wife of the steward, ye can wear scarlet and purple and gold."

"I will wear the colors of rejoicing when I have my son again," Afton answered, smoothing her hair. She fastened a small square of fabric to her head, and let her hair fall freely under it. Her heart did not glow with joy or excitement, but she was awash with simple relief that life had taken an unexpected turn for the better. She would now live in comfort, she would be able to help her mother, and she would live inside the castle walls. God must have been listening to her prayers after all.

"The groom comes!" The women shouted from the courtyard. "Hail master Josson, and good wedding day to you!"

Josson knocked timidly on the door, and Corba answered it, bowing deeply, her face wreathed in a smile. Afton bowed to Josson, too, then she put on her heavy cloak, took her groom's arm, and together they led the band of villagers to the church door.

Small children scampered in front of the couple on the way, strewing evergreen boughs in their path, and Josson pitched pennies to them from the purse at his belt. Though the wind was cold, the sun shone brightly, and Afton felt relaxed and content for the first time in years. How different was this day from the dark day when she had stood at the church door with Hubert! On that day, her life of torture had begun. Today her life of freedom would begin.

Calhoun thanked God once again that his horse was both fast and sturdy, for the stallion covered the miles with satisfying speed. *Soon I shall hold her,* Calhoun thought, *and we shall explain away the differences the years have brought between us.*

409

His heart pounded when he saw the familiar landmarks outside Margate village, and he toyed with the notion of going immediately to the castle and thanking his father for this unexpected change of heart. But love overruled reason, and he turned his horse toward the village and Corba's house. He had waited twenty-one years to claim the woman he loved, and he would not be denied one more hour.

Josson knocked at the church door, and Father Odoric answered. "A wedding, heh?" he asked, peering at the crowd with his failing eyes. "Who gives this bride to be married?" He squinted at the face before him in the veil. "Who is this bride?"

"It is Afton of Margate, and I give myself," she said clearly. The women in the crowd laughed pleasantly.

"Heh? All right, then, do you both consent to this union?" The priest squinted at Josson. "Who are you, groom?"

"I am Josson, steward at Margate Castle," Josson answered. He looked down at Afton with love in his eyes. "And I most assuredly do consent to this marriage."

"Do you, Afton, consent to marry Josson?" Father Odoric shouted, evidence that his hearing was failing as well.

"Yes, I do," Afton answered, looking up at Josson.

Father Odoric turned his ear toward her. "Say it again?"

"I do!" Afton shouted, while the crowd behind her twittered.

The wind blew harshly, blowing the women's veils and chilling the crowd. Father Odoric felt numbness in his fingers. Better hurry this wedding along before he froze to death. Perhaps there would be a warm dinner later.

Calhoun jumped off his lathered horse at Corba's cottage and strode purposefully to the door. Though he banged with all his might, there was no response. He looked around and noticed that the row of cottages seemed deserted. Mounting his horse again, he spied a small girl plucking

410

evergreen limbs from the road. "Where is Corba who lives here?" he demanded gruffly.

The girl eyed his sword and armor and her eyes widened.

"I won't hurt you," Calhoun said, wishing he had taken the time to shave his beard and make himself more presentable. "Where are the villagers from this house?"

The little girl would not answer, but she lifted her arm and pointed down the road to the church. Calhoun spurred his horse.

"All right, is there anyone here who knows of any impediment to this union?" Father Odoric asked, pretending to look through the crowd.

Josson heard the sound of an urgently galloping horse and prayed the priest would continue quickly, but Father Odoric was distracted by the sound. He lowered his prayer book and squinted past the crowd.

Josson turned reluctantly as a regal knight in armor abruptly reined in his horse in front of the church. The stallion reared, scattering women and children in the assembled group, and the knight raised his visor and peered at Josson and his bride. Josson's eyes widened.

It was Calhoun!

"Stop this union," Calhoun barked, his right hand on the hilt of his sword. "I hold claim to the woman who stands before the priest."

"Excuse me," Father Odoric's voice crackled like dead leaves. "Who are you and what have you to do with these proceedings?"

"I am Calhoun of Margate, and I love this woman," Calhoun called again, and Josson's mouth went dry when he felt Afton's hand tense in his. "I will not leave without her."

Josson stirred himself to action. "This is impossible," he cried, clinging to his bride's hand and stamping his foot in frustration. He turned toward his master's son. "She will have nothing to do with you, sir!"

"Oh yes, I will!" Her hand left his in an instant and

Josson watched, stunned, as his bride flew through the crowd as swiftly as a bird. With one movement she extended her hand, and the knight pulled her up behind him on the horse. Her arms locked around him as he spurred the black stallion and, in a whirl of dust and a breath of cold air, they were gone.

"Why, this is most unusual," Father Odoric said, peering around for the bride who seemed to have mysteriously vanished.

Josson glared at the priest, the anger of all his years of waiting burning his soul. He had spent his life serving the nobility, staying out of the way of the nobility, suffering the quirks and whims of his noble masters. For his faithful service, he had been granted a bride. And, by the heavens, he would suffer his lord's son no longer!

"He will pay for this," Josson snapped, kicking Afton's evergreen bouquet out of his way as he strode from the church. "By all the saints, the renegade Calhoun will pay for this!"

"Calm yourself, Josson," Endeline said, demurely smoothing her veil. "They will return, mark my words."

"Justice must be done!" Josson fumed, pacing in the great hall. He forgot his usual deference in the heat of his anger. "She had given me her word! We were married, until your son showed his face at the church!"

"I cannot believe my son has dishonored me in this way," Perceval muttered darkly, motioning to a servant for more ale. "I gave the woman to Josson. If Calhoun does not bring her back, my promises will be worthless among the people. My name has been dishonored, and this will not be forgiven."

"Calhoun is a traitor to Perceval's house, my lord," Ambrose added, studying the tip of his dagger in the candlelight. "He has been by himself far too long. He has lost his sense of family honor and pride."

"Not all men are as stalwart as you are," Endeline said,

placing her hand upon Ambrose's shoulders. "But Calhoun is not totally lost. Love for that woman has made him a fool throughout his life. Still, fool though he may be, he is dependable. He will return tomorrow, I assure you."

"How can you give this assurance?" Josson turned angry eyes upon her. "He will take my bride for himself tonight, and even if he returns, can I wipe his memory from her mind?"

"Your bride will return here tomorrow, undefiled," Endeline said, moving to a bench. "Calhoun may not care for our family honor, but his own honor runs deep." She glanced at Perceval and emphasized her next words: "He will not take a woman who is not his wife."

"What is to stop them from being married, then?" Perceval asked, opening his hands. "Any village priest could marry them."

"You forget one thing," Endeline said, smiling smugly. She reached for Ambrose's hand and cradled it tenderly. "Calhoun has his honor to draw him back, and Afton has Ambrose. Afton will do nothing that might endanger her son's life. They will both return here in the morning, unmarried and untouched."

"Call the council together," Perceval announced, slamming his glass upon the table. "They will face the council of judgment as soon as they return." The earl turned to Endeline. "If you are right, my wife, we shall be ready. And if you are wrong—"

"I am right," Endeline said. She laid a kiss on the tip of her finger and pressed it to Ambrose's cheek. "They will be back in the morning, then you shall all have opportunity for justice."

Oblivious to the cold, Afton clung to Calhoun as though she would never let him go. Once again he had returned to her from the dead, and this time she knew what she demanded of him. Still he had come, and willingly.

They rode for miles on a road outside Margate, and as

the sun began to set Calhoun allowed the horse to slow to a walk. "We shall have to find a place to rest," he said, his voice hoarse. "Then we must talk."

She nodded her consent, her cheek against his shoulder. When he dismounted in a forest clearing, she slid easily from the horse's back. Pulling her wedding cloak tightly around her, she watched as he built a small fire and led the horse to a nearby stream to drink. When he had finished tending the horse, he sank onto the ground beside her.

They did not touch, and Afton feared to break the silence between them. "Speak, Calhoun," she finally urged him. "I will answer anything you ask."

"Why were you about to marry my father's steward?" he asked, his eyes on the flames in front of them. "The letter from my father implied that you had agreed to marry me. For one moment at the church, I was afraid you would not come with me. If you had not—" he paused, and Afton knew what he was thinking. Public humiliation was more than Calhoun could bear.

She hoped he would turn to her and see the honesty on her face. "A letter from your father? Calhoun, I knew nothing of any letter, nor did your father approach me. Josson asked me to marry him, and I agreed because as his wife I could move to the castle."

"To be near my mother." Bitterness edged his voice. Afton knew he understood her completely.

"And to be near the son she took from me." She kicked a fallen pinecone into their small fire and watched it sizzle and glow in the heat of the flame.

"We have been tricked, then," Calhoun said, turning to her at last, resignation evident in his features. "I thought I came home to claim my love at last and I thought you had given up your desire to avenge yourself upon my mother."

"I shall never give that up!" she cried, curling her hands into fists. "You do not understand at all, Calhoun!"

He stared sadly past her into the darkness around

them, and Afton drew her knees up and buried her head in her arms. "I thought you had accepted me at last and understood my position," she sobbed. "By marrying Josson, I was prepared to sacrifice joy for mere happiness, but when I looked up, there you were, an avenging angel in armor. I was certain God had sent you to help me in my cause."

He shook his head slowly. "I cannot aid you in the cause that would destroy my mother," he said, each word an effort. "Even though your cause may be righteous."

"She stole my son!" Her voice ripped through the silence of the night. "I want him back!"

"No, you don't," Calhoun answered. "He is not the boy you sent to her. He is a man now, one after Hubert's own heart, ambitious and cunning. He is his father's son."

Afton's eyes went wide in horror and her hand struck Calhoun's face. He did not resist until she began beating his chest, then he held her arms and let her cry. "It cannot be," she cried, twisting in his grip. "You are lying, Calhoun! Please, tell me you are lying!"

He did not answer, but continued to hold her, and she knew his words were true. She had long suspected that Hubert's qualities resided in her son. As a boy, Ambrose had been charming, but devilish, and often he had unnerved her with his cunning. And, on the day she was arrested and taken from the mill, had he not been an accomplice in injustice? And for what? A pony?

She relaxed in Calhoun's grip and was surprised when he gently laid her head in his lap and stroked her hair. As she lay there, her eyes wide, she watched the cluster of flames in front of her—greedy flames that devoured every tender twig within reach and insistently lapped at the log Calhoun had placed on the fire. Endeline was just such a flame: devouring and working her way into every part of Afton's life to destroy all that was beautiful and good.

She did not know how long she lay in his arms, but after a while she stirred and sat up. "I love you, Calhoun," she said, turning her face into the firelight so he could see her clearly if he turned her way. "I have always loved you, and you alone."

"I loved a beautiful maiden called Afton," Calhoun answered softly. "Whose heart was as pure as her face."

"That girl is a woman now, with a woman's scars," Afton sighed, loosening the cloak tied around her neck. "Accept her love or leave it, the choice is yours."

Calhoun stood to his feet without even glancing in her direction. "I will keep watch while you sleep," he said, his voice flat. "We will ride back in the morning."

He stepped away from her in the darkness, and Afton spread her cloak on the ground and pillowed her head in her arms. Like a child, she cried herself to sleep.

He watched her as she slept, covering his feelings with the habitual detachment he found useful on the battlefield. He would never have dreamed it possible, but the older he grew, the more often he found himself imitating Fulk. If he needed to slit a man's throat, he did it as Fulk would have, quietly and quickly without a second thought. If he was required to whip a disobedient soldier, he wielded the lash himself, considering that Fulk had borne more blows than these without a whimper of pain or fear.

And now his mind taunted him: *Do you need to renounce your love? Do it as Fulk would have, resolutely and calmly. Take her back to the church and leave her with a man who would never be threatened by her ferocity.*

"Josson would faint if he knew the true tenor of your nature," Calhoun whispered as Afton lay sleeping. "But he will never see it, for he does not know you. While I, who adore you and would fight for you, am bound by honor to renounce you for my mother's sake."

He looked upon her with admiration, knowing some of what she had endured. She had survived marriage to Hubert, who, by all accounts, had been as brutal as Zengi. She had been falsely accused, unjustly treated, and stripped of her dignity and worth in the eyes of the entire village. Still, she stood strong and unbowed.

"Perhaps the thing I cannot overlook is the thing that has kept you alive," Calhoun whispered again in his solitary discourse. "But I am tired of strife and bloodshed, and I cannot marry a woman whose thirst for vengeance outstrips my love for her or my need for honor."

THIRTY-SEVEN

As Calhoun and Afton drew near to the castle a trumpet blew, and Calhoun knew Perceval and Endeline had been alerted to their approach. "It is time to face our actions," Calhoun told the woman who sat silently behind him. "Are you ready?"

"She can but kill me," Afton answered. "Though I suppose it is Josson's choice as to what shall be done with me."

"They may not believe we shared a chaste night together," Calhoun said, slowing the horse to a walk. "It may even be that you will be tried for adultery."

"It would not be the first false charge I have withstood," Afton said, raising her chin. "Do not worry about me, Calhoun. I have lost every battle of my life, but I have survived."

The gate creaked open for them without the welcoming herald of trumpets, and no man called out a greeting. The silence was ominous. Through the gate they rode, to the entrance of the castle, where a stableboy took hold of Calhoun's horse. Afton slid easily off the back of the animal, then waited for Calhoun. Side by side, they walked into the great hall.

Perceval and Endeline waited on the dais, and Afton's heart leapt at the sight of Ambrose sitting at Endeline's side. How handsome and tall he had grown! He was breathtakingly beautiful, a stunning boy with dusty gold hair, yet he cast impartial eyes upon Afton as if she were just another villager. Afton felt a sob rising from her heart and forced herself to look away lest she dissolve into tears.

Two rows of Perceval's nobles, called into special council for the hearing, sat as motionless as statues. Josson, the injured party, stood alone on a carpet before Perceval.

"Calhoun of Margate and Afton, widow of Hubert," Perceval called as they entered. "You are ordered to stand and hear the accusations against you."

"What are these accusations?" Calhoun demanded, placing his hand on his sword. "I would hear them and refute them."

"You stole my bride at the church door," Josson cried, taking a step toward Calhoun. He stopped abruptly. "She gave me her promise to wed and yet she left with you in fear for her life."

"I felt no fear," Afton answered clearly. "I went with Calhoun willingly."

The council members stirred, and Perceval rapped his knuckles on the table for quiet. "Josson speaks the truth," Perceval told the counselors. "I gave this woman to my honored steward as a bride." He looked steadily at his son. "She agreed to be married. Then you, Calhoun, abducted the bride, and now my name has been dishonored among the people. What say you to this charge?"

"I have in my possession a letter from you stating that this woman was free to marry," Calhoun answered, pulling the letter from his tunic. "And your injunction that I should return home. I assumed, of course, that the woman was promised to me."

"You assumed incorrectly," Ambrose sneered. Then he turned his gaze toward Afton. "Hello, Mother."

Afton felt her throat tighten. Calhoun was right, this snide boy was not the son she had surrendered eight years ago! He might have sprung from her womb, but he sat next to Endeline as Hubert reincarnated, taunting her one last time. Still, was he completely lost? He was only sixteen. Surely she had time to redirect him, if given the opportunity!

"Ambrose," she whispered, her heart breaking.

Perceval was blind to the drama between Afton and her son. He fastened his dark eyes upon Calhoun. "I would like to know your intentions regarding this woman."

"As God is my witness, my love for her is honorable," Calhoun replied, his voice steady and strong. "No dishonor has been brought to any member of this house, nor to the woman herself." He glanced briefly at Josson. "I did not touch her."

"So say you," Josson declared, his face flushing. "Who is to believe it? Lord Perceval, I demand justice!"

"God will reveal his justice," Perceval pronounced, rising to his feet. The counselors stood in unison for his judgment: "Calhoun, as of this day, you are no longer my son," Perceval announced. "This boy, Ambrose, whom we have reared in your absence, is a finer son to me than ever you were. And to validate the truthfulness of your statements, when the sun is at its highest point in the sky this day, you shall duel for this woman. If your love is honorable, God will grant you victory. If your words and spirit are false, may God grant you a mercifully quick death."

Afton felt her knees turn to water at Perceval's words, and the room began to spin slowly. The only objects that did not move were Perceval's eyes, glinting in the shadows of the hall. "Prepare yourself," he said. "I have spoken."

Calhoun's horse shifted uneasily as the field outside the castle filled with spectators. The news had spread like wildfire, and villagers, knights, tradesmen, and servants appeared from every hamlet of Perceval's lands to watch the promised spectacle. Never before had a nobleman's son dueled for the love of a common woman. "Such a thing," one laundress told her mate as she shoved her laundry aside, "may never happen again."

Calhoun checked his sword, dagger, and lance. He had fought over forty tournament duels in his lifetime, but this duel would not end until one champion lay dead. He was not worried, though. If God were truly the judge of this match, he would be victorious.

He was also comforted by the thought that Perceval's garrison contained no knights prepared to face a seasoned soldier. Knowing his father's mind, the man who faced him would likely be poor Josson, who had never lifted a lance in his lifetime. Calhoun could imagine Perceval's train of thought: Honor and duty would demand that Calhoun duel, and he would be victorious; Perceval would allow Calhoun to marry Afton; and, in time, Perceval would restore Calhoun to his rightful place.

Calhoun chuckled wryly as he gripped his sword. His father was fond of orchestrating people's fates. Now, though, he had involved Calhoun—and he was not inclined to follow anyone's direction but his own.

The crowd cheered when Perceval and Endeline appeared in their box at the top of the tower. As Perceval's chaplain lifted his arms high and prayed that God's will would be done, the villagers removed their hats and caps and bowed their heads.

"That will do," Calhoun muttered, slowly walking his horse down to the far end of the tourney field. He tightened his hand around the pole of his lance. "Let's have it over and done with." He looked through the sea of faces for Afton. Where would the guards have taken her? She would probably watch the duel from the garrison. No matter. After Calhoun's victory, he would take her far from Margate, possibly to London. Perhaps then she could leave her past behind, and they could love each other.

The trumpeters blew the warning, and Calhoun mounted his stallion, who seemed to sense that today's ride was more important than most. Calhoun checked his stirrups and his spurs, and tightened the leather band that strapped his hand and lance together.

Another trumpet blasted, and Calhoun aimed his lance at the chest of the masked rider even as the challenger thundered toward him. Calhoun leaned back on his heels, and his spurs urged the stallion forward to his target.

Flanked by a burly guard on either side, Afton stood at the wide window at the top of the tower garrison. From there she could see Calhoun, riding in his simple blue tunic, and the rider who charged in Perceval's colors. A tear rolled down her cheek. Though she had not loved Josson, she did not want to be the reason for his death.

The thunder of pounding hooves carried across the pasture. Clods of earth rose from the ground as the horses raced, but the riders seemed to sit motionless, their lances still and steadily aimed at the other's breast. The second before the two made contact, Afton turned her head, unable to watch.

Metal clashed, and a collective groan rose from the crowd. Afton peered down; the rider in Perceval's colors lay on the grassy field, his shield rammed away and his helmet thrown from his head. Calhoun sat squarely on his horse, circling the downed rider even as the man struggled to his feet.

The felled rider gained his footing and pulled the sword from his belt. He took a brave stand, but the crowd already knew his situation was hopeless. From a mounted position, Calhoun would merely have to aim the lance a second time, and the man on the ground would never land a blow.

Afton crossed herself and whispered a prayer for Josson's soul, for surely he would spend his next hour with God. The sun shone on the man's long hair, hair that gleamed like gold . . .

Afton gasped. The felled rider was not Josson, but Ambrose!

Her blood ran cold and she involuntarily clasped her hands together in the pose for prayer. Ambrose, the ruthless boy who had literally taken Calhoun's place at Margate, stood defenseless on the field—yet Calhoun did not strike.

Afton watched as Calhoun circled his quarry yet again; then he spurred his horse and rode to the opposite end of the field. Ambrose seized the advantage and sprinted to his horse, leaping upon the animal's back and charging again in wild fury.

Fulk would have loved this, Calhoun thought as Ambrose approached, his sword swinging wildly in proud fury. *My father challenges me with the one knight I cannot kill. God, give me wisdom!*

He waited until Ambrose was within fifteen feet, then turned his agile horse and spurred the stallion forward, an old trick of the elusive Saracens. Ambrose sailed past, overshooting his target, then turned his bulky horse to charge again. His mouth hung open, contorted with anger, and his face gleamed red with murderous intent.

Calhoun whirled and turned, whirled and turned, keeping his head low behind his shield. He could not kill the boy, but neither would he let himself be killed or maimed by this sixteen-year-old fledgling. Only one option remained, and Calhoun found it almost more distasteful than death.

He waited until Ambrose faced him again, then took careful aim at the boy's unprotected chest with his lance, and charged. His lance was steady, his aim sure, and in the last second, just as Ambrose went pale and his eyes widened, Calhoun deflected the point of his lance and kept his spur to the horse, galloping out of the field of contest and through the neighboring meadow.

At that point he knew his previous plans had to be forfeited. He would not marry Afton, he could not take her away, for he could not win the duel. Killing Josson would have been necessary according to Perceval's judgment, a fact he knew Afton would regret, but forgive. Had he killed Ambrose, though, she would never have forgiven him.

As he rode, his thoughts were darkened by one other realization: many of those assembled for the tourney would always believe that Calhoun, mighty knight of Margate Castle, had fled in fear for his life.

But those who knew him would know the truth.

AGNELET
1141

Praise the Lord, O my soul;
all my inmost being, praise his holy name.
Praise the Lord, O my soul,
and forget not all his benefits—
who forgives all your sins
and heals all your diseases,
who redeems your life from the pit
and crowns you with love and compassion,
who satisfies your desires with good things
so that your youth is renewed like the eagle's.
For as high as the heavens are above the earth,
so great is his love for those who fear him.

PSALM 103:1-5, 11, NIV

Thirty-Eight

As Calhoun's horse sped away, Afton's heart raced ahead of her feet and she seized the moment and slipped out of the tower garrison. The guards stood shocked and silent at the window, watching Calhoun ride away from certain victory. She slipped down the stairs noiselessly and ran through the courtyard and out of the castle. The confused crowd had begun to disperse when she reached the field, and she merged into the crowd of onlookers and mingled with them on the road, keeping her head low.

She had to find Calhoun. He had spared her son, and she owed him an immeasurable debt of gratitude. Perhaps he did still love her after all.

The crowd of peasants, disappointed and restless, trudged along the castle road toward the village. Afton forced herself to maintain their leaden pace, but as soon as the first trees obscured her from the castle tower, she bolted from the crowd and disappeared into the forest. She knew it was possible Calhoun had ridden straight away, possibly back to London, but she prayed he would not leave without telling her good-bye.

The forest surrounded her in cool darkness, and she thrashed through the tangled undergrowth in a blind hurry, searching for familiar bushes and trees. When she finally saw the leafless crest of the twin oaks, she gasped in gratitude and pressed on until she stood at the gnarled trunks. Laying a hand tenderly upon Calhoun's engraved name, she peered around the tree to see if he waited by the pool.

At first she seemed to be the only one there, but the sudden whinny of a horse assured her he was near. She stepped out into the clearing and saw him, standing away from the water, leaning against a tree. His stallion was tethered nearby, and the creature defiantly tossed his head as she approached.

"Calhoun!" She smoothed her hair and took a timid step in his direction. He looked up, but his eyes did not snap in anticipation and he did not flash the smile she had always loved. His shoulders slumped in dejection. "You saved my son's life," she said, stepping toward him again. "You are a great hero."

He grunted and looked up at the bare treetops. "A hero? No, Afton, from this day forward I will be branded as a coward. I am not only outcast from my family, but my brothers in arms will shun me as well."

"Shun you? They will admire you! You refused to strike down a child! Even though victory was in your grasp—"

"My opponent was a knight," Calhoun interrupted, sinking slowly to the ground, his armor sliding over the tender bark of a young tree. "I ran from another knight. Regardless of my reasons, the story will spread, and no knight will ever trust me in battle again."

Afton rushed to his side. "I'm tired of all this talk of knights," she cried, reaching for his hands. She sank to the ground beside him, his hands clenched tightly in hers. "It does not matter what those rusty, worn-out warriors think of you. I know you are valiant, Calhoun, and you have done a noble thing."

He would not look at her, so she pulled his face toward her until she looked into his blue eyes. "I owe you my life, most noble Calhoun. I give you my love."

He raised his hand and she closed her eyes, certain that his lips would fall upon hers. But he only removed her hand from his cheek. Without a word, he stood up. "I spared your son at great price, Afton," he said stiffly, walking toward his horse.

She darted to his side. "What do you mean? Where are you going?"

"I must go away. I have no name here, no honor, and no family."

"But I love you!"

He swung into his saddle and looked down at her. It was as though she gazed into the face of a man a thousand years old. "You would not want a man with no pride," he said finally.

He kicked his horse and the animal began to move forward.

"Go, then!" Afton screamed at his back, her voice ringing in the trees. "Take your ridiculous pride and honor and never return to this place. You will die on a battlefield alone, Calhoun, and what joy will honor bring you then?"

He did not answer, but kept moving through the trees. After a few moments, the trees stopped rustling and the dead leaves grew silent. She stood alone in the forest, then threw herself upon the cold, muddy bank of the pool and wept.

She cried until she felt sick, and she vomited quietly in the bushes, then washed her face in the pool. *Go ahead, drown yourself*, the reflection in the water taunted her. *You have no life, either. It may well be that Perceval has put a bounty upon your head, or perhaps he has given you in marriage to the vilest man in his employ. Even Josson will not have you now, for you have shamed him in front of the villagers.* Her fingers closed around a rock and she hurled it into the center of her reflection, shattering it into ever-spreading rings of water.

She rose slowly, drawing her cloak about her. She began to walk, not in the direction of the village, but deeper into the forest. She did not know where she would go, but she did not care. *There are hungry winter wolves in this forest*, she thought idly, *and it will be a mercy to me if they attack.*

She stopped ere nightfall, though, and rubbed her frozen feet. They were blue with cold, and bleeding from the rough cuts of briars and stones—yet the pain was blessedly sharp, for her physical aches distracted her from the misery of her soul.

Looking about, she took refuge in a quiet thicket, lying down to sleep on a bed of fallen leaves, shivering like the dogs that used to lie at Perceval's kitchen door in hopes of a handout.

When morning dawned, she rose and walked again, her sore feet throbbing and her stomach aching with hunger. The damp silk of her wedding tunic offered no protection from the sunless chill, and her hair tangled in the bushes and branches that surrounded her.

She did not even know in which direction she traveled, for the sun hid behind a veil of gray clouds. She felt as though she moved in an ocean of cold mist, with unseen predators lurking behind every rock and shadow. Once, when she heard the piercing snarl of an animal, she lost her sense and ran, losing her slippers and her veil in her mad rush of terror. Another time she heard men's voices and the braying of dogs, and she crawled into a rotting log to hide until the sounds faded away. The rotting wood around her put her in mind of the grave, and she shuddered violently, yet she dared not stir from the place until all was silent once again.

For two days she wandered in the woods and, on the third day, she saw light at the edge of the trees. She stumbled blindly toward it. A road stretched before her in the distance, and she staggered across a clearing, hoping to beg mercy from a passing stranger. But the winter sun shone too brightly upon her and its sudden light after the dark of the forest caused her head to swim. Weak from exhaustion and exposure to the cold, she collapsed in the field, face down, her arms extended as though in silent entreaty.

When the convent housekeeper found her, she remarked to the abbess that God had surely willed that the woman be rescued, for she had been lying in the shape of a cross.

THIRTY-NINE

"Bring her in carefully," Madame Hildegard told Trilby, holding the heavy oak door open. "Do you need help?"

"She's nothing but skin and bones," Trilby answered, shaking her head. She laid the woman carefully upon a bed in the infirmary. "She weighs no more than a sack of potatoes."

Madame Luna, who presided over the infirmary, checked the woman for wounds and then covered her with a woolen blanket. "What do you think?" Hildegard murmured quietly. "Is she mad? For what cause would a woman wander in the forest and lie in the field?"

"I do not know," Luna answered, eyeing the woman's pale face. She flicked a dead leaf off the clean blanket. "Her tunic is fine, though torn, but her hands are callused and worn. I am sure she will tell us her story when she awakens." She laid her expert hand upon the woman's forehead. "She has fever. We had better call a doctor and a priest."

"Call the doctor," Hildegard nodded, giving permission. "We will call a priest only if it is necessary."

Before Madame Luna began the devotional reading at dinner, Hildegard raised her hand for the nuns' attention. Every eye turned soundlessly in her direction. "Our prayers are needed for a woman in our infirmary," she announced, smiling gently first at the nuns on her left, then at those on her right. "I will be nursing her. She would appreciate your prayers as well."

The nuns nodded in sympathy and agreement, and Madame Luna began to read from the Holy Scripture. Down at the end of the table, Lienor sipped her clear broth and idly wondered who this woman was that had come to their infirmary.

"Madame Abbess, may I nurse the sick woman?"

Hildegard always found it hard to refuse the sincerity in Agnelet's rare requests, but she shook her head resolutely. "Madame Luna is a fine nurse. You are needed elsewhere, my child."

"But even Madame Luna cannot nurse without sleep. I could spell her during the evening hours."

Hildegard sighed. Only two years old in the religious life, Agnelet was already a stronger nun than many of those who had given their lives to God twenty years before. Still, to expose her tender soul and heart to a woman who might possibly be mad . . .

"You may relieve Madame Luna in the evening hours only. When you do so, you are to observe the grand silence and not speak."

Agnelet nodded gratefully and her smile lit up her entire face, bathing even the hideous birthmark in a serene glow. She bowed reverently and left the room, and Hildegard thought once again that she understood why God allowed the birthmark upon Agnelet's tender face. Without it, Agnelet's beauty would be flawless, and such perfection was not meant to be within the reach of mortals.

For days the woman had been delirious in fever, whispering hoarsely and crying piteously. Whoever she was, some great sorrow had torn her soul, and tears coursed down Agnelet's cheeks as she wiped the woman's gaunt face with a cool cloth. Over and over she cooled the woman's face until the cloth grew hot in her hand, then Agnelet dipped it into fresh water and began again, ministering silently to the woman in her care.

But tonight Agnelet noticed a change in her patient. At first the woman's tongue had been coated with a white substance, but on this evening it seemed raw and red. Her face burned crimson with fever, except for a pale area around her trembling mouth, and her body was spotted with a scarlet rash.

The woman had sunk deeper into delirium. "Calhoun," she whimpered once, her body curving in pain and longing, then she stiffened, and thrashed back and forth in pain. Her hands held her head, tore at her long hair, and scratched at the rash on her body. Agnelet feared the woman was dying and she moved toward the bell that would alert Trilby to fetch a priest.

Suddenly the woman sat upright in bed and her dark eyes flew open. "Don't kill my son!" she cried, staring at Agnelet, who froze, her hand on the bell rope. "Don't kill my daughter!"

Agnelet rushed toward the woman, grabbed her shoulders, and gently pushed her back down on the mattress. Though her conscience pricked at her heart, she disobeyed the grand silence: "There, there," she crooned softly, as the woman relaxed slightly. "No one is going to hurt your children."

"My babies," the woman echoed, her eyes closing again. "Don't let him kill my babies."

The woman drifted off to sleep, but her ragged breaths came in spurts, and Agnelet could hear the death rattle in the woman's throat. She moved toward the bell rope again. Surely the end was near.

But as she reached out her hand, a sudden impulse came over her. She moved back to the bed, fell on her knees, and began to pray. "Our Father," she began, lifting her eyes to the ceiling. "Don't take this woman's life. Someone has hurt her, someone has threatened her children. Loving Father, if you must take a soul, take mine, O Lord, for it knows the pain this woman feels. Don't take her from her children."

She mouthed the words over and over again, as if the

repetition of them would assure God of her sincerity. When Madame Luna came in the next morning she found Agnelet crouched by the side of the bed, her hands folded in prayer.

Beside her, the woman slept easily, her fever broken.

The doctor said Agnelet's illness was a simple case of contagion. The sick woman had brought a disease into the convent and somehow gave it to the young nun. He promptly declared the infirmary off-limits to all the nuns but Madame Luna and Abbess Hildegard.

But as she lay on a mattress next to the woman, Agnelet knew God had honored her prayer. The woman would live.

Her own head was throbbing beneath her veil and headbands the morning that the woman sat up and looked around curiously. Her eyes caught Agnelet's, and the young nun saw a momentary flash of sympathy. "I must be at a convent," the woman whispered shyly. "But near what town?"

"Margate," Agnelet replied, the whisper ripping her sore throat.

The infirmary door opened and Madame Luna's eyes widened in surprise. "You are better!" she announced. "We have prayed and waited for this day. May we send for someone to care for you? Surely someone is worried about where you are."

The woman shook her head. "No one cares for me," she answered, her dark eyes closing in resignation. "There is no one to send for."

Madame Luna bowed slightly. "As you wish. You are fortunate to be alive." Madame Luna crossed to Agnelet's bed and laid a practiced hand across the young nun's forehead. "And you, dear sister, are burning with fever. I shall call the doctor."

"Don't." Agnelet tugged at Madame Luna's sleeve. "Do not trouble him. I am in God's hands."

Madame Luna hesitated, then nodded. "As you wish," she said simply, laying a heavy woolen blanket over the young girl. "But rest." She turned back to the woman. "I shall bring you some soup and bread. You must eat your way back to health."

The woman's smile lit up her face—and Agnelet's heart.

Afton felt stronger with every passing day. Soon she was able to eat, to sit up, and to stay awake. She knew the time was coming for her to take charge of her life again, but she had no idea what she should do. Only one thing was certain: she would no longer wait for Calhoun.

As Afton grew stronger, her young companion in the infirmary grew steadily weaker. The girl's face was constantly flushed with fever, and the horrific mark across her face darkened as her fever rose. While the girl slept, Afton studied her face with undisguised and morbid curiosity. The girl would have been quite handsome, for her features were delicate and lovely, but the hideous birthmark effectively overwhelmed any beauty in the small face.

Once the young nun opened her gray eyes while Afton was studying her face. "I'm sorry," Afton apologized in embarrassment, lowering her gaze. "I thought—"

"I do not take offense," Agnelet rasped, putting her hand to her throat. "My heart is impure. Why should my face then be pure? I cannot rail against my Creator."

"You do not regret his choice?" Afton asked. "He could have made you beautiful."

The girl made an effort to swallow. "Then I would not have been brought here, and this is where I have found peace, love, and the joy that comes from knowing God."

"You were cast off from your family?" Afton shook her head in disapproval. "I would hate them forever. No loving mother would abandon her child." She thought of Ambrose, standing tall and handsome by Endeline's side, and her voice cracked. "Willingly, of course. If my mother had abandoned me willingly, I would hate her forever."

"I do not hate my mother," Agnelet said, wearily closing her eyes. "She gave me life. She directed my path to this loving place. I could not have asked for more."

Afton stared at the young girl in amazement as the nun closed her eyes in exhaustion. Even in pain, she seemed as pure and demure as a statue of the Virgin Mary. After a moment, Afton shook her head. What did this sheltered girl know of life?

"I think you have been misled," Afton said, not caring if the girl heard her. "If I were locked behind these walls, I would be angry with God. I would be furious with those who kept me here, and I would vow revenge upon the woman who brought me to this place."

The girl's eyelids fluttered, then opened. "I am sorry that such anger has found a home in your heart," she said drowsily. "But you must get better—for your children." The girl's eyes closed in sleep, and Afton stared gloomily into the gathering darkness.

Afton grew restless as she grew stronger. She wanted to walk around, to see something other than the four mud-colored walls that surrounded her, but her thin legs would not yet fully support her weight. Once when she tried to stand, her legs collapsed under her, and Madame Luna found her sprawled on the hard floor.

"God wills that you rest with us yet awhile longer," the older nun grunted, lifting Afton back onto her mattress.

"I thought my strength had returned," Afton explained.

"Though the spirit is willing, the flesh is yet weak," Madame Luna replied, tucking a rough blanket around Afton's waist. "Maybe even your spirit is not as strong as our Lord intends. Take a lesson from our dear sister and meditate upon God while your flesh gathers strength."

Afton glanced over at the sleeping form of Agnelet. She lay perfectly still, flat on her back, her arms folded neatly across the rough blanket that covered her. Her mouth occasionally twitched in the restlessness of fever, and perspiration dotted her forehead. Still, she did not moan, cry out, or call for comfort.

Afton was about to remark that Agnelet was not meditating, but sleeping, when a bell chimed from outside the infirmary to summon the nuns for prayer. Madame Luna's finger went automatically to her lips to remind Afton that speech was now forbidden, then she turned and left the room as smoothly as a shadow.

Frustrated with her weakness, Afton lay back on her mattress and stared at the ceiling as the nuns' prayers ascended to heaven. *Benedicite, O all beasts and cattle, bless the Lord,* the nuns chanted. And, in whispered response through the delirium of fever, Agnelet joined in from her sickbed:

"Cleanse my heart and lips, O Almighty God. *Munda cor meum. . . .*"

The sick girl's evident sincerity struck Afton like a sharp slap. What sins had this young girl committed? Why did she need God's forgiveness? Surely she was a victim, not an aggressor. Just as Afton had been victimized all her life by grasping, powerful people, someone had taken this girl from her rightful place and left her imprisoned in a convent.

Afton closed her eyes and settled into the fantasy that had entertained her through hours of silence in the infirmary. Though she knew any woman could have been Agnelet's mother, it was delightful to imagine that a noblewoman had brought the girl to this place, perhaps even a friend of Endeline's. The haughty, scornful woman of Afton's imagination was unwilling to love the scarred child, unwilling even to acknowledge that such imperfection could exist in a proud lineage. How fulfilling, how pleasing it would be to present Agnelet to her family and demand the girl receive her rightful dowry and position!

A wry smile crossed Afton's lips as she pictured the noble ladies who had visited Margate Castle during her younger days. Could Agnelet be the daughter of Lady Regan of York? They shared the same golden hair color. Or perhaps the woman who had shown such disdain for this sweet child was the regal Lady Udele of Berkhamsted. Lady Udele, Afton remembered, was not known for marital faithfulness.

"You are much better." Agnelet's words interrupted Afton's thoughts. She jerked her head toward the sick girl, and a blush burned Afton's cheek as she regarded the young nun. What would she say if she knew what Afton had been thinking?

"Yes, I am better," Afton replied evenly. She pursed her lips together thoughtfully and turned slightly so Agnelet would not have to move to see her face. "I was just thinking of you. I was listening to your prayer and wondering what you could possibly have to confess. Surely you have committed no sins. But you have been taken from your mother's arms, deprived of home, family, position, and . . . ," Afton paused. "Beauty. Indeed, it would seem that God should be asking *your* forgiveness."

Agnelet's gray eyes were troubled, and she made an effort to wet her lips with her swollen tongue. "God has given me nothing but grace and favor," she answered. "In his sight, I am whole. I am his child. I could want nothing more."

"What about what should be yours? Do you never want your rightful place and possessions?" Afton argued, pulling herself to a sitting position and tugging gently on Agnelet's blanket. "Since so much has been taken from you, you have a right to demand justice. Seek out those who wronged you and claim your birthright. I will help. When you are better, we can start here at Margate village, then progress to the neighboring manors until we find someone who knows something of your birth. Who knows what secrets we will uncover?"

"No," Agnelet answered softly. She extended her hand, and Afton leaned over and gently took the girl's warm hand in hers.

"No one has wronged me," Agnelet said, her voice unusually strong. "I was born into an evil world, but God in his mercy saved me from certain death and made me his child. As a child of God, I have no rights in the world and expect none. What wrongs I have known or imagined, I forgave long ago."

"And the woman who gave you birth and then cast you off?" Afton interjected. "What of her?"

"I love her," Agnelet replied simply. She paused to swallow, and Afton reached for a cup of water with her free hand and held it to Agnelet's lips. After the young girl had drunk, she put her head back on her pillow and sighed. "Do not trouble yourself for me," Agnelet whispered, her eyelids drooping in exhaustion. "I have more than the world can offer. I have peace. I know Love and call him by name. I am going to a place far better than this—"

"Don't say that!" Afton interrupted, the cup slipping from her grasp. She ignored the spilled water and clasped Agnelet's small hand in hers. "You will grow strong and stand yet with me to walk out of here. The illness is but temporary, you will see."

Agnelet's eyes closed, and Afton thought the young nun shook her head in gentle disagreement even as she smiled.

The doctor visited the infirmary every day, diligent in his concern, and Madame Hildegard began to visit the sickroom more often as the young nun grew weaker. Agnelet no longer recited prayers with the nuns, but whispered them constantly in a feverish delirium.

"Deo gratias," she would murmur. "Grace is spread abroad on thy lips." At other times she would cry out, *"Mea culpa, mea culpa,* I accuse myself!" before mumbling through a vague catalog of sins that plagued her tender conscience.

The young girl's piety continually disturbed Afton. If Agnelet, a woman who was most innocent and beautiful in spirit, was tormented by the stain of sin, how much more should Afton herself be? Pride, jealousy, bitterness, rebellion, self-pity—as Agnelet made delirious confession of each of these sins, her words struck a sensitive nerve in Afton's own soul. But she would push aside her growing sense of conviction with renewed anger. Why should she repent of anything when she was the victim?

After overhearing one of Agnelet's whispered confessions to the abbess, Afton shook her head in frustration, then caught the abbess staring at her.

"Have you had occasion to visit our chapel?" the abbess asked, absently making the sign of the cross over Agnelet. "You look familiar to me."

Afton shook her head. "No, Madame," she lied, drawing her blanket protectively around her. No one from outside the abbey had yet discovered her whereabouts, and she could not arouse the old nun's suspicion, especially since Endeline was likely to have a spy even in the convent. Afton counted herself fortunate that the threat of contagion had kept Lienor from visiting the infirmary and recognizing her.

Later that evening Madame Luna brought Afton a simple tunic, one left by a young girl entering the convent. "I am sorry, but the fine tunic you were wearing was quite ruined," Madame Luna explained. "My frugal sisters have already cut it up for scraps. We have this replacement, but I am sure you are used to finer materials than this."

"No," Afton answered, accepting the new tunic gratefully. "This tunic will be fine. I am not highborn."

"I suppose you will soon be leaving us," Madame Luna remarked casually. Her tone was more a suggestion than a question, which did not surprise Afton. She *was* surprised, however, to realize that she did not yet want to go. Agnelet was still terribly ill, and somehow it seemed wrong to go while the young girl still suffered.

"I will go soon," Afton answered slowly, unfolding the new tunic. "When I feel strong enough."

"It will be as God wills," Madame Luna answered, removing the supper bowl from the table by Afton's bed. She put it outside the door and returned with the abbess, who had come to check on Agnelet. The young girl had been silent for over an hour. Madame Luna's manner became immediately more solicitous as she bent over the young sister, and she tenderly opened the girl's mouth and nodded to the abbess. Madame Hildegard reluctantly pulled the bell rope in the corner of the room.

In a moment, Afton heard the answering bell from the convent chapel, and within half an hour Father Barton stood in the infirmary, offering the last rites for Madame Agnelet.

Afton sat on her bed, hugging her knees, as the women who had known and loved Agnelet for all the years of her life glided through the infirmary in a single line. Afton thought the nuns' detachment seemed unnatural; though tears shone in their eyes as they carried lighted candles and sang Agnelet's soul to heaven, not one pair of eyes lifted to God in reproach. Not one voice questioned God's judgment. No lips curled downward with the weight of unuttered questions.

In her last moments of life, Agnelet saw only the sweet smiles of her sisters.

Afton sat quietly on her bed, feeling uncomfortably guilty. Agnelet lay in death's stillness on her straw mattress, pale in her black habit, and Madame Hildegard anointed her with holy oil and placed within her folded hands the parchment she had signed at vesture when she gave her soul and life to God.

"Peace to this house," the priest sang in a rich baritone.

"And to all who live herein," responded the nuns, their faces shining in the semidarkness.

From her bed, Afton wept, not knowing if her tears were for the brave young nun whose face was bathed in peace, or for herself, who had known so little peace.

Afton rose and dressed in her new tunic the next morning. It was time to go, for Agnelet's suffering had ended, and Madame Luna instinctively knew Afton would be leaving. She brought a wooden tray on which rested a sparse breakfast of bread and cheese. "You will need strength for your journey," the nun ordered. "Eat."

Afton took a few bites of the tasteless bread and wished she could be more grateful. A rap at the door distracted

Madame Luna's sharp eyes, and Afton sighed in relief and stuffed a hunk of bread under the mattress.

"You have a visitor," Madame Luna said, opening the door wider so the visitor could enter. Afton drew in her breath quickly. Lienor stood in the doorway. What did this mean? Of course, Lienor must have seen her last night in the infirmary, but did she intend to reveal Afton's identity?

Lienor nodded her thanks to Madame Luna, who left the room, then she walked to a bench and sat down. "Praised be Jesus Christ," Lienor whispered.

Afton sank onto her mattress, stunned. It had been so long since she had heard Lienor's voice that the sound of it thrilled her, like an age-old memory suddenly revived. "You are free to speak?" Afton said. "Your vow of silence is ended?"

"As of today, there is no need for it," Lienor said softly, her eyes flitting to the empty mattress where Agnelet had lain. "I kept silent to protect the happiness of someone who deserved joy. Now I may speak."

"Of what?" Afton asked. "Are you going to tell the abbess who I am? I only kept my identity secret because your father—"

"Your happiness deserves to be protected, too," Lienor interrupted gently. "I will not reveal your identity. But some-one else must be—" she paused—"unmasked."

Afton couldn't help her curiosity. "Who?"

Lienor's eyes flickered again over the empty bed. "I saw her as an infant, the day she arrived here. Such a tiny baby, and I knew the old woman at the gate could not have been her mother. But even though the crimson mark marred the beauty of her face, I saw her ancestry reflected there."

"I, too, saw something familiar in her face," Afton whis-pered, leaning forward. "Can justice yet be done for this poor girl?"

Lienor looked back at Afton, and her voice dropped to a nearly indiscernible whisper. "I had seen her beauty once before. Dainty nose, soft gray eyes, stubborn chin." She smiled. "Such beautiful features could only have come from you, Afton. Madame Hildegard learned that on the same day the babe came to us you were delivered of a baby boy. I surmised that you had also been delivered of a girl."

The room began to spin, and Afton clutched her fingers into the scratchy burlap mattress. This could not be! Her baby had died! Hubert had killed the child, and the cook, too—as he had nearly killed her. "No, that can't be!" she whimpered. "It's impossible. My baby was killed!"

Pity shone in Lienor's eyes. "I knew you were married to a devil and I did not speak up at first because I feared for the child's safety. By the time I learned of Hubert's death, we had all come to love Agnelet, and she loved us. I knew then the best life for her was here at the convent. She was protected."

"*I* was her mother?" Afton gasped, the memory of her recent fantasy flooding through her soul. Oh, the stinging insults she had planned to hurl at the heartless lady who had borne the child! The pain and dismay she had wanted to inflict upon Agnelet's uncaring mother now doubled and ripped through her own heart.

Afton's arms crossed her chest and she doubled over in pain. "You knew she was my daughter?" she said, speaking through clenched teeth, uncontrollable emotions welling up within her. "You kept her from me?"

Lienor shook her head. "I tried to show you once. When you came to tell me that Calhoun had been captured, I tried to lead you to the window to see her. But you would not look."

"I thought she was dead! How could I have known?"

"It was as God willed." Lienor smiled a sweet, unruffled smile. "Agnelet would not have known happiness in the world, for it is a cruel place for those who are not beautiful." Despite her demeanor, Afton suspected that the memory of her own pain still resided in Lienor's heart.

Afton's emotions swirled like a cyclone. "If I had known, I would have made her happy! We could have gone away—"

Lienor held up her hand. "Agnelet could not run from herself. In this place she came to an understanding and acceptance of God's will. She was dearer to God than the rest of us, and that is why he drew her to himself."

"I killed her." A fresh recognition struck Afton, and she sat upright. "She lay here and forgave me—," her voice cracked and she spoke through sobs. "I killed her, and she said she loved me. While my heart was set on vengeance for her, she would have nothing of it. She loved me, Lienor! How could she do that?"

Lienor stood and placed an awkward hand on Afton's shoulder. "The mercy of God works in strange ways," she whispered softly. "Do not think ill of me for not speaking sooner. But I could not destroy her happiness."

Lienor slipped out of the room, and Afton buried her face in the burlap mattress and screamed.

FORTY

The morning of her departure from the convent, Afton knelt for three hours in the chapel, praying for comfort that would not come. When her knees were numb from grating on the stone floor, she left the convent for the road that led to the village. She took nothing from the nunnery but the cast-off tunic she wore and a knowledge too terrible to be denied.

She needed a safe place to think, a place away from the black-robed women who only reminded her of her loss. She no longer cared what fate, if any, Endeline and Perceval had planned for her, for any pain they might have intended would be eclipsed by the yawning emptiness of her heart.

Corba welcomed her home with a warm embrace and, after one look at Afton's face, asked no questions. Afton lay down on her straw mattress and slept twelve hours without stirring, then she awoke in the dead of night and sat quietly, thinking.

Agnelet had been her daughter, that much she knew for certain. As she stared into the darkness, she saw Hubert clearly, grinning as he lifted the babe from between her legs. "And God has given me a sign," he had bellowed as Afton struggled to lift her head through her pain. "For the child is marked as the offspring of an adulteress. I read your sin in the child's face."

She had been too overwhelmed with suffering to comprehend his words, but now she understood what Hubert had seen. The birthmark. The mark of Afton's sin, Hubert had called it. She lowered her head upon her arms. Was the child marked for her sin of loving Calhoun? Even though she had been physically faithful to her husband, had God punished her for loving another? Was he punishing her still, by taking her daughter from her a second time?

She could not escape her guilt. *I did not look for her,* Afton thought, driving her fist into her open palm. *I should have gone throughout England looking for her little body, but I did not! And just as I hated Corba for giving me to Endeline, so she must have hated me!*

But she did not. A cool voice of reason crossed Afton's mind. *Without ever knowing you, she loved you. She was grateful to you. She prayed for you.*

Was it possible that Agnelet had been better off in the convent? What sort of life would she have had in the village? Afton's tears began anew when she realized that Lienor was right: no matter where they had gone, Agnelet would have been feared, scorned, or even accused of being a child of the devil. Her life would not have been secure—and vain, ambitious Ambrose might have been unspeakably cruel to her.

Afton raised her eyes to the thatched roof of Corba's hut. She could not bargain with God. In infinite wisdom, he had known and chosen the best path for Agnelet. *But why,* Afton wondered, *did God choose to bring our paths together? Can he forgive me for being the instrument of her death?*

Afton mourned in silence for two days, speaking and eating little. On the evening of the second day, she clasped Corba's hands and poured out the entire story, beginning with Agnelet's birth and ending with her death. "She lived and died in peace and joy," Afton whispered, as tears flowed freely from Corba's dim eyes. "Surely that is all a mother can ask for a child."

"That is all," Corba agreed, sniffling noisily. "But heed the words of your daughter, Afton."

Afton cocked her head. "What words?"

"Didn't she tell ye to get better for the sake of your children? Ye still have a child on this earth. Do not forget Ambrose. He is not living in peace and joy, but in the castle."

Afton released Corba's hands and sank to the floor. What was she to do with Ambrose? How could she help him while he lived in the castle, the lair of ambition and vanity?

Forgive . . .

Afton frowned at the word that immediately rose within her. Suddenly, Agnelet's words echoed in her mind: *As a child of God, I have no rights in the world and expect none. What wrongs I have known or imagined, I forgave long ago.* . . .

"No!" Afton whispered heatedly, desperately. "You cannot be asking that of me! It cannot be just to forgive those who took so much away from me!"

But her only answer was silence. And a restlessness in her soul that would not go away.

On the third day, Afton rose from her bed and dressed herself, determined to go on, to live, to do what she could for her son.

FORTY-ONE

"Halt in the name of King Stephen!" the guard on the London road called hoarsely. The silver of his sword gleamed in the sun. "Identify yourself."

"Calhoun, of late in the service of the king," Calhoun answered, his hand on his own sword. "I wish to join the king's ranks for a lifetime of service."

The guard whispered to his companion, who nodded. "Proceed," the first man announced, waving Calhoun through.

Calhoun rode immediately to Stephen's palace and found a company of the king's knights preparing to ride out. He gave his horse to a page and gathered his courage to approach the castle. He did not know what, if any, news had reached Stephen in the weeks since the disastrous duel. He hoped the king had been too involved in his war with Matilda to pay any attention to rumors about a cowardly knight. In any case, Calhoun had decided to spend the rest of his life in the king's service.

He gave his name to a messenger, who reappeared shortly. "The king will see you right away," the messenger announced, raising an eyebrow in surprise. Calhoun nodded and proceeded into the main hall.

Stephen sat at dinner, flanked by his aides. "We eat on the run, Sir Calhoun," he said, acknowledging Calhoun's presence. "Matilda and her forces are on the move in the south. We go at once to stop them."

"I am at your service," Calhoun said, kneeling on the stone floor.

"What of your marriage?" Stephen asked, waving a chicken leg imperiously. "I thought you took your leave some weeks ago to be married."

"The marriage did not take place." Calhoun raised his head defiantly.

"I am not so concerned with the marriage," Stephen answered, taking a tremendous bite of chicken. He chewed thoughtfully for a moment, then swallowed. "Where have you been in the intervening time?"

Calhoun lowered his eyes to the stone floor, uncomfortably aware that the noise of forty dining knights had subsided. All eyes and ears, it seemed, were trained upon him.

"I have been riding through the countryside, collecting my thoughts," Calhoun answered. "I needed to find a new purpose for my life—"

"Have you found it?" the king questioned.

"I offer it to you," Calhoun finished. "My life and my service."

"As the son of Perceval?"

Calhoun flushed. "As myself."

The king put down his chicken and wiped his hands fastidiously on the linen tablecloth. "Before I accept this valiant offering, I want to know of your father's loyalty."

Calhoun did not waver. "My father has cast me off. I am no longer his son."

"But I asked of his loyalty." Stephen's voice was clipped, his eyes narrowed.

"He has always been loyal to the throne."

"What of his loyalty to Matilda?"

"I do not know—"

"Think, man!" Stephen slammed his hand down upon the table, and his aides jumped in surprise. Stephen took a deep breath. "Captured prisoners told my captains they have been for many months sustained by tributes from Perceval, the earl of Margate. *Do you know this to be true?*"

Calhoun knelt before the king, silently cursing the family pride that kept him from betraying Perceval's treacherous dealings.

"Do you know?" Stephen roared.

"I cannot answer."

Stephen sprang from his seat and came out from behind the table to stand in front of Calhoun. He nodded toward two guards, who moved to Calhoun's right and left hand.

Stephen made an obvious effort to lighten his voice, but he stood with his hands at his belt, his legs apart as if preparing for a duel. "I hear disturbing things, son of Perceval. You fight bravely for us, then you go home for a marriage that does not take place. Then you are to fight a knight—one sworn to Matilda—but you do not kill him. Instead, you ride off and spare the villain's life. Then you reappear here weeks later and offer yourself, all the while your father aids my sworn enemy this very hour. Does this suggest something to you?"

"He is a spy!" a bearded man at the table hissed. "Perceval sends his son to spy on us."

"He is a traitor," another man chimed in. "He bragged of killing Matilda's captain, Arnoul, but the Limb of Hell is alive and well, terrorizing the king's loyal citizens."

"Arnoul is alive?" Calhoun's astonishment showed on his face, but not plainly enough to convince his accusers.

"So it would seem." Stephen's eyes held him in an unblinking gaze, and Calhoun knew he had no defense. Who could trust a man who had turned against his family and shown mercy to the king's enemy? Both were unthinkable.

"I offer my life in service to you and to God," Calhoun spoke boldly. "My heart is true. Do with my life as you please."

A light flickered in Stephen's eyes and the trace of a smile passed across his face. "Very well, Sir Calhoun. I will have you imprisoned and hold your life as a test of your father's loyalty. That is my plan. God's plan for your life remains to be seen."

Stephen looked to the guards. "Take him to the tower," he commanded. As the guards led him out, Calhoun heard the king's parting words: "Have my company readied at once. We ride for Margate Castle within the hour."

"It is good ye are up and dressed," Corba said, offering Afton a slice of thick brown bread. "There are reports of trouble at the castle, and things may be skittish in the village." Corba's hands were shaking as she nervously wiped them on her apron. "A messenger from Matilda's troops rode through last night and demanded aid from Perceval at the castle. The men are saying that Matilda's knights may pass through here today."

"It would serve justice if they cleaned out Perceval's storehouse," Afton answered, dipping her bread in a jar of honey. "Perceval deserves it, after taxing us twice to pay for his double tributes."

"But we do not deserve to starve if they burn our village," Corba's voice trembled and she sank onto a bench at the table. "And Calhoun does not deserve to die," she added.

Afton's eyes widened. "Why would Calhoun die?" she asked. "Surely he fights for Stephen again."

Corba shook her head. "Lord Perceval and Lady Endeline pretend they do not care, but it is rumored that Calhoun is a prisoner of the king, his life held in ransom for Perceval's loyalty. If Perceval aids Matilda—"

"Shhh, mother!" Afton snapped, her brain racing at what she had heard. Her first thought was for Ambrose . . . if Matilda's men reached the castle, all would be well for Ambrose. Yet, if Stephen learned of Perceval's support for Matilda, Calhoun would surely die for his father's disloyalty. Afton shuddered. Despite Calhoun's foolish faults, he did not deserve to die for the folly of his father. He had spared her son, and if she could save his life, she would.

"Matilda's men come by day?" she asked, staring into space across the table.

"So they say," Corba answered.

"Does anyone know where Stephen's men are?"

Corba shook her head. "I'm an old woman, girl. I only know what the other women tell me."

Afton stood up and grabbed a scarf, quickly tying it around her head. She kissed Corba gently on the cheek. "Do not fear, Mother," she said, placing her hands tenderly on Corba's shoulders. "I love you."

She did not know from where Matilda's army would come, but the only clear road to Margate Castle lay through the village. She ignored the glances of the village women as she walked, and felt the familiarity of the old mill house as she passed the mill and the stream.

It was there that Agnelet and Ambrose had been born. If all went according to her plan, she and Ambrose would live there again. Now that the boy was of age, she would demand that he be released from Perceval and given his lawful inheritance. By the king's law, Ambrose was not a knight, but a miller. The mill was his, and, as his mother, she would live there with him, and all would be well.

The warm sun offered the promise of spring as she followed the road past the mill. When she came to a fork in the road, she sat on a grassy knoll and waited, untying her scarf so her hair could dance in the slight breeze. Hair, as Endeline taught her, was a marvelous distraction. For some silly reason, men seemed to be captivated by it.

There were few visitors traveling by. An itinerant priest and his companion glanced at her surreptitiously, and a passing washerwoman and her servant paused to give her a disdainful look. At last, though, her patience was rewarded. A cloud of dust appeared on the road near the horizon. As it drew closer, Afton stood and judged her surroundings again. She would have to be close enough to arouse interest, but not so close that she could be scooped up into a saddle and carried away as booty. She was well enough acquainted with men of the sword to know that it was prudent to keep her distance.

She walked ten paces into the field, a good distance from the road, and as the party of knights drew near she waved her hands in greeting. "Stop a minute," she called, aping Corba's common accent. "Be ye goin' to Margate Castle?"

A large brute in armor turned his scarred face toward her. One red scar dripped down his left cheek, and a dark patch obscured his left eye. "Aye, wench," he snarled, reining his horse in tightly. His smile turned into a gruesome grin. "Would ye like a lift?"

The other knights laughed uproariously, and Afton involuntarily stepped back. "Not with ye, sir," she answered lightly, throwing her scarf back over her head. The knight laughed again and struck his horse with the whip, and the procession moved forward.

Afton remained aware of the knights' eyes upon her, though, and she walked slowly beside them and pretended to stumble, falling to the ground. "Please," she breathed in a desperate whisper, "please, let one of you be as chivalrous as Calhoun."

She lay in the dirt for a few moments as the tramp of hooves slowly passed her by, then one horse broke from the rear of the company and cantered toward her. Upon reaching her, a young knight smiled down at her. "Are you hurt, miss? Can I offer you a ride? We will never let it be said that Matilda's knights left a maiden in peril."

"Thank you," Afton sighed, pointing to her ankle. "But I'm afraid you'll have to help me up."

The young knight dismounted and pulled her to her feet, keeping his arm around her waist. The remaining knights jeered and rode away. "Your company is leaving you," Afton remarked, placing her small hands in his.

"It does not matter," the knight smiled. "I can catch them in a moment. My horse is the swiftest in the company."

"How wonderful," Afton answered. He supported her as she limped to the left side of the horse. The knight put his hands under her arms and lifted her easily into the saddle, then placed the reins in her hands as he prepared to mount behind her. As soon as Afton felt the smooth leather of the reins, she turned the horse and kicked with all her might. The startled animal lunged away. As the knight shouted and ran after her, Afton leaned forward and urged the stallion on until she was out of reach.

Afton kept the horse at a gallop until she had passed the convent, then she allowed him to slow to a trot. She did not know where to find Stephen or Calhoun, but if mercy existed in heaven, she would find one of them—before it was too late.

She rode through the afternoon and, at each village, asked the whereabouts of Stephen's army. No one gave her an answer until one old woman took pity on her. "A rider came through this morning," the woman said, grinning toothlessly. "Stephen's forces are just north of here, making camp for the night, they tell me. But he won't have nothing to do with a woman, I can tell ye that."

"Be that as it may, I must find him," Afton answered, bowing to the old woman. "Thank you for your kindness."

"Long live the king!" the woman crowed in response, and Afton pointed her horse toward the north.

It did not take long to find the king's encampment, for campfires were already sending lazy tendrils of smoke into the sky. She left the road and moved in the direction of the fire, and soon two mounted knights hurried to intersect her path. "Who goes there?" one of them called, his sword glimmering in his hand. "Name yourself, woman."

Afton felt her stomach turn over. What was she doing? Was this impulsive action only destined to make matters worse for all? Would she be waylaid here before even reaching King Stephen?

"I am Afton of Margate Castle," she answered, reining in her horse. She held her head high. "I demand to see the king."

"Who are you to demand anything of the king?" the

other knight asked, laughing. He leaned forward in his saddle, but kept his sword at his side. "You're a pretty thing. Did the king send for you? One of the captains, perhaps?"

Afton recognized the leer of lust, for Hubert had often worn the same expression. Though she felt her cheeks flame, she answered defiantly. "I demand to see the king, for I bring news of Matilda's army."

The other knight lowered his shield. "Why is your horse arrayed in red?" he asked, suspicion in his eyes. "Red is the color of Matilda's army."

"Because it is Matilda's horse," Afton answered, with a bold toss of her head. "I stole him from her knights. Now let me pass, for I need to see the king!"

"Let her pass."

Afton whirled around to see who had spoken. Another man on horseback had quietly ridden up behind her. Afton frowned, for this man was not dressed in armor but in a simple bright tunic. He was tall and thin, with auburn hair and eyes that were deep and dreamy—not at all the eyes of a warrior—eyes that stirred Afton's memory.

"Gislebert?" she asked. "Can it be you?"

The young man, now full-grown, nodded gravely. "Yes. I will be happy to escort you to the king, my lady. I am sure what you have to tell us is of great worth."

Afton had imagined that King Stephen would travel in a magnificent shelter, but she was led to a spartan tent of coarse wool, inside which was only a rough table and a simple cot. The tent was filled with men in armor, but they all gave attention to a plain-looking man who sat on a bench enveloped in a tapestry. The man's nose and eyes were red and puffy, and he was blowing his nose with great force as Gislebert led Afton into the tent.

"It's a ruinous thing, this war," the man told his counselors as he wiped his ample nose. "It may cost England more than she knows. Not only are we killing our own fair land and its people, but the French have begun to eye us with a wary eye. How can we keep the peace abroad if we cannot maintain it at home?"

"Your Majesty," Gislebert interrupted, bowing from the waist. "I present to you Afton of Margate Castle, a free woman. She has urgent news for Your Majesty."

"Yes?" Stephen lifted bleary eyes to Afton's. "What news does she bring me?"

"Only this, sire," Afton said, kneeling low. She took a deep breath and felt her nervousness ease. Stephen was nothing like the hard and cruel Henry. In fact, she almost felt sorry for the man who was before her. "I am come to tell you that Matilda's forces are even now surrounding the castle of Margate."

Stephen motioned to one of his counselors, and the man bowed and sped away. "Thank you for that confirmation," Stephen said, nodding to her. "But that news had reached us earlier. We will travel to Margate on the morrow."

Afton took a deep breath. "There is more, Majesty," she continued. "It may be that Perceval will not be able to withstand the pressures exerted by Matilda's men. If that is the case, kind king, do not hold Perceval's weakness against his son, Calhoun, whom you hold. Calhoun's heart has always been in your hands."

Stephen cocked his head and regarded Afton carefully. She saw wariness in his eyes. "Where have you come from, woman?" he asked lightly, gazing at her dress. "You are not from the castle, though your speech and manners indicate you are highborn. Your clothing indicates poverty and ignorance, yet you have addressed a king today with grace and skill." He leaned forward and absently wiped his nose with a handkerchief. "You are either very brave or very foolish. Could it be that you are a spy, come to redeem another spy, the worthy Calhoun? If I follow your suggestions, am I walking into a trap?"

"No, Your Majesty." Afton shook her head. "My life will stand for my honesty. If you promise to send for Calhoun and spare his life, I will tell you how to surround and defeat Matilda's forces at Margate Castle."

Stephen paused for a moment, then threw back his head and laughed, stomping his foot in merriment. "A military adviser, this woman," he said, wiping tears from his eyes. He blew his nose again, then abruptly stopped laughing. "How is it you have come to know so much about the castle?"

"I spent my childhood there, as a companion for Perceval's daughter, Lienor," Afton answered. "I was torn from all I loved and reared as a child of nobility until I reached marriageable age."

Stephen gazed at her a moment more. "This company of Matilda's at Margate—how many are they?"

Afton paused only a moment. "About thirty and five."

"Mounted?"

"All."

"Led by a woman?"

"No, sire. Led by a big man, with a patch over one eye and a scar down one cheek."

Stephen slapped the table. "By St. Jude, it is Arnoul's company. It may not be Matilda herself, but it is her right arm. If we could take them—"

"It will be a great victory, Your Majesty," Gislebert inserted. "I can vouch for this woman's honesty. I knew her years ago, and I have never known her to be a liar."

"We will ride at first light," Stephen announced. "And—" he paused and waved a hand in Afton's direction, "send one rider immediately to London and bring us the prisoner Calhoun."

Afton closed her eyes in relief. "Thank you, Your Majesty."

"Spare your gratitude yet a while," Stephen answered. "If your plan is true, you win your life and the life of the knight. If you play me false, however, tomorrow's sun will be the last you shall see."

FORTY-TWO

She spent the night in a small tent with two burly guards positioned outside. Gislebert brought her a bowl of porridge, which she ate quickly, aware of his eyes following her every move. When she had finished, she put the bowl aside. "How came you to ride with the king?" she asked. "I thought you wanted to be a troubadour."

"Aye, and so I am," Gislebert answered, settling down on the ground across from her. "His Majesty's troubadour. I entertain the royal court when they are in need of a story or song."

"How came you to be in the royal court?"

Gislebert looked out the open door of her tent and lowered his voice. "When Calhoun did not return with the company from Outremer, I considered my vow to him kept." He read her question in her eyes. "Before he left for the East, Calhoun bade me swear that I would visit you and keep you from harm's way. I did this for two years, to the best of my ability."

Afton suddenly understood the many seemingly useless visits the boy had made to the mill; he had come even more often than Josson. "I thought you were just a simple dreamer," she said, smiling. She shook her head. "I did not know you were on Calhoun's errand to—"

"I was his friend," Gislebert interrupted. "We met at Warwick, and I would have followed him to Outremer, but for you. He would not leave you unprotected."

Afton turned her head away, touched by Calhoun's concern, but angered by his lack of confidence in her. How like him to think her weak and helpless! "I am sorry I came between you," she whispered. "Though it is obvious you have done well since we last met. Surely you can desire no more than a place in the king's court?"

Gislebert shook his head. "I desire much more," he said simply. "I would see Calhoun restored to safety, but Stephen is convinced he is a traitor. If I were to say otherwise, my life would also be in danger." He flushed and looked into her eyes. "Do not misunderstand. I would give my life for him, but what good could I do him in prison? So I have remained silent, that I might seize an opportunity when it was presented."

"I understand," Afton sighed.

"I also desire the hand of a certain maiden in marriage," Gislebert whispered, and Afton turned surprised eyes upon him.

"You do not know her," he inserted quickly. "My beautiful Nadine was very young when I met her at Margate, the servant girl of a visiting lady. I lost my heart the moment I saw her. When she left and I heard that Calhoun had not returned with the other knights, I knew I could not stay in Margate. I left to find her."

"Have you found this maiden?"

Gislebert shook his head. "She served a lady who moved in royal circles, so day after day I have hoped for a glimpse of her, but as of yet fortune has not smiled upon me. Still," he said with a shrug, "I do not give up. Whether my beautiful Nadine is in England or France, I will find her."

The young man turned again to the open doorway. "When I left Margate, I wandered through the country in my search and sang songs for my keep. It was not an easy life," he continued, his eyes darkening with remembered sorrow, "until I met an earl who introduced me to the king. His Majesty bid me stay at the castle and entertain the royal court, which I have done for many months now. And, while

I have heard nothing of Nadine, it was there that I learned Calhoun was alive and in the king's service, battling Matilda. I tried to find him, but he was always one step ahead of me."

Gislebert clasped his hands around his knees, and Afton thought to herself that this quiet, confident young man bore little resemblance to the mischievous boy she had known so long ago.

"One day I learned that Calhoun had gone home to be married," Gislebert went on. "'Ah,' I thought, 'I will go to Margate and wish him well with his bride. Perhaps Nadine and her lady will be among the wedding guests.' But before I was granted leave, Calhoun was back in London, imprisoned for being a spy. I have not dared to speak to him, for fear that I will be thought in collusion."

"No one would think you have anything to do with Matilda," Afton protested, throwing her hands wide. "You have no family ties—"

"The court now is like quicksand," Gislebert interrupted. "No one is trusted, and certain knights and lords rejoice when others are swept away by the king's outrage. Stephen has been especially angered by reports of Perceval's disloyalty. One of Matilda's knights would have a greater chance for Stephen's mercy than a lord who has dealt fealty with a double hand."

Gislebert looked at Afton, his face half hidden by shadows. "I have wrestled with guilt, fear, love, and my obligation to a friend," he whispered. "When I saw you, I knew an opportunity at last had come, and the least I could do was provide an entry for you to see the king."

"Without your word, I would not have made it past the guards," Afton replied, as he rose to his feet. "Thank you, then, Gislebert. And good night."

The camp broke before daylight. Stephen's men dismantled their tents and mounted their horses with astonishing speed, and the knights were assembled on the road before the day had broken. Afton rode on a sturdy mount behind the king, and she kept quiet as they rode south, knowing that her life, Calhoun's, and possibly Gislebert's hung in the balance.

Margate village appeared deserted as they rode through it; it was as though every villein had sensed the approaching clash and now hid within the safety of their huts. Afton peered into Corba's tiny courtyard as she passed and saw nothing, not even a stray chicken. Her mother had undoubtedly gone into hiding like the others.

The forest was cool and still as they rode through, and Afton's apprehension rose with every step of her horse. Soon she would see Margate Castle. If Perceval's colors still flew from the tower, would Stephen believe her assertion that Matilda had marched on the castle? And if Matilda's men were no longer ensconced at the castle, would Perceval manage to convince the king of his continued loyalty, thus making her a liar?

The forest broke from around them and Margate Castle lay before them, illuminated in the early morning sun. The fields outside the castle walls were the bright green of early spring, and Afton found it hard to believe that war could erupt in these simple fields.

"All seems peaceful enough," Stephen remarked to the knight who rode on his right hand. The king turned to look at Afton. "There are no signs of Matilda's men, lady. What say you now?"

"All is not well," Afton replied surely, glancing about. "Look, Majesty, on the towers. Perceval's colors do not fly, nor do his guards stand watch. Look in the fields, sire. This is early spring, yet there are no villeins in the fields."

The king reined in his horse and sat still in the road, carefully observing the castle. The tall enceinte seemed naked, for no guards walked the high wall and no faces peered out from the notches of the crenellations.

Stephen raised his hand. "Trumpeter," he called, "sound a warning that we approach. Let us see what the response will be."

The trumpeter blew a loud flourish that rang over the

empty pasture and echoed far back into the rolling hills. A few moments later, the castle gate opened, and a lone rider—a knight in full armor—came riding toward them. He carried Perceval's banner, and Afton recognized him at once. Jarvis.

"My king!" The knight stopped his horse and dismounted in one swift movement. He fell to one knee and smote his breast with a fist. "We are honored by your visit, but my Lord Perceval did not expect you. If you will give him a day to prepare—"

"I do not want Perceval's hospitality," Stephen answered, his wary eyes carefully scanning the tower battlements. "I want to know of his loyalty."

"My lord has always served the king," Jarvis answered, his words stilted. "He pledges his eternal love and fealty—"

"Jarvis!" Afton spoke clearly, and the knight's eyes widened in surprise as he looked up and saw her. "If you feel any loyalty to Calhoun, I beg you to tell the truth. The king knows that Matilda's knights have sojourned here."

Jarvis's face reddened and he lowered his eyes to the ground. When he spoke, his voice shook with repressed emotion. "Matilda's men arrived yesterday and are hidden in the garrison. They are ready to attack if you draw near." Jarvis spat on the ground. "Arnoul sent me to dissuade you from entering. He fears a siege and has pledged to kill Lord Perceval and Lady Endeline if he and his men are not allowed to escape."

"They will not escape," Stephen answered, drawing his sword from its sheath. "You will ride in the fore, Sir Jarvis, and take your chances fighting for your king. You, lady of Margate, shall ride in the rear with Gislebert and wait out the battle."

"Your Majesty, I do not think a direct charge upon the castle is prudent," Afton inserted. "Perceval's castle is well-supplied—"

"Shut up, woman!" Stephen turned surprisingly blue eyes on her and impatiently wiped his red nose. He motioned for his trumpeter, who blew a three-noted flourish, and the company of mounted knights fanned out into a single line across the road and into the pasture on both sides.

With his knights in position, Stephen motioned to the trumpeter again. The man blew a long, shrill blast, and the knights gripped their shields, spurred their horses, and thundered over the soft turf. Afton held her reins tightly, watching in alarm. She glanced at Gislebert, whose face had paled at the trumpet blast.

As the king's knights stormed toward the castle, the faces of Matilda's men arose along the top of the castle wall. A sheet of flaming arrows shot forth from the flared arrow loops, dastardly little holes that allowed weapons to be launched without exposing the archer. Wave after wave of deadly arrows fell upon the riders, and the knights who actually reached the wall were picked off by Matilda's marksmen.

It did not take long for Stephen and his knights to realize the futility of storming the castle. After a brief and bloody battle, Stephen's trumpeter sounded retreat, and the remaining royal knights withdrew as quickly as they had advanced. As their horses rushed past her like the hounds of hell, Afton's horse trembled and bolted after them, down the castle road and into the stillness of the forest.

The horses churned on the road in a restless melee, and Afton waved her scarf to get the king's attention. "Follow me," she cried, and Gislebert echoed her.

"Let us follow the woman," he suggested to the king, "for she knows the area."

Afton dismounted and led her trembling horse through the familiar forest. The king and his company followed in a single line, and soon she had found her landmark, the twin trees. She led her horse to the pool and noticed with relief that the other knights did likewise.

King Stephen dismounted, looking at his surroundings with approval. The knights who had escaped without injury watered the horses, then tended to the walking wounded.

Afton noticed that the group was smaller by at least ten knights, and Jarvis was among the missing.

"This foray is useless," one knight grumbled to the king. "Margate Castle is well-fortified. We cannot hope to storm it with our small number."

"Would you have Arnoul laugh at us?" the king snapped, pacing the ground. "We must take the castle. I will not have the crown sullied by such a braggart."

The king turned to face Afton. "Did you bring us here to be slaughtered?" he asked, wiping perspiration from his brow. "You will die in the morning. You, and Calhoun when he arrives."

"Your Majesty has not heard my plan," Afton answered, folding her hands into her sleeves, a calming gesture she had learned from the nuns. "It is true that Margate Castle is well-fortified, for Perceval updates it regularly. But did you know that he has installed lavatories along the wall for his knights?"

Stephen snorted. "What good do lavatories do me now?"

Afton smiled gently. "The lavatories are made with stone shafts along the outside of the wall," she said. "They are not large enough to see from the field, but a man could climb them. I did so often as a child."

"Climb them?" Stephen turned to look at one of his knights. "Could you climb a lavatory shaft?"

"It is a simple matter, Majesty," Afton said, stooping down. She drew a large circle in the dirt at the king's feet. "This is the castle wall. Here and here . . ." She drew two smaller rings. ". . . are the towers. Tucked away on the towers are the lavatory shafts. If you hide in the forest until dark, then send one man in to climb the castle walls, you can likely catch Matilda's entire force napping in the garrison . . ." She drew a large rectangle inside the circle. ". . . here. Lady Endeline and Lord Perceval will be in the castle, of course, and it is likely your dread enemy Arnoul will be there, too."

"A knight climbing the walls would be totally exposed," one of the king's knights pointed out, running a stick through her diagram. "He could not climb with his lance or shield. At most, he could carry his sword and his dagger."

"Perhaps that is all he will need," Afton answered, looking steadily into the king's eyes. "Matilda's men are tired. They think they have just won a great victory. They will drink Perceval's ale and feast on his food and they will go to the garrison for sleep. Their eyelids will be heavy, their swords at rest. If their door is unguarded and they are bottled up inside the garrison, the victory will be yours. Select your bravest knight, Your Majesty, and the strongest. If the plan fails—"

"It is suicide," the knight interrupted.

"If it fails," Afton persisted, ignoring the man, "you have lost one knight of twenty. But if it succeeds, you can capture Arnoul's entire force without bloodshed."

"Whom shall I send?" Stephen looked around at the circle of knights that had gathered.

"Send me!"

The crowd parted as a knight pushed his way through, and Afton trembled at the unexpected sound of the voice. For there before her and the king, chains binding his hands, stood Calhoun.

FORTY-THREE

Endeline watched their supper guest warily. Arnoul was brutish and coarse, but there was no denying his quick intelligence. He reminded her of a chameleon, always changing, ever rising to the challenge of the moment. It would do them no good if he suspected Perceval had been anything other than a faithful backer of Matilda. As long as Charles and Ambrose held their tongues . . .

"I suppose, now that you have routed the king's army, you will leave in the morning," Endeline said smoothly, passing Arnoul another heaping plate of veal. "But, of course, you are welcome to stay as long as we may do service to your cause."

"I suppose my purpose is done," Arnoul answered, smiling in satisfaction. "Routing the king's army was an unexpected pleasure. I had but one purpose in coming here, and that was to take the life of your son, Calhoun." Arnoul grinned, and Endeline felt her skin crawl in shock and fear.

"What?" Perceval asked dully. Endeline was not sure that Perceval had even understood the events of the last two days. His mind had not been clear since Arnoul's men had suddenly appeared on the road.

"I have nothing against you, my lord, but if Stephen heard that you were giving me aid—and I made certain that he *would* hear—then I knew the royal wrath would be kindled against Calhoun and the order would come for his death." His hard face creased in a smile that held only bitterness and hatred. "The mighty and noble Calhoun, executed in disgrace as a cursed spy, a traitor to his king. A more fitting end I could not have designed myself. It was he, you know, who took my eye and left me with this bloody scar."

"Calhoun did that?" Endeline gasped, pretending more horror than she felt.

Arnoul's face darkened. "My men and I sought refuge in a church, but your son set fire to the place. I am sure Calhoun thought me dead, but I found a trapdoor and a tunnel dug by some wandering priest, so I escaped the fate your son had planned for me."

"You came here to—?" Perceval gestured weakly, unable to follow the conversation.

"By now, Calhoun is either dead or nearly so," Arnoul said, pausing to tear a chunk of veal with his teeth. "At last, my vengeance is complete."

"Mine is not," Ambrose interrupted from the end of the table. He stared intently at Arnoul. "Calhoun ran from my sword in a duel, to show me mercy. Mercy! As though I could not have slit his throat, given the chance. I have not forgotten the insult, nor shall I."

Arnoul grinned and wagged a finger at Ambrose. "So you're the young knight who made Calhoun run! Ride with us tomorrow. Swear allegiance to Matilda and serve her well."

"No, my place is here," Ambrose answered. He looked at Endeline and smiled. "I am needed here."

"You certainly are," Endeline purred, thankful that at least Ambrose was still thinking clearly. "What would we do without you?"

The horses stomped and snorted quietly in the darkness, and Afton crept quietly to where Calhoun stood alone. He seemed thinner than when she had last seen him, and the hard look of determination in his eyes frightened her.

"I am sorry," she said when he looked at her. "I know you would rather die than owe a woman for your freedom—"

"It matters not," he cut her off. "Tonight I have a

chance to redeem myself in the eyes of my king and my fellow knights. I will succeed or die."

"Calhoun." Gislebert walked over from the clearing and extended a hand to his friend. "It is time for you to get ready."

Calhoun walked past her without another word.

Stephen's knights slept in two-hour shifts without the comfort of a campfire, and Afton could feel their uneasiness mounting as the night grew blacker. *What if your plan fails?* her thoughts railed against her. *It sounded so simple, but these are men of war, and they think you foolish! What if you are sending Calhoun to his death? What if Ambrose is killed in the fighting?*

She rose from her place at the foot of the twin trees and crept to the small circle of knights surrounding Calhoun.

"I will go over the wall at the south tower," Calhoun told the men who crouched around him. "You must follow me on foot, but keep low in the grasses. You will not be seen from the castle, for the darkness of night will cover you."

"On foot?" one knight interrupted. "We are not common foot soldiers."

"On this occasion you must be," Calhoun answered, one corner of his mouth rising in a half-smile. "Half of you will remain hidden in the trees on your horses, the other half must follow on foot. When you see that I have safely climbed over, run to the gate with your swords in hand. I will barricade Arnoul's men inside the garrison, then open the gate for you."

"One man alone cannot open the gate," Stephen inserted, shaking his head. "It is too heavy! And even if you could do it, the noise of the gate will alert the enemy. You would have Arnoul's sword in your back before even one of our knights had passed through."

"I will help Calhoun open the gate," Gislebert said, placing his hand on Calhoun's shoulder. Afton could not believe her eyes. Gentle Gislebert, poet to the king, had crept into the circle. He wore a knight's tunic and had a sword strapped to his side.

"What are you doing?" Calhoun asked, an honest smile of amusement on his face.

"I am going with you," Gislebert announced. "I can climb better in my bare feet than any knight in a suit of mail. And I know the castle. I can help open the gate after you have secured the garrison."

Stephen cocked his head. "It is a reasonable plan," he said finally. "But I shall miss you, Gislebert, if you fall in this endeavor. Calhoun—" the royal eyes narrowed, "I still do not trust. If he is lying and runs to Perceval and safety, I have lost nothing. But you, Gislebert, I would miss."

Gislebert bowed. "It is time I did the things poets only write about," he joked weakly.

"You were the shadow of my younger days," Calhoun said, looking at Gislebert with affection in his eyes. "You were always underfoot. In truth, I am glad you will be with me now. Come with me, old friend."

Afton watched as they knelt together before the king to receive his blessing. The entire company parted as the two walked resolutely out of the forest, and Afton realized they would be soon readying for battle. Soon she would know if her plan had succeeded. Soon she would know if she was to die.

She closed her eyes, hesitant to watch Calhoun and Gislebert vanish from sight. *God, are you there?* Her heart called out desperately. *Please, just this one time, have mercy. Let my beloved Calhoun and the brave Gislebert live.*

She heard no answer, no reassurance . . . but a voice from the past stirred in her memory. She frowned, looked around, then slipped away from the king's men. The nagging memory grew stronger as she crept through the forest silently, stopping occasionally to gather her bearings. She knew now what she must do. Unless her recollection failed her, there was another more secluded route into the castle. And she planned to find it.

Calhoun crept soundlessly through the tall grass of the pasture, praying the sun would hold its advent for another hour. Gislebert followed, matching him step for step, until he darted away to scale the lavatory shaft on the north tower.

Calhoun waited in the grass until he was sure no guards stared sleepily in his direction, then he sprinted for the southern tower. When he felt its aging stone beneath his fingers, he kissed the wall in relief and whispered a thanks to God. He could bear what was to follow. He had been most afraid of being stopped by an unfair arrow from the wall.

Foolish guards, Calhoun thought as he moved to the lavatory shaft and searched for a foothold. *They watch the stars and listen for hoofbeats.*

The lavatory shafts were rough and of new plaster, and Calhoun found it easy to grip the outcroppings of rock and pull himself up. He passed a slotted arrow loop and boldly peered through the narrow opening. No life stirred in the courtyard below; even the rooster in the henhouse was still dreaming.

At the top of the tower, where the shaft began, Calhoun swung fearlessly, reaching for an outcropping of the machicolations. He felt himself falling, but caught the stone in time. Without even pausing to ponder the danger he had barely avoided, he hoisted himself easily through the opening, designed for pouring oil onto attackers below.

He crept carefully along the catwalk at the top of the wall, then descended a staircase that led to the courtyard. He saw a movement in the distance and stiffened, but when the figure waved, Calhoun sighed in relief. Gislebert. The younger man ran in the shadows toward the gate, and Calhoun sprinted along the inner walls toward the garrison.

A sleepy guard sat on a bench outside the door, his head hanging over a cup of ale. Calhoun expertly slid behind him and pressed his dagger to the man's throat. At the feel of the cold metal against his skin, the man jerked his chin upward as the cup fell to the ground.

Calhoun whispered tensely: "How many are inside? Don't talk, just use your fingers."

The startled guard held up ten fingers, then clenched his fists twice more. Calhoun whispered again. "How many of Matilda's people sleep not in the garrison, but in the castle?"

The guard shrugged, and Calhoun adjusted his dagger so that its edge bit into the top layer of the man's skin. The man's eyes widened, and he lifted five fingers.

"Only five? And Arnoul is among them?"

The guard nodded carefully.

"Good. Now you are going to enter the garrison and bolt the door behind you. I will have my spear trained on this door, and if you or your fellows make a sound or come out in the next hour, you will be speared like a trout, do you understand?"

The guard nodded again, and Calhoun helped him to his feet and through the doorway. Calhoun closed the door firmly, then heard the bolt sliding gently into place. *The poor fellow's scared to death,* Calhoun thought as he dragged a bale of hay from the barn and placed it in front of the door.

He then ran to the deserted kitchen, where the supper fire still smoldered in the hearth. Scooping a red-hot coal into a copper cup, he ran to the garrison and tossed the coal into the dry hay. The hot embers gleamed, then flickered, then flamed brightly. Calhoun grinned in grim satisfaction. Anyone who tried to leave the garrison in the next several minutes would have to be willing to walk through a wall of fire.

Then Calhoun turned to stare at the castle. He knew Gislebert waited at the gate, and that Stephen and his men waited just outside. And yet . . . Arnoul was in the castle. As was Ambrose. It would be an easy thing, with the advantage of surprise, to best them both and thus prove to his father—and to himself—that he was in the right. An inner voice cautioned him—a voice reminiscent of Fulk on the night they escaped Zengi's dungeon—but he turned from it with an impatient jerk. Gislebert and King Stephen would wait for a few moments.

The time had come for Calhoun of Margate to reclaim his heritage.

"Perceval! Wake up!" Endeline shouted, shaking her husband's shoulder. "I smell smoke! Are we under attack?"

Perceval sat up, and Ambrose burst into the chamber, clad already in his hauberk. Behind him came Arnoul, his eyes squinting in the darkness. "The enemy are upon us," Arnoul snapped, flinging the covers off Perceval's bed. "Up, Lord Percy! And take us to the upper floor."

"The upper floor?" Endeline squealed, slipping into her tunic. "Morgan! Lunette! Help me dress!"

"There's no time for that!" Arnoul's rough hand grabbed Endeline's arm and thrust her toward the door. "Call your son, and all in the house."

"My son sleeps on the upper floor," she answered. "Here there are only my maids." She gestured toward the room where Morgan, Lunette, and Lizette slept. Arnoul went to rouse the maids, and Endeline stepped nearer the doorway to peer down the staircase. Was her heart the pounding sound she heard, or was someone beating on the door? Three of Arnoul's guards at the lower door looked up at her. Another knight stood on the landing and waited to lead them upstairs.

"I must have a moment with my maids," Endeline said, holding her head proudly. "A lady does not step outside her chamber without suitable clothing."

Arnoul leered at her with his one good eye, then pulled the astonished Perceval out of bed. "Quickly, then," he said, and Endeline turned to her maids and whispered hurried instructions. Lizette and Lunette quickly threw a cloak over their mistress's thin tunic. But Morgan sank back into the shadows of the room.

"We are ready," Endeline commanded imperiously, and Arnoul pushed Perceval through the doorway. Ambrose followed reluctantly, then Endeline slipped out into the hall.

Though Ambrose walked in silence beside her, Endeline shivered in fear. She had not planned anything like this. She and Perceval had been clever. Had it not been for Calhoun and his damnable loyalty to the crown, all would have been well. But now . . . Endeline fought down rage at the thought that it was her own son's actions that had provoked this attack. Why hadn't one of her children inherited her shrewdness?

She glanced to where Charles waited meekly at the top of the stairs, concerned for nothing but the next wheat crop. And Ambrose . . .

She reached out for him, her fingers gripping his arm like a vise, and brought her lips to his ear. "Do something, you fool!" she whispered intensely. "If you would be a man of Perceval's house, take action! Prove yourself!"

Ambrose's dark eyes shone in the torchlight. "What action would you have me take, precious lady?"

"Do you see this?" Endeline stopped on the stairs and swept her hand in a wide gesture. "The castle, the manor, the estates—all will be gone if Stephen defeats Arnoul now! Perceval's lands will be confiscated and we will all be hanged for treason!"

Her voice softened even as her lips brushed his cheek. "If you wish to save this for yourself, Ambrose, take action. Arnoul trusts you."

Ambrose smiled and lifted his head. "Never fear, my lady. I will do as you command." He let her pass, and then turned his most winning smile on Arnoul, who came behind Lizette and Lunette up the stairs. "Faithful Arnoul, surely you can use my services on the lower floors. Take the others to the upper floor, but let me and my fair brother Charles assist you downstairs."

Arnoul paused, but then jerked his head in agreement. Endeline watched, perplexed, as Ambrose fell out of their group and Charles came down the stairs. But before she could question the young man's request or actions, Arnoul pressed her to continue to the upper floor.

As he placed a fresh bale of hay upon the smoldering blaze at the door of the garrison, Calhoun heard sounds of movement within. Good. The knights had no escape unless they showed themselves upon the castle wall or jumped from the window to the grass of the pasture. Either way, Stephen's men would be waiting.

Now he faced a particular problem. He could not gain access to the castle keep, for the door was strongly barricaded. Could it be that his enemy Arnoul was so vengeful he would kill Perceval or Endeline? Calhoun stepped into the courtyard and looked into the castle windows. All was still, but for movement at an upper window, in the rooms where he and Charles had slept as boys.

"Surrender to the forces of King Stephen!" he called boldly over the noise of the fire. "Defeat is inevitable, Arnoul!"

Perceval's grizzled face appeared in a large upper window. Calhoun stared in amazement, barely recognizing his father. Could a man change so much in such a short period of time?

"Calhoun! Is that you?" Perceval called. His voice was that of an old man.

"It is your son," Calhoun answered, an odd feeling of pity sweeping over him so strongly that his knees threatened to buckle. He moved into the center of the open courtyard and opened his hand to his father. "Come down, Father, and meet the king."

"I don't know," Perceval answered, peering into the dimness. "I shall have to ask Lady Endeline."

Perceval disappeared from the window and another voice roared "Calhoun!" Arnoul stepped into view, his scarred visage on full display, grim evidence of his escape from the burning church. "So you are not executed!" Arnoul bellowed. "It is true, then, that King Stephen is merciful to those who least deserve mercy. Draw near, my friend, and meet your fate."

Arnoul gestured with his hand and a red-robed knight

armed with a long bow and arrow appeared next to him in the window and took aim. Calhoun stood still in the open space, transfixed. He had climbed the wall with only his sword, and there was no wagon, no wall, no animal to shield him. His hauberk would not stop the penetration of an arrow, and he doubted if he could outrun it.

"Fire when ready," Arnoul told the archer casually, stepping away.

Calhoun was close enough to see the archer smile in the early morning light. The archer stepped back, giving himself more room to maneuver in case his target should decide to run. Calhoun knew that the force of an arrow from a long bow would not only penetrate his body, but likely pin him to the ground. As the archer curled his targeting finger around the bow and inhaled, steadying the arrow for release, Calhoun felt a flash of understanding. The same enemy that had felled the mighty Fulk was about to bring him to his end. That enemy was Calhoun himself . . . his pride. Though Fulk's death had forced him to see his pride for what it was, he still had not overcome it. It had, in fact, defeated him. Closing his eyes, Calhoun accepted the inevitable.

God, I am coming to you. . . .

"No!" He heard the spring of the bowstring and a dull sound of impact, and he opened his eyes to see Perceval falling out the window. With the arrow through his body, the old man seemed to fall slowly, as if in a dream. Calhoun realized with a shock that his father had thrown himself into the path of the arrow intended for him.

The dream ended with a sickening thud. Jarred into action, Calhoun ran to where his father lay on the ground, his eyes wide open. Perceval looked at Calhoun as he clutched the arrow in his breast. "My son," he whispered, his breath rattling in his throat.

"Yes, Father, I am your son." Calhoun reached for the old man's hand and held it over his heart as the earl of Margate drew his last breath.

A scream from above caught his attention, and he

looked up to see Endeline at another window, her face frozen in horror at the sight on the ground. He opened his mouth to speak to his mother, but Arnoul's archer let a second arrow fly. Calhoun did not have time to run. He could only flinch in anticipation, and the four-foot arrow hit him squarely in his right arm, piercing the elbow.

"Skewered like a chicken, Sir Calhoun!" Arnoul's voice came from near Calhoun, and he whirled around to see his enemy standing twenty paces away in the courtyard. The castle door stood open. "Shoot no more, for I will take care of this," Arnoul called up to the archer in the castle. "Come down and aid your brothers in the garrison."

Arnoul grinned tantalizingly at Calhoun. "The door is open, my friend," he said, jerking his head toward the doorway. "I do not stand in your way. Go in and take your castle—if you can."

Calhoun tried to reach for his sword, but the long arrow in his arm struck his body, and grated across the shattered joint of his elbow. Calhoun gritted his teeth and reached across his body with his left hand to slowly draw his weapon. *Fulk*, he thought with a wry grimness, *I should have paid more attention to your lessons! Instead, this duel will be my final shame, for I have never been good at fighting left-handed.*

Arnoul held his sword in his right hand and jiggled it casually, as if this were but another mock duel at Warwick Castle. He approached with catlike steps and leered at Calhoun. "Remember the days at Warwick Castle, my friend? Remember the times you beat me? Well, this is no contest, brother knight. This is battle, and before the sun is fully risen we shall know who is the most able warrior."

Arnoul raised the hilt of his sword to his lips and kissed it. "Confess your sins and prepare to die," he intoned, eyeing Calhoun over the blade of his sword.

"I am more fit for death than you, Arnoul, and far less likely to find it," Calhoun answered, gripping his sword in his awkward left hand. At best, he could use it as an effective shield, blocking Arnoul's jabs. He tried to reach for his light

476

dagger with his right hand, but pain raked across his nerves as he flexed his fingers and willed his arm to bend. He was as ineffectual as a bird with a clipped wing, as powerless as the meek messenger pigeons of the Saracens beneath the fierce talons of the Christians' well-trained falcons.

Calhoun gritted his teeth, ignoring his limp right arm and the pain that coursed through his body. He gripped his sword more firmly. So be it. If his time had come, he would go down fighting, a man of honor to his last breath.

Afton crept quietly in the shadows of the castle wall and wiped the mud from her skirt. She shivered when a breeze struck her, for her clothing was wet and cold. The pool at the back of the castle, which was used by the washerwomen, opened up outside the castle walls. It had surprised Afton to discover she was still small enough to fit through the narrow underwater pipe that brought water into the castle courtyard.

She took a moment to wring out her heavy skirt, then froze when she heard a taunting voice. Darting toward the sound, she saw the man she recognized as Arnoul standing in the courtyard. There with him stood Calhoun, and she gasped when she saw the long, bloody arrow that hung from Calhoun's useless arm. Her heart tightened painfully at the way her beloved struggled, with his left hand, to wield his sword threateningly, while Arnoul's laughter rang from the castle walls.

Desperately, she looked around. Why didn't someone help him? Where was Gislebert? Or Ambrose? Surely Ambrose would help a fellow knight . . .

Arnoul showed no signs of advancing toward Calhoun. Instead, he seemed content to taunt him, cursing and screaming, but Afton knew the tirade would soon end. Arnoul's sword swung angrily toward Calhoun, punctuating his curses . . . Afton's eyes narrowed. Arnoul's dagger. It rested in its sheath on his right hip, untouched, seemingly forgotten. If she could only reach it without being noticed in her approach!

But if you strike Arnoul, her reason reminded her, *you will surely steal the last of Calhoun's pride. He may well hate you forever.*

"And if I do nothing," she whispered, "Calhoun will die here today." When Hubert had taken her infant daughter, she had been unable to stop him. When Endeline had taken Ambrose, there had been nothing she could do. But now . . . now she could—and would—act. Resolve flowed into her heart. "This time," she muttered, reaching down to ease off her wet slippers, "With God's help, I will do something!"

Gathering up her heavy skirts, she raced toward the two men. As her bare feet skimmed over the ground, Afton sent thanks heavenward that Arnoul's screamed curses and threats masked any sound of her approach. His bellowing crescendoed into a roar and, at the culmination of his tirade, he raised his sword and advanced to strike. Knowing the time had come, Afton ducked under the large man's upraised arm and grabbed for his dagger. He must have felt the pressure of her grasp, for with a start he turned in her direction, and she used his backward momentum to spring up under his arm.

Arnoul roared in surprise as she thrust his dagger into his heart—and sent the Limb of Hell to eternal blackness.

Calhoun held his sword aloft, intent on striking at least one blow before his head was taken from his shoulders. Then, just as something ran at Arnoul from the shadows, a voice echoed in Calhoun's mind: "You cannot save yourself; salvation must come by another."

The voice was not audible, yet Calhoun discerned it clearly. *Who speaks to me thus?* his mind questioned, even as he steadied his sword for Arnoul's attack. *God?*

Suddenly, Arnoul's face froze in a paroxysm of terror, and Calhoun watched in amazement as the villain shuddered, then fell back into the dust. Calhoun stared in bewilderment. There, above Arnoul's still form, stood Afton, her golden hair framing her face, tears streaking her cheeks, a bloody dagger clenched in her hand—she looked like an avenging angel.

Once more the words railed in Calhoun's conscience; old, familiar words that he recognized now from his childhood chaplain's catechism: "You cannot save yourself; salvation must come by another."

Calhoun let his sword fall limply to his side as the words sank deep into his soul. *Your words are true,* he answered the unseen presence silently. *I am no invincible knight. I am weak, I feel pain . . . I am mortal.* He glanced at Afton, who was staring at him, her face pale. *And now I see, as I never have before, how much my life depends on others . . . and how much I have to learn about loving this woman you have given me.*

He smiled at her then, a smile of joy and relief, for he was free at last. Pride no longer held him prisoner. "I thank you," he said, his voice hoarse with emotion. "You have saved my life."

She looked at him blankly for a moment, then cast the dagger aside and covered her face with her hands. He noticed for the first time that she was dripping wet and shivering.

"You don't have to thank me," she answered stiffly, lowering her hands from her face, keeping her eyes averted from Arnoul's still body. "I know you don't want to. I know a knight would rather be dead than owe his life to a woman—" Her voice broke then, and she looked at him, her eyes brimming with unshed tears. "But I could not let him kill you."

Calhoun lifted his face to the brightening sky and laughed. "No," he said, shaking his head. "I would not trade life for the 'honor' of this knight who kneels now at hell's door. I do thank you, Afton, most sincerely."

"You . . . thank me," she echoed softly. So this was how it was going to be. She saved his life, and he gave her polite thanks, as if she had picked up a trinket that had fallen from his lap to the floor. Had her bitterness toward Endeline made her such a fiend in his eyes that he felt nothing for her? Had her lust for revenge killed his love?

She turned away and covered her eyes with her hand, unwilling that he should see her weep. She had told him of her love, she had offered undying gratitude, and she had risked her life for his own—and still it was not enough. She had nothing else to give.

She heard the crunch of his footstep upon the gravel in the courtyard and felt him draw nearer. "I thank you," he said, his voice deep and low, "and I love you. There is no other woman in the world with your courage."

She opened her eyes, afraid to believe what she had heard. He stood within arm's reach, but he grimaced in pain, then smiled sheepishly. "I would kiss you now, but I have to help Gislebert raise the gate for King Stephen and his men," he said, pointing to the gate with his uninjured arm. "Alas, I don't think I can pull the rope." He turned toward her and smiled gently. "Will you help me?"

Afton returned his smile, and the first rays of daylight broke over the eastern wall of the castle, lighting the straggling tendrils of her hair like golden fire. "Is it not dishonorable for a knight to ask a mere woman for help?" she asked, her eyes glinting up at him.

"No," Calhoun answered, reaching out for her hand. He squeezed it gently. "My honor today lies in you, Afton."

FORTY-FOUR

Afton found dry clothing in the wardrobe and put her hands over her ears to drown out Calhoun's muffled cries of pain as the king's physician removed the arrow. When at last Calhoun was silent, she stepped into the chamber, where the physician wrapped fresh linen around her beloved's arm. "In time, the bones will knit and the arm will heal," the doctor said, smiling up at her. "He'll be wielding a sword again within the year."

"I think not," Calhoun muttered weakly, and his eyes caught Afton's. He managed a smile, a decent imitation of the mischievous grin that had sent her heart pounding in childhood days. "Shall we go downstairs, my lady, and see what the cat has dragged in?"

Her hand felt warm and safe in his as they went downstairs to the great hall, where the king and his officers sorted through their prisoners. "Ah, Calhoun," Stephen said when they entered the room. "If it were not for Arnoul's men leaping like frightened lizards from the garrison, I would have thought you a traitor. You took far too long to open the gate."

"Aye, far too long indeed," Gislebert echoed from his place by the king's side. "I was frozen in terror the entire time, fearing you had surely been killed. And when you finally appeared in the courtyard, and I saw that Arnoul would certainly strike you down, I must confess, I closed my eyes and wished to die with you."

"I am glad that you did not," Calhoun answered, smiling at his friend, "for we need fewer soldiers and more poets in this place." He bowed stiffly to King Stephen. "I am in your service, Your Highness, and I lay before you all that Margate Castle has to offer."

"Well put, good knight," Stephen replied, looking around the room. "Now let us see what that booty is."

Thirty of Matilda's men had been captured as they leapt from the burning garrison; twenty of Perceval's knights, including Ambrose, were in chains as well for fighting against Stephen. Five bodies had been found within the castle walls and now lay in the hall before the king: Perceval, Arnoul, two of Arnoul's men . . . and Charles.

Afton gasped as she recognized Calhoun's brother, who looked as if he merely slept. The soft fringe of his lashes framed lids that seemed reluctant to release the pink glow of life. A sudden cry from the doorway of the room drew Afton's attention, and she saw Endeline, sagging against the two guards who had led her into the room, her pale face registering grief and shock as she stared at her eldest son's lifeless body.

"Charles!" Endeline's voice was ragged with pain and disbelief. "With what enemy did my Charles meet?" She turned to Ambrose. "He departed in your company, Ambrose. What happened to my son?"

"Aye, Charles escaped with me," Ambrose answered calmly, then turned to the king and bowed respectfully. "Indeed, I feel bound to tell you that I do not deserve these chains, Your Majesty, for we have just undergone a terrible ordeal. All in Margate Castle were held hostage and count ourselves most fortunate that Your Glorious Majesty arrived in time to allow us to escape with our lives."

"Pray, then, can you explain this death?" Stephen commanded, pointing to Charles' body. "He wears no dagger; he carried no sword. How came a man of peace to die here this day?"

Ambrose nodded gravely. "I do not know, sire, but I

weep for him as I would a brother. Arnoul did hold us captive, but Charles and I managed to slip away. It must have been Arnoul, or one of his men, who killed Charles as he attempted to flee the castle."

Endeline moaned softly and fell on the body of her first-born son. But the company was distracted from the sad sight by the sound of shrieking from outside the hall. Two of Stephen's knights entered the room, half-carrying, half-pulling Morgan. The maid's eyes were blank in her hysteria and her body twisted frantically as she struggled to free herself from the guard.

"We found this wench hiding in the chamber storeroom," one knight explained. "She nearly scratched my eyes out as we carried her down here."

"I know this woman, she is my mother's maid," Calhoun told the king, stepping forward. He looked at Morgan and held out his hand in a comforting gesture. "Calm down, Morgan, all is well. The king has delivered the castle."

Morgan's eyes went wide. "No he 'asn't," she said, her eyes filled with fear. She pointed a trembling finger at Ambrose. "The devil is still 'ere! I see 'im! I saw 'im upstairs in the chamber. I 'id in the storeroom to guard the gold, as my mistress told me, and I saw young Ambrose lead Charles into the chamber. He killed the young master! He drew a dagger and stabbed 'im in the back, 'e did! I saw it with my own eyes!"

She spread her bloody hands before the king. "Here's 'is blood! It fell upon the ground where he lay! I tried to help 'im, but I was too late!" She collapsed on the ground, sobbing.

Stunned and horrified at the woman's accusation, Afton looked at her son, who stood as still as a statue. Standing thus, with his eyes darkly gleaming, he was the embodiment of Hubert. *My son is lost to me.* The thought hit Afton forcefully. *He never really belonged to me, for he is his father's son.* A wave of grief and loss swept over her, threatening to buckle her knees as the king turned to Ambrose.

"What say you to this charge?" the king asked, his eyes narrowing.

"I say nothing," Ambrose answered, stepping forward. He pointed at Morgan. "It is clear—this hysterical woman is a murderer. She hid in the storeroom to steal from my lord and lady and she is the one covered in blood, Your Majesty. Surely it was her dagger that killed my brother Charles."

"He was not your brother," Calhoun inserted. "And Morgan has no motive to kill the gentle Charles. But you, Ambrose, thought to inherit Perceval's estate, did you not? With Charles dead and the second son cast off—"

"—it would be easy enough to blame the death on the raging fight," the king finished Calhoun's thought. "I see the situation clearly."

Afton felt as though her heart had been dipped in ice. Ambrose's crime was too monstrous to be believed, but— try though she might—she knew of nothing in his words or character to contradict the deed. Instead, there was only more evidence that he was like his father: grasping, ambitious, and greedy. As much as she wanted to love and vindicate him, she could not deny that Calhoun's words rang true. Her knees gave way and she sank to the ground, covering her face with her hands. She and Endeline had each lost a son today.

"I find Calhoun's words reasonable," King Stephen pronounced. "And I find the maid credible. I hereby sentence you, Ambrose, to be hung by the neck in this courtyard where you once took vows of obedience and loyalty. You have proven this day that you are capable of neither. May your neck be as easily broken as were your vows."

Two of Stephen's knights seized Ambrose immediately. As they dragged him from the room, he flung angry words at Endeline: "It was you who told me to take action, to be a man! My dagger acted only to slake your bloodthirsty ambition!"

As Ambrose's words died away, King Stephen looked at the less-than-regal form of Endeline, who sat weeping by

Charles' side. "You are not without fault in this, lady. You and your husband divided your loyalties, lying both to your king and to the one who would usurp our rightful throne. You propagated the falsehood that led us to think your most noble son Calhoun a spy, and in so doing nearly brought about your own child's death. The nobles and villeins have carried the rumor that your loyalty is cheap, easily bought and easily traded. Today we see that this is true. Have you not heard that you cannot serve two masters?"

Endeline did not answer, nor did she raise her eyes to the king. Stephen's voice softened. "Your husband is now beyond the reach of man's justice; he must account of himself to God. But you, Lady Endeline, must kneel before me and confess your wrongs or pay the penalty."

Endeline clasped her hands and began to rock back and forth, her long dark hair tangled across her upturned face. But instead of answering the king, she reached out to lift Charles' cold hand and hold it tenderly. "Sweet baby mine, how long will you sleep?" she began to sing hoarsely.

Stephen's eyes widened for a moment, then filled with a sad pity. He turned his head away from the sight to look at Calhoun. He was kneeling beside Afton, who was unaware of what was happening around her, so absorbed was she in her grief over Ambrose.

"Calhoun," he said, and the young knight, upon hearing his name, rose to face his king. "Good knight, I have found only three people with honor in this entire household," Stephen said. "You, the lady Afton, and the maid, Morgan. To the maid, I grant freedom. And to the Lady Afton—"

Calhoun reached down to take Afton's hands, and she looked at him, startled. Then, realizing that King Stephen was addressing her, she rose to stand beside Calhoun. The king lifted his chin and regarded Afton with frank curiosity. "To you, fair lady, as reward for your part in the day's victory, I present the fate of this hapless woman, Endeline, who has advocated treason against king, country, and family. Perhaps she will make a more worthy slave than royal subject. Then again . . ." The king spread his hands. "Mayhap her execution would please you more. What say you regarding her?"

The room fell totally silent, and every eye turned to Afton—every eye save those of Endeline, who continued to sing a soft lullaby.

The king's question seemed to ring in Afton's ears. She glanced over at Endeline, who sat between the lifeless bodies of her husband and son, her sources of joy and pride. She had lost everything: home, family, position, power. . . . The scene should have brought Afton joy, but as she watched Endeline distractedly rub her son's dead hand, she remembered another pale hand that had reached out to her in love: Agnelet's.

A year ago Afton could have taken a dagger and plunged it with pleasure into Endeline's heart. Six months ago she could have dressed the lady in sackcloth and sent her into the forest to fend for food like a wild animal. But that was before she had met, mourned, and come to understand Agnelet . . . before she had come face-to-face with forgiveness.

Agnelet, flesh of her flesh, had suffered the lack of beauty and mother and brother, yet she had borne all through the power of faith. Instead of hatred, she had known peace; instead of vengeance, she had sought to bring joy.

Suddenly Afton knew that God's purpose in sending her to her daughter, at least in part, was to prepare her for this moment. With Endeline's fate in her hands, Afton had the opportunity to choose forgiveness or vengeance. And again, she could hear the small voice that had been beseeching her since Agnelet's death . . . but this time she understood.

She drew a deep breath before speaking: "I once thought myself a victim of this woman's evil schemes," she said slowly, looking up at the king. "My suffering blinded me to the truth of my own pride. For me to assuage that pride now—" she crossed the room, putting her hand on Endeline's shoulder—"would be a greater wrong than all those visited upon me."

Endeline did not respond to her touch, but Afton continued. "I forgive you, Lady Endeline, and pray that you would forgive the hate I have borne you these many years."

At the softness in Afton's voice, Endeline turned slowly to face her—but the dark eyes that had always been so proud and scheming now reflected only the black void of madness. Shocked, Afton withdrew her hand and stepped back.

"So what say you?" the king demanded. "What shall be done with her?"

Afton looked up into Calhoun's blue eyes, which searched hers and waited. Her face softened, and she held his eyes as she answered the king. "Let the lady be given a house on the castle grounds and a nurse to care for her," she said, walking to Calhoun's side. She placed her hand on Calhoun's arm. "And let her be kept near her son, for children and their mothers should not be forced apart."

Stephen raised his brow in surprise, then nodded. "It shall be done," he said. Then, turning to Calhoun, the king cocked his head and a pleasant, almost teasing smile crossed his features. "Can it be, Sir Knight, that this remarkable young woman is the lady you were promised in marriage?"

Calhoun dropped Afton's hands and stepped forward. "Yes, sire."

"And would it please you if I were to offer her to you now?"

Calhoun looked down at Afton, who knelt on the floor at his feet. His eyes shone with unspoken desire, and she knew he still loved her—indeed, that he had never stopped loving her. His pride had come between them, as had her bitterness, but both had at last been vanquished. They had conquered more than an enemy army in the past few hours: they had conquered the worst parts of themselves.

His voice was low and quiet. "If she will agree, sire, it would please me greatly."

The king nodded and held out his hand to Afton. "Do you agree, Lady Afton?"

She rose to her feet and laid her hands in the king's, who then transferred them to Calhoun. It was all she wanted, to stand by her beloved's side forever. Nothing else mattered—and in that instant, she knew she was, for the first time in her life, truly free.

"Yes, sire. I most surely do agree."

"Then, upon my decree, you two shall be married two days from now. For a wedding present, I endow you, Calhoun, with all the estates and lands formerly held by Perceval of Margate, to be held by you and your progeny for all time."

Gislebert clapped his hands in delight.

"So be it!" the king called out. "And now, order dinner at once, my new earl of Margate, for your king is hungry."

For the first time in his life, Calhoun broke royal protocol and did not answer. Instead, with Afton in his arms, he claimed the kisses he had sought for years.

Epilogue

So Father Odoric married them twain,
Calhoun and Afton, their love new ordained.
And later that morning, when it was day,
They prayed by the grave of sweet Agnelet.

Steward Josson married Lizette the maid,
And Margate's brave dead to their rest were laid.
A small house for two, of Margate loam,
Corba and Endeline made their new home.

Within a year's time Margate's lord found joy
In the birth of Afton's twin baby boys.
Alard and Albert, strong handsome babes both,
Were honored by knights and protected by oath.

But peace was not found on fair England's shores
Till cruel war had raged for twelve years more.
Stephen and Matilda, the crown their due,
Agreed to crown Henry, son of Anjou.

Gislebert, whose heart was heavy and sad,
Wrote tales of danger in pop'lar ballads,
Served Lord Calhoun and his fair Afton queen,
But finally left Margate to seek his Nadine.

Afton of Margate Castle

You ask what became of poor Gislebert—
The singer of ballads, the friend debonair?
His tale is daring, yet full of love's pain,
Where much love is lost before it is gained.

Alas, I have not now the time to tell
This noble man's story, though I know it well.
So for now I needs must bid you adieu,
And dedicate my song, fair listeners, to you.

Additional books by Angela Elwell Hunt

CALICO BEAR   0-8423-0302-2
A warm bedtime story that reassures children of God's love for them in a changing world.

CASSIE PERKINS SERIES   Volumes 1-9
This bright, ambitious heroine teaches junior high readers about finding God in the challenges of growing up.

LOVING SOMEONE ELSE'S CHILD   0-8423-3863-2
A supportive, practical book for adults who are taking the responsibility to care for children not their own.

THE RISE OF BABYLON *(with Charles Dyer)*   0-8423-5618-5
Dyer shows how Babylon and present-day Iraq fit into Bible prophecy, pointing to Jesus as the source of true security.